Call
to Arms

Call
to Arms

Octopus Books Limited

First published 1983 by

Octopus Books Limited
59 Grosvenor Street
London W1

Copyright © 1983 selection and arrangement

Reprinted 1984

Octopus Books Limited

Illustration by Theresa Tower

ISBN 0 7064 1964 2

Printed in Czechoslovakia
50488/2

Contents

Fair Stood The Wind For France H. E. Bates 9

How Brigadier Gerard Won His Medal Sir Arthur Conan Doyle 21

The Invaders (from 'The Last Enemy') Richard Hillary 40

The War of the Worlds H. G. Wells 50

All Quiet On The Western Front Erich Maria Remarque 63

The Battle of Borodino (from 'War and Peace') Leo Tolstoy 74

Catch 22 Joseph Heller 97

Buller's Guns Richard Hough 108

Arctic Convoy (from 'H.M.S. Ulysses') Alistair MacLean 116

The Red Badge of Courage Stephen Crane 129

Escape From Colditz (from 'They Have Their Exits') Airey Neave 148

Goodbye To All That Robert Graves 163

The Moon's A Balloon David Niven 179

The Warrior's Soul Joseph Conrad 191

Fly for Your Life   Larry Forrester   207

The Naked And The Dead   Norman Mailer   220

The Reason Why   Cecil Woodham Smith   240

The Affair at Coulter's Notch   Ambrose Bierce   257

The Fort at Zinderneuf   P. C. Wren   264
(from 'Beau Geste')

The Cruel Sea   Nicholas Monsarrat   284

Waterloo   W. M. Thackeray   301
(from 'Vanity Fair')

Enemy Coast Ahead   Guy Gibson V.C.   315

Into Battle   Frederic Manning   334
(from 'Her Privates We')

Acknowledgments   345

In peace there's nothing so becomes a man
As modest stillness and humility:
But when the blast of war blows in our ears,
Then imitate the action of the tiger;
Stiffen the sinews, summon up the blood,
Disguise fair nature with hard-favour'd rage.

Shakespeare: **Henry V** III i 3–8

Fair Stood The Wind For France

H. E. BATES

A young RAF officer shot down over occupied France is nursed back to health by a remarkable young woman after losing an arm. Determined to make their way to England to get married, the couple reach Marseilles in the company of a fellow pilot and fugitive, O'Connor .....

AS THEY WENT OUT OF MARSEILLES that night, himself, the girl and O'Connor, travelling by train, he sat by the side of the girl, she in the corner of the compartment by the window, with O'Connor opposite. Above O'Connor's head, on the rack, was the girl's attaché case, containing all their things. The train, which was supposed to be very fast, stopped many times at intervals through the night, and sometimes at these stops Franklin would lift the window-blind and look out on the darkness of a strange station, with the ghosts of hurrying people passing to and fro under shaded lights, the ghostly voluble voices excitedly babbling; or on some remote part of the track where nothing moved and nothing could be seen except red stars of signal lights in the blackness, and there was no sound but hollow echoing noises of shunting trucks and sometimes the wind tuning the telegraph wires. Occasionally at these stops there came into the carriage once again the heavy friendly smell of locomotive smoke, steamy and pungent out of the strange darkness, so that Franklin would remember the night of rowing over the river; but otherwise there was nothing but the smell of the train, of the many cheap cigarettes smoked by other passengers, and sometimes the intimate small fragrance of the girl's hair as she leaned her head on his shoulder.

He did not know at all how long the journey would take. He hoped simply for darkness at the frontier. It seemed natural that things must be easier in darkness. He remembered other frontiers, and other trains, in peace-time, and how, as far as he could recall, there was less vigilance at night. Sometimes, thinking of the girl and O'Connor and not knowing how adequate the papers of any of them were, he was worried. Then he would remember Miss Campbell and Miss Baker. At the station in Marseilles there had been an atmosphere of wild disintegration; the air was exploding into a million fragmentary rumours; and it was quite right what Miss Campbell said. Everyone was running, and it was just possible

9

that there would be a short period when everyone would be too concerned for himself to wonder where other people were running to. If the worst came you could always run in the darkness. It might even be necessary, in fact better, to be separated. He had better face that, he thought.

He sat for some time thinking about this. They had decided, since O'Connor could speak only English, and since his own accent wasn't at all perfect, never to speak to each other in the carriage except when they were alone. They had not yet been alone, and now in the carriage with them were two sailors and an elderly woman. The sailors, who had smoked heavily all the way from Marseilles, were now asleep. The woman reminded him faintly of Miss Campbell, except that she was very French where Miss Campbell had been very Anglo-Saxon, and she was much younger. But her grey face, as she continually read the book open on her knees, had the same large bland imperturbability. Under the book was a small handbag of food. Now and then she slid her hand under the book and surreptitiously took out something and ate it. The lights in the train were quite dim. She munched the food very furtively, her hand over her mouth, and whatever it was she was eating Franklin never knew.

He got up at last and looked hard at O'Connor and went out into the corridor. He looked up and down the corridor, and the motion of the train swayed him about in the empty darkness. He caught the handrail with his right hand and hung on. O'Connor came out into the corridor a moment later and shut the door.

'Anything up?' O'Connor said.

'No. I just wanted to talk, that's all.'

'What happens at the frontier?'

'That's what I wanted to talk about. I haven't the faintest idea.'

'I wish to hell we were flying,' O'Connor said.

Franklin leaned against the window. In the faint light he could see the faces of himself and O'Connor impressed in reflection on the glass. O'Connor looked disturbingly English still.

'Look,' he said. 'If we get separated.'

'If what?' O'Connor said. 'Don't talk cock. Nobody's going to separate us. Not now.'

'It's more than possible.'

'Nobody's going to separate us,' O'Connor said. He was very firm. 'I'll shoot the bastard who does.'

'You'll shoot nobody.'

'If you only knew how I've been longing to shoot somebody,' O'Connor said.

'I do know.'

'Then you understand my feelings. Nobody's going to separate us now. I'll see to that.'

10

'All right,' Franklin said. 'Just in case.'

A man came along the corridor, carrying a heavy brown suitcase. He pushed past O'Connor and Franklin, who stopped talking. The man said 'Pardon!' and O'Connor and Franklin pressed themselves against the outer glass so that he could get by.

The man swayed along the corridor, bumping the suitcase against his legs. Franklin and O'Connor watched him go.

'O.K.,' O'Connor said.

'If I should get separated from you,' Franklin said, talking in a low voice, 'take the girl to the French authorities in Madrid. If you get to England take her to my mother. Go and see my mother, anyway.'

'Right. I got the address,' O'Connor said.

'And you?'

'I'll be doing target practice somewhere.'

'Now look.'

'Now look what?' O'Connor said. 'You overruled me last time, and what happened? You got in a hell of a mess and I got in a hell of a mess. The only time you let me arrange things I got you over the river.'

'All right,' Franklin said. 'Ten to one we won't get separated. I just wanted to tell you it doesn't matter much if we do. Each can find his own way.'

'We'll cling together like the ivy,' O'Connor said.

Franklin grinned. 'All right.' There was really no arguing with O'Connor. There never really had been. Better to let him go. 'But for God's sake don't show that revolver. And whatever happens, be nice to her.'

'I'll be nice to her.' O'Connor, a little embarrassed by the effort of saying something tender, stared at his own face in the glass. 'I'll be nice to her. I know how you feel. I'm sorry you didn't find the padre.'

'Thanks. We'll find one,' Franklin said.

O'Connor did not speak. They leaned together against the glass. Franklin, who could see nothing and could only feel the darkness solidly flowing past beyond their reflected faces, felt they were very close together: closer than on any of their trips, closer than in the river with O'Connor swimming him across, closer than at the meeting in Marseilles. This closeness gave him great confidence. O'Connor was one of the imperishable ones who somehow blundered through.

There were no words for this, and he looked up and down the corridor. No one was coming and he said:

'All right. Go back and tell Françoise I want her. Don't talk and, if she's asleep, don't wake her.'

O'Connor looked through the glass division of the compartment.

'She is asleep.'

Franklin looked through the glass. The girl was sitting quite upright.

11

She had closed her eyes, the closed lids slightly paler than the sunburn of her face. It was as if she were not asleep, but really dreamily thinking through the closed lids. She might easily have been praying, too, he thought.

'All right,' he said. 'Go back, anyway. Tell her when she wakes up.'

O'Connor opened the compartment door and went in, and Franklin watched him shut it again and sit down. The girl did not seem to wake, and he turned back to stare at the night flowing beyond his reflection in the sheet of glass.

He stood there for a long time while the train rocked on in the darkness. It did not stop at all as he stood there, and he got the impression of inevitability from its constant speed in the night. Every-thing had seemed inevitable, really, since the meeting with Miss Campbell and Miss Baker. Everything, after the weeks of indecision and of looking vainly for the padre in Marseilles, had happened quickly. It was better like that. Almost everything that had happened before that now seemed increasingly confused. It was hard to recall even the most vicious moments of pain. His arm had healed very well; he supposed it was really wonderful. They would let him fly again. They had to let him fly again. It was quite impossible to consider a life without flying, and he would pull every string he knew until they did let him fly. He hung on to the handrail and the train swayed in the darkness, jerking violently, the darkness firing signal lights in a row, like tracer, as they passed a station. He remembered something Miss Campbell had said about being young and not realizing, in youth, that the going was good. He wondered how her youth had been spent; remote holidays in the Highlands, seasons in London, the spring perhaps at Hyères, the summer in Dorset. You could be very young for a long time in those days, and it would not matter if you never knew it, because of the apparent permanence of that gentle world. Now there was no gentleness left, and scarcely any youth at all. You were doing elementary physics one day and bombing somebody to hell the next. The train was smoother now in the darkness, and his face pale and immobile in the glass. He was twenty-two but he did not feel very young any more.

Miss Campbell wouldn't understand. He thought how admirable and fortunate she was. He would remember Miss Campbell for ever and the smell of tea that was all England. The train lurched again, and then in a moment the compartment door opened and he turned to find Françoise coming out.

She shut the door and smiled.

'Been to sleep?'

'No. Not really.'

'Not really?'

'Half asleep. Just thinking.'

He moved along the corridor, towards the end, the girl with him. It was the middle of the night, and in the compartments most people were sleeping. He held her with his arm in the corner at the end of the corridor and they spoke in low tones.

'Thinking of what?'

'Of what we will do when we are out of here.'

'What will we do?'

'Eat a lot.'

'What else?'

'I will learn English.'

'What else?'

'You will get a new arm. Was there something else?'

'Yes. I will call the arm George.'

'George? Because of what?'

'Because George is the name of the automatic pilot.'

'What pilot? Tell me about him. This George.'

It suddenly struck him that she was talking too much; that her sleep had been really full of truth. It seemed better once again to face the possibility of their being separated.

'Suppose we don't get out of here?' he said.

'We will get out.'

'We may get out and we may be separated.'

'We shan't get separated.' He knew that the moment was coming when he would not be able to argue against it. 'I have faith we won't get separated. I had faith we would get here and we got here. I had faith you wouldn't die after the arm and you didn't die.'

'I shall die after it,' he mocked. 'One day.'

'You shouldn't mock death,' she said.

He held her again in the corner of the corridor, glad that he had said something to make her stop talking. It seemed suddenly as if they were the only people awake on the train: very awake in a darkness unknown to them. Then lights were fired out of the night again, red and yellow and black, and the points of another station crackled explosively under the train. He held her against him and again thought, for some reason, quite inconsequentially, of Miss Campbell. The going was very good, after all. It was very good and very wonderful: the night flowing on and themselves the only people awake in it, Marseilles and the uncertainty behind them, and then beyond that, far back, all the difficulties, the nearness of death and the pain. Miss Campbell was quite right. He felt the smooth, warm arm of the girl and wanted suddenly to bury his face in her hair because of the truth of it. Only a little farther, he thought. It can't be much farther. We've come a long way and it can't be much farther. The train swung on in the night, and because of his love and confidence in her he felt himself swing forward before it. For a moment or two he was borne forward on a smooth illusion, and was at last in Spain.

In about half an hour the train stopped at a station. It was not the frontier, and Franklin and the girl went back to their seats. A few people got in and stood in the corridor. In the corner the woman with the book was still reading, and still, sometimes, furtively eating out of her bag.

O'Connor was sleeping in the corner. The girl changed her seat and sat at the right side of Franklin, leaning her head on his shoulder. He put his arm against her and held her there. He looked at O'Connor, the sailors, the woman reading, the attaché case, and persuaded himself for one moment that it was a holiday. Then the train moved on, jerking at first, then smoother and smoother, until the feeling of its inevitability grew on him again. He shut his eyes and wondered how much farther they had to go. It was colder now.

It seemed very cold when he woke and his heart turned over, sick and sour, and he saw the daylight beyond the window-blinds. He knew now there would not be darkness. The sick excitement of the moment, of knowing they were nearly there, made him almost dizzy. O'Connor was still asleep, and the girl was drowsy as Franklin moved her head away from his shoulder and got up. In the corner the woman who resembled Miss Campbell was still reading; she did not look up as he stumbled out into the corridor.

He stood by the window for some time and watched the early day going past: a white farmhouse, with a few vineyards on terraces beyond, and then fields striped brown by ploughing, and then a station house of yellow plaster by a level crossing, and then fields and fields again. The sun was coming uncertainly through grey easterly cloud and he could see a wind blowing the bare trees along the line. The land was rising to the west. Then there was another level crossing, and he saw a peasant and a boy with a brown horse and cart, waiting for the train to come through. Sitting in the cart, the boy had his coat turned up, and Franklin could see the mane of the horse tossed suddenly upwards in a wild fringe by the wind.

He felt in his pocket for his papers. It couldn't be long now. Somewhere in the night the train had stopped again, and now the corridor was empty. He had looked at his papers over and over again, putting them to all the tests. It was impossible to think they were not right.

He stood there for about ten minutes, hating the daylight. There were more houses by the track, in ones and twos, and then in small settlements of twenty or thirty, red and white. The vines were all empty beyond them. The fields were empty, and the wind continued to blow fitfully at the empty trees.

He looked into the compartment and saw the girl wake. She was awake and was combing her hair. Seeing him, she smiled and then the black hair fell over her face and for a moment she was lost. O'Connor was awake, too. The blinds on the other side of the compartment were drawn up, and Franklin could see more houses on that side, and then beyond them the crumpled faint line of mountains.

O'Connor came into the corridor. He shut the door.

'We're coming to it,' Franklin said.

'Any moment now,' O'Connor said.

'If anything happens act as if you didn't know either of us. We'll do the same.'

'Don't worry,' O'Connor said. 'If I don't get out one way I'll get out another.'

Before Franklin could speak again the train began to slow down. He saw more houses go past, and then a new concrete water-tower, and then the first sidings of a station. He stood rigid.

'Go and sit down and tell Françoise to come out a moment,' he said. 'And remember you're a Frenchman now.'

'Don't insult me,' O'Connor said. 'I might shoot myself by mistake.'

He grinned and went into the compartment, shutting the door. The girl had finished combing her hair and in a moment she came out. The train was going very slowly now.

'We must be there,' he said. 'Are you all right?'

'I am all right.' She smiled. Her hair was smooth and lovely where she had combed it.

'There may be some confusion,' he said, 'and we may get separated for a moment. But don't worry.'

'I am not worried.'

He looked up and down the corridor. It was empty.

'Would you kiss me?' he said. 'Here?'

'I will kiss you,' she said.

She kissed him briefly, her lips very warm and steadfast. He felt unsteady.

'Let's go back,' he said. 'I will get the case.'

She did not smile. Her face had the same tense assurance as when he had first seen it, and nothing, he thought, could be more sure than that. He went into the compartment and got down the attaché case from the rack. The two sailors were smoking, and the woman in the corner was still reading. He stood with the case in his hand and looked at the girl and heard the brakes on the train.

In a few more moments the train had stopped and, suddenly, what he had feared and expected and wanted to happen was happening, simply but quickly, in a way that he could not influence nor prevent. He was with the girl out on the platform. He could not see O'Connor. He gripped the case. Some hundreds of passengers seemed to have exploded from the train. For a few moments there was no order among them, and then they were drifting down the platform, and he was with them and the girl with him, and they had their papers in their hands. He was borne forward with them and felt the wind driving coldly down on to the station from the mountains. He saw it blow the dark hair of the girl wildly about her face. It blew into her eyes, so that for a moment she could not see. She brushed it out with her hand. Then he looked back, but still he couldn't see O'Connor, and then the long line of people bore him away from the train, his throat continually tight and dry, until he was in a large office, where men were examining papers and stamping them, and where the worst moment of all his life suddenly slipped past him, unexpectedly simple and brief, before he knew it, and he was walking out again into the cold wind on the station, his papers in his hand. It all seemed so simple that he wondered suddenly if it was purposely simple. He looked wildly about the station for O'Connor. The steam from under the train was blown almost flat along the platform, among the feet of the people. He could not see O'Connor. Walking back towards the coach where they had been he was suddenly torn between the need for finding O'Connor and the fear of losing sight of the girl. He looked back. In the large office behind him the girl was standing at a table. Someone was asking her questions, and he was near enough to see her mouth moving in answer. Her bare head was high up, her hair untidy where the wind had blown it. He thought in that moment how desperately he wanted to marry her. A French curé with long black habit and flat black hat went past him, carrying two bags, and into the crowd, and he wondered why he had never thought of being married in the French church. Then he knew that it could only have complicated things. Now they were almost free and it did not matter. The going is good. Miss Campbell, he thought. Are you thinking of us? We are almost through. We can be married in Madrid.

He thought all this very quickly; it was part of the moments of confusion. He still could not see O'Connor. He turned and looked swiftly into the train, but it was empty. At the far end three or four uniformed men, station officials or perhaps even gendarmes, were getting into the train. He could see their peaked caps above the crowd, and then as he moved back down the platform he saw that they were gendarmes, four of them. They were armed with short rifles.

The crowd on the station had begun to scatter itself; the long queue had been sucked into the office. It was half-past seven. The engine which had brought the train in had been detached and was whistling up the line. He took all this in very swiftly as he looked back for the girl. In that moment he could not see her. Someone else was at the table where she had been. He stared wildly towards the office. Then it was all right. He could see her. She was at another table, with another official, answering other questions.

He still could not see O'Connor. He kept midway between the train and the office. The train was still without an engine and there was plenty of time. Then he saw the Frenchwoman who resembled Miss Campbell. She had her papers in one hand and in the other a cake; she was reading the papers and eating the cake at the same time. He wanted to ask her if she had seen O'Connor, but suddeny he could not remember any words of French, and she went on and got into the train.

In the few moments before he went back the girl had disappeared. He could not see her at all. The desks in the office were occupied by other people, and he knew that she must have come out. He walked wildly about the platform. Down the line the new engine was coming on to the train, and people everywhere were getting back to their seats.

He tried to be very calm. He went back into the train. The Frenchwoman so like Miss Campbell was sitting in the corner of the compartment. She did not look up. Neither the girl nor O'Connor was there.

They must be here, he thought, they must be somewhere. They must be. He walked down two sections of the corridor and then got out on to the platform. The four gendarmes were walking up through the train. It was seven-forty now, and he looked again into the office windows. The girl was not there.

He walked up and down the train for some distance outside it, and then he got into it and walked up the corridor again. It was a very long train and he walked through seven coaches. It seemed to him that there was plenty of time. He wondered where the hell O'Connor could be. He knew that he could go on without O'Connor, but not without the girl. Nothing mattered without her – nothing, nothing, nothing at all. The thought of it filled him with sick panic, and he started to walk back up the train.

The train began to move when he was halfway along it. He knew afterwards that it was a false move; there were many people still on the platform. But he did not know it then, and he began to run. He ran up two sections of corridor, with the train still moving, before he saw O'Connor.

O'Connor was jumping off the train. He was jumping down on to the tracks as Franklin saw him, and then running across them with two of the gendarmes running after him. The train was moving fairly fast as all three of them jumped, and one of the gendarmes fell on his knees. O'Connor was running towards some coal-trucks; he went behind them and then, still running, came out again. The first gendarme was very fast, and was then about thirty yards behind O'Connor. It seemed that he would catch O'Connor very quickly. Then O'Connor made a new line, running hard across open metals between two lines of trucks, gaining a little until he reached the cover of the trucks farther on. Then Franklin saw him stop and press himself against the truck, and wait. He knew in that moment what he was going to do. The gendarme was running up past the truck, between the metals. 'Oh, you bloody fool! You bloody, crazy fool!' Franklin thought. A moment later O'Connor was firing with the revolver. 'Jesus you fool, you fool!' Franklin thought. He saw the gendarme, about twenty yards back, fall back against the truck. 'You fool, you fool!' Franklin thought. 'You poor idiotic fool! Don't shoot any more! Don't shoot!' and then he saw O'Connor shooting at the gendarme for the second and third and fourth time before running on. He saw the gendarme all the time slowly slipping down until he was almost flat against the truck where O'Connor had shot him.

The train began to slow down and then stopped again as O'Connor and the gendarmes disappeared. Franklin walked sickly back up the train. There were several excited people in the corridor, but no gendarmes at all. He pushed past, looking into all the compartments as he walked, but the girl was not there. He knew that she must be in the compartment where they had always been.

He walked back into that compartment but she was not there. Only the Frenchwoman was sitting in the corner, still reading, but not eating now. Franklin stood vaguely in the compartment, holding the attaché case in his hand, feeling as if he were the centre of an absurd and fantastic mistake. He looked frantically out of the window. The train was just beyond the station, and the wind was blowing pieces of straw and dirty paper down the tracks.

He felt lost and helpless as he turned to the woman in the corner.

'The young woman,' he said. 'The girl. Please! Please! The girl who was here. Didn't she come back?'

The woman looked up. She looked remarkably like Miss Campbell in a younger way.

'Yes. She came back.'

'For God's sake, where is she?' he said. 'Please, please, where is she?'

'She was with gendarmes,' the woman said. 'Her papers were not in order. She came back to tell you that, I think.'

'But what had she done to be with gendarmes?'

Already the train was moving, but he did not notice it.

'I don't know. But I should say not much.'

'What makes you say that?'

'She didn't look afraid.'

The train was moving quite fast now, and on the sidings, among the lines of trucks, there was no sign of O'Connor. He was desperate.

'Did she say anything?' he said. 'A message? Please!'

'There was no time,' the woman said. He was not really listening now. He looked at her wildly and then beyond the windows. A new world was racing past. 'The gendarmes took her out. There was some confusion. One of them jumped out of the train. They were all jumping about and running. Did you see? It was all very confused.'

'Yes, I saw it,' he said.

No, he hadn't seen it. Not that gendarme. Were all the gendarmes running? It did not matter. He walked out into the corridor. It was all over. It did not matter if all the gendarmes had jumped off the train. Nothing mattered. He did not want to talk about it now.

He walked frantically up the corridor, carrying the attaché case. He did not want to talk about anything. He walked through the dark intersection between the coaches, swaying blindly. Then he stood by the window on the other side. The inside of himself was dead. He felt suddenly old, bitterly and vacantly old, in a way that Miss Campbell, herself so very old, would never have understood. After a few moments he felt sick, too, and opened the window and let the wind, cold and violent, blow in on his face. The trees at the foot of the mountains, dark and grey on the sunless side, were leafless. The leaves blown from them looked harsh and dry after the heat of summer. The wind sweeping down the slopes had driven them into great brown drifts in the hollows everywhere.

He stood there for what seemed a long time before shutting the window. The cold wind blowing in so violently from the rush of the train had stung his eyes, and he shut them for a few moments, pressing his head on the glass.

When he opened them he could see the reflection of the girl's face, cloudy and unreal, beside his own in the window. It was for a moment part of the world racing past the train. Her face was very white, and he could not believe in the reality of it, and simply stood there watching it stupidly, as if she were a cloudy memory in the glass. Then he saw her breath forming on the cold glass, forming and dissolving and forming again in a small grey circle before the reflection of her mouth. He heard her breathing very quickly. She was breathing with little gasps of pain, as if she had been running to find him and was frightened, and she began to try to talk at the same time. He heard her say something about her papers and the gendarmes, and then about O'Connor. 'They were taking me off the train when he saw and began to run,' she said. She had never been able to pronounce his name in the right way, and he saw her frightened lips mumbling and faltering as she tried to say it now. 'They began running when O'Connor ran. They all left me and began running.'

'Oh God!' he said. 'Don't talk, don't talk!'

He could not bear the agony of her frightened smile or the agony of knowing what O'Connor had done. He wanted to put his arm about her, but she was standing on his left side and there was no arm there to comfort her. He only stared at her, and then rested his face against her head and watched her bright dark eyes.

She leaned against his empty sleeve and he let her go on crying for a long time, not trying to stop her, and as the train rushed on between trees bare and bright in the morning sun he knew that she was not crying for herself. She was not crying for O'Connor, shooting and being shot at, doing a stupid and wonderful thing for them, or because she was young, or for the terror of the moment or for joy or for the things she had left behind. She was not crying for France, or for the doctor, who represented France, or for her father, shot with his own revolver. She was not even crying for himself. He felt she was crying for something that he could never have understood without her, and now did understand because of her. Deep and complete, within himself, all these things were part of the same thing, and he knew that what she was really crying for was the agony of all that was happening in the world.

And as he realized it there were tears in his own eyes, and because of his tears the mountains were dazzling in the sun.

How Brigadier Gerard Won His Medal

SIR ARTHUR CONAN DOYLE

THE DUKE OF TARENTUM, or Macdonald, as his old comrades prefer to call him, was, as I could perceive, in the vilest of tempers. His grim, Scotch face was like one of those grotesque door-knockers which one sees in the Faubourg St Germain. We heard afterwards that the Emperor had said in jest that he would have sent him against Wellington in the South, but that he was afraid to trust him within the sound of the pipes. Major Charpentier and I could plainly see that he was smouldering with anger.

'Brigadier Gerard of the Hussars,' said he, with the air of the corporal with the recruit.

I saluted.

'Major Charpentier of the Horse Grenadiers.'

My companion answered to his name.

'The Emperor has a mission for you.'

Without more ado he flung open the door and announced us.

I have seen Napoleon ten times on horseback to once on foot, and I think that he does wisely to show himself to the troops in this fashion, for he cuts a very good figure in the saddle. As we saw him now he was the shortest man out of six by a good hand's breadth, and yet I am no very big man myself, though I ride quite heavy enough for a hussar. It is evident, too, that his body is too long for his legs. With his big, round head, his curved shoulders, and his clean-shaven face, he is more like a Professor at the Sorbonne than the first soldier in France. Every man to his taste, but it seems to me that, if I could clap a pair of fine light cavalry whiskers, like my own, on to him, it would do him no harm. He has a firm mouth, however, and his eyes are remarkable. I have seen them once turned on me in anger, and I had rather ride at a square on a spent horse than face them again. I am not a man who is easily daunted, either.

He was standing at the side of the room, away from the window, looking up at a great map of the country which was hung upon the wall. Berthier stood beside him, trying to look wise, and just as we entered, Napoleon snatched his sword impatiently from him and pointed with it on the map. He was talking fast and low, but I heard him say, 'The valley of the Meuse,' and twice he repeated 'Berlin'. As we entered, his aide-de-camp advanced to us, but the Emperor stopped him and beckoned us to

21

his side.

'You have not yet received the cross of honour, Brigadier Gerard?' he asked.

I replied that I had not, and was about to add that it was not for want of having deserved it, when he cut me short in his decided fashion.

'And you, Major?' he asked.

'No, sire.'

'Then you shall both have your opportunity now.'

He led us to the great map upon the wall and placed the tip of Berthier's sword on Rheims.

'I will be frank with you, gentlemen, as with two comrades. You have both been with me since Marengo, I believe?' He had a strangely pleasant smile, which used to light up his pale face with a kind of cold sunshine. 'Here at Rheims are our present headquarters on this the 14th of March. Very good. Here is Paris, distant by road a good twenty-five leagues. Blucher lies to the north, Schwarzenberg to the south.' He prodded at the map with the sword as he spoke.

'Now,' said he, 'the further into the country these people march, the more completely I shall crush them. They are about to advance upon Paris. Very good. Let them do so. My brother, the King of Spain, will be there with a hundred thousand men. It is to him that I send you. You will hand him this letter, a copy of which I confide to each of you. It is to tell him that I am coming at once, in two days' time, with every man and horse and gun to his relief. I must give them forty-eight hours to recover. Then straight to Paris! You understand me, gentlemen?'

Ah, if I could tell you the glow of pride which it gave me to be taken into the great man's confidence in this way. As he handed our letters to us I clicked my spurs and threw out my chest, smiling and nodding to let him know that I saw what he would be after. He smiled also, and rested his hand for a moment upon the cape of my dolman. I would have given half my arrears of pay if my mother could have seen me at that instant.

'I will show you your route,' said he, turning back to the map. 'Your orders are to ride together as far as Bazoches. You will then separate, the one making for Paris by Oulchy and Neuilly, and the other to the north by Braine, Soissons, and Senlis. Have you anything to say, Brigadier Gerard?'

I am a rough soldier, but I have words and ideas. I had begun to speak about glory and the peril of France when he cut me short.

'And you, Major Charpentier?'

'If we find our route unsafe, are we at liberty to choose another?' said he.

'Soldiers do not choose, they obey.' He inclined his head to show that we were dismissed, and turned round to Berthier. I do not know what he said, but I heard them both laughing.

Well, as you may think, we lost little time in getting upon our way. In half an hour we were riding down the High Street of Rheims, and it struck twelve o'clock as we passed the Cathedral. I had my little grey mare, Violette, the one which Sebastiani had wished to buy after Dresden. It is the fastest horse in the six brigades of light cavalry, and was only beaten by the Duke of Rovigo's racer from England. As to Charpentier, he had the kind of horse which a horse grenadier or a cuirassier would be likely to ride; a back like a bedstead, you understand, and legs like the posts. He is a hulking fellow himself, so that they looked a singular pair. And yet in his insane conceit he ogled the girls as they waved their handkerchiefs to me from the windows, and he twirled his ugly red moustache up into his eyes, just as if it were to him that their attention was addressed.

When we came out of the town we passed through the French camp, and then across the battle-field of yesterday, which was still covered both by our own poor fellows and by the Russians. But of the two the camp was the sadder sight. Our army was thawing away. The Guards were all right, though the young guard was full of conscripts. The artillery and the heavy cavalry were also good if there were more of them, but the infantry privates with their under officers looked like schoolboys with their masters. And we had no reserves. When one considered that there were 80,000 Prussians to the north and 150,000 Russians and Austrians to the south, it might make even the bravest man grave.

For my own part, I confess that I shed a tear until the thought came that the Emperor was still with us, and that on that very morning he had placed his hand upon my dolman and had promised me a medal of honour. This set me singing, and I spurred Violette on, until Charpentier had to beg me to have mercy on his great, snorting, panting camel. The road was beaten into paste and rutted two feet deep by the artillery, so that he was right in saying that it was not the place for a gallop.

I have never been very friendly with this Charpentier; and now for twenty miles of the way I could not draw a word from him. He rode with his brows pucked and his chin upon his breast, like a man who is heavy with thought. More than once I asked him what was on his mind, thinking that, perhaps, with my quicker intelligence I might set the matter straight. His answer always was that it was his mission of which he was thinking, which surprised me, because, although I had never thought much of his intelligence, still it seemed to me to be impossible that anyone could be puzzled by so simple and soldierly a task.

Well, we came at last to Bazoches, where he was to take the southern road and I the northern. He half turned in his saddle before he left me, and he looked at me with a singular expression of inquiry in his face.

'What do you make of it, Brigadier?' he asked.

'Of what?'

'Of our mission.'

'Surely it is plain enough.'

'You think so? Why should the Emperor tell us his plans?'

'Because he recognized our intelligence.'

My companion laughed in a manner which I found annoying.

'May I ask what you intend to do if you find these villages full of Prussians?' he asked.

'I shall obey my orders.'

'But you will be killed.'

'Very possibly.'

He laughed again, and so offensively that I clapped my hand to my sword. But before I could tell him what I thought of his stupidity and rudeness he had wheeled his horse, and was lumbering away down the other road. I saw his big fur cap vanish over the brow of the hill, and then I rode upon my way, wondering at his conduct. From time to time I put my hand to the breast of my tunic and felt the paper crackle beneath my fingers. Ah, my precious paper, which should be turned into the little silver medal for which I had yearned so long. All the way from Braine to Sermoise I was thinking of what my mother would say when she saw it.

I stopped to give Violette a meal at a wayside auberge on the side of a hill not far from Soissons – a place surrounded by old oaks, and with so many crows that one could scarce hear one's own voice. It was from the innkeeper that I learned that Marmont had fallen back two days before, and that the Prussians were over the Aisne. An hour later, in the fading light, I saw two of their vedettes upon the hill to the right, and then, as darkness gathered, the heavens to the north were all glimmering from the lights of a bivouac.

When I heard that Blucher had been there for two days, I was much surprised that the Emperor should not have known that the country through which he had ordered me to carry my precious letter was already occupied by the enemy. Still, I thought of the tone of his voice when he said to Charpentier that a soldier must not choose, but must obey. I should follow the route he had laid down for me as long as Violette could move a hoof or I a finger upon her bridle. All the way from Sermoise to Soissons, where the road dips up and down, curving among the fir woods, I kept my pistol ready and my sword-belt braced, pushing on swiftly where the path was straight, and then coming slowly round the corners in the way we learned in Spain.

When I came to the farmhouse which lies to the right of the road just after you cross the wooden bridge over the Crise, near where the great statue of the Virgin stands, a woman cried to me from the field, saying that the Prussians were in Soissons. A small party of their lancers, she said, had come in that very afternoon, and a whole division was expected before midnight. I did not wait to hear the end of her tale, but clapped spurs into Violette, and in five minutes was galloping her into the town.

Three Uhlans were at the mouth of the main street, their horses tethered, and they gossiping together, each with a pipe as long as my sabre. I saw them well in the light of an open door, but of me they could have seen only the flash of Violette's grey side and the black flutter of my cloak. A moment later I flew through a stream of them rushing from an open gateway. Violette's shoulder sent one of them reeling, and I stabbed at another but missed him. Pang, pang, went two carbines, but I had flown round the curve of the street, and never so much as heard the hiss of the balls. Ah, we were great, both Violette and I. She lay down to it like a coursed hare, the fire flying from her hoofs. I stood in my stirrups and brandished my sword. Someone sprang for my bridle. I sliced him through the arm, and I heard him howling behind me. Two horsemen closed upon me. I cut one down and outpaced the other. A minute later I was clear of the town, and flying down a broad white road with the black poplars on either side. For a time I heard the rattle of hoofs behind me, but they died and died until I could not tell them from the throbbing of my own heart. Soon I pulled up and listened, but all was silent. They had given up the chase.

Well, the first thing that I did was to dismount and to lead my mare into a small wood through which a stream ran. There I watered her and rubbed her down, giving her two pieces of sugar soaked in cognac from my flask. She was spent from the sharp chase, but it was wonderful to see how she came round with a half-hour's rest. When my thighs closed upon her again, I could tell by the spring and the swing of her that it would not be her fault if I did not win my way safe to Paris.

I must have been well within the enemy's lines now, for I heard a number of them shouting one of their rough drinking songs out of a house by the roadside, and I went round by the fields to avoid it. At another time two men came out into the moonlight (for by this time it was a cloudless night) and shouted something in German, but I galloped on without heeding them, and they were afraid to fire, for their own hussars are dressed exactly as I was. It is best to take no notice at these times, and then they put you down as a deaf man.

It was a lovely moon, and every tree threw a black bar across the road. I could see the countryside just as if it were daytime, and very peaceful it looked, save that there was a great fire raging somewhere in the north. In the silence of the night-time, and with the knowledge that danger was in front and behind me, the sight of that great distant fire was very striking and awesome. But I am not easily clouded, for I have seen too many singular things, so I hummed a tune between my teeth and thought of little Lisette, whom I might see in Paris. My mind was full of her when, trotting round a corner, I came straight upon half-a-dozen German dragoons, who were sitting round a brushwood fire by the roadside.

I am an excellent soldier. I do not say this because I am prejudiced in my own favour, but because I really am so. I can weigh every chance in a moment, and decide with as much certainty as though I had brooded for a week. Now I saw like a flash that, come what might, I should be chased, and on a horse which had already done a long twelve leagues. But it was better to be chased onwards than to be chased back. On this moonlit night, with fresh horses behind me, I must take my risk in either case; but if I were to shake them off, I preferred that it should be near Senlis than near Soissons.

All this flashed on me as if by instinct, you understand. My eyes had hardly rested on the bearded faces under the brass helmets before my rowels had touched Violette, and she was off with a rattle like a pas-de-charge. Oh, the shouting and rushing and stamping from behind us! Three of them fired and three swung themselves on to their horses. A bullet rapped on the crupper of my saddle with a noise like a stick on a door. Violette sprang madly forward, and I thought she had been wounded, but it was only a graze above the near fore-fetlock. Ah, the dear little mare, how I loved her when I felt her settle down into that long, easy gallop of hers, her hoofs going like a Spanish girl's castanets. I could not hold myself. I turned on my saddle and shouted and raved, 'Vive l'Empereur!' I screamed and laughed at the gust of oaths that came back to me.

But it was not over yet. If she had been fresh she might have gained a mile in five. Now she could only hold her own with a very little over. There was one of them, a young boy of an officer, who was better mounted than the others. He drew ahead with every stride. Two hundred yards behind him were two troopers, but I saw every time that I glanced round that the distance between them was increasing. The other three who had waited to shoot were a long way in the rear.

The officer's mount was a bay – a fine horse, though not to be spoken of with Violette; yet it was a powerful brute, and it seemed to me that in a few miles its freshness might tell. I waited until the lad was a long way in front of his comrades, and then I eased my mare down a little – a very, very little, so that he might think he was really catching me. When he came within pistol-shot of me I drew and cocked my own pistol, and laid my chin upon my shoulder to see what he would do. He did not offer to fire, and I soon discerned the cause. The silly boy had taken his pistols from his holsters when he had camped for the night. He did not seem to understand that he was at my mercy. I eased Violette down until there was not the length of a long lance between the grey tail and the bay muzzle.

'Rendez-vous!' he yelled.

'I must compliment monsieur upon his French,' said I, resting the barrel of my pistol upon my bridle-arm, which I have always found best when shooting from the saddle. I aimed at his face, and could see, even in the moonlight, how white he grew when he understood that it was all up with him. But even as my finger pressed the trigger I thought of his mother, and I put my ball through his horse's shoulder. I fear he hurt himself in the fall, for it was a fearful crash, but I had my letter to think of, so I stretched the mare into a gallop once more.

But they were not so easily shaken off, these brigands. The two troopers thought no more of their young officer than if he had been a recruit thrown in the riding-school. They left him to the others and thundered on after me. I had pulled up on the brow of a hill, thinking that I had heard the last of them; but, my faith, I soon saw there was no time for loitering; so away we went, the mare tossing her head and I my shako, to show what we thought of two dragoons who tried to catch a hussar. But at this moment, even while I laughed at the thought, my heart stood still within me, for there at the end of the long white road was a black patch of cavalry waiting to receive me. To a young soldier it might have seemed the shadow of the trees, but to me it was a troop of hussars, and, turn where I could, death seemed to be waiting for me.

Well, I had the dragoons behind me and the hussars in front. Never since Moscow have I seemed to be in such peril. But for the honour of the brigade I had rather be cut down by a light cavalryman than by a heavy. I never drew bridle, therefore, or hesitated for an instant, but I let Violette have her head. I remember that I tried to pray as I rode, but I am a little out of practice at such things, and the only words I could remember were the prayer for fine weather which we used at the school on the evening before holidays. Even this seemed better than nothing, and I was pattering it out, when suddenly I heard French voices in front of me. Ah, mon Dieu, but the joy went through my heart like a musket-ball. They were ours – our own dear little rascals from the corps of Marmont. Round whisked my two dragoons and galloped for their lives, with the moon gleaming on their brass helmets, while I trotted up to my friends with no undue haste, for I would have them understand that though a hussar may fly, it is not in his nature to fly very fast. Yet I fear that Violette's heaving flanks and foam-spattered muzzle gave the lie to my careless bearing.

Who should be at the head of the troop but old Bouvet, whom I saved at Leipzig! When he saw me his little pink eyes filled with tears, and indeed, I could not but shed a few myself at the sight of his joy. I told him of my mission, but he laughed when I said that I must pass through Senlis.

'The enemy is there,' said he. 'You cannot go.'

'I prefer to go where the enemy is,' I answered.

'But why not go straight to Paris with your despatch? Why should you choose to pass through the one place where you are almost sure to be taken or killed?'

'A soldier does not choose – he obeys,' said I, just as I had heard Napoleon say it.

Old Bouvet laughed in his wheezy way, until I had to give my moustachios a twirl and look him up and down in a manner which brought him to reason.

'Well', said he, 'you had best come along with us, for we are all bound for Senlis. Our orders are to reconnoitre the place. A squadron of Poniatowski's Polish Lancers are in front of us. If you must ride through it, it is possible that we may be able to go with you.'

So away we went, jingling and clanking through the quiet night until we came up with the Poles – fine old soldiers all of them, though a trifle heavy for their horses. It was a treat to see them, for they could not have carried themselves better if they had belonged to my own brigade. We rode together, until in the early morning we saw the lights of Senlis. A peasant was coming along with a cart, and from him we learned how things were going there.

His information was certain, for his brother was the Mayor's coachman, and he had spoken with him late the night before. There was a single squadron of Cossacks – or a polk, as they call it in their frightful language – quartered upon the Mayor's house, which stands at the corner of the market-place, and is the largest building in the town. A whole division of Prussian infantry was encamped in the woods to the north, but only the Cossacks were in Senlis. Ah, what a chance to avenge ourselves upon these barbarians, whose cruelty to our poor countryfolk was the talk at every camp fire.

We were into the town like a torrent, hacked down the vedettes, rode over the guard, and were smashing in the doors of the Mayor's house before they understood that there was a Frenchman within twenty miles of them. We saw horrid heads at the windows – heads bearded to the temples, with tangled hair and sheepskin caps, and silly, gaping mouths. 'Hourra! Hourra!' they shrieked, and fired with their carbines, but our fellows were into the house and at their throats before they had wiped the sleep out of their eyes. It was dreadful to see how the Poles flung themselves upon them, like starving wolves upon a herd of fat bucks – for, as you know, the Poles have a blood feud against the Cossacks. The most were killed in the upper rooms, whither they had fled for shelter, and the blood was pouring down into the hall like rain from a roof. They are terrible soldiers, these Poles, though I think they are a trifle heavy for their horses. Man for man, they are as big as Kellerman's cuirassiers. Their equipment is, of course, much lighter, since they are without the cuirass, back-plate, and helmet.

Well, it was at this point that I made an error – a very serious error it must be admitted. Up to this moment I had carried out my mission in a manner which only my modesty prevents me from describing as remarkable. But now I did that which an official would condemn and a soldier excuse.

There is no doubt that the mare was spent, but still it is true that I might have galloped on through Senlis and reached the country, where I should have had no enemy between me and Paris. But what hussar can ride past a fight and never draw rein? It is to ask too much of him. Besides, I thought that if Violette had an hour of rest I might have three hours the better at the other end. Then on the top of it came those heads at the windows, with their sheepskin hats and their barbarous cries. I sprang from my saddle, threw Violette's bridle over a rail-post, and ran into the house with the rest. It is true that I was too late to be of service, and that I was nearly wounded by a lance-thrust from one of these dying savages. Still, it is a pity to miss even the smallest affair, for one never knows what opportunity for advancement may present itself. I have seen more soldierly work in outpost skirmishes and little gallop-and-hack affairs of the kind than in any of the Emperor's big battles.

When the house was cleared I took a bucket of water out for Violette, and our peasant guide showed me where the good Mayor kept his fodder. My faith, but the little sweetheart was ready for it. Then I sponged down her legs, and leaving her still tethered I went back into the house to find a mouthful for myself, so that I should not need to halt again until I was in Paris.

And now I come to the part of my story which may seem singular to you, although I could tell you at least ten things every bit as queer which have happened to me in my lifetime. You can understand that, to a man who spends his life in scouting and vedette duties on the bloody ground which lies between two great armies, there are many chances of strange experiences. I'll tell you, however, exactly what occurred.

Old Bouvet was waiting in the passage when I entered, and he asked me whether we might not crack a bottle of wine together. 'My faith, we must not be long,' said he. 'There are ten thousand of Theilmann's Prussians in the woods up yonder.'

'Where is the wine?' I asked.

'Ah, you may trust two hussars to find where the wine is,' said he, and taking a candle in his hand, he led the way down the stone stairs into the kitchen.

When we got there we found another door, which opened on to a winding stair with the cellar at the bottom. The Cossacks had been there before us, as was easily seen by the broken bottles littered all over it. However, the Mayor was a *bon-vivant*, and I do not wish to have a better set of bins to pick from. Chambertin, Graves, Alicante, white wine and red, sparkling and still, they lay in pyramids peeping coyly out of sawdust. Old Bouvet stood with his candle looking here and peeping there, purring in his throat like a cat before a milk-pail. He had picked upon a Burgundy at last, and had his hand outstretched to the bottle when there came a roar of musketry from above us, a rush of feet, and such a yelping and screaming as I have never listened to. The Prussians were upon us!

Bouvet is a brave man: I will say that for him. He flashed out his sword and away he clattered up the stone steps, his spurs clinking as he ran. I followed him, but just as we came out into the kitchen passage a tremendous shout told us that the house had been recaptured.

'It is all over,' I cried, grasping at Bouvet's sleeve.

'There is one more to die,' he shouted, and away he went like a madman up the second stair. In effect, I should have gone to my death also had I been in his place, for he had done very wrong in not throwing out his scouts to warn him if the Germans advanced upon him. For an instant I was about to rush up with him, and then I bethought myself that, after all, I had my own mission to think of, and that if I were taken the important letter of the Emperor would be sacrificed. I let Bouvet die alone, therefore, and I went down into the cellar again, closing the door behind me.

Well, it was not a very rosy prospect down there either. Bouvet had dropped the candle when the alarm came, and I, pawing about in the darkness, could find nothing but broken bottles. At last I came upon the candle, which had rolled under the curve of a cask, but, try as I would with my tinderbox, I could not light it. The reason was that the wick had been wet in a puddle of wine, so suspecting that this might be the case, I cut the end off with my sword. Then I found that it lighted easily enough. But what to do I could not imagine. The scoundrels upstairs were shouting themselves hoarse, several hundred of them from the sound, and it was clear that some of them would soon want to moisten their throats. There would be an end to a dashing soldier, and of the mission and of the medal. I thought of my mother and I thought of the Emperor. It made me weep to think that the one would lose so excellent a son and the other the best light cavalry officer he ever had since Lasalle's time. But presently I dashed the tears from my eyes. 'Courage!' I cried, striking myself upon the chest. 'Courage, my brave boy. Is it possible that one who has come safely from Moscow without so much as a frost-bite will die in a French wine-cellar?' At the thought I was up on my feet and clutching at the letter in my tunic, for the crackle of it gave me courage.

My first plan was to set fire to the house, in the hope of escaping in the confusion. My second to get into an empty wine-cask. I was looking round to see if I could find one, when suddenly, in the corner, I espied a little low door, painted of the same grey colour as the wall, so that it was only a man with quick sight who would have noticed it. I pushed against it, and at first I imagined that it was locked. Presently, however, it gave a little, and then I understood that it was held by the pressure of something on the other side. I put my feet against a hogshead of wine, and gave such a push that the door flew open and I came down with a crash upon my back, the candle flying out of my hands, so that I found myself in darkness once more. I picked myself up and stared through the black archway into the gloom beyond.

There was a slight ray of light coming from some slit or grating. The dawn had broken outside, and I could dimly see the long, curving sides of several huge casks, which made me think that perhaps this was where the Mayor kept his reserves of wine while they were maturing. At any rate, it seemed to be a safer hiding-place than the outer cellar, so gathering up my candle, I was just closing the door behind me, when I suddenly saw something which filled me with amazement, and even, I confess, with the smallest little touch of fear.

I have said that at the further end of the cellar there was a dim grey fan of light striking downwards from somewhere near the roof. Well, as I peered through the darkness, I suddenly saw a great, tall man skip into this belt of daylight, and then out again into the darkness at the further end. My word, I gave such a start that my shako nearly broke its chin-strap! It was only a glance, but, none the less, I had time to see that the fellow had a hairy Cossack cap on his head, and that he was a great, long-legged, broad-shouldered brigand, with a sabre at his waist. My faith, even Etienne Gerard was a little staggered at being left alone with such a creature in the dark.

But only for a moment. 'Courage!' I thought. 'Am I not a hussar, a brigadier, too, at the age of thirty-one, and the chosen messenger of the Emperor?' After all, this skulker had more cause to be afraid of me than I of him. And then suddenly I understood that he was afraid – horribly afraid. I could read it from his quick step and his bent shoulders as he ran among the barrels, like a rat making for its hole. And, of course, it must have been he who had held the door against me, and not some packing-case or wine-cask as I had imagined. He was the pursued then, and I the pursuer. Aha, I felt my whiskers bristle as I advanced upon him through the darkness! He would find that he had no chicken to deal with, this robber from the North. For the moment I was magnificent.

At first I had feared to light my candle lest I should make a mark of myself, but now, after cracking my shin over a box, and catching my spurs in some canvas, I thought the bolder course the wiser. I lit it, therefore, and then advanced with long strides, my sword in my hand. 'Come out, you rascal!' I cried. 'Nothing can save you. You will at last meet with your deserts.'

I held my candle high, and presently I caught a glimpse of the man's head staring at me over a barrel. He had a gold chevron on his black cap, and the expression of his face told me in an instant that he was an officer and a man of refinement.

'Monsieur,' he cried, in excellent French, 'I surrender myself on a promise of quarter. But if I do not have your promise, I will then sell my life as dearly as I can.'

'Sir,' said I, 'a Frenchman knows how to treat an unfortunate enemy. Your life is safe.' With that he handed his sword over the top of the barrel, and I bowed with the candle on my heart. 'Whom have I the honour of capturing?' I asked.

'I am the Count Boutkine, of the Emperor's own Don Cossacks,' said he. 'I came out with my troop to reconnoitre Senlis, and as we found no sign of your people we determined to spend the night here.'

'And would it be an indiscretion,' I asked, 'if I were to inquire how you came into the back cellar?'

'Nothing more simple,' said he. 'It was our intention to start at early dawn. Feeling chilled after dressing, I thought that a cup of wine would do me no harm, so I came down to see what I could find. As I was rummaging about, the house was suddenly carried by assault so rapidly that by the time I had climbed the stairs it was all over. It only remained for me to save myself, so I came down here and hid myself in the back cellar, where you have found me.'

I thought of how old Bouvet had behaved under the same conditions, and the tears sprang to my eyes as I contemplated the glory of France. Then I had to consider what I should do next. It was clear that this Russian Count, being in the back cellar while we were in the front one, had not heard the sounds which would have told him that the house was once again in the hands of his own allies. If he should once understand this the tables would be turned, and I should be his prisoner instead of he being mine. What was I to do? I was at my wits' end, when suddenly there came to me an idea so brilliant that I could not but be amazed at my own invention.

'Count Boutkine,' said I, 'I find myself in a most difficult position.'

'And why?' he asked.

'Because I have promised you your life.'

His jaw dropped a little.

'You would not withdraw your promise?' he cried.

'If the worst comes to the worst I can die in your defence,' said I; 'but the difficulties are great.'

'What is it, then?' he asked.

'I will be frank with you,' said I. 'You must know that our fellows, and especially the Poles, are so incensed against the Cossacks that the mere sight of the uniform drives them mad. They precipitate themselves instantly upon the wearer and tear him limb from limb. Even their officers cannot restrain them.'

The Russian grew pale at my words and the way in which I said them.

'But this is terrible,' said he.

'Horrible!' said I. 'If we were to go up together at this moment I cannot promise how far I could protect you.'

'I am in your hands,' he cried. 'What would you suggest that we should do? Would it not be best that I should remain here?'

'That worst of all.'

'And why?'

'Because our fellows will ransack the house presently, and then you would be cut to pieces. No, no, I must go and break it to them. But even then, when once they see that accursed uniform, I do not know what may happen.'

'Should I then take the uniform off?'

'Excellent!' I cried. 'Hold, we have it! You will take your uniform off and put on mine. That will make you sacred to every French soldier.'

'It is not the French I fear so much as the Poles.'

'But my uniform will be a safeguard against either.'

'How can I thank you?' he cried. 'But you – what are you to wear?'

'I will wear yours.'

'And perhaps fall a victim to your generosity?'

'It is my duty to take the risk,' I answered; 'but I have no fears. I will ascend in your uniform. A hundred swords will be turned upon me. "Hold!" I will shout, "I am the Brigadier Gerard!" Then they will see my face. They will know me. And I will tell them about you. Under the shield of these clothes you will be sacred.'

His fingers trembled with eagerness as he tore off his tunic. His boots and breeches were much like my own, so there was no need to change them, but I gave him my hussar jacket, my dolman, my shako, my sword-belt, and my sabre-tasche, while I took in exchange his high sheepskin cap with the gold chevron, his fur-trimmed coat, and his crooked sword. Be it well understood that in changing the tunics I did not forget to change my thrice-precious letter also from my old one to my new.

'With your leave,' said I, 'I shall now bind you to a barrel.'

He made a great fuss over this, but I have learned in my soldiering never to throw away chances, and how could I tell that he might not, when my back was turned, see how the matter really stood, and break in upon my plans? He was leaning against a barrel at the time, so I ran six times round it with a rope, and then tied it with a big knot behind. If he wished to come upstairs he would, at least, have to carry a thousand litres of good French wine for a knapsack. I then shut the door of the back cellar behind me, so that he might not hear what was going forward, and tossing the candle away I ascended the kitchen stair.

There were only about twenty steps, and yet, while I came up them, I seemed to have time to think of everything that I had ever hoped to do. It was the same feeling that I had at Eylau when I lay with my broken leg and saw the horse artillery galloping down upon me. Of course, I knew that if I were taken I should be shot instantly as being disguised within the enemy's lines. Still, it was a glorious death – in the direct service of the Emperor – and I reflected that there could not be less than five lines, and perhaps seven, in the *Moniteur* about me. Palaret had eight lines, and I am sure that he had not so fine a career.

When I made my way out into the hall, with all the nonchalance in my face and manner that I could assume, the very first thing that I saw was Bouvet's dead body, with his legs drawn up and a broken sword in his hand. I could see by the black smudge that he had been shot at close quarters. I should have wished to salute as I went by, for he was a gallant man, but I feared lest I should be seen, and so I passed on.

The front of the hall was full of Prussian infantry, who were knocking loopholes in the wall, as though they expected that there might be yet another attack. Their officer, a little man, was running about giving directions. They were all too busy to take much notice of me, but another officer, who was standing by the door with a long pipe in his mouth, strode across and clapped me on the shoulder, pointing to the dead bodies of our poor hussars, and saying something which was meant for a jest, for his long beard opened and showed every fang in his head. I laughed heartily also, and said the only Russian words that I knew. I learned them from little Sophie, at Wilna, and they meant: 'If the night is fine we shall meet under the oak tree, but if it rains we shall meet in the byre.' It was all the same to this German, however, and I have no doubt that he gave me credit for saying something very witty indeed, for he roared laughing, and slapped me on my shoulder again. I nodded to him and marched out of the hall-door as coolly as if I were the commandant of the garrison.

There were a hundred horses tethered about outside, most of the them belonging to the Poles and hussars. Good little Violette was waiting with the others, and she whinnied when she saw me coming towards her. But I would not mount her. No. I was much too cunning for that. On the contrary, I chose the most shaggy little Cossack horse that I could see, and I sprang upon it with as much assurance as though it had belonged to my father before me. It had a great bag of plunder slung over its neck, and this I laid upon Violette's back, and led her along beside me. Never have you seen such a picture of the Cossack returning from the foray. It was superb.

Well, the town was full of Prussians by this time. They lined the side-walks and pointed me out to each other, saying, as I could judge from their gestures, 'There goes one of those devils of Cossacks. They are the boys for foraging and plunder.'

One or two officers spoke to me with an air of authority, but I shook my head and smiled, and said, 'If the night is fine we shall meet under the oak tree, but if it rains we shall meet in the byre,' at which they shrugged their shoulders and gave the matter up. In this way I worked along until I was beyond the northern outskirt of the town. I could see in the roadway two lancer vedettes with their black and white pennons, and I knew that when I was once past these I should be a free man once more. I made my pony trot, therefore, Violette rubbing her nose against my knee all the time, and looking up at me to ask how she had deserved that this hairy doormat of a creature should be preferred to her. I was not more than a hundred yards from the Uhlans when, suddenly, you can imagine my feelings when I saw a real Cossack coming galloping along the road towards me.

Ah, my friend, you read this, if you have any heart, you will feel for a man like me, who had gone through so many dangers and trials, only at this very last moment to be confronted with one which appeared to put an end to everything. I will confess that for a moment I lost heart, and was inclined to throw myself down in my despair, and to cry out that I had been betrayed. But, no; I was not beaten even now. I opened two buttons of my tunic so that I might get easily at the Emperor's message, for it was my fixed determination when all hope was gone to swallow the letter and then die sword in hand. Then I felt that my little, crooked sword was loose in its sheath, and I trotted on to where the vedettes were waiting. They seemed inclined to stop me, but I pointed to the other Cossack, who was still a couple of hundred yards off, and they, understanding that I merely wished to meet him, let me pass with a salute.

I dug my spurs into my pony then, for if I were only far enough from the lancers I thought I might manage the Cossack without much difficulty. He was an officer, a large, bearded man, with a gold chevron in his cap, just the same as mine. As I advanced he unconsciously aided me by pulling up his horse, so that I had a fine start of the vedettes. On I came for him, and I could see wonder changing to suspicion in his brown eyes as he looked at me and at my pony, and at my equipment. I do not know what it was that was wrong, but he saw something which was as it should not be. He shouted out a question, and then when I gave no answer he pulled out his sword. I was glad in my heart to see him do so, for I had always rather fight than cut down an unsuspecting enemy. Now I made at him full tilt, and, parrying his cut, I got my point in just under the fourth button of his tunic. Down he went, and the weight of him nearly took me off my horse before I could disengage. I never glanced at him to see if he were living or dead, for I sprang off my pony and on to Violette, with a shake of my bridle and a kiss of my hand to the two Uhlans behind me. They galloped after me, shouting, but Violette had had her rest, and was just as fresh as when she started. I took the first side road to the west and then the first to the south, which would take me away from the enemy's country. On we went and on, every stride taking me further from my foes and nearer to my friends. At last, when I reached the end of a long stretch of road, and looking back from it could see no sign of any pursuers, I understood that my troubles were over.

And it gave me a glow of happiness, as I rode, to think that I had done to the letter what the Emperor had ordered. What would he say when he saw me? What could he say which would do justice to the incredible way in which I had risen above every danger? He had ordered me to go through Sermoise, Soissons, and Senlis, little dreaming that they were all three occupied by the enemy. And yet I had done it. I had borne his letter in safety through each of these towns. Hussars, dragoons, lancers, Cossacks, and infantry – I had run the gauntlet of all of them, and had come out unharmed.

When I had got as far as Dammartin I caught a first glimpse of our own outposts. There was a troop of dragoons in a field, and of course I could see from the horsehair crests that they were French. I galloped towards them in order to ask them if all was safe between there and Paris, and as I rode I felt such a pride at having won my way back to my friends again, that I could not refrain from waving my sword in the air.

At this a young officer galloped out from among the dragoons, also brandishing his sword, and it warmed my heart to think that he should come riding with such ardour and enthusiasm to greet me. I made Violette caracole, and as we came together I brandished my sword more gallantly than ever, but you can imagine my feelings when he suddenly made a cut at me which would certainly have taken my head off if I had not fallen forward with my nose in Violette's mane. My faith, it whistled just over my cap like an east wind. Of course, it came from this accursed Cossack uniform which, in my excitement, I had forgotten all about, and this young dragoon had imagined that I was some Russian champion who was challenging the French cavalry. My word, he was a frightened man when he understood how near he had been to killing the celebrated Brigadier Gerard.

Well, the road was clear, and about three o'clock in the afternoon I was at St Denis, though it took me a long two hours to get from there to Paris, for the road was blocked with commissariat waggons and guns of the artillery reserve, which was going north to Marmont and Mortier. You cannot conceive the excitement which my appearance in such a costume made in Paris, and when I came to the Rue de Rivoli I should think I had a quarter of a mile of folk riding or running behind me. Word had got about from the dragoons (two of whom had come with me), and everybody knew about my adventures and how I had come by my uniform. It was a triumph – men shouting and women waving their handkerchiefs and blowing kisses from the windows.

Although I am a man singularly free from conceit, still I must confess that, on this one occasion, I could not restrain myself from showing that this reception gratified me. The Russian's coat had hung very loose upon me, but now I threw out my chest until it was as tight as a sausage-skin. And my little sweetheart of a mare tossed her mane and pawed with her front hoofs, frisking her tail about as though she said, 'We've done it together this time. It is to us that commissions should be entrusted.' When I kissed her between the nostrils as I dismounted at the gate of the Tuileries, there was as much shouting as if a bulletin had been read from the Grand Army.

I was hardly in costume to visit a King; but, after all, if one has a soldierly figure one can do without all that. I was shown up straight away to Joseph, whom I had often seen in Spain. He seemed as stout, as quiet, and as amiable as ever. Talleyrand was in the room with him, or I suppose I should call him the Duke of Benevento, but I confess that I like old names best. He read my letter when Joseph Buonaparte handed it to him, and then he looked at me with the strangest expression in those funny little, twinkling eyes of his.

'Were you the only messenger?' he asked.

'There was one other, sir,' said I. 'Major Charpentier, of the Horse Grenadiers.'

'He has not yet arrived,' said the King of Spain.

'If you had seen the legs of his horse, sire, you would not wonder at it,' I remarked.

'There may be other reasons,' said Talleyrand, and he gave that singular smile of his.

Well, they paid me a compliment or two, thought they might have said a good deal more and yet have said too little. I bowed myself out, and very glad I was to get away, for I hate a Court as much as I love a camp. Away I went to my old friend Chaubert, in the Rue Miromesnil, and there I got his hussar uniform, which fitted me very well. He and Lisette and I supped together in his rooms, and all my dangers were forgotten. In the morning I found Violette ready for another twenty-league stretch. It was my intention to return instantly to the Emperor's headquarters, for I was, as you may well imagine, impatient to hear his words of praise, and to receive my reward.

I need not say that I rode back by a safe route, for I had seen quite enough of Uhlans and Cossacks. I passed through Meaux and Château Thierry, and so in the evening I arrived at Rheims, where Napoleon was still lying. The bodies of our fellows and of St Prest's Russians had all been buried, and I could see changes in the camp also. The soldiers looked better cared for; some of the cavalry had received remounts, and everything was in excellent order. It was wonderful what a good general can effect in a couple of days.

When I came to the headquarters I was shown straight into the

Emperor's room. He was drinking coffee at a writing-table, with a big plan drawn out on paper in front of him. Berthier and Macdonald were leaning, one over each shoulder, and he was talking so quickly that I don't believe that either of them could catch a half of what he was saying. But when his eyes fell upon me he dropped the pen on to the chart, and he sprang up with a look in his pale face which struck me cold.

'What the deuce are you doing here?' he shouted. When he was angry he had a voice like a peacock.

'I have the honour to report to you, sire,' said I, 'that I have delivered your despatch safely to the King of Spain.'

'What!' he yelled, and his two eyes transfixed me like bayonets. Oh, those dreadful eyes, shifting from grey to blue, like steel in the sunshine. I can see them now when I have a bad dream.

'What has become of Charpentier?' he asked.

'He is captured,' said Macdonald.

'By whom?'

'The Russians.'

'The Cossacks?'

'No, a single Cossack.'

'He gave himself up?'

'Without resistance.'

'He is an intelligent officer. You will see that the medal of honour is awarded to him.'

When I heard those words I had to rub my eyes to make sure that I was awake.

'As to you,' cried the Emperor, taking a step forward as if he would have struck me, 'you brain of a hare, what do you think that you were sent upon this mission for? Do you conceive that I would send a really important message by such a hand as yours, and through every village which the enemy holds? How you came through them passes my comprehension; but if your fellow-messenger had had but as little sense as you, my whole plan of campaign would have been ruined. Can you not see, coglione, that this message contained false news, and it was intended to deceive the enemy whilst I put a very different scheme into execution?'

When I heard those cruel words and saw the angry, white face which glared at me, I had to hold the back of a chair, for my mind was failing me and my knees would hardly bear me up. But then I took courage as I reflected that I was an honourable gentleman, and that my whole life had been spent in toiling for this man and for my beloved country.

'Sire,' said I, and the tears would trickle down my cheeks whilst I spoke, 'when you are dealing with a man like me you would find it wiser to deal openly. Had I known that you had wished the despatch to fall into the hands of the enemy, I would have seen that it came there. As I believed that I was to guard it, I was prepared to sacrifice my life for it. I do not believe, sire, that any man in the world ever met with more toils and perils than I have done in trying to carry out what I thought was your will.'

I dashed the tears from my eyes as I spoke, and with such fire and spirit as I could command I gave him an account of it all, of my dash through Soissons, my brush with the dragoons, my adventure in Senlis, my rencontre with Count Boutkine in the cellar, my disguise, my meeting with the Cossack officer, my flight, and how at the last moment I was nearly cut down by a French dragoon. The Emperor, Berthier, and Macdonald listened with astonishment on their faces. When I had finished Napoleon stepped forward and he pinched me by the ear.

'There, there!' said he. 'Forget anything which I may have said. I would have done better to trust you. You may go.'

I turned to the door, and my hand was upon the handle, when the Emperor called upon me to stop.

'You will see,' said he, turning to the Duke of Tarentum, 'that Brigadier Gerard has the special medal of honour, for I believe that if he has the thickest head he has also the stoutest heart in my army.'

The Invaders
RICHARD HILLARY

As young pilots fresh from university, Hillary and his friends are now eagerly awaiting their first experience of combat after the frustrating months of the 'phoney war' . . . . .

AFTER KICKING OUR HEELS for two days at Turnhouse, a reaction set in. We were like children with the promise of a trip to the seaside, broken because of rain. On the third day I allowed myself to be persuaded against my better judgment to take up a gun again.

The Duke of Hamilton, the Station CO, had offered the Squadron a couple of days grouse-shooting on his estate. Colin, of course, was eager to go as were two other 'A' Flight pilots, Sheep Gilroy and Black Morton. Sheep was a Scotsman and a farmer, with a port-wine complexion and features which gave rise to his name. I finally agreed to go in place of Peter Pease, who was on duty, and the four of us set off. It was pouring with rain when we arrived, to be greeted by the usual intimidating band of beaters, loaders, gillies, and what-not. We set off at once for the butts, an uphill climb across the moors of a mere couple of miles, the others apparently in no way put out by the weather. We climbed in single file, I bringing up the protesting rear, miserable, wet, and muddy from repeated falls into the heather. After about an hour we reached the top and disposed ourselves in four butts, while the beaters, loaders, gillies, and what-not squelched away into the mist. After the first half-hour, during which my hands turned blue and my feet lost all feeling, I sat down and resigned myself to the sensation of the wet earth steadily seeping through my breeches. From time to time I got up and looked over at the others, alert, guns gripped firmly, staring eagerly into the mist, and I was ashamed of my craven spirit: I chid myself. Were there not gentlemen – and the right type of gentlemen too – who paid £30 a day for the privilege of just such suffering? My musings were interrupted by a series of animal cries, and from out of the mist emerged the beaters, beating. As a result of this lengthy co-ordination of effort one hare and two rather tired-looking birds put in an apologetic short-lived appearance, to be summarily dispatched by our withering fire. The prospect of lunch cheered me, and my hunger was such that I was undismayed at the thought of the long walk back, but my illusions were rudely shattered when we set off purposefully for a second lot of butts where a larger flock, flight, covey, or what-have-you was expected. Once again the beaters vanished into the mist, once again we were left damply to our meditations, and once again a discreet flutter of wings rewarded our vigil. This time my cries of hunger were accorded a grudging attention and we set off for the brake, parked some miles away and containing whisky and sandwiches. Sheep and Black Morton had to return to Turnhouse that evening for duty, but Colin and I were to stay overnight and shoot again in the morning (on condition it wasn't raining). Back at the lodge I got out of my wet clothes and sank gratefully into a hot bath, allowing the steam to waft away the more acute memories of the day's discomforts. Colin at dinner stretched out his legs contentedly, and his face wore the rapt expression of the madman who, when asked why he banged his head against the wall, replied that it was such fun when he stopped.

We retired early to bed and slept until, at two o'clock in the morning, a gillie banged on the door. Colin got up, took from the gillie's hand a telegram, opened it, and read it aloud. It said: SQUADRON MOVING SOUTH STOP CAR WILL FETCH YOU AT EIGHT OCLOCK DENHOLM. For us, the war began that night.

At ten o'clock we were back at Turnhouse. The rest of the Squadron were all set to leave; we were to move down to Hornchurch, an aerodrome twelve miles east of London on the Thames Estuary. Four machines would not be serviceable until the evening, and Broody Benson, Pip Cardell, Colin, and I were to fly them down. We took off at four o'clock, some five hours after the others, Broody leading, Pip and I to each side, and Colin in the box, map-reading. Twenty-four of us flew south that tenth day of August 1940: of those twenty-four, eight were to fly back.

We landed at Hornchurch at about seven o'clock to receive our first shock. Instead of one section there were four squadrons at readiness; 603 Squadron were already in action. They started coming in about half an hour after we landed, smoke stains along the leading edges of the wings showing that all the guns had been fired. They had acquitted themselves well although caught at a disadvantage of height.

'You don't have to look for them,' said Brian. 'You have to look for a way out.'

From this flight Don MacDonald did not return.

At this time the Germans were sending over comparatively few bombers. They were making a determined attempt to wipe out our entire fighter force, and from dawn till dusk the sky was filled with Messerschmitts 109s and 110s.

Half a dozen of us always slept over at the dispersal hut to be ready for a surprise enemy attack at dawn. This entailed being up by four-thirty and by five o'clock having our machines warmed up and the oxygen, sights and ammunition tested. The first Hun attack usually came over about breakfast-time and from then until eight o'clock at night we were almost continuously in the air. We ate when we could, baked beans and bacon and eggs being sent over from the mess.

On the morning after our arrival I walked over with Peter Howes and Broody. Howes was at Hornchurch with another squadron and worried because he had as yet shot nothing down. Every evening when we came into the mess he would ask us how many we had got and then go over miserably to his room. His squadron had had a number of losses and was due for relief. If ever a man needed it, it was Howes. Broody, on the other hand, was in a high state of excitement, his sharp eager face grinning from ear to ear. We left Howes at his dispersal hut and walked over to where our machines were being warmed up. The voice of the controller came unhurried over the loud-speaker, telling us to take off, and in a few seconds we were running for our machines. I climbed into the cockpit of my plane and felt an empty sensation of suspense in the pit of my stomach. For one second time seemed to stand still and I stared blankly in front of me. I knew that that morning I was to kill for the first time. That I might be killed or in any way injured did not occur to me. Later, when we were losing pilots regularly, I did consider it in an abstract way when on the ground; but once in the air, never. I knew it could not happen to me. I suppose every pilot knows that, knows it cannot happen to him; even when he is taking off for the last time, when he will not return, he knows that he cannot be killed. I wondered idly what he was like, this man I would kill. Was he young, was he fat, would he die with the Fuehrer's name on his lips, or would he die alone, in that last moment conscious of himself as a man? I would never know. Then I was being strapped in, my mind automatically checking the controls, and we were off.

We ran into them at 18,000 feet, twenty yellow-nosed Messerschmitt 109s, about 500 feet above us. Our squadron strength was eight, and as they came down on us we went into line astern and turned head on to them. Brian Carbury, who was leading the Section, dropped the nose of his machine, and I could almost feel the leading Nazi pilot push forward on his stick to bring his guns to bear. At the same moment Brian hauled hard back on his own control stick and led us over them in a steep climbing turn to the left. In two vital seconds they lost their advantage. I saw Brian let go a burst of fire at the leading plane, saw the pilot put his machine into a half roll, and knew that he was mine. Automatically, I kicked the rudder to the left to get him at right angles, turned the gun-button to 'Fire', and let go in a four-second burst with full deflection. He came right through my sights and I saw the tracer from all eight guns thud home. For a second he seemed to hang motionless; then a jet of red flame shot upwards and he spun out of sight.

For the next few minutes I was too busy looking after myself to think of anything, but when, after a short while, they turned and made off over the Channel, and we were ordered to our base, my mind began to work again.

It had happened.

My first emotion was one of satisfaction, satisfaction at a job adequately done, at the final logical conclusion of months of specialized training. And then I had a feeling of the essential rightness of it all. He was dead and I was alive; it could so easily have been the other way round; and that would somehow have been right too. I realized in that moment just how lucky a fighter pilot is. He has none of the personalized emotions of the soldier, handed a rifle and bayonet and told to charge. He does not even have to share the dangerous emotions of the bomber pilot who night after night must experience that childhood longing for smashing things. The fighter pilot's emotions are those of the duellist – cool, precise, impersonal. He is privileged to kill well. For if one must either kill or be killed, as now one must, it should, I feel, be done with dignity. Death should be given the setting it deserves; it should never be a pettiness; and for the fighter pilot it never can be.

From this flight Broody Benson did not return.

During that August-September period we were always so outnumbered that it was practically impossible, unless we were lucky enough to have the advantage of height, to deliver more than one squadron attack. After a few seconds we always broke up, and the sky was a smoke trail of individual dog-fights. The result was that the Squadron would come home individually, machines landing one after the other at intervals of about two minutes. After an hour, Uncle George would make a check-up on who was missing. Often there would be a telephone-call from some pilot to say that he had made a forced landing at some other aerodrome, or in a field. But the telephone wasn't always so welcome. It would be a rescue squad announcing the number of a crashed machine; then Uncle George would check it, and cross another name off the list. At that time, the losing of pilots was somehow extremely impersonal; nobody, I think, felt any great emotion – there simply wasn't time for it.

After the hard lesson of the first two days, we became more canny and determined not to let ourselves be caught from above. We would fly on the reciprocal of the course given us by the controller until we got to 15,000 feet, and then fly back again, climbing all the time. By this means we usually saw the Huns coming in below us, and were in a perfect position to deliver a squadron attack. If caught at a disadvantage, they would never stay to fight, but always turned straight back for the Channel. We arranged a system whereby two pilots always flew together – thus if one should follow a 'plane down the other stayed 500 feet or so above, to protect him from attack in the rear.

Often machines would come back to their base just long enough for the ground staff, who worked with beautiful speed, to refuel them and put in a new oxygen bottle and more ammunition before taking off again. Uncle George was shot down several times but always turned up unhurt; once we thought Rusty was gone for good, but he was back leading his flight the next day; one sergeant pilot in 'A' Flight was shot down four times, but he seemed to bear a charmed life.

The sun and the great height at which we flew often made it extremely difficult to pick out the enemy machines, but it was here that Sheep's experience on the moors of Scotland proved invaluable. He always led the guard section and always saw the Huns long before anyone else. For me the sun presented a major problem. We had dark lenses on our glasses, but I, as I have mentioned before, never wore mine. They gave me a feeling of claustrophobia.

With spots on the wind-screen, spots before the eyes, and a couple of spots which might be Messerschmitts, blind spots on my goggles seemed too much of a good thing; I always slipped them up on to my forehead before going into action. For this and for not wearing gloves I paid a stiff price.

I remember once going practically to France before shooting down a 109. There were two of them, flying at sea-level and headed for the French coast. Raspberry was flying beside me and caught one half-way across. I got right up close behind the second one and gave it a series of short bursts. It darted about in front, like a startled rabbit, and finally plunged into the sea about three miles off the French coast.

On another occasion I was stupid enough actually to fly over France: the sky appeared to be perfectly clear but for one returning Messerschmitt, flying very high. I had been trying to catch him for about ten minutes and was determined that he should not get away. Eventually I caught him inland from Calais and was just about to open fire when I saw a squadron of twelve Messerschmitts coming in on my right. I was extremely frightened, but turned in towards them and opened fire at the leader. I could see his tracer going past underneath me, and then I saw his hood fly off, and the next moment they were past. I didn't wait to see any more, but made off for home, pursued for half the distance by eleven very determined Germans. I landed a good hour after everyone else to find Uncle George just finishing his check-up. From this flight Larry Cunningham did not return.

After about a week of Hornchurch, I woke late one morning to the noise of machines running up on the aerodrome. It irritated me: I had a headache.

Having been on every flight the previous day, the morning was mine to do with as I pleased. I got up slowly, gazed dispassionately at my tongue in the mirror, and wandered over to the mess for breakfast. It must have been getting on for twelve o'clock when I came out on to the aerodrome to find the usual August heat haze forming a dull pall over everything. I started to walk across the aerodrome to the dispersal point on the far side. There were only two machines on the ground so I concluded that the Squadron was already up. Then I heard a shout, and our ground crew drew up in a lorry beside me. Sergeant Ross leaned out:

'Want a lift, sir? We're going round.'

'No, thanks, Sergeant. I'm going to cut across.'

This was forbidden for obvious reasons, but I felt like that.

'O.K., sir. See you round there.'

The lorry trundled off down the road in a cloud of dust. I walked on across the landing ground. At that moment I heard the emotionless voice of the controller.

'Large enemy bombing formation approaching Hornchurch. All personnel not engaged in active duty take cover immediately.'

I looked up. They were still not visible. At the dispersal point I saw Bubble and Pip Cardell make a dash for the shelter. Three Spitfires had just landed, turned about and came past me with a roar to take off down-wind. Our lorry was still trundling along the road, maybe half-way round, and seemed suddenly an awfully long way from the dispersal point.

I looked up again, and this time I saw them – about a dozen slugs, shining in the bright sun and coming straight on. At the rising scream of the first bomb I instinctively shrugged up my shoulders and ducked my head. Out of the corner of my eye I saw the three Spitfires. One moment they were about twenty feet up in close formation; the next catapulted apart as though on elastic. The leader went over on his back and ploughed along the runway with a rending crash of tearing fabric; No. 2 put a wing in and spun around on his airscrew, while the plane on the left was blasted wingless into the next field. I remember thinking stupidly, 'That's the shortest flight he's ever taken,' and then my feet were nearly knocked from under me, my mouth was full of dirt, and Bubble, gesticulating like a madman from the shelter entrance, was yelling, 'Run, you bloody fool, run!' I ran. Suddenly awakened by the lunacy of my behaviour, I covered the distance to the shelter as if impelled by a rocket and shot through the entrance while once again the ground rose up and hit me, and my head smashed hard against one of the pillars. I subsided on a heap of rubble and massaged it.

'Who's here?' I asked, peering through the gloom.

'Cardell and I and three of our ground crew,' said Bubble, 'and, by the Grace of God, you!'

I could see by his mouth that he was still talking, but a sudden concentration of the scream and crump of falling bombs made it impossible to hear him.

The air was thick with dust and the shelter shook and heaved at each explosion, yet somehow held firm. For about three minutes the bedlam continued, and then suddenly ceased. In the utter silence which followed nobody moved. None of us wished to be the first to look on the devastation which we felt must be outside. Then Bubble spoke. 'Praise God!' he said, 'I'm not a civilian. Of all the bloody frightening things I've ever done, sitting in that shelter was the worst. Me for the air from now on!'

It broke the tension and we scrambled out of the entrance. The runways were certainly in something of a mess. Gaping holes and great gobbets of earth were everywhere. Right in front of us a bomb had landed by my Spitfire, covering it with a shower of grit and rubble.

I turned to the aircraftman standing beside me. 'Will you get hold of Sergeant Ross and tell him to have a crew give her an inspection.'

I followed his glance and saw the lorry, the roof about twenty yards away, lying grotesquely on its side. I climbed into the cockpit, and, feeling faintly sick, tested out the switches. Bubble poked his head over the side.

'Let's go over to the mess and see what's up: all our machines will be landing down at the reserve landing field, anyway.'

I climbed out and walked over to find that the three Spitfire pilots were quite unharmed but for a few superficial scratches, in spite of being machine-gunned by the bombers. 'Operations' was undamaged: no hangar had been touched and the Officers' Mess had two windows broken.

The Station Commander ordered every available man and woman on to the job of repairing the aerodrome surface and by four o'clock there was not a hole to be seen. Several unexploded bombs were marked off, and two lines of yellow flags were laid down to mark the runways. At five o'clock our Squadron, taking off for a 'flap' from the reserve field, landed without incident on its home base. Thus, apart from four men killed in the lorry and a network of holes on the landing surface, there was nothing to show for ten minutes' really accurate bombing from 12,000 feet, in which several dozen sticks of bombs had been dropped. It was a striking proof of the inefficacy of their attempts to wipe out our advance fighter aerodromes.

Brian had a bullet through his foot, and as my machine was still out of commission, I took his place in readiness for the next show. I had had enough of the ground for one day.

Six o'clock came and went, and no call. We started to play poker and I was winning. It was agreed that we should stop at seven: should there be a 'flap' before then, the game was off. I gazed anxiously at the clock. I am always unlucky at cards, but when the hands pointed to 6.55 I really began to feel my luck was on the change. But sure enough at that moment came the voice of the controller: '603 Squadron take off and patrol base: further instructions in the air.'

We made a dash for our machines and within two minutes were off the ground. Twice we circled the aerodrome to allow all twelve planes to get in formation. We were flying in four sections of three: Red Section leading, Blue and Green to right and left, and the three remaining planes forming a guard section above and behind us. I was flying No. 2 in the Blue Section.

Over the radio came the voice of the controller: 'Hullo, Red Leader,' followed by instructions on course and height.

As always, for the first few minutes we flew on the reciprocal of the course given until we reached 15,000 feet. We then turned about and flew on 110° in an all-out climb, thus coming out of the sun and gaining height all the way.

During the climb Uncle George was in constant touch with the ground. We were to intercept about twenty enemy fighters at 25,000 feet. I glanced across at Stapme and saw his mouth moving. That meant he was singing again. He would sometimes do this with his radio set on 'send', with the result that, mingled with our instructions from the ground, we would hear a raucous rendering of 'Night and Day'. And then quite clearly over the radio I heard the Germans excitedly calling to each other. This was a not infrequent occurrence and it made one feel that they were right behind, although often they were some distance away. I switched my set to 'send' and called out '*Halt's Maul!*' and as many other choice pieces of German invective as I could remember. To my delight I heard one of them answer: 'You feelthy Englishman, we will teach you how to speak to a German.' I am aware that this sounds a tall story, but several others in the Squadron were listening out and heard the whole thing.

I looked down. It was a completely cloudless sky and way below lay the English countryside, stretching lazily into the distance, a quite extraordinary picture of green and purple in the setting sun.

I took a glance at my altimeter. We were at 28,000 feet. At that moment Sheep yelled 'Tallyho' and dropped down in front of Uncle George in a slow dive in the direction of the approaching planes. Uncle George saw them at once: 'O.K. Line astern.'

I drew in behind Stapme and took a look at them. They were about 2,000 feet below us, which was a pleasant change, but they must have spotted us at the same moment, for they were forming a protective circle, one behind the other, which is a defence formation hard to break.

'Echelon starboard,' came Uncle George's voice.

We spread out fanwise to the right.

'Going down!'

One after the other we peeled off in a power dive. I picked out one machine and switched my gun-button to 'Fire'. At 300 yards I had him in my sights. At 200 I opened up in a long four-second burst and saw the tracer going into his nose. Then I was pulling out, so hard that I could feel my eyes dropping through my neck. Coming round in a slow climbing turn, I saw that we had broken them up. The sky was now a mass of individual dog-fights. Several of them had already been knocked down. One I hoped was mine, but on pulling up I had not been able to see the result. To my left I saw Peter Pease make a head-on attack on a Messerschmitt. They were headed straight for each other and it looked as though the fire of both was striking home. Then at the last moment the Messerschmitt pulled up, taking Peter's fire full in the belly. It rolled on to its back, yellow flames pouring from the cockpit, and vanished.

The next few minutes were typical. First the sky a bedlam of machines; then suddenly silence and not a plane to be seen. I noticed then that I was very tired and very hot. The sweat was running down my face in rivulets. But this was no time for vague reflections. Flying around the sky on one's own at that time was not a healthy course of action.

I still had some ammunition left. Having no desire to return to the aerodrome until it had all been used to some good purpose, I took a look around the sky for some friendly fighters. About a mile away over Dungeness I saw a formation of about forty Hurricanes on patrol at 20,000 feet. Feeling that there was safety in numbers, I set off in their direction. When about 200 yards from the rear machine, I looked down and saw 5,000 feet below another formation of fifty machines flying in the same direction. Flying stepped like this was an old trick of the Huns, and I was glad to see we were adopting the same tactics. But as though hit by a douche of cold water, I suddenly woke up. There were far more machines flying together than we could ever muster over one spot. I took another look at the rear machine in my formation, and sure enough, there was the Swastika on its tail. Yet they all seemed quite oblivious of my presence. I had the sun behind me and a glorious opportunity. Closing in to 150 yards I let go a three-second burst into the rear machine. It flicked on to its back and spun out of sight. Feeling like an irresponsible schoolboy who has perpetrated some crime which must inevitably be found out, I glanced round me. Still nobody seemed disturbed. I suppose I could have repeated the performance on the next machine, but I felt that it was inadvisable to tempt Providence too far. I did a quick half roll and made off home, where I found to my irritation that Raspberry, as usual, had three planes down to my one.

There was to be a concert on the station that night, but as I had to be up at five the next morning for Dawn Readiness, I had a quick dinner and two beers, and went to bed, feeling not unsatisfied with the day.

Perhaps the most amusing though painful experience which I had was when I was shot down acting as 'Arse-end Charlie' to a squadron of Hurricanes. Arse-end Charlie is the man who weaves backwards and forwards above and behind the squadron to protect them from attack from the rear. There had been the usual dog-fights over the South Coast, and the squadron had broken up. Having only fired one snap burst, I climbed up in search of friendly Spitfires, but found instead a squadron of Hurricanes flying round the sky at 18,000 feet in sections of stepped-up threes, but with no rear-guard. So I joined in. I learned within a few seconds the truth of the old warning, 'Beware of the Hun in the Sun'. I was making pleasant little sweeps from side to side, and peering earnestly into my mirror when, from out of the sun and dead astern, bullets started appearing along my port wing. There is an appalling tendency to sit and watch this happen without taking any action, as though mesmerized by a snake; but I managed to pull myself together and go into a spin, at the same time attempting to call up the Hurricanes and warn them, but I found that my radio had been shot away. At first there appeared to be little damage done and I started to climb up again, but black smoke began pouring out of the engine and there was an unpleasant smell of escaping glycol. I thought I had better get home while I could; but as the wind-screen was soon covered with oil I realized that I couldn't make it and decided instead to put down at Lympne, where there was an aerodrome. Then I realized that I wasn't going to make Lympne either – I was going at full boost and only clocking ninety miles per hour, so I decided that I had better put down in the nearest field before I stalled and spun in. I chose a cornfield and put the machine down on its belly. Fortunately nothing caught fire, and I had just climbed out and switched off the petrol, when to my amazement I saw an ambulance coming through the gate. This I thought was real service, until the corporal and two orderlies who climbed out started cantering away in the opposite direction, their necks craned up to the heavens. I looked up and saw about fifty yards away a parachute, and suspended on the end, his legs dangling vaguely, Colin. He was a little burned about his face and hands but quite cheerful.

We were at once surrounded by a bevy of officers and discovered that we had landed practically in the back garden of a Brigade cocktail party. A salvage crew from Lympne took charge of my machine, a doctor took charge of Colin, and the rest took charge of me, handing me double whiskies for the nerves at a laudable rate. I was put up that night by the Brigadier, who thought I was suffering from a rather severe shock, largely because by dinner-time I was so pie-eyed that I didn't dare open my mouth but answered all his questions with a glassy stare. The next day I went up to London by train, a somewhat incongruous figure, carrying a helmet and parachute. The prospect of a long and tedious journey by tube to Hornchurch did not appeal to me, so I called up the Air Ministry and demanded a car and a WAAF. I was put on to the good lady in charge of transport, a sergeant, who protested apologetically that she must have the authorization of a Wing Commander. I told her forcibly that at this moment I was considerably more important than any Wing Commander, painted a vivid picture of the complete disorganization of Fighter Command in the event of my not being back at Hornchurch within an hour, and clinched the argument by telling her that my parachute was a military secret which must on no account be seen in a train. By the afternoon I was flying again.

That evening there was a terrific attack on Hornchurch and, for the first time since coming south, I saw some bombers. There were twelve Dornier 215s flying in close formation at about 12,000 feet, and headed back for France. I was on my way back to the aerodrome when I first sighted them about 5,000 feet below me. I dived straight down in a quarter head-on attack. It seemed quite impossible to miss, and I pressed the button. Nothing happened; I had already fired all my ammunition. I could not turn back, so I put both my arms over my head and went straight through the formation, never thinking I'd get out of it unscratched. I landed on the aerodrome with the machine, quite serviceable, but a little draughty.

From this flight Bubble Waterson did not return.

And so August drew to a close with no slackening of pressure in the enemy offensive. Yet the Squadron showed no signs of strain, and I personally was content. This was what I had waited for, waited for nearly a year, and I was not disappointed. If I felt anything, it was a sensation of relief. We had little time to think, and each day brought new action. No one thought of the future: sufficient unto the day was the emotion thereof. At night one switched off one's mind like an electric light.

It was one week after Bubble went that I crashed into the North Sea.

The War of the Worlds

H.G. WELLS

The day after the landing of the first Martian cylinder, although several people are dead and the newspapers and armed forces have been alerted to the threat of all-out invasion, the ordinary routines of English suburban life continue – but not for long .....

SATURDAY LIVES IN MY memory as a day of suspense. It was a day of lassitude too, hot and close, with, I am told, a rapidly fluctuating barometer. I had slept but little, though my wife had succeeded in sleeping, and I rose early. I went into my garden before breakfast, and stood listening, but towards the common there was nothing stirring but a lark.

The milkman came as usual. I heard the rattle of his chariot, and I went round to the side gate to ask the latest news. He told me that during the night the Martians had been surrounded by troops, and that guns were expected. Then, a familiar reassuring note, I heard a train running towards Woking.

'They aren't to be killed,' said the milkman, 'if that can posibly be avoided.'

I saw my neighbour gardening, chatted with him for a time, and then strolled in to breakfast. It was a most unexceptional morning. My neighbour was of opinion that the troops would be able to capture or to destroy the Martians during the day.

'It's a pity they make themselves so unapproachable,' he said. 'It would be curious to learn how they live on another planet; we might learn a thing or two.'

He came up to the fence and extended a handful of strawberries, for his gardening was as generous as it was enthusiastic. At the same time he told me of the burning of the pine-woods about the Byfleet Golf Links.

'They say,' said he, 'that there's another of those blessed things fallen there – number two. But one's enough, surely. This lot'll cost the insurance people a pretty penny before everything's settled.' He laughed with an air of the greatest good-humour as he said this. The woods, he said, were still burning, and pointed out a haze of smoke to me. 'They will be hot under foot for days on account of the thick soil of pine-needles and turf,' he said, and then grew serious over 'poor Ogilvy'.

After breakfast, instead of working, I decided to walk down towards the common. Under the railway bridge I found a group of soldiers – sappers, I think, men in small round caps, dirty red jackets unbuttoned, and showing their blue shirts, dark trousers, and boots coming to the calf. They told me no one was allowed over the canal, and, looking along the road towards the bridge, I saw one of the Cardigan men standing sentinel there. I talked with these soldiers for a time; I told them of my sight of the Martians on the previous evening. None of them had seen the Martians, and they had but the vaguest ideas of them, so that they plied me with questions. They said that they did not know who had authorized the movements of the troops; their idea was that a dispute had arisen at the Horse Guards. The ordinary sapper is a great deal better educated than the common soldier, and they discussed the peculiar conditions of the possible fight with some acuteness. I described the Heat-Ray to them, and they began to argue among themselves.

'Crawl up under cover and rush 'em, say I,' said one.

'Get aht!' said another. 'What's cover against this 'ere 'eat? Sticks to cook yer! What we got to do is to go as near as the ground'll let us, and then drive a trench.'

'Blow yer trenches! You always want trenches; you ought to ha' been born a rabbit, Snippy.'

'Ain't they got any necks, then?' said a third abruptly – a little, contemplative, dark man, smoking a pipe.

I repeated my description.

'Octopuses,' said he, 'that's what I calls 'em. Talk about fishers of men – fighters of fish it is this time!'

'It ain't no murder killing beasts like that,' said the first speaker.

'Why not shell the darned things strite off and finish 'em?' said the little dark man. 'You carn tell what they might do.'

'Where's your shells?' said the first speaker. 'There ain't no time. Do it in a rush, that's my tip, and do it at once.'

So they discussed it. After a while I left them, and went on to the railway-station to get as many morning papers as I could.

But I will not weary the reader with a description of that long morning and of the longer afternoon. I did not succeed in getting a glimpse of the common, for even Horsell and Chobham church towers were in the hands of the military authorities. The soldiers I addressed didn't know anything; the officers were mysterious as well as busy. I found people in the town quite secure again in the presence of the military, and I heard for the first time from Marshall, the tobacconist, that his son was among the dead on the common. The soldiers had made the people on the outskirts of Horsell lock up and leave their houses.

I got back to lunch about two, very tired, for, as I have said, the day was extremely hot and dull, and in order to refresh myself I took a cold bath in the afternoon. About half-past four I went up to the railway-station to get an evening paper, for the morning papers had contained only a very inaccurate description of the killing of Stent, Henderson, Ogilvy, and the others. But there was little I didn't know. The Martians did not show an inch of themselves. They seemed busy in their pit, and there was a sound of hammering and an almost continuous streamer of smoke. Apparently, they were busy getting ready for a struggle. 'Fresh attempts have been made to signal, but without success,' was the stereotyped formula of the papers. A sapper told me it was done by a man in a ditch with a flag on a long pole. The Martians took as much notice of such advances as we should of the lowing of a cow.

I must confess the sight of all this armament, all this preparation, greatly excited me. My imagination became belligerent, and defeated the invaders in a dozen striking ways; something of my schoolboy dreams of battle and heroism came back. It hardly seemed a fair fight to me at that time. They seemed very helpless in this pit of theirs.

About three o'clock there began the thud of a gun at measured intervals from Chertsey or Addlestone. I learnt that the smouldering pine-wood into which the second cylinder had fallen was being shelled, in the hope of destroying that object before it opened. It was only about five, however, that a field-gun reached Chobham for use against the first body of Martians.

About six in the evening, as I sat at tea with my wife in the summer-house talking vigorously about the battle that was lowering upon us, I heard a muffled detonation from the common, and immediately after a gust of firing. Close on the heels of that came a violent, rattling crash, quite close to us, that shook the ground; and, starting out upon the lawn, I saw the tops of the trees about the Oriental College burst into smoky red flame, and the tower of the little church beside it slide down into ruin. The pinnacle of the mosque had vanished, and the roof-line of the college itself looked as if a hundred-ton gun had been at work upon it. One of our chimneys cracked as if a shot had hit it, flew, and the piece of it came clattering down the tiles and made a heap of broken red fragments upon the flower-bed by my study window.

I and my wife stood amazed. Then I realized that the crest of Maybury Hill must be within range of the Martians' Heat-Ray now that the college was cleared out of the way.

At that I gripped my wife's arm, and without ceremony ran her out into the road. Then I fetched out the servant, telling her I would go upstairs myself for the box she was clamouring for.

'We can't possibly stay here,' I said; and as I spoke the firing reopened for a moment upon the common.

'But where are we to go?' said my wife in terror.

I thought, perplexed. Then I remembered her cousins at Leatherhead.

'Leatherhead!' I shouted above the sudden noise.

She looked away from me downhill. The people were coming out of their houses astonished.

'How are we to get to Leatherhead?' she said.

Down the hill I saw a bevy of hussars ride under the railway bridge; three galloped through the open gates of the Oriental College; two others dismounted, and began running from house to house. The sun, shining through the smoke that drove up from the tops of the trees, seemed blood-red, and threw an unfamiliar lurid light upon everything.

'Stop here,' said I; 'you are safe here;' and I started off at once for the Spotted Dog, for I knew the landlord had a horse and dog-cart. I ran, for I perceived that in a moment everyone upon this side of the hill would be moving. I found him in his bar, quite unaware of what was going on behind his house. A man stood with his back to me, talking to him.

'I must have a pound,' said the landlord, 'and I've no one to drive it.'

'I'll give you two,' said I, over the stranger's shoulder.

'What for?'

'And I'll bring it back by midnight,' I said.

'Lord!' said the landlord, 'what's the hurry? I'm selling my bit of a pig. Two pounds, and you bring it back? What's going on now?'

I explained hastily that I had to leave my home, and so secured the dog-cart. At the time it did not seem to me nearly so urgent that the landlord should leave his. I took care to have the cart there and then, drove it off down the road, and, leaving it in charge of my wife and servant, rushed into my house and packed a few valuables, such plate as we had, and so forth. The beech trees below the house were burning while I did this, and the palings up the road glowed red. While I was occupied in this way, one of the dismounted hussars came running up. He was going from house to house, warning people to leave. He was going on as I came out of my front door, lugging my treasures, done up in a table-cloth. I shouted after him:

'What news?'

He turned, stared, bawled something about 'crawling out in a thing like a dish-cover', and ran on to the gate of the house at the crest. A sudden whirl of black smoke driving across the road hid him for a moment. I ran to my neighbour's door, and rapped to satisfy myself, what I already knew, that his wife had gone to London with him, and had locked up their house. I went in again according to my promise to get my servant's box, lugged it out, clapped it beside her on the tail of the dog-cart, and then caught the reins and jumped up into the driver's seat beside my wife. In another moment we were clear of the smoke and noise, and spanking down the opposite slope of Maybury Hill towards Old Woking.

In front was a quiet sunny landscape, a wheat-field ahead on either side of the road, and the Maybury Inn with its swinging sign. I saw the doctor's cart ahead of me. At the bottom of the hill I turned my head to look at the hillside I was leaving. Thick streamers of black smoke shot with threads of red fire were driving up into the still air, and throwing dark shadows upon the green tree-tops eastward. The smoke already extended far away to the east and west – to the Byfleet pine-woods eastward, and to Woking on the west. The road was dotted with people running towards us. And very faint now, but very distinct through the hot, quiet air, one heard the whirr of a machine-gun that was presently stilled, and an intermittent cracking of rifles. Apparently, the Martians were setting fire to everything within range of their Heat-Ray.

I am not an expert driver, and I had immediately to turn my attention to the horse. When I looked back again the second hill had hidden the black smoke. I slashed the horse with the whip, and gave him a loose rein until Woking and Send lay between us and that quivering tumult. I overtook and passed the doctor between Woking and Send.

Leatherhead is about twelve miles from Maybury Hill. The scent of hay was in the air through the lush meadows beyond Pyrford, and the hedges on either side were sweet and gay with multitudes of dog-roses. The heavy firing that had broken out while we were driving down Maybury Hill ceased as abruptly as it began, leaving the evening very peaceful and still. We got to Leatherhead without misadventure about nine o'clock, and the horse had an hour's rest while I took supper with my cousins and commended my wife to their care.

My wife was curiously silent throughout the drive, and seemed oppressed with forebodings of evil. I talked to her reassuringly, pointing out that the Martians were tied to the pit by sheer heaviness, and, at the utmost, could but crawl a little out of it, but she answered only in monosyllables. Had it not been for my promise to the innkeeper, she would, I think, have urged me to stay in Leatherhead that night. Would that I had! Her face, I remember, was very white as we parted.

For my own part, I had been feverishly excited all day. Something very like the war fever, that occasionally runs through a civilized community, had got into my blood, and in my heart I was not so very sorry that I had to return to Maybury that night. I was even afraid that the last fusillade I had heard might mean the extermination of our invaders from Mars. I can best express my state of mind by saying that I wanted to be in at the death.

It was nearly eleven when I started to return. The night was unexpectedly dark; to me, walking out of the lighted passage of my cousins' house, it seemed indeed black, and it was as hot and close as the day. Overhead the clouds were driving fast, albeit not a breath stirred the shrubs about us. My cousins' man lit both lamps. Happily, I knew the road intimately. My wife stood in the light of the doorway, and watched me until I jumped up into the dogcart. Then abruptly she turned and went in, leaving my cousins side by side wishing me good hap.

I was a little depressed at first with the contagion of my wife's fears, but very soon my thoughts reverted to the Martians. At that time I was absolutely in the dark as to the course of the evening's fighting. I did not know even the circumstances that had precipitated the conflict. As I came through Ockham (for that was the way I returned, and not through Send and Old Woking) I saw along the western horizon a blood-red glow, which, as I drew nearer, crept slowly up the sky. The driving clouds of the gathering thunderstorm mingled there with masses of black and red smoke.

Ripley Street was deserted, and except for a lighted window or so the village showed not a sign of life; but I narrowly escaped an accident at the corner of the road to Pyrford, where a knot of people stood with their backs to me. They said nothing to me as I passed. I do not know what they knew of the things happening beyond the hill, nor do I know if the silent houses I passed on my way were sleeping securely, or deserted and empty, or harassed and watching against the terror of the night.

From Ripley until I came through Pyrford I was in the valley of the Wey, and the red glare was hidden from me. As I ascended the little hill beyond Pyrford Church the glare came into view again, and the trees about me shivered with the first intimation of the storm that was upon me. Then I heard midnight pealing out from Pyrford Church behind me, and then came the silhouette of Maybury Hill, with its tree-tops and roofs black and sharp against the red.

Even as I beheld this a lurid green glare lit the road about me, and showed the distant woods towards Addlestone. I felt a tug at the reins. I saw that the driving clouds had been pierced as it were by a thread of green fire, suddenly lighting their confusion and falling into the fields to my left. It was the Third Falling Star!

Close on its apparition, and blindingly violet by contrast, danced out the first lightning of the gathering storm, and the thunder burst like a rocket overhead. The horse took the bit between his teeth and bolted.

A moderate incline runs down towards the foot of Maybury Hill, and down this we clattered. Once the lightning had begun, it went on in as rapid a succession of flashes as I have ever seen. The thunder-claps, treading one on the heels of another and with a strange crackling accompaniment, sounded more like the working of a gigantic electric machine than the usual detonating reverberations. The flickering light was blinding and confusing, and a thin hail smote gustily at my face as I drove down the slope.

At first I regarded little but the road before me, and then abruptly my attention was arrested by something that was moving rapidly down the opposite slope of Maybury Hill. At first I took it for the wet roof of a house, but one flash following another showed it to be in swift rolling movement. It was an elusive vision – a moment of bewildering darkness, and than a flash like daylight, the red masses of the Orphanage near the crest of the hill, the green tops of the pine trees, and this problematical object came out clear and sharp and bright.

And this thing I saw! How can I describe it? A monstrous tripod, higher than many houses, striding over the young pine trees, and smashing them aside in its career; a walking engine of glittering metal, striding now across the heather; articulate ropes of steel dangling from it, and the clattering tumult of its passage mingling with the riot of the thunder. A flash, and it came out vividly, heeling over one way with two feet in the air, to vanish and reappear almost instantly as it seemed, with the next flash, a hundred yards nearer. Can you imagine a milking-stool tilted and bowled violently along the ground? That was the impression those instant flashes gave. But instead of a milking-stool imagine it a great body of machinery on a tripod stand.

Then suddenly the trees in the pine-wood ahead of me were parted, as brittle reeds are parted by a man thrusting through them; they were snapped off and driven headlong, and a second huge tripod appeared, rushing, as it seemed, headlong towards me. And I was galloping hard to meet it! At the sight of the second monster my nerve went altogether. Not stopping to look again, I wrenched the horse's head hard round to the right, and in another moment the dog-cart had heeled over upon the horse; the shafts smashed noisily, and I was flung sideways and fell heavily into a shallow pool of water.

I crawled out almost immediately, and crouched, my feet still in the water, under a clump of furze. The horse lay motionless (his neck was broken, poor brute!), and by the lightning flashes I saw the black bulk of the overturned dog-cart, and the silhouette of the wheel still spinning slowly. In another moment the colossal mechanism went striding by me, and passed up-hill towards Pyrford.

Seen nearer, the thing was incredibly strange, for it was no mere insensate machine driving on its way. Machine it was, with a ringing metallic pace, and long flexible glittering tentacles (one of which gripped a young pine tree) swinging and rattling about its strange body. It picked its road as it went striding along, and the brazen hood that surmounted it moved to and fro with the inevitable suggestion of a head looking about it. Behind the main body was a huge thing of white metal like a gigantic fisherman's basket, and puffs of green smoke squirted out from the joints of the limbs as the monster swept by me. And in an instant it was gone.

So much I saw then, all vaguely for the flickering of the lightning, in blinding high lights and dense black shadows.

As it passed it set up an exultant deafening howl that drowned the thunder: 'Aloo! aloo!' and in another minute it was with its companion, and half a mile away, stooping over something in the field. I have no doubt this thing in the field was the third of the ten cylinders they had fired at us from Mars.

For some minutes I lay there in the rain and darkness watching, by the intermittent light, these monstrous beings of metal moving about in the distance over the hedge-tops. A thin hail was now beginning, and as it came and went, their figures grew misty and then flashed into clearness again. Now and then came a gap in the lightning, and the night swallowed them up.

I was soaked with hail above and puddle-water below. It was some time before my blank astonishment would let me struggle up the bank to a drier position, or think at all of my imminent peril.

Not far from me was a little one-roomed squatter's hut of wood, surrounded by a patch of potato-garden. I struggled to my feet at last, and, crouching and making use of every chance of cover, I made a run for this. I hammered at the door, but I could not make the people hear (if there were any people inside), and after a time I desisted, and, availing myself of a ditch for the greater part of the way, succeeded in crawling, unobserved by these monstrous machines, into the pine-wood towards Maybury.

Under cover of this I pushed on, wet and shivering now, towards my own house. I walked among the trees trying to find the footpath. It was very dark indeed in the wood, for the lightning was now becoming infrequent, and the hail, which was pouring down in a torrent, fell in columns through the gaps in the heavy foliage.

If I had fully realized the meaning of all the things I had seen I should have immediately worked my way round through Byfleet to Street Cobham, and so gone back to rejoin my wife at Leatherhead. But that night the strangeness of things about me, and my physical wretchedness, prevented me, for I was bruised, weary, wet to the skin, deafened and blinded by the storm.

I had a vague idea of going on to my own house, and that was as much motive as I had. I staggered through the trees, fell into a ditch and bruised my knees against a plank, and finally splashed out into the lane that ran down from the College Arms. I say splashed, for the storm water was sweeping the sand down the hill in a muddy torrent. There in the darkness a man blundered into me and sent me reeling back.

He gave a cry of terror, sprung sideways, and rushed on before I could gather my wits sufficiently to speak to him. So heavy was the stress of the storm just at this place that I had the hardest task to win my way up the hill. I went close up to the fence on the left and worked my way along its palings.

Near the top I stumbled upon something soft, and, by a flash of lightning, saw between my feet a heap of black broadcloth and a pair of boots. Before I could distinguish clearly how the man lay, the flicker of light had passed. I stood over him waiting for the next flash. When it came, I saw that he was a sturdy man, cheaply but not shabbily dressed; his head was bent under his body, and he lay crumpled up close to the fence, as though he had been flung violently against it.

Overcoming the repugnance natural to one who had never before touched a dead body, I stooped and turned him over to feel for his heart. He was quite dead. Apparently his neck had been broken. The lightning flashed for a third time, and his face leapt upon me. I sprang to my feet. It was the landlord of the Spotted Dog, whose conveyance I had taken.

I stepped over him gingerly and pushed on up the hill. I made my way by the police station and the College Arms towards my own house. Nothing was burning on the hillside, though from the common there still came a red glare and a rolling tumult of ruddy smoke beating up against the drenching hail. So far as I could see by the flashes, the houses about me were mostly uninjured. By the College Arms a dark heap lay in the road.

Down the road towards Maybury Bridge there were voices and the sound of feet, but I had not the courage to shout or to go to them. I let myself in with my latch-key, closed, locked and bolted the door, staggered to the foot of the staircase and sat down. My imagination was full of those striding metallic monsters, and of the dead body smashed against the fence.

I crouched at the foot of the staircase with my back to the wall, shivering violently.

I have said already that my storms of emotion have a trick of exhausting themselves. After a time I discovered that I was cold and wet, and with little pools of water about me on the staircarpet. I got up almost mechanically, went into the dining-room and drank some whisky, and then I was moved to change my clothes.

After I had done that I went upstairs to my study, but why I did so I do not know. The window of my study looks over the trees and the railway towards Horsell Common. In the hurry of our departure this window had been left open. The passage was dark, and, by contrast with the picture the window-frame enclosed, that side of the room seemed impenetrably dark. I stopped short in the doorway.

The thunderstorm had passed. The towers of the Oriental College and the pine trees about it had gone, and very far away, lit by a vivid red glare, the common about the sand-pits was visible. Across the light, huge black shapes, grotesque and strange, moved busily to and fro.

It seemed, indeed, as if the whole country in that direction was on fire –

a broad hillside set with minute tongues of flame, swaying and writhing with the gusts of the dying storm, and throwing a red reflection upon the cloud scud above. Every now and then a haze of smoke from some nearer conflagration drove across the window and hid the Martian shapes. I could not see what they were doing, nor the clear form of them, nor recognize the black objects they were busied upon. Neither could I see the nearer fire, though the reflections of it danced on the wall and ceiling of the study. A sharp, resinous twang of burning was in the air.

I closed the door noiselessly and crept towards the window. As I did so, the view opened out until, on the one hand, it reached to the houses about Woking Station, and on the other to the charred and blackened pine-woods of Byfleet. There was a light down below the hill, on the railway, near the arch, and several of the houses along the Maybury road and the streets near the station were glowing ruins. The light upon the railway puzzled me at first; there was a black heap and a vivid glare, and to the right of that a row of yellow oblongs. Then I perceived this was a wrecked train, the fore part smashed and on fire, the hinder carriages still upon the rails.

Between these three main centres of light, the houses, the train, and the burning country towards Chobham, stretched irregular patches of dark country, broken here and there by intervals of dimly-glowing and smoking ground. It was the strangest spectacle, that black expanse set with fire. It reminded me, more than anything else, of the Potteries seen at night. People at first I could distinguish none, though I peered intently for them. Later I saw against the light of Woking Station a number of black figures hurrying one after the other across the line.

And this was the little world in which I had been living securely for years, this fiery chaos! What had happened in the last seven hours I still did not know, nor did I know, though I was beginning to guess, the relation between these mechanical colossi and the sluggish lumps I had seen disgorged from the cylinder. With a queer feeling of impersonal interest I turned my desk-chair to the window, sat down, and stared at the blackened country, and particularly at the three gigantic black things that were going to and fro in the glare about the sand-pits.

They seemed amazingly busy. I began to ask myself what they could be. Were they intelligent mechanisms? Such a thing I felt was impossible. Or did a Martian sit within each, ruling, directing, using, much as a man's brain sits and rules in his body? I began to compare the things to human machines, to ask myself for the first time in my life how an ironclad or a steam-engine would seem to an intelligent lower animal.

The storm had left the sky clear, and over the smoke of the burning land the little facing pin-point of Mars was dropping into the west, when the soldier came into my garden. I heard a slight scraping at the fence, and rousing myself from the lethargy that had fallen upon me, I looked down and saw him dimly clambering over the palings. At the sight of another human being my torpor passed, and I leant out of the window eagerly.

'Hist!' said I in a whisper.

He stopped astride of the fence in doubt. Then he came over and across the lawn to the corner of the house. He bent down and stepped softly.

'Who's there?' he said, also whispering, standing under the window and peering up.

'Where are you going?' I asked.

'God knows.'

'Are you trying to hide?'

'That's it.'

'Come into the house,' I said.

I went down, unfastened the door and let him in, and locked the door again. I could not see his face. He was hatless, and his coat was unbuttoned.

'My God!' he said as I drew him in.

'What has happened?' I asked.

'What hasn't?' In the obscurity I could see he made a gesture of despair. 'They wiped us out – simply wiped us out,' he repeated again and again.

He followed me, almost mechanically, into the dining-room.

'Take some whisky,' I said, pouring out a stiff dose.

He drank it. Then abruptly he sat down before the table, put his head on his arms, and began to sob and weep like a little boy, in a perfect passion of emotion, while I, with a curious forgetfulness of my own despair, stood beside him wondering.

It was a long time before he could steady his nerves to answer my questions, and then he answered perplexingly and brokenly. He was a driver in the artillery, and had only come into action about seven. At that time firing was going on across the common, and it was said the first party of Martians were crawling towards their second cylinder under cover of a metal shield.

Later this shield staggered up on tripod legs, and became the first of the fighting machines I had seen. The gun he drove had been unlimbered near Horsell, in order to command the sand-pits, and its arrival had precipitated the action. As the limber gunners went to the rear, his horse trod in a rabbit-hole and came down, throwing him into a depression of the ground. At the same moment the gun exploded behind him, the ammunition blew up, and there was fire all about him, and he found himself lying under a heap of charred dead men and horses.

'I lay still,' he said, 'scared out of my wits, with the fore-quarter of a horse atop of me. We'd been wiped out. And the smell – good God! Like burnt meat! I was hurt across the back by the fall of the horse, and there I had to lie until I felt better. Just like parade it had been a minute before – then stumble, bang, swish!'

'Wiped out!' he said.

He had hid under the dead horse for a long time, peeping out furtively across the common. The Cardigan men had tried a rush, in skirmishing order, at the pit, simply to be swept out of existence. Then the monster had risen to its feet, and had begun to walk leisurely to and fro across the common, among the few fugitives, with its head-like hood turning about exactly like the head of a cowled human being. A kind of arm carried a complicated metallic case, about which green flashes scintillated, and out of the funnel of this there smote the Heat-Ray.

In a few minutes there was, so far as the soldier could see, not a living thing left upon the common, and every bush and tree upon it that was not already a blackened skeleton was burning. The hussars had been on the road beyond the curvature of the ground, and he saw nothing of them. He heard the Maxims rattle for a time, and then become still. The giant saved Woking Station and its cluster of houses until last; then in a moment the Heat-Ray was brought to bear, and the town became a heap of fiery ruins. Then the thing shut off the Heat-Ray, and, turning its back upon the artilleryman, began to waddle away towards the smouldering pine-woods that sheltered the second cylinder. As it did so, a second glittering Titan built itself up out of the pit.

The second monster followed the first, and at that the artilleryman began to crawl very cautiously across the hot heather ash towards Horsell. He managed to get alive into the ditch along by the side of the road, and so escaped to Woking. There his story became ejaculatory. The place was impassable. It seems there were a few people alive there, frantic for the most part, and many burnt and scalded. He was turned aside by the fire, and hid among some almost scorching heaps of broken wall as one of the Martian giants returned. He saw this one pursue a man, catch him up in one of its steely tentacles, and knock his head against the trunk of a pine tree. At last, after nightfall, the artilleryman made a rush for it and got over the railway embankment.

Since then he had been skulking along towards Maybury, in the hope of getting out of danger Londonwards. People were hiding in trenches and cellars, and many of the survivors had made off towards Woking Village and Send. He had been consumed with thirst until he found one of the water mains near the railway arch smashed, and the water bubbling out like a spring upon the road.

That was the story I got from him bit by bit. He grew calmer telling me and trying to make me see the things he had seen. He had eaten no food since mid-day, he told me early in his narrative, and I found some mutton and bread in the pantry and brought it into the room. We lit no lamp, for fear of attracting the Martians, and ever and again our hands would touch upon bread or meat. As he talked, things about us came darkly out of the darkness, and the trampled bushes and broken rose trees outside the window grew distinct. It would seem that a number of men or animals had rushed across the lawn. I began to see his face, blackened and haggard, as no doubt mine was also.

When we had finished eating we went softly upstairs to my study, and I looked again out of the open window. In one night the valley had become a valley of ashes. The fires had dwindled now. Where flames had been there were now streamers of smoke; but the countless ruins of shattered and gutted houses and blasted and blackened trees that the night had hidden stood out now gaunt and terrible in the pitiless light of dawn. Yet here and there some object had had the luck to escape – a white railway signal here, the end of a greenhouse there, white and fresh amidst the wreckage. Never before in the history of warfare had destruction been so indiscriminate and so universal. And, shining with the growing light of the east, three of the metallic giants stood about the pit, their cowls rotating as though they were surveying the desolation they had made.

It seemed to me that the pit had been enlarged, and ever and again puffs of vivid green vapour streamed up out of it towards the brightening dawn – streamed up, whirled, broke and vanished.

Beyond were the pillars of fire about Chobham. They became pillars of bloodshot smoke at the first touch of day.

All Quiet
On The Western Front

ERICH MARIA REMARQUE

At 18, Remarque was called up into the Kaiser's army for World War I. Coming to terms with squalor and suffering, the young man at the same time found friendship and a depth of sympathy undreamt of by most people of his age . . . . .

WE HAVE TO GO UP ON WIRING fatigue. The motor lorries roll up after dark. We climb in. It is a warm evening and the twilight seems like a canopy under whose shelter we feel drawn together. Even the stingy Tjaden gives me a cigarette and then a light.

We stand jammed in together, shoulder to shoulder, there is no room to sit. But we do not expect that. Müller is in a good mood for once; he is wearing his new boots.

The engines drone, the lorries bump and rattle. The roads are worn and full of holes. We dare not show a light so we lurch along and are often almost pitched out. That does not worry us, however. It can happen if it likes; a broken arm is better than a hole in the guts, and many a man would be thankful enough for such a chance of finding his home way again.

Beside us stream the munition-columns in long files. They are making the pace, they overtake us continually. We joke with them and they answer back.

A wall becomes visible, it belongs to a house which lies on the side of the road. I suddenly prick up my ears. Am I deceived? Again I hear distinctly the cackle of geese. A glance at Katczinsky – a glance from him to me; we understand one another.

'Kat, I hear some aspirants for the frying-pan over there.'

He nods. 'It will be attended to when we come back. I have their number.'

Of course Kat has their number. He knows all about every leg of goose within a radius of fifteen miles.

The lorries arrive at the artillery lines. The gun-emplacements are camouflaged with bushes against aeriel observation, and look like a kind of military Feast of the Tabernacles. These branches might seem gay and cheerful were not cannon embowered there.

63

The air becomes acrid with the smoke of the guns and the fog. The fumes of powder taste bitter on the tongue. The roar of the guns makes our lorry stagger, the reverberation rolls raging away to the rear, everything quakes. Our faces change imperceptibly. We are not, indeed, in the front-line, but only in the reserves yet in every face can be read: This is the front, now we are within its embrace.

It is not fear. Men who have been up as often as we have become thick skinned. Only the young recruits are agitated. Kat explains to them: 'That was a twelve-inch. You can tell by the report; now you'll hear the burst.'

But the muffled thud of the burst does not reach us. It is swallowed up in the general murmur of the front: Kat listens: 'There'll be a bombardment to-night.'

We all listen. The front is restless. 'The Tommies are firing already,' says Kropp.

The shelling can be heard distinctly. It is the English batteries to the right of our section. They are beginning an hour too soon. According to us they start punctually at ten o'clock.

'What's got them?' says Müller, 'their clocks must be fast.'

'There'll be a bombardment, I tell you. I can feel it in my bones.' Kat shrugs his shoulders.

Three guns open fire close beside us. The burst of flame shoots across the fog, the guns roar and boom. We shiver and are glad to think that we shall be back in the huts early in the morning.

Our faces are neither paler nor more flushed than usual; they are not more tense nor more flabby – and yet they are changed. We feel that in our blood a contact has shot home. That is no figure of speech; it is fact. It is the front, the consciousness of the front, that makes this contact. The moment that the first shells whistle over and the air is rent with the explosions there is suddenly in our veins, in our hands, in our eyes a tense waiting, a watching, a heightening alertness, a strange sharpening of the senses. The body with one bound is in full readiness.

It often seems to me as though it were the vibrating, shuddering air that with a noiseless leap springs upon us; or as though the front itself emitted an electric current which awakened unknown nerve-centres.

Every time it is the same. We start out for the front plain soldiers, either cheerful or gloomy: then come the first gun-emplacements and every word of our speech has a new ring.

When Kat stands in front of the hut and says: 'There'll be a bombardment,' that is merely his own opinion; but if he says it here, then the sentence has the sharpness of a bayonet in the moonlight, it cuts clean through the thought, it thrusts nearer and speaks to this unknown thing that is awakened in us, a dark meaning – 'There'll be a bombardment.' Perhaps it is our inner and most secret life that shivers and falls on guard.

To me the front is a mysterious whirlpool. Though I am in still water far away from the centre, I feel the whirl of the vortex sucking me slowly, irresistibly, inescapably into itself.

From the earth, from the air, sustaining forces pour into us – mostly from the earth. To no man does the earth mean so much as to the soldier. When he presses himself down upon her long and powerfully, when he buries his face and his limbs deep in her from the fear of death by shell-fire, then she is his only friend, his brother, his mother; he stifles his terror and his cries in her silence and her security; she shelters him and releases him for ten seconds to live, to run, ten seconds of life; receives him again and often for ever.

Earth! – Earth! – Earth!

Earth with thy folds, and hollows, and holes, into which a man may fling himself and crouch down. In the spasm of terror, under the hailing of annihilation, in the bellowing death of the explosions, O Earth, thou grantest us the great resisting surge of a new-won life. Our being, almost utterly carried away by the fury of the storm, streams back through our hands from thee, and we, thy redeemed ones, bury ourselves in thee, and through the long minutes in a mute agony of hope bite into thee with our lips!

At the sound of the first droning of the shells we rush back, in one part of our being, a thousand years. By the animal instinct that is awakened in us we are led and protected. It is not conscious; it is far quicker, much more sure, less fallible, than consciousness. One cannot explain it. A man is walking along without thought or heed; – suddenly he throws himself down on the ground and a storm of fragments flies harmlessly over him; – yet he cannot remember either to have heard the shell coming or to have thought of flinging himself down. But had he not abandoned himself to the impulse he would now be a heap of mangled flesh. It is this other, this second sight in us, that has thrown us to the ground and saved us, without our knowing how. If it were not so, there would not be one man alive from Flanders to the Vosges.

We march up, moody or good-tempered soldiers – we reach the zone where the front begins and become on the instant human animals.

An indigent looking wood receives us. We pass by the soup-kitchens. Under cover of the wood we climb out. The lorries turn back. They are to collect us again in the morning before dawn.

Mist and the smoke of guns lie breast-high over the fields. The moon is shining. Along the road troops file. Their helmets gleam softly in the moonlight. The heads and the rifles stand out above the white mist, nodding heads, rocking barrels.

Farther on the mist ends. Here the heads become figures; coats, trousers, and boots appear out of the mist as from a milky pool. They become a column. The column marches on, straight ahead, the figures resolve themselves into a block, individuals are no longer recognizable, the dark wedge presses onward, fantastically topped by the heads and weapons floating on the milky pool. A column – not men at all.

Guns and munition wagons are moving along a cross-road. The backs of the horses shine in the moonlight, their movements are beautiful, they toss their heads, and their eyes gleam. The guns and the wagons float past the dim background of the moonlit landscape, the riders in their steel helmets resemble knights of a forgotten time; it is strangely beautiful and arresting.

We push on to the pioneer dump. Some of us load our shoulders with pointed and twisted iron stakes; others thrust smooth iron rods through rolls of wire and go off with them. The burdens are awkward and heavy.

The ground becomes more broken. From ahead come warnings: 'Look out, deep shell-hole on the left' – 'Mind, trenches' –

Our eyes peer out, our feet and our sticks feel in front of us before they take the weight of the body. Suddenly the line halts; I bump my face against the roll of wire carried by the man in front and curse.

There are some shell-smashed lorries in the road. Another order: 'Cigarettes and pipes out.' We are near the line.

In the meantime it has become pitch dark. We skirt a small wood and then have the front-line immediately before us.

An uncertain red glow spreads along the skyline from one end to the other. It is in perpetual movement, punctuated with bursts of flame from the nozzles of the batteries. Balls of light rise up high above it, silver and red spheres which explode and rain down in showers of red, white, and green stars. French rockets go up, which unfold a silk parachute to the air and drift slowly down. They light up everything as bright as day, their light shines on us and we see our shadows sharply outlined on the ground. They hover for the space of a minute before they burn out. Immediately fresh ones shoot up in the sky, and again green, red, and blue stars.

'Bombardment,' says Kat.

The thunder of the guns swells to a single heavy roar and then breaks up again into separate explosions. The dry bursts of the machine-guns rattle. Above us the air teems with invisible swift movement, with howls, pipings, and hisses. They are smaller shells; – and amongst them, booming through the night like an organ, go the great coalboxes and the heavies. They have a hoarse, distant bellow like a rutting stag and make their way high above the howl and whistle of the smaller shells. It reminds me of flocks of wild geese when I hear them. Last autumn the wild geese flew day after day across the path of the shells.

The searchlights begin to sweep the dark sky. They slide along it like gigantic tapering rulers. One of them pauses, and quivers a little.

Immediately a second is beside him, a black insect is caught between them and tries to escape – the airman. He hesitates, is blinded and falls.

At regular intervals we ram in the iron stakes. Two men hold a roll and the others spool off the barbed wire. It is that awful stuff with close-set, long spikes. I am not used to unrolling it and tear my hand.

After a few hours it is done. But there is still some time before the lorries come. Most of us lie down and sleep. I try also, but it has turned too chilly. We know we are not far from the sea because we are constantly waked by the cold.

Once I fall fast asleep. Then wakening suddenly with a start I do not know where I am. I see the stars, I see the rockets, and for a moment have the impression that I have fallen asleep at a garden fête. I don't know whether it is morning or evening, I lie in the pale cradle of the twilight, and listen for soft words which will come, soft and near – am I crying? I put my hand to my eyes, it is so fantastic, am I a child? Smooth skin; – it lasts only a second, then I recognize the silhouette of Katczinsky. The old veteran, he sits quietly and smokes his pipe – a covered pipe of course. When he sees I am awake, he says: 'That gave you a fright. It was only a nose-cap, it landed in the bushes over there.'

I sit up, I feel myself strangely alone. It's good Kat is there. He gazes thoughtfully at the front and says:

'Mighty fine fire-works if they weren't so dangerous.'

One lands behind us. Some recruits jump up terrified. A couple of minutes later another comes over, nearer this time. Kat knocks out his pipe. 'We're in for it.'

Then it begins in earnest. We crawl away as well as we can in our haste. The next lands fair amongst us. Two fellows cry out. Green rockets shoot up on the sky-line. Barrage. The mud flies high, fragments whizz past. The crack of the guns is heard long after the roar of the explosions.

Beside us lies a fair-headed recruit in utter terror. He has buried his face in his hands, his helmet has fallen off. I fish hold of it and try to put it back on his head. He looks up, pushes the helmet off and like a child creeps under my arm, his head close to my breast. The little shoulders heave. Shoulders just like Kemmerich's. I let him be. So that the helmet should be of some use I stick it on his behind; – not for a jest, but out of consideration, since that is his highest part. And though there is plenty of meat there, a shot in it can be damned painful. Besides, a man has to lie for months on his belly in the hospital, and afterwards he would be almost sure to have a limp.

It's got someone pretty badly. Cries are heard between the explosions.

At last it grows quiet. The fire has lifted over us and is now dropping on the reserves. We risk a look. Red rockets shoot up to the sky. Apparently there's an attack coming.

Where we are it is still quiet. I sit up and shake the recruit by the shoulder. 'All over, kid! It's all right this time.'

He looks round him dazedly. 'You'll get used to it soon,' I tell him.

He sees his helmet and puts it on. Gradually he comes to. Then suddenly he turns fiery red and looks confused. Cautiously he reaches his hand to his behind and looks at me dismally.

I understand at once: Gun-shy. That wasn't the reason I had stuck his helmet over it. 'That's no disgrace,' I reassure him: 'Many's the man before you has had his pants full after the first bombardment. Go behind that bush there and throw your underpants away. Get along – '

He goes off. Things become quieter, but the cries do not cease. 'What's up, Albert?' I ask.

'A couple of columns over there have got it in the neck.'

The cries continued. It is not men, they could not cry so terribly.

'Wounded horses,' says Kat.

It's unendurable. It is the moaning of the world, it is the martyred creation, wild with anguish, filled with terror, and groaning.

We are pale. Detering stands up. 'God! For God's sake! Shoot them.'

He is a farmer and very fond of horses. It gets under his skin. Then as if deliberately the fire dies down again. The screaming of the beasts becomes louder. One can no longer distinguish whence in this now quiet silvery landscape it comes; ghostly, invisible, it is everywhere, between heaven and earth it rolls on immeasurably. Detering raves and yells out: 'Shoot them! Shoot them, can't you? damn you again!'

'They must look after the men first,' says Kat quietly.

We stand up and try to see where it is. If we could only see the animals we should be able to endure it better. Müller has a pair of glasses. We see a dark group, bearers with stretchers, and larger black clumps moving about. Those are the wounded horses. But not all of them. Some gallop away in the distance, fall down, and then run on farther. The belly of one is ripped open, the guts trail out. He becomes tangled in them and falls, then he stands up again.

Detering raises his gun and aims. Kat hits it in the air. 'Are you mad – ?'

Detering trembles and throws his rifle on the ground.

We sit down and hold our ears. But this appalling noise, these groans and screams penetrate, they penetrate everywhere.

We can bear almost anything. But now the sweat breaks out on us. We must get up and run no matter where, but where these cries can no longer be heard. And it is not men, only horses.

From the dark group stretchers move off again. Then single shots crack out. The black heap convulses and then sinks down. At last! But still it is not the end. The men cannot overtake the wounded beasts which fly in their pain, their wide open mouths full of anguish. One of the men goes down on his knee, a shot – one horse drops – another. The last one props itself on its forelegs and drags itself round in a circle like a merry-go-round; squatting, it drags round in circles on its stiffened forelegs, apparently its back is broken. The soldier runs up and shoots it. Slowly, humbly, it sinks to the ground.

We take our hands from our ears. The cries are silenced. Only a long-drawn, dying sigh still hangs on the air.

Then only again the rockets, the singing of the shells and the stars there – most strange.

Detering walks up and down cursing: 'Like to know what harm they've done.' He returns to it once again. His voice is agitated, it sounds almost dignified as he says: 'I tell you it is the vilest baseness to use horses in the war.'

We go back. It is time we returned to the lorries. The sky is become brighter. Three o'clock in the morning. The breeze is fresh and cool, the pale hour makes our faces look grey.

We trudge onwards in single file through the trenches and shell-holes and come again to the zone of mist. Katczinsky is restive, that's a bad sign.

'What's up, Kat?' says Kropp.

'I wish I were back home.' Home – he means the huts.

'We'll soon be out of it, Kat.'

He is nervous. 'I don't know, I don't know – '

We come to the communication-trench and then to the open fields. The little wood reappears; we know every foot of ground here. There's the cemetery with the mounds and the black crosses.

That moment it breaks out behind us, swells, roars, and thunders. We duck down – a cloud of flame shoots up a hundred yards ahead of us.

The next minute under a second explosion part of the wood rises slowly in the air, three or four trees sail up and then crash to pieces. The shells begin to hiss like safety-valves – heavy fire –

'Take cover!' yells somebody – 'Cover!'

The fields are flat, the wood is too distant and dangerous – the only cover is the graveyard and the mounds. We stumble across in the dark and as though he had been spat there every man lies glued behind a mound.

Not a moment too soon. The dark goes mad. It heaves and raves. Darknesses blacker than the night rush on us with giant strides, over us and away. The flames of the explosions light up the graveyard.

There is no escape anywhere. By the light of the shells I try to get a view of the fields. They are a surging sea, daggers of flame from the explosions leap up like fountains. It is impossible for anyone to break

69

through it.

The wood vanishes, it is pounded, crushed, torn to pieces. We must stay here in the graveyard.

The earth bursts before us. It rains clods. I feel a smack. My sleeve is torn away by a splinter. I shut my fist. No pain. Still that does not reassure me: wounds don't hurt till afterwards. I feel the arm all over. It is grazed but sound. Now a crack on the skull, I begin to lose consciousness. Like lightning the thought comes to me: Don't faint! I sink down in the black broth and immediately come up to the top again. A splinter slashes into my helmet, but has already travelled so far that it does not go through. I wipe the mud out of my eyes. A hole is torn up in front of me. Shells hardly ever land in the same hole twice, I'll get into it. With one lunge, I shoot as flat as a fish over the ground; there it whistles again, quickly I crouch together, claw for cover, feel something on the left, shove in beside it, it gives way, I groan, the earth leaps, the blast thunders in my ears, I creep under the yielding thing, cover myself with it, draw it over me, it is wood, cloth, cover, cover, miserable cover against the whizzing splinters.

I open my eyes – my fingers grasp a sleeve, an arm. A wounded man? I yell to him – no answer – a dead man. My hand gropes farther, splinters of wood – now I remember again that we are lying in the graveyard.

But the shelling is stronger than everything. It wipes out the sensibilities, I merely crawl still farther under the coffin, it shall protect me, though Death himself lies in it.

Before me gapes the shell-hole. I grasp it with my eyes as with fists. With one leap I must be in it. There, I get a smack in the face, a hand clamps on to my shoulder – has the dead man waked up? – The hand shakes me, I turn my head, in the second of light I stare into the face of Katczinsky, he has his mouth wide open and is yelling. I hear nothing, he rattles me, comes nearer, in a momentary lull his voice reaches me: 'Gas – Gaas – Gaaas – Pass it on.'

I grab for my gas-mask. Some distance from me there lies someone. I think nothing but this: That fellow there must know: Gaaas – Gaaas –

I call, I lean toward him, I swipe at him with the satchel, he doesn't see – once again, again – he merely ducks – it's a recruit – I look at Kat desperately, he has his mask on – I pull out mine, too, my helmet falls to one side, it slips over my face, I reach the man, his satchel is on the side nearest me, I seize the mask, pull it over his head, he understands, I let go and with a jump drop into the shell hole.

The dull thud of the gas-shells mingles with the crashes of the high explosives. A bell sounds between the explosions, gongs, and metal clappers warning everyone – Gas – Gas – Gaas.

Someone plumps down behind me, another. I wipe the goggles of my mask clear of the moist breath. It is Kat, Kropp, and someone else. All four of us lie there in heavy, watchful suspense and breathe as lightly as possible.

These first minutes with the mask decide between life and death: is it air-tight? I remember the awful sights in the hospital: the gas patients who in day-long suffocation cough up their burnt lungs in clots.

Cautiously, the mouth applied to the valve, I breathe. The gas still creeps over the ground and sinks into all hollows. Like a big, soft jelly-fish it floats into our shell-hole and lolls there obscenely. I nudge Kat, it is better to crawl out and lie on top than to stay where the gas collects most. But we don't get as far as that; a second bombardment begins. It is no longer as though shells roared; it is the earth itself raging.

With a crash something black bears down on us. It lands close beside us; a coffin thrown up.

I see Kat move and I crawl across. The coffin has hit the fourth man in our hole on his out-stretched arm. He tries to tear off his gas-mask with the other hand. Kropp seizes him just in time, twists the hand sharply behind his back and holds it fast.

Kat and I proceed to free the wounded arm. The coffin lid is loose and burst open, we are easily able to pull it off, we toss the corpse out, it slides down to the bottom of the shell-hole, then we try to loosen the under-part.

Fortunately the man swoons and Kropp is able to help us. We no longer have to be careful, but work away till the coffin gives with a sigh before the spade that we have dug in under it.

It has grown lighter. Kat takes a piece of the lid, places it under the shattered arm, and we wrap all our bandages round it. For the moment we can do no more.

Inside the gas-mask my head booms and roars – it is nigh bursting. My lungs are tight, they breathe always the same hot, used-up air, the veins on my temples are swollen. I feel I am suffocating.

A grey light filters through to us. I climb out over the edge of the shell-hole. In the dirty twilight lies a leg torn clean off; the boot is quite whole, I take that all in at a glance. Now something stands up a few yards distant. I polish the windows, in my excitement they are immediately dimmed again. I peer through them, the man there no longer wears his mask.

I wait some seconds – he has not collapsed – he looks around and makes a few paces – rattling in my throat I tear my mask off too and fall down, the air streams into me like cold water, my eyes are bursting the wave sweeps over me and extinguishes me.

The shelling has ceased, I turn towards the crater and beckoning to the others. They take off their masks. We lift up the wounded man, one taking his splinted arm. And so we stumble off hastily.

The graveyard is a mass of wreckage. Coffins and corpses lie strewn about. They have been killed once again; but each of them that was flung up saved one of us.

The hedge is destroyed, the rails of the light railway are torn up and rise stiffly in the air in great arches. Someone lies in front of us. We stop; Kropp goes on alone with the wounded man.

The man on the ground is a recruit. His hip is covered with blood; he is so exhausted that I feel for my water-bottle where I have rum and tea. Kat restrains my hand and stoops over him.

'Where's it got you comrade?'

His eyes move. He is too weak to answer.

We slit open his trousers carefully. He groans. 'Gently, gently, it is much better – '

If he has been hit in the stomach he oughtn't to drink anything. There's no vomiting, that's a good sign. We lay the hip bare. It is one mass of mincemeat and bone splinters. The joint has been hit. This lad won't walk any more.

I wet his temples with a moistened finger and give him a swig. His eyes move again. We see now that the right arm is bleeding as well.

Kat spreads out two wads of dressing as wide as possible so that they will cover the wound. I look for something to bind loosely round it. We have nothing more, so I slit up the wounded man's trouser leg still farther in order to use a piece of his underpants as a bandage. But he is wearing none. I now look at him closely. He is the fair-headed boy of a little while ago.

In the meantime Kat has taken a bandage from a dead man's pocket and we carefully bind the wound. I say to the youngster who looks at us fixedly: 'We're going for a stretcher now – '

Then he opens his mouth and whispers: 'Stay here – '

'We'll be back again soon,' says Kat, 'We are only going to get a stretcher for you.'

We don't know if he understands. He whimpers like a child and plucks at us: 'Don't go away – '

Kat looks around and whispers: 'Shouldn't we just take a revolver and put an end to it?'

The youngster will hardly survive the carrying, and at the most he will only last a few days. What he has gone through so far is nothing to what he's in for till he dies. Now he is numb and feels nothing. In an hour he will become one screaming bundle of intolerable pain. Every day that he can live will be a howling torture. And to whom does it matter whether he has them or not –

I nod. 'Yes, Kat, we ought to put him out of his misery.'

He stands still a moment. He has made up his mind. We look round – but we are no longer alone. A little group is gathering, from the shell-holes and trenches appear heads.

We get a stretcher.

Kat shakes his head. 'Such a kid – ' He repeats it 'Young innocents – '

Our losses are less than was to be expected – five killed and eight wounded. It was in fact quite a short bombardment. Two of our dead lie in the upturned graves. We merely throw the earth in on them.

We go back. We trot off silently in single file one behind the other. The wounded are taken to the dressing-station. The morning is cloudy. The bearers make a fuss about numbers and tickets, the wounded whimper. It begins to rain.

An hour later we reach our lorries and climb in. There is more room than there was.

The rain becomes heavier. We take out waterproof sheets and spread them over our heads. The rain rattles down, and flows off at the sides in streams. The lorries bump through the holes, and we rock to and fro in a half-sleep.

Two men in the front of the lorry have long forked poles. They watch for telephone wires which hang crosswise over the road so low that they might easily pull our heads off. The two fellows take them at the right moment on their poles and lift them over behind us. We hear their call 'Mind – wire – ,' dip the knee in a half-sleep and straighten up again.

Monotonously the lorries sway, monotonously come the calls, monotonously falls the rain. It falls on our heads and on the heads of the dead up in the line, on the body of the little recruit with the wound that is so much too big for his hip; it falls on Kemmerich's grave; it falls in our hearts.

An explosion sounds somewhere. We wince, our eyes become tense, our hands are ready to vault over the side of the lorry into the ditch by the road.

Nothing happens – only the monotonous cry: 'Mind – wire,' – our knees bend – we are again half asleep.

The Battle of Borodino

LEO TOLSTOY

On the morning of 7 September, 1812 Count Peter Ivanovitch Bézoukhov finds himself infected by the excitement of battle and becomes involved in the fight against the French invader which costs the life of his old friend and rival, Prince Andrew Bolkonsky . . . . .

IT WAS A BRILLIANT, DELICIOUS morning, dew-drops sparkled everywhere; the sun sent level rays through the curtain of cloud, and a shaft of light fell across the roof and through the hanging mist, on the dusty road just moist with the dew, on the walls of the houses, the rough wood palings, and the horses standing saddled at the door. The roar of the cannon grew louder and louder.

'Make haste, count, if you want to be in time!' shouted an aide-de-camp as he galloped past.

Peter started on foot, his man leading the horses, and made his way by the road as far as the knoll from whence he had surveyed the field the day before. This mamelon was crowded with military; the staff-officers could be heard talking French, and conspicuous among them all was Koutouzow's grey head under a white cap bound with red, his fat neck sunk in his broad shoulders. He was studying the distance through a field-glass.

As he climbed the slope Peter was struck by the scene that spread before him. It was the same landscape that he had seen yesterday, but swarming now with an imposing mass of troops, wrapped in wreaths of smoke and lighted up by the low sun which was rising on the left and filling the pure upper air with quivering rose and gold, while on the earth lay long masses of black shadow. The clumps of trees that bordered the horizon might have been hewn out of some sparkling yellow-green gem, and beyond them again, far away, the Smolensk road could be made out, covered with troops. Close to the knoll the golden fields and dewy slopes were bathed in shimmering light, and everywhere to the right and left were soldiers and still soldiers. It was animated, grandiose and unexpected; but what expecially interested Peter was the actual field of battle – Borodino and the valley of the Kolotcha through which the river ran.

Above the stream, over Borodino, just where the Voïna makes its way through vast marshes to join the Kolotcha, rose one of those mists which, melting and dissolving before the sun's rays, gives an enchanted aspect and colour to the landscape it transforms rather than hides.

The morning light glowed on this mist, and in the smoke which mixed with it here and there, and sparkled on the water, the dew, the bayonets, even on Borodino. Through that transparent veil could be seen the white church, the hovel roofs of the village, and on every side serried masses of soldiers, green caissons and guns. From the valley, from the heights, and the slopes, from the woods, from the fields, came cannon-shots, now singly, now in volleys, followed by puffs of smoke which wreathed, mingled, and faded away. And strange as it may appear, this smoke and cannonade were the most attractive features of the spectacle. Puff! and a tight round cloud of smoke changing from violet to grey, to milky-white would be seen, and – *boom*! a second later one would hear the sound; *puff, puff*! two smokes would rise jostling each other and then blending into each other, and – boom, boom! – sound would confirm what the eye had seen. Peter turned to look at the first cloud of smoke, which he had left as a firm round ball, and already in place of it were balloons of smoke drifting aside; and 'puff' (a pause) 'puff, puff!' three or four more would rise, and to each one with the same pauses 'boom, boom, boom' answered a full, firm, fine sound. Sometimes it seemed as if these smokes moved, and at others as if they were stationary and the forests, fields and shining bayonets moved past them. To the left over the fields and bushes, they were constantly appearing, these large puffs of smoke with their majestic echoes, and nearer in the lower ground and in the woods, smaller and more frequent puffs of musket smoke with no time to form into balloon-shapes flashed out, giving also place to smaller echo. Tra-ta-ta-ta-ta rattled the muskets, frequently but irregularly, and thinly, compared to the rich noise of the big guns. Peter was chafing to be there among the smoke, and the sparkling bayonets, in the midst of the movement, close to the guns.

He turned to compare his own feelings with those which Koutouzow and his staff might be expected to feel at such a moment, and found on every face that suppressed excitement which he had noticed before, but which he had not understood until after his conversation with Prince Andrew.

'Go, my friend, go,' said Koutouzow to a general standing near him, 'and God go with you.' And the general who had taken the order went past Peter down the hill.

'To the bridge!' he answered in reply to a question from another officer.

'And I, too,' thought Peter, following him. The general mounted his horse which a Cossack was holding, and Peter, going up to his servant, asked which of his two steeds was the quietest to ride. Then, clutching the beast's mane, leaning over his neck and clinging on by his heels, off he started. He felt that his spectacles were going; however, as he would not, and indeed could not, leave go of the bridle or the mane, away he went after the general, past the rest of the officers who gazed at him with amusement.

The general led the way down the hill and turned off sharp to the left; Peter lost sight of him and found himself riding through the ranks of an infantry regiment; he tried in vain to get out of the midst of the men, who surrounded him on all sides and looked with angry surprise at this fat man in a white hat, who was knocking them about so heedlessly, and at such a critical moment.

'Why the devil do you ride through a battalion?' asked one: and another gave the horse a prod with the butt-end of his musket. Peter, clutching the saddle-bow and holding in his frightened steed as best he might, was carried on at a furious speed, and presently found himself in an open space. In front of him was a bridge guarded by infantry firing briskly; without knowing it he had come down to the bridge between Gorky and Borodino which the French, after taking the village, had come down to attack. On both sides of the river, and in the hayfields he had seen from afar, soldiers were struggling frantically; still Peter could not believe that he was witnessing the first act of a battle. He did not hear the bullets that were whistling about his ears, nor the balls that flew over his head; and it did not occur to him that the men on the other side of the river were the enemy, or that those who lay on the ground were wounded or killed.

'What on earth is he doing in front of the line?' shouted a voice. 'Left! left! turn to the left!'

Peter turned to the right, and ran up against an aide-de-camp of General Raïevsky's; the officer looked furious, and was about to abuse him roundly, when he recognised him.

'What brings you here?' said he, and he rode away.

Peter, with a vague suspicion that he was not wanted there, and fearing he might be in the way, galloped after him.

'Is it here? May I follow you?' he asked.

'In a minute – wait a minute,' said his friend, tearing down into the meadows to meet a burly colonel to whom he was carrying orders. Then he came back to Peter.

'Tell me what on earth you have come here for? To look on I suppose?'

'Just so,' said Peter, while the officer wheeled his horse round and was starting off again.

'Here, it is not such warm work yet, thank God! but there, where Bagration is to the left, they are getting it hot.'

'Really!' said Peter. 'Where?'

'Come up the hill with me; you will see very well from thence, and it is still bearable. Are you coming?'

'After you,' said Peter, looking round for his servant; then, for the first time, his eye fell on the wounded men who were dragging themselves to the rear, or being carried on litters; one poor little soldier, with his hat lying by his side, was stretched motionless on the field where the mown hay exhaled its stupefying scent.

'Why have they left that poor fellow?' Peter was on the point of saying; but the aide-de-camp's look of pain as he turned away stopped the question on his lips. As he could nowhere see his servant he rode on, across the flat as far as Raïevsky's battery; but his horse could not keep up with the officer's and shook him desperately.

'You are not used to riding, I see,' said the aide-de-camp.

'Oh! it is nothing,' said Peter, 'his pace is bad.'

'The poor beast has had his off leg wounded just above the knee – a bullet must have caught him there. Well, I congratulate you, count – it is your baptism of fire.'

After passing the Sixth Corps they got, through dense smoke, to the rear of the artillery, which held an advanced position and kept up an incessant and deafening fire. At last they found themselves in a little copse where the mild autumn air was clear of smoke. They dismounted and climbed the little hill.

'Is the general here?' asked the aide-de-camp.

'Just gone,' was the answer. The officer turned to Peter; he did not know what to do with him.

'Do not trouble yourself with me,' said Bésoukhow. 'I will go on to the top.'

'Yes, do – and stay there; you will see everything and it is comparatively safe. I will come back for you.'

So they parted, and never again met, and only much later did Peter hear that the aide-de-camp had an arm shot off that day. He went up to the battery that held the famous knoll which came to be known to the Russians as the 'Mamelon battery or Raïevsky's redoubt'; and to the French – who regarded it as the key of the position – as 'the great redoubt,' or 'the fatal redoubt,' or the 'centre redoubt.' At its foot fell tens of thousands.

The works were thrown up on a mamelon surrounded with trenches on three sides. Ten heavy guns poured forth death through the embrasures of a breastwork, while other pieces, continuing the line, never paused in their fire. The infantry stood somewhat farther back.

Peter had no suspicion of the paramount value of this point, but supposed it to be, on the contrary, of quite secondary importance. He sat down on the edge of the earthwork that screened the battery and looked about with a smile of innocent satisfaction; now and then he got up to see

what was going on, trying to keep out of the way of the men who were re-
loading the guns and pushing them forward each time, and of those who
went to and fro carrying the heavy cartridges. The guns of this battery
kept up a constant fire, one after the other, deafening those near and
clouding the surrounding country by their smoke. Quite unlike the
infantry outside whose duty it was to protect the redoubt, the gunners
standing on this speck of earth that was enclosed by its semicircle of
trenches, and apart from the rest of the battle seemed bound together in a
kind of fraternal responsibility; and the appearance in their midst of a
civilian like Peter was by no means pleasing to them. They looked at him
askance and seemed almost alarmed at his presence; a tall pock-marked
artillery officer came close up to him and looked at him inquisitively, and
a quite young lieutenant, rosy and baby-faced, who was in charge of two
guns, turned round and said very severely:

'You must have the goodness to go away, sir; you cannot remain here.'

The gunners continued to shake their heads disapprovingly; but when
they saw that the man in a white hat did not get in the way, that he was
content to sit still, or walk up and down in the face of the enemy's fire, as
coolly as if it were a boulevard, that he stood aside politely to make room
for them with a shy smile – their ill-humour gave place to sympathetic
cordiality, such as soldiers are apt to feel for the dogs, cocks, or other
animals that march with the regiment. They adopted him, as it were, and
laughing at him among themselves gave him the name of 'our
gentleman'.

A ball fell within a couple of yards of Peter, who only shook off the dust
with which he was covered and smiled as he looked round.

'And you are really not afraid, master?' asked a stalwart, red-faced
artilleryman, showing his white teeth in a grin.

'Well, are you afraid?'

'Ah, but you know they will have no respect for you. If one of them
knocks you down it will kick your inside out! How can you help being
afraid?' he added with a laugh.

Two or three more had stopped to look at Peter; they had jolly, friendly
faces, and seemed quite astonished to hear him talk like themselves.

'It is our business, master. But as for you, it is not at all the same thing,
and it is wonderful . . .'

'Now then – serve the guns!' cried the young lieutenant, who was
evidently on duty of this kind for the first or second time in his life, he was
so extravagantly anxious to be blameless in his conduct to his chief and to
his men.

The continual thunder of guns and musketry grew louder and louder,
especially on the left, round Bagration's advanced work; but Peter's
attention was taken up with what was going on close to him, and the
smoke prevented his seeing the progress of the action. His first impulse of

gratified excitement had given way to a very different feeling, roused in the first instance by the sight of the little private in the hay-field. Seated on the earthwork he was now engrossed in watching the faces of those round him. It was scarcely ten o'clock yet; twenty men had been carried away from the battery, and two guns were silenced. The enemy's missiles fell thicker and faster, and spent balls dropped about them with a buzz and a thud. The artillerymen did not seem to heed them; they were full of jest and high spirits.

'Look out my beauty! Not this way, try the infantry!' cried one man to a shell that spun across above their heads.

'Yes, go to the infantry,' echoed a second; and he laughed as he saw the bomb explode among the foot soldiers.

'Hallo! Is that an acquaintance of yours?' cried a third, to a peasant who bowed low as a ball came past.

A knot of men had gathered close to the breastwork to look at something in the distance.

'Do you see? the advanced posts are retiring, they are giving way!' said one.

'Mind your own business,' cried an old sergeant. 'If they are retiring it is because there is something for them to do elsewhere.' He took one of them by the shoulders and shoved him forward with his knee. They all laughed.

'Forward No 5!' was shouted from the other end.

'A long pull and a pull all together!' answered the men who were serving the gun.

'Hallo! That one nearly had "our gentleman's" hat off!' said a wag addressing Peter. 'Ah! you brute!' he added as the ball hit the wheel of a gun-carriage and took off a man's leg.

'Here, you foxes!' cried another to the militiamen who had been charged with the duty of removing the wounded, and who now crept forward, bent almost double. 'This is not quite the sauce you fancy!'

'Look at those crows!' added a third to a party of the militia who had stopped short in their horror at the sight of the man who had lost his leg.

Peter observed that every ball that hit, and every man that fell, added to the general excitement. The soldiers' faces grew more fierce and more eager, as lightnings played round a thunder-cloud, and as though in defiance of that other storm that was raging around them. Peter felt that this glow was infectious.

At ten o'clock the infantry sharpshooters, placed among the scrub in front of the battery, and along the Kamenka brook, began to give way; he could see them running and carrying the wounded on their gun-stocks. A general came up the mamelon, exchanged a few words with the colonel in command, shot a wrathful scowl at Peter, and went away again, after ordering the infantry men to fire lying down, so as to expose a smaller front. There was a sharp rattle of drums in the regiment below, and the line rushed forward. Peter's attention was caught by the pale face of a young officer, who was marching with them backwards, holding his sword point downwards, and looking behind him uneasily; in a minute they were lost to sight in the smoke, and Peter only heard a confusion of cries, and the steady rattle of well-sustained firing. Then, in a few minutes, the wounded were brought out of the mêlée on stretchers.

In the redoubt projectiles were falling like hail, and several men were laid low; the soldiers were working with increased energy; no one heeded Peter. Once or twice he was told to get out of the way, and the old commanding officer walked up and down from one gun to another, with his brows knit. The boy lieutenant, with flaming cheeks, was giving his orders more incisively than ever; the gunners brought up the cartridges, loaded and fired with passionate celerity and zeal. They no longer walked; they sprang about as if they were moved by springs. The thundercloud was close overhead. Every face seemed to flash fire, and Peter, now standing by the old colonel, felt as if the explosion was at hand; then the young lieutenant came up to the chief, and saluted with his hand to the peak of his cap.

'I have the honour to inform you that there are only eight rounds left. Must we go on?'

'Grape-shot!' cried the colonel, instead of answering him; and at the moment the little lieutenant gave a cry, and dropped like a bird shot on the wing.

Everything whirled and swam before Peter's eyes. A rain of ball was clattering on the breastwork, the men, and the guns. Peter, who had not thought much about it hitherto, now heard nothing else. On the right some soldiers were running and shouting Hurrah! – but backwards, surely, not forwards. A ball hit the earthwork close to where he was standing, and made the dust fly: at the same instant a black object seemed to leap up and bury itself in something soft. The militiamen made the best of their way down the slope again.

'Grape-shot!' repeated the old commander. A sergeant in much agitation ran to him and told him, in terrified undertones, that the ammunition was all spent. He might have been a house-steward telling his master that wine had run short.

'Rascals! what are they about?' cried the officer; he looked round at Peter; his heated face streaming with perspiration, and his eyes flashing with a fever of excitement. 'Run down to the reserve, and fetch up a caisson,' he added furiously to one of the soldiers.

'I will go,' said Peter.

The officer did not answer, but stepped aside. 'Wait – don't fire.'

The man who had been ordered to fetch up the caisson ran against Peter.

'It is not your place, master!' he said; and he set off as fast as he could go, down the slope. Peter ran after him, taking care to avoid the spot where the boy lieutenant was lying. Two, three, balls flew over his head, and fell close to him.

'Where am I going?' he suddenly asked himself, when he was within a few feet of the ammunition stores. He stopped, not knowing where to go. At the same instant a tremendous shock flung him face downwards on the ground, a sheet of flame blinded him, and a terrific shriek ending in an explosion and rattle all round him, completely stunned him. When he presently recovered his senses, he was lying on the ground with his arms spread out. The caisson he had before seen had vanished; in its place the scorched grass was strewn with green boards, half-burnt up, and with rags of clothing; one horse, shaking off the remains of his shafts, started away at a gallop; his mate, mortally injured, lay whinnying piteously.

Peter, half crazy with terror, started to his feet, and ran back to the battery, as being the only place where he could find shelter from all these catastrophes. As he went he was surprised to hear no more firing, and to find the work occupied by a number of new-comers, whom he could not recognise. The colonel was leaning over the breastwork, as though he were looking down at something, and a soldier, struggling in the hands of some others, was shouting for help. He had not had time to understand that the commanding officer was dead, and the soldier a prisoner, when another was killed under his eyes by a bayonet thrust in the back. Indeed he had scarcely set foot in the redoubt, when a man in a dark-blue uniform, with a lean, brown face, threw himself on him, sword in hand. Peter instinctively dodged and seized his assailant by the neck and shoulder. It was a French officer; but he dropped his sword, and took Peter by the collar. They stood for a few seconds face to face, each looking more astonished than the other at what he had just done.

'Am I his prisoner, or is he mine?' was the question in both their minds.

The Frenchman was inclined to accept the first alternative, for Peter's powerful hand was tightening its clutch on his throat. He seemed to be trying to speak, when a ball came singing close over their heads, and Peter almost thought it had carried off his prisoner's, he ducked it with such amazing promptitude. He himself did the same, and let go. The Frenchman, being no longer curious to settle which was the other's prize, fled into the battery, while Peter made off down the hill, stumbling over the dead and wounded, and fancying in his panic that they clutched at his garments.

As he got to the bottom he met a dense mass of Russians, running as if they were flying from the foe, but all rushing towards the battery. This was the attack for which Yermolow took all the credit, declaring to all who would listen to him that his good star and daring alone could have carried it through. He pretended that he had had his pockets full of crosses of St. George, which he had strewn all over the mamelon. The French, who had captured the redoubt, now in their turn fled, and the Russians pursued them with such desperate determination, that it was impossible to stop them.

The prisoners were led away from the spot; among them was a wounded general, who was at once surrounded by Russian officers. Hundreds of wounded, French and Russians, their faces drawn with anguish, were carried off the mamelon, or dragged themselves away. Once more Peter went up; but those who had been his friends were gone; he found only a heap of slain, for the most part unknown to him, though he saw the young lieutenant still in the same place by the earthwork, sunk in a heap in a pool of blood; the ruddy-faced gunner still moved convulsively, but was too far gone to be carried away. Peter fairly took to his heels: 'They must surely leave off now,' he thought. 'They must be horrified at what they have done.' And he mechanically followed in the wake of the procession of litters which were quitting the field of action.

The sun, shrouded in the cloud of smoke, was still high above the horizon. Away to the left, and particularly round Séménovski, a confused mass swayed and struggled in the distance, and the steady roar of cannon and musketry, far from diminishing, swelled louder and louder; it was like the wild despairing effort of a man who collects all his strength for a last furious cry.

The principal scene of action had been over a space of about two versts, lying between Borodino and the advanced works held by Bagration. Beyond this radius the cavalry of Ouvarow had made a short diversion in the middle of the day, and behind Outitza Poniatowski and Toutchkow had come to blows; but these were relatively trifling episodes. It was on the plain, between the village and Bagration's entrenchment, a tract of open ground almost clear of copse or brushwood, that the real engagement was fought, and in the simplest way. The signal to begin was given on each side by the firing of several hundred cannon. Then, as the smoke rolled down in a thick cloud, the divisions under Desaix and Compans attacked Bagration, while the viceroy's marched on Borodino. It was about a verst[1] from Bagration's position to Schevardino, where Napoleon had posted himself; and more than two, as the crow flies, from those advanced works to Borodino. Napoleon could not therefore be aware of what was going on there, for the whole valley was shrouded in smoke. Desaix's men were invisible as soon as they got into the hollow, and when they had once disappeared they could be seen no more, as the opposite slope was hidden from view. Here and there a black mass, or a

[1] Two-thirds of a mile.

few bayonets, might be seen; still, from the redoubt at Schevardino no one could be certain whether the hostile armies were moving or standing still. The slanting rays of a glorious sun lighted up Napoleon's face, and he screened his eyes with his hand to examine the defences opposite. Shouts rose now and then above the rattle of musketry, but the smoke thickened and curtained everything from view. Napoleon, standing on the hillock, looked through a telescope, and in the little circle of the spy-glass saw smoke and moving people – now his own men, now Russians; but where it all was when he looked again with the bare eye he could not tell. He went down from the eminence and walked up and down, stopping now and then to listen to the artillery, and looking at the field of battle; but neither from where he stood, nor from the knoll – where he had left his generals – nor from the entrenchments, which had fallen into the hands of the French and the Russians alternately, could anything that was happening be discovered. For several hours in succession, now the French came into view and now the Russians – now the infantry, and now the cavalry, they seemed to surge up, to fall, struggle, jostle, and then, not knowing what to do shouted and ran forwards or backwards. Napoleon's aides-de-camp, the orderly officers of his marshals, rode up every few minutes to report progress; but these reports were necessarily fictitious because, in the turmoil and fire, it was impossible to know exactly how matters stood, and because most of the aides-de-camp were content to repeat what was told them, without going themselves to the scene of action; because, too, during the few minutes that it took them to ride back again, everything changed, and what had been true was then false. Thus, one of the viceroy's aides-de-camp flew to tell the emperor that Borodino was taken, that the bridge over the Kolotcha was held by the French, and to ask Napoleon whether troops should be made to cross it or no. Napoleon's commands were to form in line on the other side and wait; but even while he was giving this order, and at the very time when the aide-de-camp was leaving Borodino, the bridge had been recaptured and burnt by the Russians in the conflict with which Peter had got mixed up at the beginning of the engagement. Another aide-de-camp came riding up, with a scared face, to say that the attack on the advanced works had been repulsed, that Compans was wounded, and Davoust killed; while in fact, the entrenchments had been recaptured by fresh troops, and Davoust had only been bruised.

As the outcome of these reports, which were inevitably inaccurate by the mere force of circumstances, Napoleon made fresh arrangements, which, if they had not been anticipated by prompt action on the spot, must have come too late. The marshals and generals in command, who were nearer to the struggle than he was, and who now and then exposed themselves to fire, took steps without waiting to refer to the emperor, directed the artillery, and brought up the cavalry on this side or the infantry on that. Often, however, their orders were only half-executed, or not heeded at all. The ranks that were ordered to advance flinched and turned tail as soon as they smelt grape-shot; those who ought to have stood firm, fled or rushed on as they saw the foe rise up before them; and the cavalry, again, would bolt off to catch the Russian fugitives. In this way two regiments of cavalry charged across the ravine of Séménovski, dashed up the hill, turned right round and pelted back again, while the infantry performed much the same feat, allowing itself to be completely carried away. Hence all the decisions necessitated by the events of the moment were taken by those in immediate command, without waiting for orders from Ney, Davoust, or Murat – much less from Napoleon. They did not hesitate, indeed, to take the responsibility since, during the struggle, a man's sole idea is to escape with his life, and in seeking his own safety he rushes forward or back, and acts under the immediate influence of his own personal excitement.

On the whole, after all, these various movements resulting from mere chance neither helped, nor even altered, the attitude of the troops. Their attacks and blows did little harm: it was the round shot and shell flying across the wide plain that brought death and wounds. As soon as the men were out of range of the cannon their leaders had them in hand, formed them into line, brought them under discipline; and, by sheer force of that discipline, led them back into the ring of iron and fire, where they again lost their presence of mind, and fled headlong, dragging one another into the stampede.

Davoust, Murat, and Ney had led forward their troops under fire again and again, in enormous masses and in perfect order, but instead of seeing the enemy take to flight, as in so many previous battles, these disciplined troops turned back disbanded and panic-stricken; in vain they re-formed their ranks, their numbers perceptibly dwindled. About noon Murat sent a message to Napoleon to ask for reinforcements. Napoleon was sitting at the foot of the knoll drinking punch. When the aide-de-camp came up and said the Russians could certainly be routed if his majesty would send a reinforcement, Napoleon looked stern and astonished:

'Reinforcements?' he cried, as if he did not understand the meaning of the request, and he looked up at the handsome lad with long black hair, curled in imitation of Murat. 'Reinforcements!' he repeated to himself in an undertone. 'What more can they want of me when they have half of the army at their disposal in front of the Russian left wing which has not even an entrenchment? Tell the King of Naples that it is not yet noon, and I do not see my way on the chessboard. Go.'

The handsome young fellow sighed, and with his hand still up to his shako rode back into the fire. Napoleon rose and called Caulaincourt and Berthier, with whom he discussed various matters not relating to the battle. In the middle of the conversation Berthier's attention was attracted by seeing a general riding a horse covered with foam, and coming towards the mamelon with his staff. This was Belliard. He dismounted, and hastening towards the emperor, explained to him, in loud and positive tones, that the reinforcements must be sent up. He swore on his honour that the Russians would be utterly cut up if the emperor would only send forward one division. Napoleon shrugged his shoulders and said nothing, still walking up and down, while Belliar vehemently expressed his opinions to the generals who stood around him.

'Belliard, you are too hot-headed,' said Napoleon. 'It is so easy to make a mistake in the thick of the fray. Go back, look again, and then return!'

Belliard had hardly disappeared, when another messenger arrived from the scene of action.

'Well, what now?' said Napoleon, in the tone of a man irritated by constant importunities.

'Your majesty, the prince ...'

'Wants reinforcements, I suppose?' interrupted Napoleon with an angry gesture.

The aide-de-camp bowed affirmatively. Napoleon turned away, went forward a step or two, turned back, and addressed Berthier.

'We must send them the reserves – what do you think? Whom can we send to help?' he said, addressing Berthier – 'that gosling whom I have made into an eagle,' as he called him later.

'Let us send Claparède's division, sire,' replied Berthier, who knew every division, regiment, and battalion by name.

The emperor nodded approval; the aide-de-camp went off at a gallop towards Claparède's division, and a few minutes later the regiment known as the Jeune Garde (in contradistinction to the Vieille Garde), which stood in reserve behind the mamelon, began to move forward. Napoleon stood looking at it.

'No,' he said suddenly, 'I cannot send Claparède – send Friant.'

Though there was nothing to be gained by moving the second rather than the first, and in fact, the immediate result was great delay, this order was carried out exactly. Napoleon though he little suspected it, was dealing with his army like a doctor, who impedes the course of nature by the application of remedies: a method he was always ready to criticise severely in others. Friant's division was soon lost to sight in the smoke, with the rest, while aides-de-camp came in from every point of the action, as if they had conspired to make the same demand. All reported that the Russians stood firm in the their positions, and were keeping up a terrific fire under which the French were fairly melting away. Napoleon continued to sit in a brown study in his folding chair. Monsieur de Beausset, who was still fasting, went up to the emperor, and respectfully suggested breakfast.

'I fancy I may congratulate your majesty on a victory?' he said.

Napoleon shook his head. Monsieur de Beausset, thinking that his negative referred to the assumed victory, took the liberty of remarking, in a half-jesting tone, that there could be no mortal reason against their having some breakfast as soon as it might be possible.

'Go to ...' Napoleon suddenly began angrily and he turned away.

A smile of pity and dejection was Beausset's comment, as he left the emperor and joined the officers.

Napoleon was going through the painful experience of a gambler who, after a long run of luck, has calculated every chance and staked handfuls of gold – and then finds himself beaten after all, just because he has played too elaborately. The troops and commanders were the same as of old; his plans well laid; his address short and vigorous; he was sure of himself, and of his experience, his genius which had ripened with years; the enemy in front was the same as at Austerlitz and Friedland; he had counted on falling on him tooth and nail – and the stroke had failed as if by magic. He was wont to see his designs crowned with success. To-day, as usual, he had concentrated his fire on a single point, had thrown forward his reserves and his cavalry – men of steel – to break through the Russian lines, and yet victory held aloof. From all sides came the cry for reinforcements, the news that generals were killed or wounded, that the regiments were demoralised, that it was impossible to move the Russians. On other occasions, after two or three moves, and two or three orders hastily given, aides-de-camp and marshals had come to him beaming, to announce with compliments and congratulations that whole corps had been taken prisoners, to bring in sheaves of standards and eagles taken from the foe; trains of cannon had rattled up behind them, and Murat had asked leave to charge the baggage-wagons with cavalry! This was how things had gone at Lodi, at Marengo, at Arcola, at Jena, at Austerlitz, at Wagram. To-day something strange was in the air – the Russian advanced works, to be sure, had been taken by storm – still, he felt it, and he knew that all his staff felt it too. Every face was gloomy; each man avoided catching his neighbour's eye; only Beausset alone did not perhaps understand what was happening and Napoleon himself knew better than anyone what was the meaning of a struggle that had lasted eight hours and had not yet resulted in victory, though all his forces had been engaged. He knew that it was a drawn game, and that even now the smallest turn of fortune might, at this critical moment, involve him and his army in ruin.

As he thought over this weird campaign in Russia – in which, during two months' fighting, not a battle had been won, not a flag, not a gun, not a company of men had been captured – the dismal faces of his courtiers, and their lamentations over the obstinacy of the Russians, oppressed him like a nightmare. The Russians might at any moment fall on his left wing, or break through his centre. A spent ball might even hit him. All these things were possible. He had been used to look forward to none but happy chances; to-day, on the contrary, an endless series of chances, all against him, rose before his fancy. Yes, it was like a nightmare, in which, one sees somebody approaching with evil intent and strikes out with all one's might, knowing that the blow must destroy, and then feels that the hand is helpless, that it falls limply like a rag, and all the horror of instant inevitable destruction seizes upon one. When he heard that the left wing was, in fact, attacked by the enemy, he was panic-stricken. Berthier came up and suggested that he should ride round and judge for himself of the state of affairs.

'What? What did you say? Ah! yes, to be sure; call for my horse....' And he started towards Séménovski.

All along the road nothing was to be seen but horses and men, singly or in heaps, lying in pools of blood: neither Napoleon nor his generals had ever seen so many slain within so small a space. The hollow roar of the cannon, which had never ceased for ten hours, and of which the ear was weary, made a sinister accompaniment to the scene. Having reached the height above Séménovski he could see in the distance, across the smoke, close lines of uniforms of unfamiliar colours: these were the Russians. They stood in compact masses behind the village and the knoll, and their guns still thundered unremittingly all along the line: it was not a battle; it was butchery, equally fruitless to both sides. Napoleon stopped and relapsed into the reverie from which Berthier had roused him. It was impossible to put an end to the slaughter, and yet he it was who, to the world, was the respnsible authority; this first repulse brought home to him all the horror and waste of such massacres.

One of the generals ventured to suggest that the Old Guard should be sent forward; Ney and Berthier exchanged glances and smiled in contempt for so preposterous a notion. Napoleon sat in silence, with his head down.

'We are eight hundred leagues from home,' he suddenly exclaimed, 'and I will not have my Guards cut to pieces!' Then turning his horse, he galloped back to Schevardino.

Koutouzow, with his head bent and sunk all into a heap from his own weight, sat all day where Peter had seen him in the morning, on a bench covered with a rug; he gave no orders but merely approved or disapproved of what was suggested to him.

'That is it – yes, yes, do so,' he would say, or; 'Go and see, my good friend, go and see!' or, again: 'That is of no use; we must wait....'

But he listened to all he was told, and gave the requisite orders without seeming to take any interest in what was said. But something else, something in the expression and tone of the speaker seemed to interest him. His long experience and hoary wisdom had taught him that no one man can direct the movements of a hundred thousand others, fighting for life and death. He knew that it was neither the plans of the commander, nor the placing of the troops, nor the number of guns, nor the amount of slain which decide the victory, but that imponderable force called the Spirit of the Army, which he tried to control and guide as far as possible. The calm, grave expression of his face was in startling contrast to the weakness of his aged frame.

At eleven in the forenoon a messenger came to say that the redoubt taken by the French had been recaptured, but that Bagration was wounded. Koutouzow exclaimed loudly and shook his head.

'Go and fetch up Prince Peter Ivanovitch,' he said to an aide-de-camp; then turning to the Prince of Wurtemberg he said: 'Would your highness at once take the command of the Second Army?'

The prince rode off, but before he reached the village of Séménovski he sent back his aide-de-camp to ask for reinforcements. Koutouzow frowned; then he sent Dokhtourow forward to take command, instead of the prince, whom he begged to return, as he found that he could not dispense with his advice under such serious circumstances. When he was told that Murat had been taken prisoner he smiled; his staff eagerly congratulated him.

'Wait a little, gentlemen,' he said. 'Wait. The battle is certainly ours, and the news that Murat is taken is not so very astonishing; but we must not crow too soon.'

However, he sent an aide-de-camp to make the fact known to the troops. Somewhat later Scherbinine arrived to tell him that the outworks at Séménovski had been taken once more by the French, and Koutouzow understood from the expression of his face, and the rumours that reached him from the scene of action, that things were going badly. He rose and led him away.

'My good fellow,' he said to Yermolow 'go and see what can be done.'

Koutouzow was at Gorky, the very centre of the Russian position; Napoleon's attack on the Russian left had been bravely repulsed, but in the centre his troops had not got beyond Borodino, and on his left flank Ouvarow's cavalry had made the French run. By three o'clock the French had given up attacking and Koutouzow could read acute excitement on the faces of those who came up from the field, as well as of those who remained with him. The success was far beyond his hopes, but his strength was beginning to fail; his head drooped, and he kept dropping asleep. Some dinner was brought to him; while he was eating, Woltzogen came to talk to him; it was he who had said in Prince Andrew's hearing that the war must have room to spread, and who was hated by Bagration. He had come by Barclay's request, to report progress as to the military operations of the left wing. The wiseacre

Barclay, seeing a crowd of fugitives and wounded, while the farthest line had given way, had come to the conclusion that the battle was lost, and had sent off his favourite aide-de-camp to carry the news to Koutouzow. The commander-in-chief was munching a piece of roast fowl, and he looked complacently up at Woltzogen who approached him with an air of indifference and a superficial smile, and saluted him with affected grace; he looked as though he would convey: 'I, as an experienced and distinguished soldier, may leave it to the Russians to offer incense to this useless old dotard, whom I know how to estimate at his true worth!'

'The old gentleman' – the Germans always spoke of Koutouzow as 'the old gentleman' – 'is making himself comfortable' thought Woltzogen, glancing at the plate; and he proceeded to report on the situation of the left flank as he had been desired, and as he himself had believed that he had seen it.

'All the chief points of our position are in the enemy's hands; we cannot dislodge them for lack of men. Our troops are flying, and it is impossible to stop them.'

Koutouzow ceased eating, and looked up astonished; he seemed not to understand the words. Woltzogen saw that he was much moved and went on with a smile:

'I do not think I should be justified in concealing from your highness what I saw. The troops are completely routed.'

'You saw! you saw that?' cried Koutouzow, starting up with a fierce frown; with his trembling hands he gesticulated threats, and almost choking, exclaimed:

'How dare you, sir, tell me such a thing as that? You know nothing about it! Go and tell your general that it is false and that I know the true state of things better than he does.'

Woltzogen would have interrupted him, but Kouitouzow went on: 'The enemy's left is driven back, and his right badly damaged. If you saw wrongly, that is no reason to tell a falsehood. Go and tell General Barclay that I intend to renew the attack to-morrow!' No one spoke; there was not a sound, but the old man's hard breathing: 'He is repulsed on all sides,' he added, 'and I thank God, and our brave troops! The victory is ours, and to-morrow we will cast him forth from the sacred soil of Russia.' He crossed himself, and ended with a sob.

Woltzogen shrugged his shoulders and smile sardonically. He turned on his heels, not even attempting to conceal his astonishment at 'the old gentleman's' wilful blindness. At this moment another officer – a particularly pleasant-looking man, came up the hill.

'Ah! here is my hero!' said Koutouzow.

This was Raïevsky. He had been all day in the hottest place in the field. His report was that the Russians were holding their own, and that the French did not dare to renew the attack.

'Then you do not think, as some others do, that we are forced to retire?' asked Koutouzow in French.

'On the contrary, highness. In a doubtful action the side that stands steady longest is the conqueror, and in my opionion ...'

'Kaïssarow!' exclaimed the commander-in-chief, 'make out the order of the day for me. And you,' he added to another officer, 'ride down the lines and say that we attack to-morrow.'

Meanwhile Woltzogen had been to Barclay and come back again, and he now said that his chief begged to have the orders he had carried confirmed by writing. Koutouzow, without even looking at him, at once had the order written out, which relieved the ex-commander-in-chief of all responsibility.

By that mysterious moral intuition which is known as *esprit de corps*, Koutouzow's order of the day was communicated instantaneously to the furthest corner of the field. Not, of course, that the original words were exactly repeated; in fact the expressions given to Koutouzow were not his at all; but everyone understood their purport and bearing. They were not the utterance, indeed, of a more or less skilful orator, but they perfectly expressed the feeling of the commander-in-chief – a sentiment that found an echo in the breast of every Russian. All these weary, doubting soldiers, when they were told that they were to attack the foe on the morrow, felt that what they wished to believe was really true; this comforted them and revived their courage.

Prince Andrew's regiment was one of those kept in reserve and inactive till about two o'clock, behind Séménovski, under heavy fire. At that time, when the regiment had already lost more than 200 men, it was ordered forward on to the open ground between Séménovski and the mamelon battery. Thousands had fallen in the course of the day on this spot, on which the fire of some hundred of the enemy's guns was now steadily directed. Without stirring an inch or firing a shot, the regiment was soon reduced by a third more. In front, and especially on the right, the cannon were thundering through a wall of smoke, and thowing out a hail of shot and shell without one instant of respite. From time to time the storm passed over their heads, the projectiles singing through the air; but then, again, several men were hit in the course of a few seconds – the dead were laid aside, and the wounded carried to the rear. Each explosion diminished the chances of life for the survivors. The regiment was drawn up in columns of battalions, three hundred paces in length; but, in spite of this length of line, all the men were equally and painfully impressed. They were all gloomy and silent; at most they spoke a few words in an undertone, and even those died on their lips as each ball took effect, and as they heard their comrades calling for the hospital men.

The officers had given orders that the men should keep their ranks sitting on the ground. One was carefully tying and untying the runner in the lining of his cap; another, breaking up the dry clay into a powder, polished up his bayonet with it; a third loosened and buckled the straps of his bag; a fourth was diligently turning down his boot-tops, and pulling them on and off; some were scraping out a hollow shelter in the earth, and some were aimlessly plaiting straws. They all seemed absorbed in their occupations, and when a comrade rolled over close by, wounded or dead – when the litters touched their heads – when through the rolling vapour they had a glimpse of the foe, no one took any notice; only if they saw the Russian artillery or cavalry move forward, or fancied the infantry were being marched about, remarks of approval were heard on all sides. Then, the moment after, all their attention was centred once more on trifles that had nothing to do with the drama going on around them. It was as if their moral force was exhausted, and had to be revived by a return to the details of daily life. An artillery train presently passed by; one of the horses harnessed to a caisson had got his leg caught in the traces.

'Look out there, at one of your team – take care! He will be down! Have they no eyes!' was shouted on all sides.

Again, the general attention was claimed by a small brown dog, which had come nobody knew whence, and trotted busily along the line with his tail steadily kept aloft. A ball fell close to him, and he ran off with a melancholy yelp, his tail between his legs, and the whole regiment roared with laughter. But such diversions only lasted a moment, and the men, whose anxious and pallid faces seemed to grow greyer and more pinched as time went on, sat there for eight hours, without food, and in the very jaws of death.

Prince Andrew, as pale as his men, walked up and down the meadow from end to end, his head bent and his hands behind his back; everything that had to be done was carried out without any orders from him; the dead were removed, the wounded taken to the rear, and the ranks closed up. At the beginning of the day he had thought it his duty to encourage his men and walk down the ranks; but he soon saw that he could teach them nothing. All the energies of his soul like those of every soldier there, were directed to keeping his thoughts off from the horrors of the situation. He dragged his feet over the trampled grass, looking mechanically at the dust on his boots; now and then, taking long strides, he tried to pace the ridges left by the mower's scythe; then he would calculate how many went to a verst; or he would pull the tufts of wormwood that grew by the hedgerow, and bruise them in his fingers, and sniff the bitter wild perfume. All the thoughts of the previous evening had left no trace in his mind; in fact he was thinking of nothing, and listened wearily to the unceasing noise, always the same – the crackling of shells and musketry. Now and then he looked round at the foremost battalion: 'Ah! here it comes – straight at us,' he would say to himself, as he heard the sharp whistle of a ball through the smoke. 'Here is another. Down it comes! No, it has passed overhead ... There, that one has fallen!' and then he would count his paces once more – sixteen across to the edge of the meadow.

Suddenly a ball flew past and buried itself in the earth, not five yards away. He shuddered involuntarily, and looked down the line; several men had no doubt been struck, for he saw a great bustle close to the second battalion.

'Tell the men not to huddle together so much!' he said to an aide-de-camp.

The order was transmitted, and the aide-de-camp came back to Prince Andrew at the very moment when the major rode up on the other side.

'Look out!' cried a terrified soldier, and a shell came flying down like a bird alighting on the ground, whizzing and shrieking, just at the feet of the major's horse, and not two yards from Prince Andrew. The horse did not pause to consider whether or not it were dignified to betray his fear; he reared, neighing with alarm, and flung himself on one side, almost throwing his rider.

'Lie down!' shouted the aide-de-camp.

But Prince Andrew stood still, doubting; the shell spun round like an enormous top, the fuse smoking and fizzing, close to a shrub of wormwood between himself and the aide-de-camp.

'Can this really mean death?' he thought, looking with a vague feeling of regret at the wormwood plant, and the black whirling object. 'I do not want to die – I like life, I like this earth. ...' These were the words in his mind, and yet he understood only too well what it was that he saw.

'Aide-de-camp,' he began, 'I should be ashamed ...'

But the sentence was never finished. There was a tremendous explosion followed by a strange clatter like that of smashing glass; a fountain of fire leapt into the air, and fell as a shower of iron; the air was full of the smell of gunpowder. Prince Andrew was jerked forward with his arms out, and fell heavily on his face. Some officers rushed up; on his right there was a pool of blood; the militiamen were called to help, but waited behind the group of officers; Prince Andrew lay with his face in the grass, breathing hard.

'Come on – come!' said someone. The peasants drew near, and lifted him by the head and feet; he groaned – the men looked at each other, and laid him down again.

'Pick him up; it must be done!' said another.

They raised him once more and got him on to a stretcher.

'Good God! what has happened? In the stomach? Then he is done for!' said the officers.

'It actually grazed my ear!' said the aide-de-camp.

The bearers went off quickly along a path they had kept open to the ambulance in the rear.

'Keep step ... you!' shouted an officer seizing the men by the shoulders and stopping the unevenly carried stretcher.

'Eh, suit your step, Fedor' said the foremost man.

'That's better,' beamed the man at the back having succeeded in suiting his step to that of the man in front.

'Excellency – my prince?' murmured Timokhine, in a tremulous voice, running by the stretcher.

Prince Andrew opened his eyes and looked at the speaker; then he closed them again.

Prince Andrew was carried into the wood where the ambulance carts stood, and the hospital tents, three in number, had been pitched close to a plantation of young birches. The horses were in harness, and very contentedly munching their oats, sparrows fluttered down to pick up the seeds they let drop, and crows, scenting blood, flew from tree to tree croaking impatiently. All round the tents, sat, lay, or stood men in blood-stained uniforms; the litter-bearers crowded about them, and could hardly be persuaded to move. They were staring at them with down-cast looks; deaf to the commands of the officers, they leaned over the wounded, wondering, as it seemed, what could be the meaning of this appalling spectacle. Inside the tents sobs of rage or pain might be heard, mingled with more plaintive groans; now and then a surgeon rushed out to fetch water, and pointed out which were to be taken in next of the wounded men who were waiting their turn – screaming, swearing, weeping, or clamouring for brandy. Some were already delirious.

Prince Andrew, as a commanding officer, was carried through this crowd to the first tent, and his bearers paused for further orders. He opened his eyes, not understanding what was going on around him: the meadow, the wormwood scrub, the mowed field, the whirling black top, the sudden longing to live that had come over him – all recurred to his mind. Quite near him a tall and finely-built corporal was talking very loud, and attracting everybody's attention; his black eyes shone from under a bandage which half-covered them, and he was propped up against the branch of a tree; he had been wounded in the head and in the foot. He had an eager audience.

'We gave him such a dose of it that he made off, leaving everything behind! We took the king himself prisoner!' he was saying, his eyes sparkling brightly.

'Ah! if the reserves had but come up, there would not have been a man of them left, I swear!'

Prince Andrew heard too, and felt comforted.

'But what can it matter to me now?' he thought. 'What has happened to me? And why am I here? Why am I in such despair at the idea of

93

dying? There is something in life after all that I have failed to understand.'

One of the surgeons, whose hands and apron were covered with blood, came out of the tent; he held a cigar between his thumb and his little finger in order to keep it from getting soiled. He looked up and away, over the heads of the wounded men; it was evident that he desperately wanted a moment of breathing time; but he almost immediately looked down at the scene at hand. He sighed and half-closed his eyes.

'In a minute,' he replied, to an assistant who pointed out Prince Andrew, and he had him carried into the tent.

There was a murmur among the rest of the victims.

'Why, you might fancy these gentlemen were the only folks that have a right to live, even in the other world!'

Prince Andrew was laid on an operating table that had but just been cleared; a surgeon was sponging it down. The prince could not clearly make out who was in the tent. The cries and moans on one hand, and the agonising pain he felt in his side, stomach and back, paralysed his faculties. Everything was mixed up in his mind into one single impression of naked, bloodstained flesh, filling the low tent; and that, again, was one with the scene he had witnessed, that scorching August day, in the pool on the Smolensk road. Yes, it was this very '*chair à canon*' which had then filled him with sickening and prophetic horror.

There were three tables in the tent; two were occupied; Prince Andrew was placed on the third, and left to himself for a few minutes, during which he was at leisure to look at the other two. On the nearest, a Tartar was sitting up – a Cossack it seemed from the uniform that lay near him. Four soldiers were holding him, while a doctor in spectacles was probing under the swarthy skin of his muscular back.

'Oh,' roared the Tartar, and suddenly raising his tanned face, with its wide forehead and flat nose, he gave a piercing yell, and flung himself from side to side to shake off the men who held him.

The farther table was surrounded with people. A tall, strongly-built man was stretched upon it, his head thrown back; there was something familiar to Prince Andrew in the colour of his curling hair, and the shape of his head. Several hospital attendants were leaning on him with all their weight to keep him from stirring. One leg – fat and white – was constantly twitching with a convulsive movement, and his whole body shook with violent and choking sobs. Two surgeons, one quite pale and tremulous, were busy over his other leg.

Having finished operating on the Tartar, who was covered up in his cloak, the surgeon in spectacles wiping his hands came across to Prince Andrew; he glanced at him and turned away.

'Take his clothes off! What are you thinking of?' he exclaimed angrily to one of his assistants.

When Prince Andrew felt himself in the hands of the attendant who, with his sleeves turned back, hastily unbuttoned his uniform, all the memory of his childhood flashed upon his mind. The surgeon bent down, examined his wound, and sighed deeply; then he called another to help him, and the next instant Prince Andrew lost consciousness from the intense agony he suddenly felt. When he came to himself the pieces of his broken thigh, with the torn flesh still clinging to them, had been extracted from his wound and it had been dressed. He opened his eyes; water was being sprinkled on his face; the doctor bent over him, kissed him silently, and went away without looking back at him.

After that fearful torture a feeling of indescribable comfort came over him. His fancy reverted to the happiest days of his infancy, especially to those hours when, after he had been undressed and put into his little bed, his old nurse had sung him to sleep. He was glad to be alive – that past seemed to have become the present. The surgeons were still busy over the man he had fancied he recognised; they were supporting him in their arms, and trying to soothe him.

'Show it me – show it me!' he said; fairly crying with pain.

Prince Andrew as he heard him felt ready to cry too. Was it because he was dying ingloriously, or because he regretted life? Was it by reason of these memories of his childhood? or because he had suffered so acutely himself, that tears of pity rose to his eyes when he saw others suffer.

They showed the other man his amputated leg, with the blood-stained boot still on it.

'Oh!' he exclaimed, and wept as bitterly as a woman.

Just then the doctor moved. 'My God! What is this? Why is he here?' said Prince Andrew to himself. He could see that the miserable creature who lay sobbing and exhausted by his side, was Anatole Kouraguine, his old adversary and rival.

A hospital servant was lifting him, and holding a glass of water to the swollen and quivering lips that could not close on the rim. 'Yes, certainly it is he – that man is bound to me by some painful association – but what is it?' He asked himself, but could find no reply, till suddenly, like a vision from an ideal world of love and purity, Natacha seemed to stand before him; Natacha as he had first seen her at the ball in 1810, with her thin bust and arms, and her radiant, half-scared, enthusiastic face – and his own love and tenderness woke up, deeper, warmer than ever. Now he knew what the link was between himself and the man whose eyes, red and dim with tears, were fixed on him. Prince Andrew remembered everything, and tender pitifulness rose up in his heart which was full of peace. He could not control those tears of compassion and charity which flowed for all humanity, for himself, for his own weakness, and for that of this hapless creature. 'Yes,' said he to himself. 'This is the pity, the charity, the love of my neighbour, the love of those that hate us as well as of those who love us, which God preached on earth, and which Maria used to talk about – but I did not understand it then. This was what I had yet to learn in this life and what makes me regret it. But now, I feel, it comes too late!'

Catch 22

JOSEPH HELLER

An island off the coast of Italy, towards the end of the Second World War. For Captain Yossarian and his colleagues, veterans of thirty, forty, fifty increasingly suicidal bombing missions, it seems the only chance of survival is to be declared unfit for further active service and sent home. Having received a leg wound, Yossarian lies in hospital with some of his friends, awaiting, with increasing exasperation, the decision of those in command . . . . .

NURSE SUE ANN DUCKETT was a tall, spare, mature, straight-backed woman with a prominent, well-rounded ass, small breasts and angular, ascetic New England features that came equally close to being very lovely and very plain. Her skin was white and pink, her eyes small, her nose and chin slender and sharp. She was able, prompt, strict and intelligent. She welcomed responsibility and kept her head in every crisis. She was adult and self-reliant, and there was nothing she needed from anyone. Yossarian took pity and decided to help her.

Next morning while she was standing bent over smoothing the sheets at the foot of his bed, he slipped his hand stealthily into the narrow space between her knees and, all at once, brought it up swiftly under her dress as far as it would go. Nurse Duckett shrieked and jumped into the air a mile, but it wasn't high enough, and she squirmed and vaulted and seesawed back and forth on her divine fulcrum for almost a full fifteen seconds before she wiggled free finally and retreated frantically into the aisle with an ashen, trembling face. She backed away too far, and Dunbar, who had watched from the beginning, sprang forward on his bed without warning and flung both arms around her bosom from behind. Nurse Duckett let out another scream and twisted away, fleeing far enough from Dunbar for Yossarian to lunge forward and grab her by the snatch again. Nurse Duckett bounced out across the aisle once more like a ping-pong ball with legs. Dunbar was waiting vigilantly, ready to pounce. She remembered him just in time and leaped aside. Dunbar missed completely and sailed by her over the bed to the floor, landing on his skull with a soggy, crunching thud that knocked him cold.

He woke up on the floor with a bleeding nose and exactly the same distressful head symptoms he had been feigning all along. The ward was in a chaotic uproar. Nurse Duckett was in tears, and Yossarian was consoling her apologetically as he sat beside her on the edge of a bed. The commanding colonel was wroth and shouting at Yossarian that he would not permit his patients to take indecent liberties with his nurses.

'What do you want from him?' Dunbar asked plaintively from the floor, wincing at the vibrating pains in his temples that his voice set up. 'He didn't do anything.'

'I'm talking about you!' the thin, dignified colonel bellowed as loudly as he could. 'You're going to be punished for what you did.'

'What do you want from him?' Yossarian called out. 'All he did was fall on his head.'

'And I'm talking about you too!' the colonel declared, whirling to rage at Yossarian. 'You're going to be good and sorry you grabbed Nurse Duckett by the bosom.'

'I didn't grab Nurse Duckett by the bosom,' said Yossarian.

'*I* grabbed her by the bosom,' said Dunbar.

'Are you both crazy?' the doctor cried shrilly, backing away in paling confusion.

'Yes, he really is crazy, Doc,' Dunbar assured him. 'Every night he dreams he's holding a live fish in his hands.'

The doctor stopped in his tracks with a look of elegant amazement and distaste, and the ward grew still. '*He does what?*' he demanded.

'He dreams he's holding a live fish in his hand.'

'What kind of fish?' the doctor inquired sternly of Yossarian.

'I don't know,' Yossarian answered. 'I can't tell one kind of fish from another.'

'In which hand do you hold them?'

'It varies,' answered Yossarian.

'It varies with the fish,' Dunbar added helpfully.

The colonel turned and stared down at Dunbar suspiciously with a narrow squint. 'Yes? And how come you seem to know so much about it?'

'I'm in the dream,' Dunbar answered without cracking a smile.

The colonel's face flushed with embarrassment. He glared at them both with cold, unforgiving resentment. 'Get up off the floor and into your bed,' he directed Dunbar through thin lips. 'And I don't want to hear another word about this dream from either one of you. I've got a man on my staff to listen to disgusting bilge like this.'

'Just why do you think,' carefully inquired Major Sanderson, the soft and thickset smiling staff psychiatrist to whom the colonel had ordered Yossarian sent, 'that Colonel Ferredge finds your dream disgusting?'

Yossarian replied respectfully. 'I suppose it's either some quality in the dream or some quality in Colonel Ferredge.'

'That's very well put,' applauded Major Sanderson, who wore squeaking GI shoes and had charcoal-black hair that stood up almost straight. 'For some reason,' he confided, 'Colonel Ferredge has always reminded me of a sea gull. He doesn't put much faith in psychiatry, you know.'

'You don't like sea gulls, do you?' inquired Yossarian.

'No, not very much,' admitted Major Sanderson with a sharp, nervous laugh and pulled at his pendulous second chin lovingly as though it were a long goatee. 'It think your dream is charming, and I hope it recurs frequently so that we can continue discussing it. Would you like a cigarette?' He smiled when Yossarian declined. 'Just why do you think,' he asked knowingly, 'that you have such a strong aversion to accepting a cigarette from me?'

'I put one out a second ago. It's still smoldering in your ash tray.'

Major Sanderson chuckled. 'That's a very ingenious explanation. But I suppose we'll soon discover the true reason.' He tied a sloppy double bow in his opened shoelace and then transferred a lined yellow pad from his desk to his lap. 'This fish you dream about. Let's talk about that. It's always the same fish, isn't it?'

'I don't know,' Yossarian replied. 'I have trouble recognizing fish.'

'What does the fish remind you of?'

'Other fish.'

'And what do other fish remind you of?'

'Other fish.'

Major Sanderson sat back disappointedly. 'Do you like fish?'

'Not especially.'

'Just why do you think you have such a morbid aversion to fish?' asked Major Sanderson triumphantly.

'They're too bland,' Yossarian answered. 'And too bony.'

Major Sanderson nodded understandingly, with a smile that was agreeable and insincere. 'That's a very interesting explanation. But we'll soon discover the true reason, I suppose. Do you like this particular fish? The one you're holding in your hand?'

'I have no feelings about it either way.'

'Do you dislike the fish? Do you have any hostile or aggressive emotions toward it?'

'No, not at all. In fact, I rather like the fish.'

'Then you do like the fish.'

'Oh, no. I have no feelings toward it either way.'

'But you just said you liked it. And now you say you have no feelings toward it either way. I've just caught you in a contradiction. Don't you see?'

'Yes, sir. I suppose you have caught me in a contradiction.'

Major Sanderson proudly lettered 'Contradiction' on his pad with his thick black pencil. 'Just why do you think,' he resumed when he had finished, looking up, 'that you made those two statements expressing contradictory emotional responses to the fish?'

'I suppose I have an ambivalent attitude toward it.'

Major Sanderson sprang up with joy when he heard the words 'ambivalent attitude'. 'You do understand!' he exclaimed, wringing his hands together ecstatically. 'Oh, you can't imagine how lonely it's been for me, talking day after day to patients who haven't the slightest knowledge of psychiatry, trying to cure people who have no real interest in me or my work! It's given me such a terrible feeling of inadequacy.' A shadow of anxiety crossed his face. 'I can't seem to shake it.'

'Really?' asked Yossarian, wondering what else to say. 'Why do you blame yourself for gaps in the education of others?'

'It's silly, I know,' Major Sanderson replied uneasily, with a giddy, involuntary laugh. 'But I've always depended very heavily on the good opinion of others. I reached puberty a bit later than all the other boys my age, you see, and it's given me sort of – well, all sorts of problems. I just know I'm going to enjoy discussing them with you. I'm so eager to begin that I'm almost reluctant to digress now to your problem, but I'm afraid I must. Colonel Ferredge would be cross if he knew we were spending all our time on me. I'd like to show you some ink blots now to find out what certain shapes and colours remind you of.'

'You can save yourself the trouble, Doctor. Everything reminds me of sex.'

'Does it?' cried Major Sanderson with delight, as though unable to believe his ears. 'Now we're *really* getting somewhere! Do you ever have any good sex dreams?'

'My fish dream is a sex dream.'

'No, I mean real sex dreams – the kind where you grab some naked bitch by the neck and pinch her and punch her in the face until she's all bloody and then throw yourself down to ravish her and burst into tears because you love her and hate her so much you don't know what else to do. That's the kind of sex dreams I like to talk about. Don't you ever have sex dreams like that?'

Yossarian reflected a moment with a wise look. 'That's a fish dream,' he decided.

Major Sanderson recoiled as though he had been slapped. 'Yes, of course,' he conceded frigidly, his manner changing to one of edgy and defensive antagonism. 'But I'd like you to dream one like that anyway just to see how you react. That will be all for today. In the meantime, I'd also like you to dream up the answers to some of those questions I asked you. These sessions are no more pleasant for me than they are for you, you know.'

'I'll mention it to Dunbar,' Yossarian replied.

'Dunbar?'

'He's the one who started it all. It's his dream.'

'Oh, Dunbar.' Major Sanderson sneered, his confidence returning. 'I'll bet Dunbar is that evil fellow who really does all those nasty things you're always being blamed for, isn't he?'

'He's not so evil.'

'And yet you'll defend him to the very death, won't you?'

'Not that far.'

Major Sanderson smiled tauntingly and wrote 'Dunbar' on his pad. 'Why are you limping?' he asked sharply, as Yossarian moved to the door. 'And what the devil is that bandage doing on your leg? Are you mad or something?'

'I was wounded in the leg. That's what I'm in the hospital for.'

'Oh, no, you're not,' gloated Major Sanderson maliciously. 'Your in the hospital for a stone in your salivary gland. So you're not so smart after all, are you? You don't even know what you're in the hospital for.'

'I'm in the hospital for a wounded leg,' Yossarian insisted.

Major Sanderson ignored his argument with a sarcastic laugh. 'Well, give my regards to your friend Dunbar. And you will tell him to dream that dream for me, won't you?'

But Dunbar had nausea and dizziness with his constant headache and was not inclined to co-operate with Major Sanderson. Hungry Joe had nightmares because he had finished sixty missions and was waiting again to go home, but he was unwilling to share any when he came to the hospital to visit.

'Hasn't anyone got any dreams for Major Sanderson?' Yossarian asked. 'I hate to disappoint him. He feels so rejected already.'

'I've been having a very peculiar dream ever since I learned you were wounded,' confessed the chaplain. 'I used to dream every night that my wife was dying or being murdered or that my children were choking to death on morsels of nutritious food. Now I dream that I'm out swimming in water over my head and a shark is eating my left leg in exactly the same place where you have your bandage.'

'That's a wonderful dream,' Dunbar declared. 'I bet Major Sanderson will love it.'

'That's a horrible dream!' Major Sanderson cried. 'It's filled with pain and mutilation and death. I'm sure you had it just to spite me. You know, I'm not even sure you belong in the Army, with a disgusting dream like that.'

Yossarian thought he spied a ray of hope. 'Perhaps you're right, sir,' he suggested slyly. 'Perhaps I ought to be grounded and returned to the States.'

'Hasn't it ever occurred to you that in your promiscuous pursuit of women you are merely trying to assuage your subconscious fears of sexual impotence?'

'Yes, sir, it has.'

'Then why do you do it?'

'To assuage my fears of sexual impotence.'

'Why don't you get yourself a good hobby instead?' Major Sanderson inquired with friendly interest. 'Like fishing. Do you really find Nurse Duckett so attractive? I should think she was rather bony. Rather bland and bony, you know. Like a fish.'

'I hardly know Nurse Duckett.'

'Then why did you grab her by the bosom? Merely because she has one?'

'Dunbar did that.'

'Oh, don't start that again,' Major Sanderson exclaimed with vitriolic scorn, and hurled down his pencil disgustedly. 'Do you really think that you can absolve yourself of guilt by pretending to be someone else? I don't like you, Fortiori. Do you know that? I don't like you at all.'

Yossarian felt a cold, damp wind of apprehension blow over him. 'I'm not Fortiori, sir,' he said timidly. 'I'm Yossarian.'

'You're who?'

'My name is Yossarian, sir. And I'm in the hospital with a wounded leg.'

'Your name is Fortiori,' Major Sanderson contradicted him belligerently. 'And you're in the hospital for a stone in your salivary gland.'

'Oh, come on, Major!' Yossarian exploded. 'I ought to know who I am.'

'And I've got an official Army record here to prove it,' Major Sanderson retorted. 'You'd better get a grip on yourself before it's too late. First you're Dunbar. Now you're Yossarian. The next thing you know you'll be claiming you're Washington Irving. Do you know what's wrong with you? You've got a split personality, that's what's wrong with you.'

'Perhaps you're right, sir,' Yossarian agreed diplomatically.

'I know I'm right. You've got a bad persecution complex. You think people are trying to harm you.'

'People are trying to harm me.'

'You see? You have no respect for excessive authority of obsolete traditions. You're dangerous and depraved, and you ought to be taken outside and shot!'

'Are you serious?'

'You're the enemy of the people!'

'Are you nuts?' Yossarian shouted.

'No, I'm not nuts,' Dobbs roared furiously back in the ward, in what he imagined was a furtive whisper. 'Hungry Joe saw them, I tell you. He saw them yesterday when he flew to Naples to pick up some black-market air conditioners for Colonel Cathcart's farm. They've got a big replacement center there and it's filled with hundreds of pilots, bombardiers and gunners on the way home. They've got forty-five missions, that's all. A few with Purple Hearts have even less. Replacement crews are pouring in from the States into the other bomber groups. They want everyone to serve overseas at least once, even administrative personnel. Don't you read the papers? We've got to kill him now!'

'You've got only two more missions to fly,' Yossarian reasoned with him in a low voice. 'Why take a chance?'

'I can get killed flying them, too,' Dobbs answered pugnaciously in his rough, quavering, overwrought voice. 'We can kill him the first thing tomorrow morning when he drives back from his farm. I've got the gun right here.'

Yossarian goggled with amazement as Dodds pulled a gun out of his pocket and displayed it high in the air. 'Are you crazy? he hissed frantically. 'Put it away. And keep your idiot voice down.'

'What are you worried about?' Dobbs asked with offended innocence. 'No one can hear us.'

'Hey, knock it off down there,' a voice rang out from the far end of the ward. 'Can't you see we're trying to nap?'

'What the hell are you, a wise guy?' Dobbs yelled back and spun around with clenched fists, ready to fight. He whirled back to Yossarian and, before he could speak, sneezed thunderously six times, staggering sideways on rubbery legs in the intervals and raising his elbows ineffectively to fend each seizure off. The lids of his watery eyes were puffy and inflamed. 'Who does he think,' he demanded, sniffing spasmodically and wiping his nose with the back of his sturdy wrist, 'he is, a cop or something?'

'He's a C.I.D. man,' Yossarian notified him tranquilly. 'We've got three here now and more on the way. Oh, don't be scared. They're after a forger named Washington Irving. They're not interested in murderers.'

'Murderers?' Dobbs was affronted. 'Why do you call us murderers? Just because we're going to murder Colonel Cathcart?'

'Be quiet, damn you!' directed Yossarian. 'Can't you whisper?'

'I am whispering. I – '

'You're still shouting.'

'No, I'm not. I – '

'Hey, shut up down there, will you?' patients all over the ward began hollering at Dobbs.

'I'll fight you all!' Dobbs screamed back at them, and stood up on a rickety wooden chair, waving the gun wildly. Yossarian caught his arm and yanked him down. Dobbs began sneezing again. 'I have an allergy,' he apologized when he had finished, his nostrils running and his eyes streaming with tears.

'That's too bad. You'd make a great leader of men without it.'

'Colonel Cathcart's the murderer,' Dobbs complained hoarsely when he had shoved away a soiled, crumpled khaki handkerchief. 'Colonel

103

Cathcart's the one who's going to murder us all if we don't do something to stop him.'

'Maybe he won't raise the missions any more. Maybe sixty is as high as he'll go.'

'He always raises the missions. You know that better than I do.' Dunbar swallowed and bent his intense face very close to Yossarian's, the muscles in his bronze, rocklike jaw bunching up into quivering knots. 'Just say it's okay and I'll do the whole thing tomorrow morning. Do you understand what I'm telling you? I'm whispering now, ain't I?'

Yossarian tore his eyes away from the gaze of burning entreaty Dobbs had fastened on him. 'Why the goddam hell don't you just go out and do it?' he protested. 'Why don't you stop talking to me about it and do it alone?'

'I'm afraid to do it alone. I'm afraid to do anything alone.'

'Then leave me out of it. I'd have to be crazy to get mixed up in something like this now. I've got a million-dollar leg wound here. They're going to send me home.'

'Are you crazy?' Dobbs exclaimed in disbelief. 'All you've got there is a scratch. He'll have you back flying combat missions the day you come out, Purple Heart and all.'

'Then I really will kill him,' Yossarian vowed. 'I'll come looking for you and we'll do it together.'

'Then let's do it tomorrow while we've still got the chance,' Dobbs pleaded. 'The chaplain says he's volunteered the group for Avignon again. I may be killed before you get out. Look how these hands of mine shake. I can't fly a plane. I'm not good enough.'

Yossarian was afraid to say yes. 'I want to wait and see what happens first.'

'The trouble with you is that you just won't do anything,' Dobbs complained in a thick, infuriated voice.

'I'm doing everything I possibly can,' the chaplain explained softly to Yossarian after Dobbs had departed. 'I even went to the medical tent to speak to Doc Daneeka about helping you.'

'Yes, I can see.' Yossarian suppressed a smile. 'What happened?'

'They painted my gums purple,' the chaplain replied sheepishly.

'They painted his toes purple, too,' Nately added in outrage. 'And then they gave him a laxative.'

'But I went back again this morning to see him.'

'And they painted his gums purple again,' said Nately.

'But I did get to speak to him,' the chaplain argued in a plaintive tone of self-justification. 'Doctor Daneeka seems like such an unhappy man. He suspects that someone is plotting to transfer him to the Pacific Ocean. All this time he's been thinking of coming to *me* for help. When I told him I needed *his* help, he wondered if there wasn't a chaplain *I* couldn't go see.' The chaplain waited in patient dejection when Yossarian and Dunbar both broke into laughter. 'I used to think it was immoral to be unhappy,' he continued, as though keening aloud in solitude. 'Now I don't know what to think any more. I'd like to make the subject of immorality the basis of my sermon this Sunday, but I'm not sure I ought to give any sermon at all with these purple gums. Colonel Korn was very displeased with them.'

'Chaplain, why don't you come into the hospital with us for a while and take it easy?' Yossarian invited. 'You could be very comfortable here.'

The brash iniquity of the proposal tempted and amused the chaplain for a second or two. 'No, I don't think so,' he decided reluctantly. 'I want to arrange for a trip to the mainland to see a mail clerk named Wintergreen. Doctor Daneeka told me he could help.'

'Wintergreen is probably the most influential man in the whole theater of operations. He's not only a mail clerk, but he has access to a mimeograph machine. But he won't help anybody. That's one of the reasons he'll go far.'

'I'd like to speak to him anyway. There must be somebody who will help you.'

'Do it for Dunbar, Chaplain,' Yossarian corrected with a superior air. 'I've got this million-dollar leg wound that will take me out of combat. If that doesn't do it, there's a psychiatrist who thinks I'm not good enough to be in the Army.'

'I'm the one who isn't good enough to be in the Army,' Dunbar whined jealously. 'It was my dream.'

'It's not the dream, Dunbar,' Yossarian explained. 'He likes your dream. It's my personality. He thinks it's split.'

'It's split right down the middle,' said Major Sanderson, who had laced his lumpy GI shoes for the occasion and had slicked his charcoal-dull hair down with some stiffening and redolent tonic. He smiled ostentatiously to show himself reasonable and nice. 'I'm not saying that to be cruel and insulting,' he continued with cruel and insulting delight. 'I'm not saying it because I hate you and want revenge. I'm not saying it because you rejected me and hurt my feelings terribly. No, I'm a man of medicine and I'm being coldly objective. I have very bad news for you. Are you man enough to take it?'

'God, no!' screamed Yossarian. 'I'll go right to pieces.'

Major Sanderson flew instantly into a rage. 'Can't you even do one thing right?' he pleaded, turning beet-red with vexation and crashing the sides of both fists down upon his desk together. 'The trouble with you is that you think you're too good for me too, just because I arrived at puberty late. Well, do you know what you are? You're a frustrated, unhappy, disillusioned, undisciplined, maladjusted young man!' Major

Sanderson's disposition seemed to mellow as he reeled off the uncomplimentary adjectives.

'Yes, sir,' Yossarian agreed carefully. 'I guess you're right.'

'Of course I'm right. You're immature. You've been unable to adjust to the idea of war.'

'Yes, sir.'

'You have a morbid aversion to dying. You probably resent the fact that you're at war and might get your head blown off any second.'

'I more than resent it, sir. I'm absolutely incensed.'

'You have deep-seated survival anxieties. And you don't like bigots, bullies, snobs or hypocrites. Subconsciously there are many people you hate.'

'Consciously, sir, consciously,' Yossarian corrected in an effort to help. 'I hate them consciously.'

'You're antagonistic to the idea of being robbed, exploited, degraded, humiliated or deceived. Misery depresses you. Ignorance depresses you. Persecution depresses you. Violence depresses you. Slums depress you. Greed depresses you. Crime depresses you. Corruption depresses you. You know, it wouldn't surprise me if you're a manic-depressive!'

'Yes, sir. Perhaps I am.'

'Don't try to deny it.'

'I'm not denying it, sir,' said Yossarian, pleased with the miraculous rapport that finally existed between them. 'I agree with all you've said.'

'Then you admit you're crazy, do you?'

'Crazy?' Yossarian was shocked. 'What are you talking about? Why am I crazy? You're the one who's crazy!'

Major Sanderson turned red with indignation again and crashed both fists down upon his thighs. 'Calling me crazy,' he shouted in a spluttering rage, 'is a typically sadistic and vindictive paranoiac reaction! You really are crazy!'

'Then why don't you send me home?'

'And I'm going to send you home!'

'They're going to send me home!' Yossarian announced jubilantly, as he hobbled back into the ward.

'Me too!' A. Fortiori rejoiced. 'They just came to my ward and told me.'

'What about me?' Dunbar demanded petulantly of the doctors.

'You?' they replied with asperity. 'You're going with Yossarian. Right back into combat!'

And back into combat they both went. Yossarian was enraged when the ambulance returned him to the squadron, and he went limping for justice to Doc Daneeka, who glared at him glumly with misery and disdain.

'You!' Doc Daneeka exclaimed mournfully with accusing disgust, the egg-shaped pouches under both eyes firm and censurous. 'All you ever think of is yourself. Go take a look at the bomb line if you want to see what's been happening since you went to the hospital.'

Yossarian was startled. 'Are we losing?'

'Losing?' Doc Daneeka cried. 'The whole military situation has been going to hell ever since we captured Paris. I knew it would happen.' He paused, his sulking ire turning to melancholy, and frowned irritably as though it were all Yossarian's fault. 'American troops are pushing into German soil. The Russians have captured back all of Romania. Only yesterday the Greeks in the Eighth Army captured Rimini. The Germans are on the defensive everywhere!' Doc Daneeka paused again and fortified himself with a huge breath for a piercing ejaculation of grief. 'There's no more Luftwaffe left!' he wailed. He seemed ready to burst into tears. 'The whole Gothic line is in danger of collapsing!'

'So?' asked Yossarian. 'What's wrong?'

'What's wrong?' Doc Daneeka cried. 'If something doesn't happen soon, Germany may surrender. And then we'll all be sent to the Pacific!'

Yossarian gawked at Doc Daneeka in grotesque dismay. 'Are you crazy? Do you now what you're saying?'

'Yeah, it's easy for you laugh,' Doc Daneeka sneered.

'Who the hell is laughing?'

'At least you've got a chance. You're in combat and might get killed. But what about me? I've got nothing to hope for.'

'You're out of your goddam head!' Yossarian shouted at him emphatically, seizing him by the shirt front. 'Do you know that? Now keep your stupid mouth shut and listen to me.'

Doc Daneeka wrenched himself away. 'Don't you dare talk to me like that. I'm a licensed physician.'

'Then keep your stupid licensed physician's mouth shut and listen to what they told me up at the hospital. I'm crazy. Did you know that?'

'So?'

'Really crazy.'

'So?'

'I'm nuts. Cuckoo. Don't you understand? I'm off my rocker. They sent someone else home in my place by mistake. They've got a licensed psychiatrist up at the hospital who examined me, and that was his verdict. I'm really insane.'

'So?'

'So?' Yossarian was puzzled by Doc Daneeka's inability to comprehend. 'Don't you see what that means? Now you can take me off combat duty and send me home. They're not going to send a crazy man out to be killed, are they?'

'Who else will go?'

Buller's Guns

RICHARD HOUGH

After a disastrous engagement in the Boer War, Commander Archy Buller and his naval forces, inexperienced in the use of artillery on land and unsupported by their senior Commander, Buller's arch-rival and enemy Marchmount, have fallen back from their guns, which lie under the scorching South African sun . . . . .

AT ELEVEN O'CLOCK, COMMANDER Marchmount rode up to the donga, where the survivors of the Naval Battery had been lying for four hours in the heat, without food or water beyond what was left in their bottles. Buller saw him coming with Lieutenant Windsor at his side, two figures shimmering and unnaturally tall in the heat distortion. When they were nearer, Buller, who was some distance from any of his men, asked out loud, 'How on earth does he do it? For God's sake, he's not even *dusty!*'

'Commander Buller, what do you propose to do about your guns?'

'I have no immediate plans.'

'You mean the Navy is to present them to the enemy?'

Buller could hardly believe his ears. The man was not joking, there was no irony in the question, which had been asked rather more sharply than was customary to an officer of equal rank.

'I mean we've no ammunition and too few men left to man them. I take it that the attack has failed. Your guns have ceased fire. There's no sign of the infantry. The Boers are still entrenched in the kopjes. And my men are awaiting orders. They are also done in.'

Buller looked up at Marchmount on his horse as he recited this message coldly. Marchmount was gazing about the donga as if inspecting the quarterdeck for tarnished brightwork and finding the scene disagreeable.

'The orders are that we must save the guns.'

Now Buller rediscovered that old enemy, his temper, an enemy that had lain low for so many years. It was rising uncontrollably, just as if he were a boy again. 'What do you mean, "save the guns"? You put your head out there in the open, Marchmount. You'll see the frying corpses of our men. You'll see them, if the Mausers don't get you first. And where're the oxen and the Kaffirs? Do you expect my men to drag the guns back –

108

what's left of them?' He stared up at the impassive figure in his recently pressed white morning dress uniform, as if Marchmount was ready to have his Admiral piped on board. 'You're mad. The sun's done in your brain.'

Marchmount turned his head slowly towards his Lieutenant and spoke in a calm voice: 'Kindly note those words, Mr. Windsor. I have no doubt that they will be used in evidence at the court-martial after this is over.'

'And I know who'll be the accused, Marchmount – dereliction of duty, cowardice in the face of the enemy, and a few other charges.' Buller's words were pouring out uncontrollably. Marchmount snapped back, as if not listening, 'I understand the Army saved some of its guns. What the Army can do – '

'They saved two guns and lost more than half their men. Go and look for yourself – and count the corpses.'

'With respect, sir. With your permission, sir . . .' A third voice broke in, a voice with a strong Geordie accent, hoarse now with dryness. Buller turned and saw Rod at attention, capless, sweat-streaked, and filthy. Marchmount nodded permission, and Rod continued. 'I don't think we can recover the guns, sir. But we might deny them to the enemy.'

'How's that, Chief Gunner?'

'We could wait until dark and incapacitate the guns. Take out the strikers from the breechblocks, sir. The Boers are unlikely to have spares – not of naval long-twelve-pounders.'

'What do you think, Mr. Windsor?'

'Well, sir – it's a compromise.'

A shrapnel shell burst overhead, the steel fragments rattling against the rocks and causing the two horses to rear. A second later a heavy common shell burst just beyond the lip of the donga, throwing up a cloud of dust and rock fragments.

While still settling his horse, and speaking more rapidly than before, Marchmount said to Buller, 'Commander Buller, will you be so good as to have your Chief Gunner and a small party proceed to your abandoned' – and he laid special emphasis on the word – 'your abandoned guns and recover the strikers. I would like them by luncheon time, please.'

With the intervention of Rod, Buller had succeeded in controlling himself. 'I will gladly do that tonight and report when the operation has been completed. Meanwhile, may I please request – '

'Now, not after dark. That may be too late. The General has cancelled the attack and the Boers may overrun this ground later today.'

Buller listened aghast to this calm pronouncement, but determined not to repeat the weak stroke of losing his temper. 'They won't last two minutes out there, Marchmount. There are more than a thousand Boer Mausers within range.'

Marchmount ignored him and addressed Rod as if Buller had not spoken. 'Chief Gunner, will you form a party without delay and send back a message when completed.' Then, without another glance at the surviving officers and ratings lying about the donga, or at Buller, he pulled round his horse and trotted away, Lieutenant Windsor trailing him like a dog at heel.

'You're under my orders now, Guns,' Buller said grimly, 'and you are forming no party of my men. Those Boers wouldn't leave their safe positions, cross the river, and advance over open ground in a million years. Not against a single battalion, let alone half the British Army.'

'I'm not afraid, sir. The job's to be done, but I'll do it alone.' He smiled up at Buller: 'I'm nippy with the striker – you know that, sir.'

'Don't talk rubbish, Midge. The job needn't be done, but it will be done. And it'll be done by me and no one else. Then I shall have the greatest pleasure in serving the strikers, not for luncheon but for dinner to Commander Marchmount, along with his best quality mutton chops.'

Rod laughed. 'We could make it for luncheon, sir, if we hurry.'

'You're not coming, Guns.'

'Not "Guns", sir. "Lucky Midge." Remember what Lord Charles calls me. You won't get along without me.'

As they were lying out there, the sun burnt down on them as if the sky were a blast furnace poised above the veldt, cruel, implacable, fierce, agonizing. Once, Buller glanced up at it in the old belief that you should know your enemy, and all that he saw was a searing white glow that filled the heavens and possessed no definition.

The only way to retain your senses was to talk. They had run from the donga before Marchmount and Windsor were out of sight, unarmed for speed and without even water bottles, deciding that it would be done quickly or not at all. Buller had told only one of his two surviving Lieutenants, leaving him in command.

They were halfway to the guns before some sharp-eyed burgher spotted the two figures 800 years distant and fired the first shot. More shots followed within seconds, rising to a soaring, rattling climax – hundreds of Mauser bullets in the air at once – before they dropped behind the limbers.

Momentarily, as he lay there panting, Buller's mind again went back twenty-five years, to those boyhood dreams of hearing a shot fired in anger. Well, today at least, and not for the first time, those dreams were being fulfilled – 'Yes, in full measure, full measure!' he told himself with a touch of self-mockery.

Later, they moved a few feet to gain the benefit of the shelter of one of the gun's wheels. Only partial shelter, from the sun as well as from the musket fire. It saved their lives, but there was no question of moving farther, of working on the guns' breechblocks and removing the strikers, let alone of returning to the donga. That would have resulted not just in being hit but of being riddled and torn apart within half a second.

There, secure in trenches and emplacements, behind rocks, were those hundreds of Boers, dirty, bearded, in their filthy old slouch hats, and no doubt as hot as they were. But each one a crack shot with his Mauser or Lee-Metford and with nothing else to shoot at but two mad Englishmen lying trapped out there within comfortable range. Even now, two hours later, they continued to shoot. But, evidently uncertain of their enemies' fate and anxious to avoid wasting ammunition, the Boers' volleys were only intermittent.

Yes, talk. Talk could save your mind, even if it further dried your parched throat.

Awhile back – it seemed like days ago – Buller had said, 'Tell me about your family, Midge. Three children, you once told me, is that right?'

Then, later, Buller said, 'Yes, I've three – Lucy, Harry, and another boy of four, Richard.' And later still: 'Tell me about your home – in Newcastle, Midge.'

Rod moved an inch to the right, to keep his neck in the shadow of the gun carriage's wheel. 'Just a little place. Two rooms up, two down. But we like it there. It's friendly. Though it can be hard, on the Tyne. A lot of hunger.'

'Like us now.'

Rod said, 'Worse and for longer.' And Buller felt ashamed of his flippancy. He could not remember ever having been hungry, except puppy hungry as a boy and in the *Britannia*, and always soon satisfied. And, of course, among his friends, four rooms for a family of five was beyond consideration as a house.

They talked then, and more easily, of their Navy life, of the chance that had got Rod past the height minimum, of life in the *Implacable*, of voyages about the world, of friends and enemies; and when Rod pressed him, Buller told of life in the Cotswolds, of hunting and hunt balls, of house parties, of the eccentricities of naval officers and those of noble birth, including his own father-in-law.

They laughed and fell silent for a few minutes. The heat beat down, surely worse than ever, but as if by some unspoken promise, neither uttered a word of complaint. Shortly after three o'clock and for no apparent reason, a heavy gun from far behind the nearest kopje opened fire and landed three shells very close, covering them with dirt and fragments of a eucalyptus tree that had stood fifty yards away.

Then Rod began to talk again, his voice very hoarse now, and strained. 'How often have you been frightened, before this, sir? When you were in the water that time? At Alexandria?'

Buller was surprised by the question and bought time by saying with a laugh that was more a croak, 'Out here – like this – with our Maker so close – we can drop the "sir".'

'Yes, sir. I mean – '

'Just call me Buller. Only a few people call me Archy and it's a terrible name.'

But Rod just stopped saying 'sir', and even that seemed unnatural.

'Since you ask me, I have to say I don't know. I remember long ago taking a big gate on my father's hunter – I wasn't more than ten. And one of my elder brothers told me I ought to have been scared, and I didn't understand what he meant. And I was supposed to feel scared standing on the old *Britannia*'s truck one evening when I was a cadet. But I just felt rather good up there.'

When Buller moved, even an inch or two, it was like shifting from red-hot steel plate onto white-hot steel plate, and the stones seemed to drill through his puttees like pokers from a fire into his skin. He noticed that Midge, Guns, Warrant Officer Roderick Maclewin, far from his wife Rosie and his three little children and his smoke-blackened four-roomed house on the banks of the Tyne – Midge was looking awful: two days' beard dusty red over gaunt white cheeks; eyes unnaturally large and wandering – wandering like those of an Arab he had once picked up in the desert on the point of death. He was suffering much worse than Buller was. 'Not the same reserves as me.'

Poor little Midge. 'Lucky Midge' sounded mocking in its inaccuracy now. Nice name Rosie. Can't have her a widow.

Then Rod seemed to revive. But his question was even more unexpected than the last one. 'Have you always loved your wife?'

'Oh yes.' Buller thought it as well to reply at once. For the sake of truth, he conditioned this. 'Of course I've had lots of affairs, like everyone else. So has she. But, yes. Oh yes, we love one another. I mean, we're married.'

'That's very interesting. I mean life is very interesting.' Rod's voice was low and Buller lost several words as some Boer marksman, with nothing else to do, loosed off a couple of rounds at them.

'We're about the same age, you and me,' Rod continued huskily and almost inaudibly. 'Both in the Navy all our lives, both gunners, both been in tight corners like this – and together. Both married. Both love our wives and children. And now stuck behind this damn gun in this damn heat with this damn thirst. As we're probably both going to die, it doesn't much matter what we say.'

'And both friends. I hope,' added Buller. He had never heard Rod swear before. Clean-tongued young man, unlike most sailors. Clean-living, too. No slipping in and out of other women's beds. No delicious flirtations at dances. Or, for that matter, no putting a hundred guineas on a throw at baccarat, and laughing at the loss, and lighting up the third big Havana of the evening, and ordering another jeroboam of Mumms Extra Dry from Charles at the Marlborough at three in the morning. No inherited title in the family, along with acres of best Cotswold farming land and a house in Belgravia, no ...

'Oh my God, how much the same we are!' exclaimed Buller to himself, with the afternoon sun torturing his head, his shoulders and back, the back of his legs, even the bottom of his feet through his boots. 'How much the same we are, this steady Warrant Officer from Northumberland, and me. And, my God, how different!'

Buller felt impelled to express this thought to Rod, and turned his head. His old friend was lying still, on his right side, slightly curled up, only the top of his head in the shade, one hand lying in the dust, the other against the gun carriage wheel, eyes half-open and seeming to see nothing.

His lips, dry and cracked as ancient parchment, moved to prove that he was alive and that he could talk. But all he said was to repeat, now with a note of delirium, 'Life is very interesting.'

'He is burning to death, this friend of mine,' Buller told himself. 'This little Chief Gunner who is my friend and who saved my life and has a wife called Rosie – he is burning to death. And I am his senior officer, and I brought him here.'

Very slowly, Buller sat up and stripped off his shirt. Then, even more slowly he secured one sleeve to a length of torn leather harness and the other through a spoke in the wheel. 'A jury rig, but it'll have to do.' Then he drew on the leather and secured that, creating shade for Rod from the waist up.

Any number of corpses, as he had pointed out to Marchmount. No shortage. And no shortage of water bottles attached to them. It had crossed his mind earlier, but the calculation of survival odds seemed as high as drawing four aces in a row. Now the odds did not seem to matter. Rod would not last until dusk, would not last for another hour without water and shade.

Buller moved so slowly, like a lethargic veldt mole snake, that he raised no dust, not a grain of dust, head up only high enough now and again to check his direction. Like a frying mutton chop. That's what he was, a sizzling, frying mutton chop. It took him fifteen minutes to reach the nearest corpse. It happened to be a rating named Wilf Robinson, a particularly happy-go-lucky leading seaman from Goole on the Humber, whom Buller had always liked, although it was difficult to recognize the blackened face and the sightless eyes as his. It was typically frugal of the man that he had not touched his water bottle.

Buller unstrapped it, and that took another five minutes. Then he began scraping his way back to the 12-pounder, over the same rocks. He even saw some of his own blood, already hardened and congealed like a healing wound; and he followed the red trail with his eyes. 'Very convenient,' he told himself. 'This way I don't even have to raise my

113

head.'

It took longer to get back, not because he was being even more careful to avoid raising dust or be observed moving, but because his strength was beginning to drain away. 'Like a damn ship's boilers when the bunkers are empty,' he said softly to himself, thinking of old Lord Huntley. He could even hear his father-in-law's voice, the words slurred: 'What happens when the bunkers are empty, eh?'

But there was never any doubt that he would complete the journey. 'Can't waste all this good Buller blood. And all this good Wilf Robinson water. And all this time ... My God, Buller, you're going delirious, too. Pull yourself together.' He laughed soundlessly. 'No, don't do that. It'll cause dust, and Mauser bullets.'

Rod's eyes were closed. He was very light to hold up, against his chest. And to hell with being seen now. We've got to get this water down.

When Buller attempted to unscrew the felt-covered cap, he noticed to his astonishment that his hand was shaking. Shaking! He held it up for a moment, the wicked sun casting the shadows of his fingers against Rod's face, and the shadows were shaking, too. 'I am,' he said aloud, half unbelievingly, half knowing it to be true, 'I am shaking with fear! Not just from weariness and strain, but from *fear*!'

At the same time, he felt a chill coursing through his body, as if the temperature had turned Arctic from tropic. It was a new sensation, a new experience, like the ache in his crotch and the prickling sensation beneath his tortured skin.

A few shots were fired from the kopje as the sun went down and a few more after it had set, the muzzle flashes like distant sparks, as if the Boers wished to remind the English once again, 'This is the sunset of the British Empire. We are here now as we were this morning and as we shall be tomorrow morning.'

Later, when it was dark, Buller quickly unscrewed the 12-pounders' strikers, working from one gun to the next. Press the knob of the spring catch, revolve the striker one sixth of a turn to the left. Then withdraw firmly.

He tied them together round his neck with a length of severed trace, the steel still hot from the day's sun. When he picked Rod up, he seemed to weigh little more than these hardened steel spikes, Buller hoisted him onto his own burnt back and held his arms over his shoulders.

Rod groaned and seemed to utter a few words. Buller, thinking his mind was wandering, said nothing in reply. But in this new dark silence of the veldt, the words were spoken again, insistently and more clearly.

Buller said, 'What is it, Midge?'

'I said, "That makes it two to one, sir."'

Buller's laugh was like the stirring of gravel. Then he began to feel his way across the veldt, taking it steadily, scraping against a harsh shrub here, avoiding a rock there, the strikers jabbing the torn flesh of his chest and knocking against one another like a clanking steel anthem of survival.

Arctic Convoy

ALISTAIR MACLEAN

Ordered to escort the vital convoy FR77 to Murmansk, H.M.S. Ulysses
*and her crew, having survived the rigours of an Arctic storm, come face to
face with disaster and the ruthless intransigence of Admiralty leadership in
London . . . . .*

ABOARD THE MERCHANT ships, crews lined the decks as the *Ulysses* steamed
up between the port and centre lines. Lined the decks and looked and
wondered – and thanked their Maker they had been wide of the path of
that great storm. The *Ulysses*, seen from another deck, was a strange
sight: broken-masted, stripped of her rafts, with her boat falls hauled taut
over empty cradles, she glistened like crystal in the morning light: the
great wind had blown away all snow, had abraded and rubbed and
polished the ice to a satin-smooth, transparent gloss: but on either side of
the bows and before the bridge were huge patches of crimson, where the
hurricane sand-blaster of that long night had stripped off camouflage and
base coats, exposing the red lead below.

The American escort was small – a heavy cruiser with a seaplane for
spotting, two destroyers and two near-frigates of the coastguard type.
Small, but sufficient: there was no need of escort carriers (although these
frequently sailed with the Atlantic convoys) because the Luftwaffe could
not operate so far west, and the wolf-packs, in recent months, had moved
north and east of Iceland: there, they were not only nearer base – they
could more easily lie astride the converging convoy routes to Murmansk.

ENE. they sailed in company, freighters, American warships and the
Ulysses until, late in the afternoon, the box-like silhouette of an escort
carrier bulked high against the horizon. Half an hour later, at 1600, the
American escorts slowed, dropped astern and turned, winking farewell
messages of good luck. Aboard the *Ulysses*, men watched them depart
with mixed feelings. They knew these ships had to go, that another
convoy would already be mustering off the St. Lawrence. There was none
of the envy, the bitterness one might expect – and had indeed been
common enough only a few weeks ago – among these exhausted men who
carried the brunt of the war. There was instead a careless acceptance of
things as they were, a quasi-cynical bravado, often a queer, high

nameless pride that hid itself beneath twisted jests and endless grumbling.

The 14th Aircraft Carrier Squadron – or what was left of it – was only two miles away now. Tyndall, coming to the bridge, swore fluently as he saw that a carrier and minesweeper were missing. An angry signal went out to Captain Jeffries of the *Stirling*, asking why orders had been disobeyed, where the missing ships were.

An Aldis flickered back its reply. Tyndall sat grim-faced and silent as Bentley read out the signal to him. The *Wrestler*'s steering gear had broken down during the night. Even behind Langanes the weather position had been severe, had worsened about midnight when the wind had veered to the north. The *Wrestler*, even with two screws, had lost almost all steering command, and, in zero visiblity and an effort to maintain position, had gone too far ahead and grounded on the Vejle bank. She had grounded on the top of the tide. She had still been there, with the minesweeper *Eager* in attendance, when the squadron had sailed shortly after dawn.

Tyndall sat in silence for some minutes. He dictated a W.T. signal to the *Wrestler*, hesitated about breaking radio silence, countermanded the signal, and decided to go to see for himself. After all, it was only three hours' steaming distance. He signalled the *Stirling*: 'Take over squadron command: will rejoin in the morning,' and ordered Vallery to take the *Ulysses* back to Langanes.

Vallery nodded unhappily, gave the necessary orders. He was worried, badly so, was trying hard not to show it. The least of his worries was himself, although he knew, but never admitted to anyone, that he was a very sick man. He thought wryly that he didn't have to admit it anyway – he was amused and touched by the elaborate casualness with which his officers sought to lighten his load, to show their concern for him.

He was worried, too, about his crew – they were in no fit state to do the lightest work, to survive that killing cold, far less sail the ship and fight her through to Russia. He was depressed, also, over the series of misfortunes that had befallen the squadron since leaving Scapa: it augured ill for the future, and he had no illusions as to what lay ahead for the crippled squadron. And always, a gnawing torment at the back of his mind, he worried about Ralston.

Ralston – that tall throwback to his Scandinavian ancestors, with his flaxen hair and still blue eyes. Ralston, whom nobody understood, with whom nobody on the ship had an intimate friendship, who went his own unsmiling, self-possessed way. Ralston, who had nothing left to fight for, except memories, who was one of the most reliable men in the *Ulysses*, extraordinarily decisive, competent and resourceful in any emergency – and who again found himself under lock and key. And for nothing that any reasonable and just man could call fault of his own.

Under lock and key – that was what hurt. Last night, Vallery had gladly seized the excuse of bad weather to release him, had intended to forget the matter, to let sleeping dogs lie. But Hastings, the Master-At-Arms, had exceeded his duty and returned him to cells during the forenoon watch. Masters-At-Arms – disciplinary Warrant Officers, in effect – had never been particularly noted for a humane, tolerant and ultra-kindly attitude to life in general or the lower deck in particular – they couldn't afford to be. But even amongst such men, Hastings was an exception – a machine-like seemingly emotionless creature, expressionless, unbending, strict, fair according to his lights, but utterly devoid of heart and sympathy. If Hastings were not careful, Vallery mused, he might very well go the same way as Lister, until recently the highly unpopular Master-At-Arms of the *Blue Ranger*. Not, when he came to think of it, that anyone knew what had happened to Lister, except that he had been so misguided as to take a walk on the flight-deck on a dark and starless night....

Vallery sighed. As he had explained to Foster, his hands were tied. Foster, the Captain of Marines, with an aggrieved and incensed Colour-Sergeant Evans standing behind him, had complained bitterly at having his marines withdrawn for guard duty, men who needed every minute of sleep they could snatch. Privately, Vallery had sympathised with Foster, but he couldn't afford to countermand his original order – not, at least, until he had held a Captain's Defaulters and placed Ralston under open arrest. ... He sighed again, sent for Turner and asked him to break out grass lines, a manila and five-inch wire on the poop. He suspected that they would be needed shortly, and, as it turned out, his preparations were justified.

Darkness had fallen when they moved up to the Vejle bank, but locating the *Wrestler* was easy – her identification challenge ten minutes ago had given her approximate position, and now her squat bulk loomed high before them, a knife-edged silhouette against the pale afterglow of sunset. Ominously, her flight deck raked perceptibly towards the stern, where the *Eager* lay, apparently at anchor. The sea was almost calm here – there was only a gentle swell running.

Aboard the *Ulysses*, a hooded, pin-hole Aldis started to chatter.

'Congratulations! How are you fast?'

From the *Wrestler*, a tiny light flickered in answer. Bentley read aloud as the message came.

'Bows aft 100 feet.'

'Wonderful,' said Tyndall bitterly. 'Just wonderful! Ask him, "How is steering-gear?"''

Back came the answer: 'Diver-down: transverse fracture of post: dockyard job.'

'My God!' Tyndall groaned. 'A dockyard job! That's handy. Ask him,

"What steps have you taken?" '

'All fuel and water pumped aft. Kedge anchor. *Eager* towing. Full astern, 1200–1230.'

The turn of the high tide, Tyndall knew. 'Very successful, very successful indeed,' he growled. 'No, you bloody fool, don't send that. Tell him to prepare to receive towing wire, bring own towing chain aft.'

'Message understood,' Bentley read.

'Ask him, "How much excess squadron fuel have you?" '

'800 tons.'

'Get rid of it.'

Bentley read, 'Please confirm.'

'Tell him to empty the bloody stuff over the side!' Tyndall roared.

The light of the *Wrestler* flickered and died in hurt silence.

At midnight the *Eager* steamed slowly ahead of the *Ulysses*, taking up the wire that led back to the cruiser's fo'c'sle capstan: two minutes later, the *Ulysses* began to shudder as the four great engines boiled up the shallow water into a seething mudstained cauldron. The chain from the poop-deck to the *Wrestler*'s stern was a bare fifteen fathoms in length, angling up at 30°. This would force the carrier's stern down – only a fraction, but in this situation every ounce counted – and give more positive buoyancy to the grounded bows. And much more important – for the racing screws were now aerating the water, developing only a fraction of their potential thrust – the proximity of the two ships helped the *Ulysses*'s screws reinforce the action of the *Wrestler*'s in scouring out a channel in the sand and mud beneath the carrier's keel.

Twenty minutes before high tide, easily, steadily, the *Wrestler* slid off. At once the blacksmith on the *Ulysses* bows knocked off the shackle securing the *Eager*'s towing wire, and the *Ulysses* pulled the carrier, her engines shut down, in a big half-circle to the east.

By one o'clock the *Wrestler* was gone, the *Eager* in attendance and ready to pass a head rope for bad weather steering. On the bridge of the *Ulysses*, Tyndall watched the carrier vanish into the night, zig-zagging as the captain tried to balance the steering on the two screws.

'No doubt they'll get the hang of it before they get to Scapa,' he growled. He felt cold, exhausted and only the way an Admiral can feel when he has lost three-quarters of his carrier force. He sighed wearily and turned to Vallery.

'When do you reckon we'll overtake the convoy?'

Vallery hesitated: not so the Kapok Kid.

'0805,' he answered readily and precisely. 'At twenty-seven knots, on the intersection course I've just pencilled out.'

'Oh, my God!' Tyndall groaned. 'That stripling again. What did I ever do to deserve him. As it happens, young man, it's imperative that we overtake before dawn.'

'Yes, sir.' The Kapok Kid was imperturbable. 'I thought so myself. On my alternative course, 33 knots, thirty minutes before dawn.'

'I thought so myself! Take him away!' Tyndall raved. 'Take him away or I'll wrap his damned dividers round ...' He broke off, climbed stiffly out of his chair, took Vallery by the arm. 'Come on, Captain. Let's go below. What the hell's the use of a couple of ancient has-beens like us getting in the way of youth?' He passed out the gate behind the Captain, grinning tiredly to himself.

The *Ulysses* was at dawn Action Stations as the shadowy shapes of the convoy, a bare mile ahead, lifted out of the greying gloom. The great bulk of the *Blue Ranger*, on the starboard quarter of the convoy, was unmistakable. There was a moderate swell running, but not enough to be uncomfortable: the breeze was light, from the west, the temperature just below zero, the sky chill and cloudless. The time was exactly 0700.

At 0702, the *Blue Ranger* was torpedoed. The *Ulysses* was two cable-lenths away, on her starboard quarter: those on the bridge felt the physical shock of the twin explosions, heard them shattering the stillness of the dawn as they saw two searing columns of flame fingering skywards, high above the *Blue Ranger*'s bridge and well aft of it. A second later they heard a signalman shouting something unintelligible, saw him pointing forwards and downwards. It was another torpedo, running astern of the carrier, trailing its evil phosphorescent wake across the heels of the convoy, before spending itself in the darkness of the Arctic.

Vallery was shouting down the voice-pipe, pulling round the *Ulysses*, still doing upwards of twenty knots, in a madly heeling, skidding turn to avoid collision with the slewing carrier. Three sets of Aldis lamps and the fighting lights were already stuttering out the 'Maintain Position' code signal to ships in the convoy. Marshall, on the phone, was giving the stand-by order to the depth-charge L.T.O.: gun barrels were already depressing, peering hungrily into the treacherous sea. The signal to the *Sirrus* stopped short, unneeded: the destroyer, a half-seen blue in the darkness, was already knifing its way through the convoy, white water piled high at its bows, headed for the estimated position of the U-boat.

The *Ulysses* sheered by parallel to the burning carrier, less than 150 feet away; travelling so fast, heeling so heavily and at such close range, it was impossible to gather more than a blurred impression, a tangled, confused memory of heavy black smoke laced with roaring columns of flame, appalling in that near-darkness, of a drunkenly listing flight-deck, of Grummans and Corsairs cartwheeling grotesquely over the edge to splash icy clouds of spray in shocked faces, as the cruiser slewed away; and then the *Ulysses* was round, heading back south for the kill.

Within a minute, the signal-lamp of the *Vectra*, up front with the convoy, started winking. 'Contact, Green 70, closing: Contact, Green 70, closing.'

'Acknowledge,' Tyndall ordered briefly.

The Aldis had barely begun to clack when the *Vectra* cut through the signal.

'Contacts, repeat contacts. Green 90, Green 90. Closing. Very close. Repeat contacts, contacts.'

Tyndall cursed softly.

'Acknowledge. Investigate.' He turned to Vallery. 'Let's join him, Captain. This is it. Wolf-pack Number One – and in force. No bloody right to be here,' he added bitterly. 'So much for Admiralty Intelligence!'

The *Ulysses* was round again, heading for the *Vectra*. It should have been growing lighter now, but the *Blue Ranger*, her squadron fuel tanks on fire, a gigantic torch against the eastern horizon, had the curious effect of throwing the surrounding sea into heavy darkness. She lay almost athwart of the flagship's course for the *Vectra*, looming larger every minute. Tyndall had his night glasses to his eyes, kept on muttering: 'The poor bastards, the poor bastards!'

The *Blue Ranger* was almost gone. She lay dead in the water, heeled far over to starboard, ammunition and petrol tanks going up in a constant series of crackling reports. Suddenly, a succession of dull, heavy explosions rumbled over the sea: the entire bridge island structure lurched crazily sideways, held, then slowly, ponderously, deliberately, the whole massive body of it toppled majestically into the glacial darkness of the sea. God only knew how many men perished with it, deep down in the Arctic, trapped in its iron walls. They were the lucky ones.

The *Vectra*, barely two miles ahead now, was pulling round south in a tight circle. Vallery saw her, altered course to intercept. He heard Bentley shouting something unintelligible from the fore corner of the compass platform. Vallery shook his head, heard him shouting again, his voice desperate with some nameless urgency, his arm pointing frantically over the windscreen, and leapt up beside him.

The sea was on fire. Flat, calm, burdened with hundreds of tons of fuel oil, it was a vast carpet of licking, twisting flames. That much, for a second, and that only, Vallery saw: then with heart-stopping shock, with physical sickening abruptness, he saw something else again: the burning sea was alive with swimming, struggling men. Not a handful, not even dozens, but literally hundreds, soundlessly screaming, agonisingly dying in the barbarous contrariety of drowning and cremation.

'Signal from *Vectra*, sir.' It was Bentley speaking, his voice abnormally matter-of-fact. ' "Depth-charging. 3, repeat 3 contacts. Request immediate assistance." '

Tyndall was at Vallery's side now. He heard Bentley, looked a long second at Vallery, following his sick, fascinated gaze into the sea ahead.

For a man in the sea, oil is an evil thing. It clogs his movements, burns his eyes, sears his lungs and tears away his stomach in uncontrollable paroxysms of retching; but oil on fire is a hellish thing, death by torture, a slow, shrieking death by drowning, by burning, by asphyxiation – for the flames devour all the life-giving oxygen on the surface of the sea. And not even in the bitter Arctic is there the merciful extinction by cold, for the insulation of an oil-soaked body stretches a dying man on the rack for eternity, carefully preserves him for the last excruciating refinement of agony. All this Vallery knew.

He knew, too, that for the *Ulysses* to stop, starkly outlined against the burning carrier, would have been suicide. And to come sharply round to starboard, even had there been time and room to clear the struggling, dying men in the sea ahead, would have wasted invaluable minutes, time and to spare for the U-boats ahead to line up firing-tracks on the convoy; and the *Ulysses*'s first responsibility was to the convoy. Again all this Vallery knew. But, at that moment, what weighed most heavily with him was common humanity. Fine off the port bow, close in to the *Blue Ranger*, the oil was heaviest, the flames fiercest, the swimmers thickest: Vallery looked back over his shoulder at the Officer of the Watch.

'Port 10!'

'Port 10, sir.'

'Midships!'

'Midships, sir.'

'Steady as she goes!'

For ten, fifteen seconds the *Ulysses* held her course, arrowing through the burning sea to the spot where some gregariously atavistic instinct for self-preservation held two hundred men knotted together in a writhing, seething mass, gasping out their lives in hideous agony. For a second a great gout of flame leapt up in the centre of the group, like a giant, incandescent magnesium flare, a flame that burnt the picture into the hearts and minds of the men on the bridge with a permanence and searing clarity that no photographic plate could ever have reproduced: men on fire, human torches beating insanely at the flames that licked, scorched and then incinerated clothes, hair and skin: men flinging themselves almost out of the water, backs arched like tautened bows, grotesque in convulsive crucifixion: men lying dead in the water, insignificant, featureless little oil-stained mounds in an oil-soaked plain: and a handful of fear-maddened men, faces inhumanly contorted, who saw the *Ulysses* and knew what was coming, as they frantically thrashed their way to a safety that offered only a few more brief seconds of unspeakable agony before they gladly died.

'Starboard 30!' Vallery's voice was low, barely a murmur, but it carried clearly through the shocked silence on the bridge.

'Starboard 30, sir.'

For the third time in ten minutes, the *Ulysses* slewed crazily round in a racing turn. Turning thus, a ship does not follow through the line of the bows cutting the water; there is a pronounced sideways or lateral motion, and the faster and sharper the turn, the more violent the broadside skidding motion, like a car on ice. The side of the *Ulysses*, still at an acute angle, caught the edge of the group on the port bow: almost on the instant, the entire length of the swinging hull smashed into the heart of the fire, into the thickest press of dying men.

For most of them, it was just extinction, swift and glad and merciful. The tremendous concussion and pressure waves crushed the life out of them, thrust them deep down into the blessed oblivion of drowning, thrust them down and sucked them back into the thrashing vortex of the four great screws....

On board the *Ulysses*, men for whom death and destruction had become the stuff of existence, to be accepted with the callousness and jesting indifference that alone kept them sane – these men clenched impotent fists, mouthed meaningless, useless curses over and over again and wept heedlessly like little children. They wept as pitiful, charred faces, turned up towards the *Ulysses* and alight with joy and hope, petrified into incredulous staring horror, as realisation dawned and the water closed over them; as hate-filled men screamed insane invective, both arms raised aloft, shaking fists white-knuckled through the dripping oil as the *Ulysses* trampled them under: as a couple of young boys were sucked into the mælstrom of the propellors, still giving the thumbs-up sign: as a particularly shocking case, who looked as if he had been barbecued on a spit and had no right to be alive, lifted a scorified hand to the blackened hole that had been his mouth, flung to the bridge a kiss in token of endless gratitude; and wept, oddly, most of all, at the inevitable humorist who lifted his fur cap high above his head and bowed gravely and deeply, his face into the water as he died.

Suddenly, mercifully, the sea was empty. The air was strangely still and quiet, heavy with the sickeing stench of charred flesh and burning Diesel, and the *Ulysses*'s stern was swinging wildly almost under the black pall overhanging the *Blue Ranger* amidships, when the shells struck her.

The shells – three 3.7s – came from the *Blue Ranger*. Certainly, no living gun-crews manned these 3.7s – the heat must have ignited the bridge fuses in the cartridge cases. The first shell exploded harmlessly against the armour-plating: the second wrecked the bosun's store, fortunately empty: the third penetrated No. 3 Low Power Room via the deck. There were nine men in there – an officer, seven ratings and Chief-Torpedo Gunner's Mate Noyes. In that confined space, death was instantaneous.

Only seconds later a heavy rumbling explosion blew out a great hole along the waterline of the *Blue Ranger* and she fell slowly, wearily right over on her starboard side, her flight-deck vertical to the water, as if content to die now that, dying, she had lashed out at the ship that had destroyed her crew.

123

On the bridge, Vallery still stood on the yeoman's platform, leaning over the starred, opaque windscreen. His head hung down, his eyes were shut and he was retching desperately, the gushing blood – arterial blood – ominously bright and scarlet in the erubescent glare of the sinking carrier. Tyndall stood there helplessly beside him, not knowing what to do, his mind numbed and sick. Suddenly, he was brushed unceremoniously aside by the Surgeon-Commander, who pushed a white towel to Vallery's mouth and led him gently below. Old Brooks, everyone knew, should have been at his Action Stations position in the Sick Bay: no one dared say anything.

Carrington straightened the *Ulysses* out on course, while he waited for Turner to move up from the after Director tower to take over the bridge. In three minutes the cruiser was up with the *Vectra*, methodically quartering for a lost contact. Twice the ships regained contact, twice they dropped heavy patterns. A heavy oil slick rose to the surface: possibly a kill, probably a ruse, but in any event, neither ship could remain to investigate further. The convoy was two miles ahead now, and only the *Stirling* and *Viking* were there for its protection – a wholly inadequate cover and powerless to save the convoy from any determined attack.

It was the *Blue Ranger* that saved FR77. In these high latitudes, dawn comes slowly, interminably: even so, it was more than half-light, and the merchant ships, line ahead through that very gentle swell, lifted clear and sharp against a cloudless horizon, a U-boat Commander's dream – or would have been, had he been able to see them. But, by this time, the convoy was completely obscured from the wolf-pack lying to the south: the light westerly wind carried the heavy black smoke from the blazing carrier along the southern flank of the convoy, at sea level, the perfect smoke-screen, dense, impenetrable. Why the U-boats had departed from their almost invariable practice of launching dawn attacks from the north, so as to have their targets between themselves and the sunrise, could only be guessed. Tactical surprise, probably, but whatever the reason it was the saving of the convoy. Within an hour, the thrashing screws of the convoy had left the wolf-pack far behind – and FR77, having slipped the pack, was far too fast to be overtaken again.

Aboard the flagship, the W.T. transmitter was chattering out a coded signal to London. There was little point, Tyndall had decided, in maintaining radio silence now; the enemy knew their position to a mile. Tyndall smiled grimly as he thought of the rejoicing in the German Naval High Command at the news that FR77 was without any air cover whatsoever; as a starter, they could expect Charlie within the hour.

The signal read: 'Admiral, 14 A.C.S.: To D.N.C., London. Rendezvoused FR77 1030 yesterday. Weather conditions extreme. Severe damage to Carriers: *Defender*, *Wrestler* unserviceable, returning base under escort: *Blue Ranger* torpedoed 0702, sunk 0730 to-day: Convoy

Escorts now *Ulysses, Stirling, Sirrus, Vectra, Viking*: no minesweepers – *Eager* to base, minesweeper from Hvalfjord failed rendezvous: Urgently require air support: Can you detach carrier battle squadron: Alternatively, permission return base. Please advise immediately.'

The wording of the message, Tyndall pondered, could have been improved. Especially the bit at the end – probably sounded sufficiently like a threat to infuriate old Starr who would only see in it pusillanimous confirmation of his conviction of the *Ulysses*'s – and Tyndall's – unfitness for the job. ... Besides, for almost two years now – since long before the sinking of the *Hood* by the *Bismark* – it had been Admiralty policy not to break up the Home Fleet squadrons by detaching capital ships or carriers. Old battleships, too slow for modern inter-naval surface action – vessels such as the *Ramillies* and the *Malaya* – were used for selected Arctic convoys: with that exception, the official strategy was based on keeping the Home Fleet intact, containing the German Grand Fleet – and risking the convoys. ... Tyndall took a last look round the convoy, sighed wearily and eased himself down to the duckboards. What the hell, he thought, let it go. If it wasted his time sending it, it would also waste old Starr's time reading it.

He clumped his way heavily down the bridge ladders, eased his bulk through the door of the Captain's cabin, hard by the F.D.R. Vallery, partly undressed, was lying in his bunk, between very clean, very white sheets: their knife-edged ironing crease-marks contrasted oddly with the spreading crimson stain. Vallery himself, gaunt-cheeked and cadaverous beneath dark stubble of beard, red eyes sunk deep in great hollow sockets, looked corpse-like, already dead. From one corner of his mouth blood trickled down a parchment cheek. As Tyndall shut the door, Vallery lifted a wasted hand, all ivory knuckles and blue veins, in feeble greeting.

Tyndall closed the door carefully, quietly. He took his time, time and to spare to allow the shock to drain out of his face. When he turned round, his face was composed, but he made no attempt to disguise his concern.

'Thank God for old Socrates!' he said feelingly. 'Only man in the ship who can make you see even a modicum of sense.' He parked himself on the edge of the bed. 'How do you feel, Dick?'

Vallery grinned crookedly. There was no humour in his smile.

'All depends what you mean, sir. Physically or mentally? I feel a bit worn out – not really ill, you know. Doc says he can fix me up – temporarily anyway. He's going to give me a plasma transfusion – says I've lost too much blood.'

'Plasma?'

'Plasma. Whole blood would be a better coagulant. But he thinks it may prevent – or minimise – future attacks. ...' He paused, wiped some

125

froth off his lips, and smiled again, as mirthlessly as before. 'It's not really a doctor and medicine I need, John – it's a padre – and forgiveness.' His voice trailed off into silence. The cabin was very quiet.

Tyndall shifted uncomfortably and cleared his throat noisily. Rarely had he been so conscious that he was, first and last, a man of action.

'Forgiveness? What on earth do you mean, Dick?' He hadn't meant to speak so loudly, so harshly.

'You know damn' well what I mean,' Vallery said mildly. He was a man who was rarely heard to swear, to use the most innocuous oath. 'You were with me on the bridge this morning.'

For perhaps two minutes neither man said a word. Then Vallery broke into a fresh paroxysm of coughing. The towel in his hand grew dark, sodden, and when he leaned back on his pillow Tyndall felt a quick stab of fear. He bent quickly over the sick man, sighed in soundless relief as he heard the quick, shallow breathing.

Vallery spoke again, his eyes still closed.

'It's not so much the men who were killed in the Low Power Room.' He seemed to be talking to himself, his voice a drifting murmur. 'My fault, I suppose – I took the *Ulysses* too near the *Ranger*. Foolish to go near a sinking ship, especially if she's burning. . . . But just one of these things, just one of the risks . . . they happen. . . .' The rest was a blurred, dying whisper. Tyndall couldn't catch it.

He rose abruptly to his feet, pulling his gloves on.

'Sorry, Dick,' he apologised. 'Shouldn't have come – shouldn't have stayed so long. Old Socrates will give me hell.'

'It's the others – the boys in the water.' Vallery might never have heard him. 'I hadn't the right – I mean, perhaps some of them would . . .' Again his voice was lost for a moment, then he went on strongly: 'Captain Richard Vallery, D.S.O. – judge, jury and executioner. Tell me, John, what am I going to say when *my* turn comes?'

Tyndall hesitated, heard the authoritative rap on the door and jerked round, his breath escaping in a long, inaudible sigh of thankfulness.

'Come in,' he called.

The door opened and Brooks walked in. He stopped short at the sight of the Admiral, turned to the white-coated assistant behind him, a figure weighed down with stands, bottles, tubing and various paraphernalia.

'Remain outside, Johnson, will you?' he asked. 'I'll call you when I want you.'

He closed the door, crossed the cabin and pulled a chair up to the Captain's bunk. Vallery's wrist between his fingers, he looked coldly across at Tyndall. Nicholls, Brooks remembered, was insistent that the Admiral was far from well. He looked tired, certainly, but more unhappy than tired. . . . The pulse was very fast, irregular.

'You've been upsetting him,' Brooks accused.

'Me? Good God, no!' Tyndall was injured. 'So help me, Doc, I never said – '

'Not guilty, Doc.' It was Vallery who spoke, his voice stronger now. 'He never said a word. *I'm* the guilty man – guilty as hell.'

Brooks looked at him for a long moment. Then he smiled, smiled in understanding and compassion.

'Forgiveness, sir. That's it, isn't it?' Tyndall started in surprise, looked at him in wonder.

Vallery opened his eyes. 'Socrates!' he murmured. 'You would know.'

'Forgiveness,' Brooks mused. 'Forgiveness. From whom – the living, the dead – or the Judge?'

Again Tyndall started. 'Have you – have you been listening outside? How can you – ?'

'From all three, Doc. A tall order, I'm afraid.'

'From the dead, sir, you are quite right. There would be no forgiveness: only their blessing, for there is nothing to forgive. I'm a doctor, don't forget – I saw those boys in the water ... you sent them home the easy way. As for the Judge – you know, "The Lord giveth, the Lord taketh away. Blessed be the name of the Lord" – the Old Testament conception of the Lord who takes away in His own time and His own way, and to hell with mercy and charity.' He smiled at Tyndall. 'Don't look so shocked, sir. I'm not being blasphemous. If that were the Judge, Captain, neither you nor I – nor the Admiral – would ever want any part of him. But you know it isn't so. . . .'

Vallery smiled faintly, propped himself up on his pillow. 'You make good medicine, Doctor. It's a pity you can't speak for the living also.'

'Oh, can't I?' Brooks smacked his hand on his thigh, guffawed in sudden recollection. 'Oh, my word, it was magnificent!' He laughed again in genuine amusement. Tyndall looked at Vallery in mock despair.

'Sorry,' Brooks apologised. 'Just fifteen minutes ago a bunch of sympathetic stokers deposited on the deck of the Sick Bay the prone and extremely unconscious form of one of their shipmates. Guess who? None other than our resident nihilist, our old friend Riley. Slight concussion and assorted facial injuries, but he should be restored to the bosom of his mess-deck by nightfall. Anyway, he insists on it – claims his kittens need him.'

Vallery looked up, amused, curious.

'Fallen down the stokehold again, I presume?'

'Exactly the question I put, sir – although it looked more as if he had fallen into a concrete mixer. "No, sir," says one of the stretcher-bearers. "He tripped over the ship's cat." "Ship's cat?" I says. "What ship's cat?" So he turns to his oppo and says: "Ain't we got a ship's cat, Nobby?" Whereupon the stoker yclept Nobby looks at him pityingly and says: "'E's got it all wrong, sir. Poor old Riley just came all over queer – took a weak turn, 'e did. I 'ope 'e ain't 'urt 'isself?" He sounded quite anxious.'

'What had happened?' Tyndall queried.

'I let it go at that. Young Nicholls took two of them aside, promised no action and had it out of them in a minute flat. Seems that Riley saw in this morning's affair a magnificent opportunity for provoking trouble. Cursed you for an inhuman, cold-blooded murderer and, I regret to say, cast serious aspersions on your immediate ancestors – and all of this, mind you, where he thought he was safe – among his own friends. His friends half-killed him.... You know, sir, I envy you....'

He broke off, rose abruptly to his feet.

'Now, sir, if you'll just lie down and roll up your sleeve ... Oh, damn!'

'Come in.' It was Tyndall who answered the knock. 'Ah, for me, young Chrysler. Thank you.'

He looked up at Vallery. 'From London – in reply to my signal.' He turned it over in his hand two or three times. 'I suppose I have to open it some time,' he said reluctantly.

The Surgeon-Commander half-rose to his feet.

'Shall I –'

'No, no, Brooks. Why should you? Besides, it's from our mutual friend, Admiral Starr. I'm sure you'd like to hear what he's got to say, wouldn't you?'

'No, I wouldn't.' Brooks was very blunt. 'I can't imagine it'll be anything good.'

Tyndall opened the signal, smoothed it out.

'D.N.O. to Admiral Commanding 14 A.C.S.,' he read slowly. '*Tirpitz* reported preparing to move out. Impossible detach Fleet carrier: FR77 vital: proceed Murmansk all speed: good luck: Starr.' Tyndall paused, his mouth twisted. 'Good luck! He might have spared us that!'

For a long time the three men looked at each other, silently, without expression. Characteristically, it was Brooks who broke the silence.

'Speaking of forgiveness,' he murmured quietly, 'what I want to know is – who on God's earth, above or below it, is ever going to forgive that vindictive old bastard?'

The Red Badge of Courage
STEPHEN CRANE

A raw recruit in the Yankee army, Henry Fleming, finds himself and his courage tested to the utmost in his first experience of the bloody and chaotic conflict of the American Civil War .....

THE YOUTH'S REGIMENT WAS marched to relieve a command that had lain long in some damp trenches. The men took positions behind a curving line of rifle pits that had been turned up, like a large furrow, along the line of woods. Before them was a level stretch, peopled with short, deformed stumps. From the woods beyond came the dull popping of the skirmishers and pickets, firing in the fog. From the right came the noise of a terrific fracas.

The men cuddled behind the small embankment and sat in easy attitudes awaiting their turn. Many had their backs to the firing. The youth's friend lay down, buried his face in his arms, and almost instantly, it seemed, he was in a deep sleep.

The youth leaned his breast against the brown dirt and peered over at the woods and up and down the line. Curtains of trees interfered with his ways of vision. He could see the low line of trenches but for a short distance. A few idle flags were perched on the dirt hills. Behind them were rows of dark bodies with a few heads sticking curiously over the top.

Always the noise of skirmishers came from the woods on the front and left, and the din on the right had grown to frightful proportions. The guns were roaring without an instant's pause for breath. It seemed that the cannon had come from all parts and were engaged in a stupendous wrangle. It became impossible to make a sentence heard.

The youth wished to launch a joke – a quotation from newspapers. He desired to say, 'All quiet on the Rappahannock,' but the guns refused to permit even a comment upon their uproar. He never successfully concluded the sentence. But at last the guns stopped, and among the men in the rifle pits rumours again flew, like birds, but they were now for the most part black creatures who flapped their wings drearily near to the ground and refused to rise on any wings of hope. The men's faces grew doleful from the interpreting of omens. Tales of hesitation and uncertainty on the part of those high in place and responsibility came to their ears.

129

Stories of disaster were borne into their minds with many proofs. This din of musketry on the right, growing like a released genie of sound, expressed and emphasized the army's plight.

The men were disheartened and began to mutter. They made gestures expressive of the sentence: 'Ah, what more can we do?' And it could always be seen that they were bewildered by the alleged news and could not fully comprehend a defeat.

Before the grey mists had been totally obliterated by the sun-rays, the regiment was marching in a spread column that was retiring carefully through the woods. The disordered, hurrying lines of the enemy could sometimes be seen down through the groves and little fields. They were yelling shrill and exultant.

At this sight the youth forgot many personal matters and became greatly enraged. He exploded in loud sentences. 'B'jiminey, we're generaled by a lot 'a lunkheads.'

'More than one feller has said that t'-day,' observed a man.

His friend, recently aroused, was still very drowsy. He looked behind him until his mind took in the meaning of the movement. Then he sighed. 'Oh, well, I s'pose we got licked,' he remarked sadly.

The youth had a thought that it would not be handsome for him to freely condemn other men. He made an attempt to restrain himself, but the words upon his tongue were too bitter. He presently began a long and intricate denunciation of the commander of the forces.

'Mebbe, it wa'n't all his fault – not all together. He did th' best he knowed. It's our lock t' git licked often,' said his friend in a weary tone. He was trudging along with stooped shoulders and shifting eyes like a man who has been caned and kicked.

'Well, don't we fight like the devil? Don't we do all that men can?' demanded the youth loudly.

He was secretly dumbfounded at this sentiment when it came from his lips. For a moment his face lost its valour and he looked guiltily about him. But no one questioned his right to deal in such words, and presently he recovered his air of courage. He went on to repeat a statement he had heard going from group to group at the camp that morning. 'The brigadier said he never saw a new reg'ment fight the way we fought yesterday, didn't he? And we didn't do better than many another reg'ment, did we? Well, then, you can't say it's th' army's fault, can you?'

In his reply, the friend's voice was stern. ''A course not,' he said. 'No man dare say we don't fight like th' devil. No man will ever dare say it. Th' boys fight like hell-roosters. But still – still, we don't have no luck.'

'Well, then, if we fight like the devil an' don't ever whip, it must be the general's fault,' said the youth grandly and decisively. 'And I don't see any sense in fighting and fighting and fighting, yet always losing through some derned old lunkhead of a general.'

130

A sarcastic man who was tramping at the youth's side, then spoke lazily. 'Mebbe yeh think yeh fit th' hull battle yestirday, Fleming,' he remarked.

The speech pierced the youth. Inwardly he was reduced to an abject pulp by these chance words. His legs quaked privately. He cast a frightened glance at the sarcastic man.

'Why, no,' he hastened to say in a conciliating voice, 'I don't think I fought the whole battle yesterday.'

But the other seemed innocent of any deeper meaning. Apparently, he had no information. It was merely his habit. 'Oh!' he replied in the same tone of calm derision.

The youth, nevertheless, felt a threat. His mind shrank from going near to the danger, and thereafter he was silent. The significance of the sarcastic man's words took from him all loud moods that would make him appear prominent. He became suddenly a modest person.

There was low-toned talk among the troops. The officers were impatient and snappy, their countenances clouded with the tales of misfortune. The troops, sifting through the forest, were sullen. In the youth's company once a man's laugh rang out. A dozen soldiers turned their faces quickly towards him and frowned with vague displeasure.

The noise of firing dogged their footsteps. Sometimes, it seemed to be driven a little way, but it always returned again with increased insolence. The men muttered and cursed, throwing black looks in its direction.

In a clear space the troops were at last halted. Regiments and brigades, broken and detached through their encounters with thickets, grew together again and lines were faced toward the pursuing bark of the enemy's infantry.

This noise, following like the yellings of eager, metallic hounds, increased to a loud and joyous burst, and then, as the sun went serenely up the sky, throwing illuminating rays into the gloomy thickets, it broke forth into prolonged pealings. The woods began to crackle as if afire.

'Whoop-a-dadee,' said a man, 'here we are! Everybody fightin'. Blood an' destruction.'

'I was willin' t' bet they'd attack as soon as th' sun got fairly up,' savagely asserted the lieutenant who commanded the youth's company. He jerked without mercy at his little moustache. He strode to and fro with dark dignity in the rear of his men, who were lying down behind whatever protection they had collected.

A battery had trundled into position in the rear and was thoughtfully shelling the distance. The regiment, unmolested as yet, awaited the moment when the grey shadows of the woods before them should be slashed by the lines of flame. There was much growling and swearing.

'Good Gawd,' the youth grumbled, 'we're always being chased around like rats! It makes me sick. Nobody seems to know where we go or why we go. We just get fired around from pillar to post and get licked here and get licked there, and nobody knows what it's done for. It makes a man feel like a damn' kitten in a bag. Now, I'd like to know what the eternal thunders we was marched into these woods for anyhow, unless it was to give the rebs a regular pot shot at us. We came in here and got our legs all tangled up in these cussed briers, and then we begin to fight and the rebs had an easy time of it. Don't tell me it's just luck! I know better. It's this derned old – '

The friend seemed jaded, but he interrupted his comrade with a voice of calm confidence. 'It'll turn out all right in th' end,' he said.

'Oh, the devil it will! You always talk like a dog-hanged parson. Don't tell me! I know – '

At this time there was an interposition by the savage-minded lieutenant, who was obliged to vent some of his inward dissatisfaction upon his men. 'You boys shut right up! There's no need a' your wastin' your breath in long-winded arguments about this an' that an' th' other. You've been jawin' like a lot a' old hens. All you've got t' do is to fight, an' you'll get plenty a' that t' do in about ten minutes. Less talkin' an' more fightin' is what's best for you boys. I never saw sech gabbling jackasses.'

He paused, ready to pounce upon any man who might have the temerity to reply. No words being said, he resumed his dignified pacing.

'There's too much chin music an' too little fightin' in this war, anyhow,' he said to them, turning his head for a final remark.

The day had grown more white, until the sun shed his full radiance upon the thronged forest. A sort of gust of battle came sweeping toward that part of the line where lay the youth's regiment. The front shifted a trifle to meet it squarely. There was a wait. In this part of the field there passed slowly the intense moments that precede the tempest.

A single rifle flashed in a thicket before the regiment. In an instant it was joined by many others. There was a mighty song of clashes and crashes that went sweeping through the woods. The guns in the rear, aroused and enraged by shells that had been thrown burrlike at them, suddenly involved themselves in a hideous altercation with another band of guns. The battle roar settled to a rolling thunder, which was a single, long explosion.

In the regiment there was a peculiar kind of hesitation denoted in the attitudes of the men. They were worn, exhausted, having slept but little and labored much. They rolled their eyes toward the advancing battle as they stood awaiting the shock. Some shrank and flinched. They stood as men tied to stakes.

This advance of the enemy had seemed to the youth like a ruthless hunting. He began to fume with rage and exasperation. He beat his foot upon the ground, and scowled with hate at the swirling smoke that was approaching like a phantom flood. There was a maddening quality in this seeming resolution of the foe to give him no rest, to give him no time to sit down and think. Yesterday he had fought and had fled rapidly. There had been many adventures. For to-day he felt that he had earned opportunities for contemplative repose. He could have enjoyed portraying to uninitiated listeners various scenes at which he had been a witness or ably discussing the processes of war with other proved men. Too it was important that he should have time for physical recuperation. He was sore and stiff from his experiences. He had received his fill of all exertions, and he wished to rest.

But those other men seemed never to grow weary; they were fighting with their old speed. He had a wild hate for the relentless foe. Yesterday, when he had imagined the universe to be against him, he had hated it, little gods and big gods; to-day he hated the army of the foe with the same great hatred. He was not going to be badgered of his life, like a kitten chased by boys, he said. It was not well to drive men into final corners; at those moments they could all develop teeth and claws.

He leaned and spoke into his friend's ear. He menaced the woods with a gesture. 'If they keep on chasing us, by Gawd, they'd better watch out. Can't stand *too* much."

The friend twisted his head and made a calm reply. 'If they keep on a-chasin' us they'll drive us all inteh th' river.'

The youth cried out savagely at this statement. He crouched behind a little tree, with his eyes burning hatefully and his teeth set in a curlike snarl. The awkward bandage was still about his head, and upon it, over his wound, there was a spot of dry blood. His hair was wondrously tousled, and some straggling, moving locks hung over the cloth of the bandage down toward his forehead. His jacket and shirt were open at the throat, and exposed his young bronzed neck. There could be seen spasmodic gulpings at his throat.

His fingers twined nervously about his rifle. He wished that it was an engine of annihilating power. He felt that he and his companions were being taunted and derided from sincere convictions that they were poor and puny. His knowledge of his inability to take vengeance for it made his rage into a dark and stormy spectre, that possessed him and made him dream of abominable cruelties. The tormentors were flies sucking insolently at his blood, and he thought that he would have given his life for a revenge of seeing their faces in pitiful plights.

The winds of battle had swept all about the regiment, until the one rifle, instantly followed by others, flashed in its front. A moment later the regiment roared forth its sudden and valiant retort. A dense wall of smoke settled slowly down. It was furiously slit and slashed by the knifelike fire from the rifles.

To the youth the fighters resembled animals tossed for a death struggle into a dark pit. There was a sensation that he and his fellows, at bay, were pushing back, always pushing fierce onslaughts of creatures who were slippery. Their beams of crimson seemed to get no purchase upon the bodies of their foes; the latter seemed to evade them with ease, and come through, between, around, and come through, between, around, and about with unopposed skill.

When, in a dream, it occurred to the youth that his rifle was an impotent stick, he lost sense of everything but his hate, his desire to smash into pulp the glittering smile of victory which he could feel upon the faces of his enemies.

The blue smoke-swallowed line curled and writhed like a snake stepped upon. It swung its ends to and fro in an agony of fear and rage.

The youth was not conscious that he was erect upon his feet. He did not know the direction of the ground. Indeed, once he even lost the habit of balance and fell heavily. He was up again immediately. One thought went through the chaos of his brain at the time. He wondered if he had fallen because he had been shot. But the suspicion flew away at once. He did not think more of it.

He had taken up a first position behind the little tree, with a direct determination to hold it against the world. He had not deemed it possible that his army could that day succeed, and from this he felt the ability to fight harder. But the throng had surged in all ways, until he lost directions and locations, save that he knew where lay the enemy.

The flames bit him, and the hot smoke broiled his skin. His rifle barrel grew so hot that ordinarily he could not have borne it upon his palms; but he kept on stuffing cartridges into it, and pounding them with his clanking, bending ramrod. If he aimed at some changing form through the smoke, he pulled his trigger with a fierce grunt, as if he were dealing a blow of the fist with all his strength.

When the enemy seemed falling back before him and his fellows, he went instantly forward, like a dog who, seeing his foes lagging, turns and insists upon being pursued. And when he was compelled to retire again, he did it slowly, sullenly, taking steps of wrathful despair.

Once he, in his intent hate, was almost alone, and was firing, when all those near him had ceased. He was so engrossed in his occupation that he was not aware of a lull.

He was recalled by a hoarse laugh and a sentence that came to his ears in a voice of contempt and amazement. 'Yeh infernal fool, don't yeh know enough t' quit when there ain't anything t' shoot at? Good Gawd!'

He turned then and, pausing with his rifle thrown half into position, looked at the blue line of his comrades. During this moment of leisure they seemed all to be engaged in staring with astonishment at him. They had become spectators. Turning to the front again he saw, under the lifted smoke, a deserted ground.

He looked bewildered for a moment. Then there appeared upon the glazed vacancy of his eyes a diamond point of intelligence. 'Oh,' he said, comprehending.

He returned to his comrades and threw himself upon the ground. He sprawled like a man who had been thrashed. His flesh seemed strangely on fire, and the sounds of the battle continued in his ears. He groped blindly for his canteen.

The lieutenant was crowing. He seemed drunk with fighting. He called out to the youth: 'By heavens, if I had ten thousand wild cats like you I could tear th' stomach outa this war in less'n a week!' He puffed out his chest with large dignity as he said it.

Some of the men muttered and looked at the youth in awestruck ways. It was plain that he had gone on loading and firing and cursing without the proper intermission, they had found time to regard him. And they now looked upon him as a war devil.

The friend came staggering to him. There was some fright and dismay in his voice. 'Are yeh all right, Fleming? Do yeh feel all right? There ain't nothin' th' matter with yeh, Henry, is there?'

'No,' said the youth with difficulty. His throat seemed full of knobs and burrs.

These incidents made the youth ponder. It was revealed to him that he had been a barbarian, a beast. He had fought like a pagan who defends his religion. Regarding it, he saw that it was fine, wild, and, in some ways, easy. He had been a tremendous figure, no doubt. By the struggle he had overcome obstacles which he had admitted to be mountains. They had fallen like paper peaks, and he was now what he called a hero. And he had not been aware of the process. He had slept and, awakening, found himself a knight.

He lay and basked in the occasional stares of his comrades. Their faces were varied in degrees of blackness from the burned powder. Some were utterly smudged. They were reeking with perspiration, and their breaths came hard and wheezing. And from these soiled expanses they peered at him.

'Hot work! Hot work!' cried the lieutenant deliriously. He walked up and down, restless and eager. Sometimes his voice could be heard in a wild, incomprehensible laugh.

When he had a particularly profound thought upon the science of war he always unconsciously addressed himself to the youth.

There was some grim rejoicing by the men. 'By thunder, I bet this army'll never see another new reg'ment like us?'

'You bet!'

> 'A dog, a woman, an' a walnut tree,
> Th' more yeh beat 'em, th' better they be!

That's like us.'

'Lost a piler men, they did. If an ol' woman swep' up th' woods she'd git a dustpanful.'

'Yes, an' if she'll come around ag'in in 'bout an hour she'll git a pile more.'

The forest still bore its burden of clamour. From off under the trees came the rolling clatter of the musketry. Each distant thicket seemed a strange porcupine with quills of flame. A cloud of dark smoke, as from smouldering ruins, went up toward the sun now bright and gay in the blue, enamelled sky.

The ragged line had respite for some minutes, but during its pause in the struggle in the forest became magnified until the trees seemed to quiver from the firing and the ground to shake from the rushing of the men. The voices of the cannon were mingled in a long and interminable row. It seemed difficult to live in such an atmosphere. The chests of the men strained for a bit of freshness, and their throats craved water.

There was one shot through the body, who raised a cry of bitter lamentation when came this lull. Perhaps he had been calling out during the fighting also, but at that time no one had heard him. But now the men turned at the woeful complaints of him upon the ground.

'Who is it? Who is it?'

'It's Jimmie Rogers. Jimmie Rogers.'

When their eyes first encountered him there was a sudden halt, as if they feared to go near. He was thrashing about in the grass, twisting his shuddering body into many strange postures. He was screaming loudly. This instant's hesitation seemed to fill him with a tremendous, fantastic contempt, and he damned them in shrieked sentences.

The youth's friend had a geographical illusion concerning a stream, and he obtained permission to go for some water. Immediately canteens were showered upon him. 'Fill mine, will yeh?' 'Bring me some, too.' 'And me, too.' He departed, laden. The youth went with his friend, feeling a desire to throw his heated body onto the stream, and soaking there, drink quarts.

They made a hurried search for the supposed stream, but did not find it. 'No water here,' said the youth. They turned without delay and began to retrace their steps.

From their position as they again faced towards the place of the fighting, they could of course comprehend a greater amount of the battle than when their visions had been blurred by the hurling smoke of the line. They could see dark stretches winding along the land, and on one cleared space there was a row of guns making grey clouds, which were filled with large flashes of orange-coloured flame. Over some foliage they could see the roof of a house. One window, glowing a deep murder red, shone squarely through the leaves. From the edifice a tall leaning tower of smoke went far into the sky.

Looking over their own troops, they saw mixed masses slowly getting into regular form. The sunlight made twinkling points of the bright steel. To the rear there was a glimpse of a distant roadway as it curved over a slope. It was crowded with retreating infantry. From all the interwoven forest arose the smoke and bluster of the battle. The air was occupied by a blaring.

Near where they stood shells were flip-flapping and hooting. Occasional bullets buzzed in the air and spanged into tree trunks. Wounded men and other stragglers were slinking through the woods.

Looking down an aisle of the grove, the youth and his companion saw a jangling general and his staff almost ride upon a wounded man, who was crawling on his hands and knees. The general reined strongly at his charger's opened and foamy mouth and guided it with dexterous horsemanship past the man. The latter scrambled in wild and torturing haste. His strength evidently failed him as he reached a place of safety. One of his arms suddenly weakened, and he fell, sliding over upon his back. He lay stretched out, breathing gently.

A moment later the small, creaking cavalcade was directly in front of the two soldiers. Another officer, riding with the skillful abandon of a cowboy, galloped his horse to a position directly before the general. The two unnoticed foot soldiers made a little show of going on, but they lingered near in the desire to overhear the conversation. Perhaps, they thought, some great inner historical things would be said.

The general, whom the boys knew as the commander of their division, looked at the other officer and spoke coolly, as if he were criticising his clothes. 'Th' enemy's formin' over there for another charge,' he said. 'It'll be directed against Whiterside, an' I fear they'll break through there unless we work like thunder t' stop them.'

The other swore at his restive horse, and then cleared his throat. He made a gesture towards his cap. 'It'll be hell t' pay stoppin' them,' he said shortly.

'I presume so,' remarked the general. Then he began to talk rapidly and in a lower tone. He frequently illustrated his words with a pointing finger. The two infantrymen could hear nothing until finally he asked: 'What troops can you spare?'

The officer who rode like a cowboy reflected for an instant. 'Well,' he said, 'I had to order in th' 12th to help th' 76th, an' I haven't really got any. But there's th' 304th. They fight like a lot a' mule drivers. I can spare them best of any.'

The youth and his friend exchanged glances of astonishment.

The general spoke sharply. 'Get 'em ready, then. I'll watch developments from here, an' send you word when t'start them. It'll happen in five minutes.'

137

As the other officer tossed his fingers toward his cap and wheeling his horse, started away, the general called out to him in a sober voice: 'I don't believe many of your mule drivers will get back.'

The other shouted something in reply. He smiled.

With scared faces, the youth and his companion hurried back to the line.

These happenings had occupied an incredibly short time, yet the youth felt that in them he had been made aged. New eyes were given to him. And the most startling thing was to learn suddenly that he was very insignificant. The officer spoke of the regiment as if he referred to a broom. Some part of the woods needed sweeping, perhaps, and he merely indicated a broom in a tone properly indifferent to its fate. It was war, no doubt, but it appeared strange.

As the two boys approached the line, the lieutenant perceived them and swelled with wrath. 'Fleming – Wilson – how long does it take yeh to git water, anyhow – where yeh been to?'

But his oration ceased as he saw their eyes, which were large with great tales. 'We're goin' t' charge – we're goin' t' charge!' cried the youth's friend, hastening with his news.

'Charge?' said the lieutenant. 'Charge? Well, b' Gawd! Now; this is real fightin'.' Over his soiled countenance there was a boastful smile. 'Charge? Well, b' Gawd!'

A little group of soldiers surrounded the two youths. 'Are we, sure 'nough? Well, I'll be derned! Charge? What fer? What at? Wilson, you're lyin'.'

'I hope to die,' said the youth, pitching his tones to the key of angry remonstrance. 'Sure as shooting, I tell you.'

And his friend spoke in re-enforcement. 'Not by a blame sight, he ain't lyin'. We heard 'em talkin'.'

They caught sight of two mounted figures a short distance from them. One was the colonel of the regiment and the other was the officer who had received orders from the commander of the division. They were gesticulating at each other. The soldier, pointing at them, interpreted the scene.

One man had a final objection: 'How could yeh hear 'em talkin'?' But the men, for a large part, nodded, admitting that previously the two friends had spoken truth.

They settled back into reposeful attitudes with airs of having accepted the matter. And they mused upon it, with a hundred varieties of expression. It was an engrossing thing to think about. Many tightened their belts carefully and hitched at their trousers.

A moment later the officers began to bustle among the men, pushing them into a more compact mass and into a better alignment. They chased those that straggled and fumed at a few men who seemed to show by their attitudes that they had decided to remain at that spot. They were like critical shepherds struggling with sheep.

Presently, the regiment seemed to draw itself up and heave a deep breath. None of the men's faces were mirrors of large thoughts. The soldiers were bended and stooped like sprinters before a signal. Many pairs of glinting eyes peered from the grimy faces toward the curtains of the deeper woods. They seemed to be engaged in deep calculations of time and distance.

They were surrounded by the noises of the monstrous altercation between the two armies. The world was fully interested in other matters. Apparently, the regiment had its small affair to itself.

The youth, turning, shot a quick, inquiring glance at his friend. The latter returned to him the same manner of look. They were the only ones who possessed an inner knowledge. 'Mule drivers – hell t' pay – don't believe many will get back.' It was an ironical secret. Still, they saw no hesitation in each other's faces, and they nodded a mute and unprotesting assent when a shaggy man near them said in a meek voice: 'We'll git swallowed.'

The youth stared at the land in front of him. Its foliages now seemed to veil powers and horrors. He was aware of the machinery of orders that started the charge, although from the corners of his eyes he saw an officer, who looked like a boy a-horseback, come galloping, waving his hat. Suddenly he felt a straining and heaving among the men. The line fell slowly forward like a toppling wall, and, with a convulsive gasp that was intended for a cheer, the regiment began its journey. The youth was pushed and jostled for a moment before he understood the movement at all, but directly he lunged ahead and began to run.

He fixed his eye upon a distant and prominent clump of trees where he had concluded the enemy were to be met, and he ran towards it as towards a goal. He had believed throughout that it was a mere question of getting over an unpleasant matter as quickly as possible, and he ran desperately, as if pursued for a murder. His face was drawn hard and tight with the stress of his endeavor. His eyes were fixed in a lurid glare. And with his soiled and disordered dress, his red and inflamed features surmounted by the dingy rag with its spot of blood, his wildly swinging rifle and banging accoutrements, he looked to be an insane soldier.

As the regiment swung from its position out into a cleared space the woods and thickets before it awakened. Yellow flames leaped towards it from many directions. The forest made a tremendous objection.

The line lurched straight for a moment. Then the right wing sprung forwards; it in turn was surpassed by the left. Afterwards the centre careered to the front until the regiment was a wedge-shaped mass, but an instant later the opposition of the bushes, trees, and uneven places on the ground split the command and scattered it into detached clusters.

The youth, light-footed, was unconsciously in advance. His eyes still kept note of the clump of trees. From all places near it the clannish yell of the enemy could be heard. The little flames of rifles leaped from it. The song of the bullets was in the air and shells snarled among the tree-tops. One tumbled directly into the middle of a hurrying group and exploded in crimson fury. There was an instant's spectacle of a man, almost over it, throwing up his hands to shield his eyes.

Other men, punched by bullets, fell in grotesque agonies. The regiment left a coherent trail of bodies.

They had passed into a clearer atmosphere. There was an effect like a revelation in the new appearance of the landscape. Some men working madly at a battery were plain to them, and the opposing infantry lines were defined by the grey walls and fringes of smoke.

It seemed to the youth that he saw everything. Each blade of the green grass was bold and clear. He thought that he was aware of every change in the thin, transparent vapour that floated idly in sheets. The brown or grey trunks of the trees showed each roughness of their surfaces. And the men of the regiment, with their starting eyes and sweating faces, running madly, or falling, as if thrown headlong, [in] to queer, heaped-up corpses – all were comprehended. His mind took a mechanical but firm impression, so that afterwards everything was pictured and explained to him, save why he himself was there.

But there was a frenzy made from this furious rush. The men pitching forwards insanely, had burst into cheerings, moblike and barbaric, but tuned in strange keys that can arouse the dullard and the stoic. It made a mad enthusiasm that, it seemed, would be incapable of checking itself before granite and brass. There was the delirium that encounters despair and death, and is heedless and blind to the odds. It is a temporary but sublime absence of selfishness. And because it was of this order was the reason, perhaps, why the youth wondered, afterward, what reasons he could have had for being there.

Presently the straining pace ate up the energies of the men. As if by agreement, the leaders began to slacken their speed. The volleys directed against them had had a seeming windlike effect. The regiment snorted and blew. Among some stolid trees it began to falter and hesitate. The men, staring intently, began to wait for some of the distant walls of smoke to move and disclose to them the scene. Since much of their strength and their breath had vanished, they returned to caution. They were become men again.

The youth had a vague belief that he had run miles, and he thought, in a way, that he was now in some new and unknown land.

The moment the regiment ceased its advance the protesting splutter of musketry became a steadied roar. Long and accurate fringes of smoke spread out. From the top of a small hill came level belchings of yellow flame that caused an inhuman whistling in the air.

The men, halted, had opportunity to see some of their comrades dropping with moans and shrieks. A few lay under foot, still or wailing. And now for an instant the men stood, their rifles slack in their hands, and watched the regiment dwindle. They appeared dazed and stupid. This spectacle seemed to paralyze them, overcome them with a fatal fascination. They stared woodenly at the sights, and, lowering their eyes, looked from face to face. It was a strange pause, and a strange silence.

Then, above the sounds of the outside commotion, arose the roar of the lieutenant. He strode suddenly forth, his infantile features black with rage.

'Come on, yeh fools!' he bellowed. 'Come on! Yeh can't stay here. Yeh must come on.' He said more, but much of it could not be understood.

He started rapidly forwards, with his head turned towards the men. 'Come on,' he was shouting. The men stared with blank and yokel-like eyes at him. He was obliged to halt and retrace his steps. He stood then with his back to the enemy and delivered gigantic curses into the faces of the men. His body vibrated from the weight and force of his imprecations. And he could string oaths with the facility of a maiden who strings beads.

The friend of the youth aroused. Lurching suddenly forwards and dropping to his knees, he fired an angry shot at the persistent woods. This action awakened the men. They huddled no more like sheep. They seemed suddenly to bethink them of their weapons, and at once commenced firing. Belaboured by their officers, they began to move forward. The regiment, involved like a cart involved in mud and muddle, started unevenly with many jolts and jerks. The men stopped now every few paces to fire and load, and in this manner moved slowly on from trees to trees.

The flaming opposition in their front grew with their advance until it seemed that all forward ways were barred by the thin leaping tongues, and off to the right an ominous demonstration could sometimes be dimly discerned. The smoke lately generated was in confusing clouds that made it difficult for the regiment to proceed with intelligence. As he passed through each curling mass the youth wondered what would confront him on the other side.

The command went painfully forward until an open space interposed between them and the lurid lines. Here, crouching and cowering behind some trees, the men clung with desperation, as if threatened by a wave. They looked wild-eyed, and as if amazed at this furious disturbance they had stirred. In the storm there was an ironical expression of their importance. The faces of the men, too, showed a lack of a certain feeling of responsibility for being there. It was as if they had been driven. It was the dominant animal failing to remember in the supreme moments the forceful causes of various superficial qualities. The whole affair seemed incomprehensible to many of them.

As they halted thus the lieutenant again began to bellow profanely. Regardless of the vindictive threats of the bullets, he went about coaxing, berating, and bedamning. His lips, that were habitually in a soft and childlike curve, were now writhed into unholy contortions. He swore by all possible deities.

Once he grabbed the youth by the arm. 'Come on, yeh lunkhead!' he roared. 'Come on! We'll all git killed if we stay here. We've on'y got t' go across that lot. An' then' – the remainder of his idea disappeared in a blue haze of curses.

The youth stretched forth his arm. 'Cross there?' His mouth was puckered in doubt and awe.

'Certainly. Jest 'cross th' lot! We can't ståy here,' screamed the lieutenant. He poked his face close to the youth and waved his bandaged hand. 'Come on!' Presently he grappled with him as if for a wrestling bout. It was as if he planned to drag the youth by the ear on to the assault.

The private felt a sudden unspeakable indignation against his officer. He wrenched fiercely and shook him off.

'Come on yerself, then,' he yelled. There was a bitter challenge in his voice.

They galloped together down the regimental front. The friend scrambled after them. In front of the colours the three men began to bawl: 'Come on! come on!' They danced and gyrated like tortured savages.

The flag, obedient to these appeals, bended its glittering form and swept toward them. The men wavered in indecision for a moment, and then with a long, wailful cry the dilapidated regiment surged forward and began its new journey.

Over the field went the scurrying mass. It was a handful of men splattered into the faces of the enemy. Toward it instantly sprang yellow tongues. A vast quantity of blue smoke hung before them. A mighty banging made ears valueless.

The youth ran like a madman to reach the woods before a bullet could discover him. He ducked his head low, like a football player. In his haste his eyes almost closed, and the scene was a wild blur. Pulsating saliva stood at the corners of his mouth.

Within him, as he hurled himself forward, was born a love, a despairing fondness for this flag which was near him. It was a creation of beauty and invulnerability. It was a goddess, radiant, that bended its form with an imperious gesture to him. It was a woman, red and white, hating and loving, that called him with the voice of his hopes. Because no harm could come to it he endowed it with power. He kept near, as if it could be a saver of lives, and an imploring cry went from his mind.

In the mad scramble he was aware that the colour sergeant flinched suddenly, as if struck by a bludgeon. He faltered, and then became motionless, save for his quivering knees.

He made a spring and a clutch at the pole. At the same instant his friend grabbed it from the other side. They jerked at it, stout and furious, but the colour sergeant was dead, and the corpse would not relinquish its trust. For a moment there was a grim encounter. The dead man, swinging with bended back, seemed to be obstinately tugging, in ludicrous and awful ways, for the possession of the flag.

It was past in an instant of time. They wrenched the flag furiously from the dead man, and, as they turned again, the corpse swayed forward with bowed head. One arm swung high, and the curved hand fell with heavy protest on the friend's unheeding shoulder.

When the two youths turned with the flag they saw that much of the regiment had crumbled away, and the dejected remnant was coming back. The men, having hurled themselves in projectile fashion, had presently expended their forces. They slowly retreated, with their faces still toward the spluttering woods, and their hot rifles still replying to the din. Several officers were giving orders, their voices keyed to screams.

'Where in hell yeh goin'?' the lieutenant was asking in a sarcastic howl. And a red-bearded officer, whose voice of triple brass could plainly be heard, was commanding: 'Shoot into 'em! Shoot into 'em! Gawd damn their souls!' There was a *mêlée* of screeches, in which the men were ordered to do conflicting and impossible things.

The youth and his friend had a small scuffle over the flag. 'Give it t' me!' 'No, let me keep it!' Each felt satisfied with the other's possession of it, but each felt bound to declare, by an offer to carry the emblem, his willingness to further risk himself. The youth roughly pushed his friend away.

The regiment fell back to the solid trees. There it halted for a moment to blaze at some dark forms that had begun to steal upon its track. Presently it resumed its march again, curving among the tree trunks. By the time the depleted regiment had again reached the first open space they were receiving a fast and merciless fire. There seemed to be mobs all about them.

The greater part of the men, discouraged, their spirits worn by the turmoil, acted as if stunned. They accepted the pelting of the bullets with bowed and weary heads. It was of no purpose to strive against walls. It was of no use to batter themselves against granite. And from this consciousness that they had attempted to conquer an unconquerable thing there seemed to arise a feeling that they had been betrayed. They glowered with bent brows, but dangerously, upon some of the officers, more particularly upon the red-bearded one with the voice of triple brass.

However, the rear of the regiment was fringed with men, who continued to shoot irritably at the advancing foes. They seemed resolved to make every trouble. The youthful lieutenant was perhaps the last man in the disordered mass. His forgotten back was toward the enemy. He had been shot in the arm. It hung straight and rigid. Occasionally he would cease to remember it, and be about to emphasize an oath with a sweeping gesture. The multiplied pain caused him to swear with incredible power.

The youth went along with slipping, uncertain feet. He kept watchful eyes rearward. A scowl of mortification and rage was upon his face. He had thought of a fine revenge upon the officer who had referred to him and his fellows as mule drivers. But he saw that it could not come to pass. His dreams had collapsed when the mule drivers, dwindling rapidly, had wavered and hesitated on the little clearing, and then had recoiled. And now the retreat of the mule drivers was a march of shame to him.

A dagger-pointed gaze from without his blackened face was held toward the enemy, but his greater hatred was riveted upon the man, who, not knowing him, had called him a mule driver.

When he knew that he and his comrades had failed to do anything in successful ways that might bring the little pangs of a kind of remorse upon the officer, the youth allowed the rage of the baffled to possess him. This cold officer upon a monument, who dropped epithets unconcernedly down, would be finer as a dead man, he thought. So grievous did he think it that he could never possess the secret right to taunt truly in answer.

He had pictured red letters of curious revenge. 'We *are* mule drivers, are we?' And now he was compelled to throw them away.

He presently wrapped his heart in the cloak of his pride and kept the flag erect. He harangued his fellows, pushing against their chests with his free hand. To those he knew well he made frantic appeals, beseeching them by name. Between him and the lieutenant, scolding and near to losing his mind with rage, there was felt a subtle fellowship and equality. They supported each other in all manner of hoarse, howling protests.

But the regiment was a machine run down. The two men babbled at a forceless thing. The soldiers who had heart to go slowly were continually shaken in their resolves by a knowledge that comrades were slipping with speed back to the lines. It was difficult to think of reputation when others were thinking of skins. Wounded men were left crying on this black journey.

The smoke fringes and flames blustered always. The youth, peering once through a sudden rift in a cloud, saw a brown mass of troops, interwoven and magnified until they appeared to be thousands. A fierce-hued flag flashed before his vision.

Immediately, as if the uplifting of the smoke had been prearranged, the discovered troops burst into a rasping yell, and a hundred flames jetted toward the retreating band. A rolling grey cloud again interposed as the regiment doggedly replied. The youth had to depend again upon his misused ears, which were trembling and buzzing from the *mêlée* of musketry and yells.

The way seemed eternal. In the clouded haze men became panic-stricken with the thought that the regiment had lots its path, and was proceeding in a perilous direction. Once the men who headed the wild procession turned and came pushing back against their comrades, screaming that they were being fired upon from points which they had considered to be toward their own lines. At this cry a hysterical fear and dismay beset the troops. A soldier, who heretofore had been ambitious to make the regiment into a wise little band that would proceed calmly amid the huge-appearing difficulties, suddenly sank down and buried his face in his arms with an air of bowing to a doom. From another a shrill lamentation rang out filled with profane illusions to a general. Men ran hither and thither, seeking with their eyes roads of escape. With serene regularity, as if controlled by a schedule, bullets buffed into men.

The youth walked stolidly into the midst of the mob, and with his flag in his hands took a stand as if he expected an attempt to push him to the ground. He unconsciously assumed the attitude of the colour bearer in the fight of the preceding day. He passed over his brow a hand that trembled. His breath did not come freely. He was choking during this small wait for the crisis.

His friend came to him. 'Well, Henry, I guess this is good-bye – John.'

'Oh, shut up, you damned fool!' replied the youth, and he would not look at the other.

The officers laboured like politicians to beat the mass into a proper circle to face the menaces. The ground was uneven and torn. The men curled into depressions and fitted themselves snugly behind whatever would frustrate a bullet.

The youth noted with vague surprise that the lieutenant was standing mutely with his legs far apart and his sword held in the manner of a cane. The youth wondered what had happened to his vocal organs that he no more cursed.

There was something curious in this little intent pause of the lieutenant. He was like a babe which, having wept its fill, raises its eyes and fixes upon a distant toy. He was engrossed in this contemplation, and the soft under lip quivered from self-whispered words.

Some lazy and ignorant smoke curled slowly. The men, hiding from the bullets, waited anxiously for it to lift and disclose the plight of the regiment.

The silent ranks were suddenly thrilled by the eager voice of the youthful lieutenant bawling out: 'Here they come! Right on to us, b' Gawd!' His further words were lost in a roar of wicked thunder from the men's rifles.

The youth's eyes had instantly turned in the direction indicated by the awakened and agitated lieutenant, and he had seen the haze of teachery disclosing a body of soldiers of the enemy. They were so near that he could see their features. There was a recognition as he looked at the types of faces. Also he perceived with dim amazement that their uniforms were rather gay in effect, being light grey, accented with a brilliant-hued facing. Too, the clothes seemed new.

These troops had apparently been going forward with caution, their rifles held in readiness, when the youthful lieutenant had discovered them and their movement had been interrupted by the volley from the blue regiment. From the moment's glimpse, it was derived that they had been unaware of the proximity of their dark-suited foes or had mistaken the direction. Almost instantly they were shut utterly from the youth's sight by the smoke from the energetic rifles of his companions. He strained his vision to learn the accomplishment of the volley, but the smoke hung before him.

The two bodies of troops exchanged blows in the manner of a pair of boxers. The fast angry firings went back and forth. The men in blue were intent with the despair of their circumstances and they seized upon the revenge to be had at close range. Their thunder swelled loud and valiant. Their curving front bristled with flashes and the place resounded with the clangor of their ramrods. The youth ducked and dodged for a time and achieved a few unsatisfactory views of the enemy. There appeared to be many of them and they were replying swiftly. They seemed moving toward the blue regiment, step by step. He seated himself gloomily on the ground with his flag between his knees.

As he noted the vicious, wolflike temper of his comrades he had a sweet thought that if the enemy was about to swallow the regimental broom as a large prisoner, it could at least have the consolation of going down with bristles forward.

But the blows of the antagonist began to grow more weak. Fewer bullets ripped the air, and finally, when the men slackened to learn of the fight, they could see only dark, floating smoke. The regiment lay still and gazed. Presently some chance whim came to the pestering blur, and it began to coil heavily away. The men saw a ground vacant of fighters. It would have been an empty stage if it were not for a few corpses that lay thrown and twisted into fantastic shapes upon the sward.

At sight of this tableau, many of the men in blue sprang from behind their covers and made an ungainly dance of joy. Their eyes burned and a hoarse cheer of elation broke from their dry lips.

It had begun to seem to them that events were trying to prove that they were impotent. These little battles had evidently endeavoured to demonstrate that the men could not fight well. When on the verge of submission to these opinions, the small duel had showed them that the proportions were not impossible, and by it they had revenged themselves upon their misgivings and upon the foe.

The impetus of enthusiasm was theirs again. They gazed about them with looks of uplifted pride, feeling new trust in the grim, always confident weapons in their hands. And they were men.

Escape From Colditz

AIREY NEAVE

Christmas 1941. In the infamous prisoner-of-war camp at Colditz a long-prepared escape is about to begin. Unknown to the Germans, the stage of the theatre in which the camp pantomime has just taken place conceals a trapdoor, leading to a passage outside the compound and perhaps – ultimately – to freedom . . . . .

THE PANTOMIME WAS OVER, and in the next week before Christmas snow fell thickly in the courtyard. In the British quarters, we ate plum pudding and drank a highly alcoholic brew distilled from dried fruits upon the kitchen stove. Quantities of this mixture had been stored for the occasion and there was great hilarity among the prisoners on Christmas Eve. Some danced, some vomited, some fell unconscious for hours. In the midst of the orgy the door opened and a German officer entered to wish us a German Christmas. The laughter ceased abruptly and there was a silence so deliberate and terrible, that it struck the German like a blow in the face. He looked blankly about him, saluted, and disconsolately withdrew.

The prisoners walked unsteadily into the courtyard and paraded for *Appel* in the snow. From somewhere beyond the gates came the sound of German voices singing Christmas hymns and in the courtyard the strains of 'Auld Lang Syne'. By a prearranged plan, the prisoners shuffled their feet within the ranks so that an immense 'V' sign was formed in the snow. When the parade was over we ran up to our quarters to look down on the courtyard. A small group of Germans were standing motionless, looking balefully at the ground before them. The great 'V' sign was there in the snow, a symbol of hope and defiance.

On the morning of 5th January, 1942, Luteyn and I were ready to escape. We held a conference with Pat Reid and Hank Wardle and decided to try immediately after the nine o'clock *Appel* that evening. Our compasses, maps and a small bundle of notes were ready for hiding inside our bodies. The uniforms were now intact beneath the stage and our civilian clothes had so far escaped detection in their 'hide.' In a moment of supreme confidence, I collected the addresses of relatives of my companions. Then flushed and excited, I lay down to sleep throughout the afternoon and early evening.

A few minutes before nine I went down to the courtyard, when the snow was falling lightly. The turrets cast long shadows in the light of the moon and the steep walls enfolded me for what I believed to be the last time. There was once more the eternal sound of hundreds of men taking their meagre exercise in clogs. I stood waiting for the *Appel*, eyeing the Dutch contingent where Luteyn was waiting ready to join me. We wore cardboard leggings painted with black polish. I wore my usual combination of battledress and sweater, and my Army boots, being brown, were also darkened with black polish. Underneath I had my 'civilian clothes' with a pair of R.A.F. trousers. I had an overpowering sense that this was my last evening in the castle. The certainty grew with every minute, making me composed and determined.

There was a sharp order of dismissal and mingling with the dispersing prisoners, Pat Reid, 'Hank' Wardle, Luteyn and I hurried quickly into the senior officers' quarters. In the darkness of the theatre, we felt our way beneath the stage, then carefully prised up the loose floorboards. Pat Reid lifted the trap called 'Shovewood' which, on its underside was whitewashed, disguising the hole in the ceiling of the passage below. I could see the strong, determined lines on his face as he worked in the glow of a cigarette-lighter. The trap removed, the mattress-cover rope was let down through the hole in the ceiling. Cautiously we climbed down, holding the boxes of uniforms, and landed with soft bumps on the floor of the passage.

The bright lights from the courtyard shone through the cobwebbed windows in the outer wall of the passage. Treading softly in our socks, we reached the door of the gate-bridge. Pat Reid, shining his lighter on the lock, swiftly picked it. It opened without a sound for he had oiled the hinges earlier in the week. We were in the half-light of a narrow corridor. We walked quietly across it and stopped at the door that led to the guard-house.

The German uniform overcoats were unpacked in silence and we put them over our workmen's clothes, leaving our battledress in the boxes. As we pulled on our boots there was no sound except the grating of Pat Reid's wire searching in the lock. A minute passed, and suddenly came fear and exasperation. The door would not open. Beneath our feet we could hear the creaking of the gates and the voices of sentries changing guard. We stood motionless, fully dressed as German officers, and waited with pounding hearts. Pat Reid spoke in a hoarse whisper.

'I'm afraid I can't get it open!'

He continued turning the wire in the lock. I could hear the wire rasping against the rusty metal as he tried again and again to open it. Ten minutes passed in terrible suspense. Through the cobwebbed window I could see the snow falling. I folded my arms and waited.

Suddenly there was the noise of old hinges creaking. A quick snap and the door swung open, showing us the dim interior of the attic.

'Good luck,' said Pat Reid, and shook hands.

We waited till the door was locked behind us and we could no longer hear his muffled steps. Then we crept carefully to the top of stone spiral stairs at an open door on the other side of the attic. A wireless in the guard-room on the ground floor was playing organ music. It was the moment to go down, for the music was loud. We walked quickly down the first flight of stairs, past the door of the officers' mess on the first floor where a light showed beneath. We waited, then stepped confidently down through darkness, into the passage beside the guard-room. The guard-room door was half-open, and I caught a glimpse of German uniforms inside, as we marched smartly into the blinding whiteness of the snow under the arc lights.

The testing time had come. I strode through the snow trying to look like a Prussian. There stood the sentry, the fallen snow covering his cap and shoulders, stamping his feet, just as I had pictured him. He saluted promptly, but he stared at us, and as our backs were turned I felt him watching. We walked on beneath the first archway and passed the second sentry without incident. Then, between the first and second archways, two under-officers talking loudly came from the Kommandantur. They began to march behind us. I felt Luteyn grow tense beside me. I clasped my hands behind my back with an air of unconcern. I might have been casually pacing an English parade ground. In a moment of excitement I had forgotten my part. 'March with your hands at your sides, you bloody fool,' came a fierce sharp whisper from my companion.

Again I saw the bicycles near the clock tower. Could they be ridden fast in this thick snow? We passed beneath the tower, saluted by the sentry, and came to the fateful wicket-gate. As Luteyn opened it I watched the under-officers, their heads bowed to the driving snow, march on across the moat bridge. Down we went into the moat, stumbling and slipping, until we reached its bed. A soldier came towards us from the married quarters. He reached us, stopped and stared deliberately. I hesitated for a moment ready to run, but Luteyn turned on him quickly and in faultless German said crossly, 'Why do you not salute?'

The soldier gaped. He saluted still looking doubtful and began to walk up the side of the moat towards the wicket-gate. We did not look back but hastened up to the path on the far side, and passing the married quarters, came to the high oak paling which bordered the pathway above the park. We were still within the faint glare of searchlights. Every moment that we stayed on the pathway was dangerous. Lifting ourselves quickly over the paling, we landed in thick snow among the tangle of trees. My cardboard belt was torn and broken and with it into the darkness vanished the holster.

Groping among the trees we struggled through frozen leaves down the steep bank and made for the outer stone wall. It was five minutes before we were at the bottom of the slope. Helped by Luteyn, I found a foothold in the stones of the wall and sat astride the coping. The wall, descending steeply with the tree-covered slope, was shrouded in snow and ice. Each time that I tried to pull Luteyn on top, I lost my foothold and slid backwards through the steep angle of the wall. Then with numbed hands, I caught him beneath the armpits and, after great efforts, hoisted him up beside me. For a minute we sat breathless in the cold air clinging to the coping, and then jumped a distance of twelve feet. We fell heavily on the hard ground in the woods outside the castle grounds. I was bruised and shaken and frightened. I stood leaning against a tree looking at Luteyn. Another minute passed in the falling snow.

'Let's go,' I said, and we began to climb towards the east seeking the direction of Leisnig, a small town six miles away.

At ten o'clock the snow was falling less thickly and the moon showed us a way through the trees as we continued to climb towards the road to Leisnig. Beyond the trees we stumbled over frozen fields with hearts uplifted. The headlights of a car, yellow in the bright moonlight, turned in our direction. We lay flat in the snowdrifts till the lights swung towards the east. As we felt the hard surface of the road, I turned up the collar of my dark blue jacket against the cold. I had left the warm green overcoat behind me buried with the rest of the uniform beneath a pile of leaves and snow. The blue jacket was made from an officer's uniform of the Chasseurs Alpins. Shorn of silver galons and badges it became a rough workman's coat of serviceable cloth. I was given it by a Jewish officer, Captain Boris, who sacrificed his smart uniform for my escape. Boris was an elderly business man, a reserve officer in the Chasseur Alpins and a great patriot. Such was the splendid comradeship of Colditz and one of the results of my interference in the Jewish Row.

On my head I wore a ski cap made of blanket and my Royal Air Force trousers were now turned down over my Army boots. From this moment Luteyn and I were Dutch electrical workers with papers permitting us to change our place of occupation from Leipzig to Ulm in South-Western Germany. Leipzig was twenty-two miles from the castle. We planned to reach it by walking the six miles to Leisnig, and there to take an early workman's train. Foreign workers, it was said, were numerous in Leipzig and some were to be transferred to the south.

We had no papers for the journey to Leipzig. Success depended on our safe arrival at the main station for the south. Pausing a while beside the road, we recovered money, maps and papers from the containers concealed in our bodies and then trudged smartly along the road. After two hours we passed a row of cottages close to Leisnig and came to what

151

appeared to be a barracks. A faint light shone from the entrance gate and in the moonlight we saw a sentry. We stopped, turned from the road, and floundered through deep snow towards a belt of trees on higher ground. We stood there, sheltering among the trees against the sharp winds of the night. The ingenious Dutch officers in Colditz had acquired by bribery a timetable of the trains from Leisnig to Leipzig. We therefore knew that the first workmen's train was due to start at five o'clock. Three hours passed. It was too cold to talk. We waited silently for the train, looking towards the town and listening to the sound of shunting on the railway.

There was not a stir in all that crystal stillness as we climbed down the slope, broke through a hedge, and came back to the road. The road descended into a valley and walking boldly down the main street to the station we passed an early morning traveller and exchanged greetings. There was peace in the little town with its spires and snow-covered roof-tops. I thought of an illustration to the children's tale, *The Tailor of Gloucester* where a lone figure walks through the sleeping city. We had half an hour to wait. There was no one at the station so we walked away to the outskirts of the town unnoticed.

When the train was due we came slowly back to the entrance of the station where a small group of German working people had collected at the gate. As is the custom, the travellers were not allowed on the platform until the train was due to start. We stood silently aside from the others sheltering from the cold beside a wooden hut. When it was nearly five o'clock the doors opened, and the crowd surged forward to the ticket office. We followed in their wake and Luteyn, who spoke the best German, stopped at the *guichet* and bought two workmen's tickets to Leipzig. I followed him on to the platform where we stood apart from the others, men and women carrying small baskets or bags of tools.

The orange front light of an engine appeared. It was a scene of true romance. Here were we, escaped enemy prisoners of war, standing on the platform of the little station, mingling with ordinary people travelling to their daily work. The train, puffing with determination through the snow, halted and we climbed into a wooden carriage.

We were herded together in the semi-darkness of air-raid precautions. The warmth inside the carriage covered the windows with moisture so that I could hardly see the dawn. I bowed my head and dozed beside an old, and evil-smelling market-woman. Suddenly I was awakened by a sharp kick on my shins and looked up in fear. I met the half-smiling eyes of Luteyn. He sat hunched in a short tight overcoat, his ski cap on one side. Then I realised that I must have been talking English in my sleep. No one had noticed or even listened to my murmurs. I watched the thin, strained faces of the working-men as they dozed shoulder to shoulder, and saw the dawn slowly appear through the sweaty windows.

I felt ashamed that Luteyn was more alert and awake. He was

strongly-built with humorous grey eyes and long dark hair. He was a strong and buoyant character whose life was spent in laughter and good fellowship. Yet he had a Dutch quality of thoroughness which made him a great escaper. He had staying power and resourcefulness and his great advantage lay in his superior knowledge of Germany and its language, so that he could take each fence with boldness and aplomb. He had a gay, attractive manner of speaking which disarmed the enemy and saved us both in the many dangerous situations which were to follow. For my part, rebellious by temperament though I was, I found him easy to work with and we seldom argued with each other.

At six o'clock we drew in to the great station of Leipzig. The travellers, woken by shrill whistles, began to yawn and swear in low exhausted voices. We looked around us and followed the crowd towards a barrier where we gave up our tickets. There came upon me a sense of alarm and bewilderment. It was twenty months since I had seen the outside world, except for my adventures in the wild desolate country of Poland. Here, among the silent crowds of people moving in the dim light of the station, I was aghast at my helplessness. I felt like a peasant come for the first time to a city, unable to comprehend the paraphernalia of civilisation.

We wandered timidly round the station watching the indicators for a train to Ulm and found that no train left until 10.30 in the evening. It slowly dawned on us that we must stay in Leipzig with nowhere to shelter or sleep for many hours. We tried to find refreshment. Entering a tea-room we ordered coffee, supplied with a small envelope of saccharine. This was all we could obtain, for every other article of food required coupons. The coffee warmed us as we looked shyly at each other, smiling a little, and not daring to speak in any language. After paying for our coffee we wandered to a waiting-room crowded with travellers, mostly poor, who sat among their luggage and children, silent and obedient. I looked at these victims of Hitler's war and felt a great pity. The hopelessness in their faces brought a stark realisation of suffering. We had heard rumours of their plight in the cmap, they were now confirmed beyond our belief. Musing I took from my pocket a huge bar of Red Cross chocolate and began to eat.

A young woman with fierce hysterical eyes, gazed at the chocolate as if she had seen a ghost. I stared back at her uncomprehending. She spoke to an old woman beside her and they looked at me in anger. Immediately the crowd near us began to talk in threatening whispers. I heard the word *tchokalade* many times. Luteyn turned to me and frowned angrily. Slowly realising the danger of my position, I put the chocolate back in my pocket. I had committed a terrible blunder. Chocolate had been unknown to working Germans for many months. Goering himself may well have tasted little. We British prisoners were well supplied. To sit eating this forbidden delicacy in the waiting-room of a great station made one not only an object of envy but of deep suspicion. We rose awkwardly and walked out of the waiting-room into the town.

Leipzig at nine in the morning on January the 6th, 1942. The snow was cleared from the streets and there was a distant hum of traffic in the sunshine. Military vehicles sped by us filled with hard-looking men in steel helmets who ignored the civilians. The sidewalks were a mass of field-grey and the mauve-blue of the Luftwaffe. We stared into the shop windows, gazing like children at expensive dresses and furs. Around us stiff, bourgeois, young men in uniform tapped their smart black boots on the pavement, as they stood before the shops. Blonde girls, in short skirts, looked up at the soldiers with fiercely possessive blue eyes and clutched them tightly.

We entered a big emporium and moved among bright lights and dance music and tinsel finery. We watched the people strolling by the counters. The Germans were young, confident and hopeful and we, mere beggars with a few bars of precious chocolate, had only our own high courage between us and the enemy on every side. Only a few sad civilians of an older generation, shabby and worn, crept among the counters like wraiths. The Nazi Revolution of Destruction was at hand.

We were bitterly disappointed to see no sign of bombing, yet the civilians looked hungry and unhappy. We threaded our way through the crowd and came to a square of gardens where a few old men and women walked in the sunshine with their dachshunds. I could read memories in their worn faces and their hatred of Hitler's New Order. I sat beside Luteyn on a seat watching their slow, hopeless perambulation among the snowbound flower beds and shrubs. For me the months of imprisonment were gone and past. I was a detached spectator watching Life go by. New sights and sounds, fresh and clear, came to me after the darkness of prison. Elderly business men and lawyers with briefcases under their arms marched past muttering sombrely to each other. A girl left the procession of Life and sat beside me.

She was young and blonde and plainly of the working class. She looked at me sharply as she sat on the wooden seat. She wore a torn old overcoat and her short tight skirt was above her bare knees. She looked down at her shoes with *ersatz* wooden heels and kicked at a heap of snow. Her mouth was set in a hard determined line. I struggled to look at her calmly but with an inwardly beating heart. Her prominent blue eyes had ruthlessness.

'Good morning,' she said.

I dared not answer or risk conversation. She pouted.

'You are unsociable, my friend.'

I turned to see Luteyn had already risen from the seat and was walking slowly away. I followed him in dismay and embarrassment and, for a moment, turned towards the girl. She was looking hard at us. I felt her blue eyes watching, deep with suspicion and annoyance. We hurried away and wandered among the side streets of Leipzig till it was noon.

A cinema in enemy territory is a fine hiding place for the fugitive. After a lunch of *ersatz* coffee we came to a cheap stuffy cinema at the bottom of an arcade. Luteyn bought the tickets. Our small stock of German marks was enough for only the cheapest seats. We stood, obediently waiting for the performance, regimented by a commissionaire. In a few minutes, we took our seat among German soldiers and sailors and their girls and waited for the curtain, and, as the lights went out, a tall young German officer came in alone and sat next to me.

We saw first on the programme a news-film of events in Libya. Rommel, standing beside a staff car in the desert, talking decisively; then excellent shots of panzers in action and a British plane being shot down. Close ups followed of a British pilot taken prisoner by the Germans and waving encouragement to his friends still in the air. In my excitement I clutched the seat in front of me and was rewarded by the occupant turning round with a harsh whisper of protest.

The feelings of a prisoner who for many months has been shut out from the war and accustomed only to the crudest enemy propaganda, are hard to describe. I could have wept from joy. At least the war was not yet lost. In the next part of the news-film there came a most shattering revelation. The scene was set in a Russian winter. Up a long snow-bound hill German soldiers struggled against the blizzard, dragging guns and vehicles. There were photographs of frozen bodies and men's limbs swollen to unrecognisable size with frost-bite. If Goebbels wanted to impress the Germans with the sufferings of their troops to inspire them to greater sacrifices at home, he hid no detail of their hardships.

There was a shocked silence when the news-film came to an end. The lights went up in the shabby hall while martial music played from a cracked loudspeaker. Young men and girls chanted Nazi songs and around us their clear voices sounded in perfect harmony. Only the old people were glum and quiet. The music changed to

'We are marching against England!'

For a moment I caught my companion's eye and, with a faint grin on our faces, Luteyn and I sang loudly with the rest.

The remainder of the programme was a film set in early nineteenth-century Germany. The heroine, a hard-faced simpering creature, was surrounded by heavy Prussian admirers. The scene which won the most applause was that in which the witty girl took refuge in an earth closet at the bottom of the garden to repel their advances. It was a hut with two heart-shaped holes cut in the door to which she pointed knowingly as she entered. The Germans roared without restraint and we, unimpressed by their lavatory humour, were constrained to do the same for fear of detection.

In the early afternoon the snow began to fall again and the streets of Leipzig seemed full of foreboding for us. A policeman watched us, and followed stealthily until we evaded him among dark alleyways. Working our way back towards the big shops and the crowds, we came to another cinema where there was an atmosphere of plush warmth, antiseptic, and wurlitzer music. We saw the same news-film again as we sat high in the gallery among more German troops on leave. Then came a royal fanfare of trumpets and Hermann Goering appeared on the screen appealing for higher output for the war. He wore the grey uniform in which I was later to see him in his cell at Nuremberg, but with a lavish display of decorations. His throaty voice rasped out propaganda to an audience which remained quiet if respectful. When his vulgar performance had lasted ten minutes there came shots of goose-stepping battalions of Nazis and someone struck up the *Horst Wessel Lied*. But the singing was cheerless and half-hearted.

From the cinema we walked again into the blackout of the city. The moon had not yet risen and only the soft whiteness of the snow guided us through public gardens to the main station. Often at corners of the streets we caught the faint reflection of a policeman's polished helmet and edged away among the crowds or dodged the trams to cross the street.

We came again to the station waiting-room and sat there tired and cold and anxious. The numerous passengers in the waiting-room, many poor and infirm, assembled for the night trains. Then came the men in uniform, elbowing all the civilians aside. I watched them closely. The bullying S.S. men, the clod-like infantrymen, and the pale, and spectacled administrative clerks. All in uniform, they tramped over the gloomy station like locusts, demanding refreshment or newspapers or anything they wanted. Such is total war.

Luteyn bought the tickets to Ulm. We had decided to change there and, if all went well, to take tickets to the Swiss frontier. At the barrier of the platform for the train to the south, military police stood to check the soldiers but there seemed no control of civilians. We waited beside the train before it started, preferring to find standing room than risk conversation in a compartment. As it began to move we climbed the steps of a carriage and stood in the corridor.

The compartment opposite was occupied by a single figure in the uniform of the S.S. I could see the man as we stood outside, a great ape-like person with a heavy jaw. His uniform was new and spotless and he crossed his legs which were in fine black boots as he read a newspaper with screaming red and black headlines. I caught only the word 'Rommel'. So that he should not watch us, we moved into the shadow at the end of the corridor and looked into the darkness where only a few pin-points of light showed the effective blackout of the city. The train jolted over the points and gathered speed with piercing whistles. Above its rattle I heard the door of the compartment open, and turning my head saw the big S.S. man standing in the doorway. His hands were on each side of the entrance door and he spoke to us in a soft voice.

'Are you Jews?'

'Certainly not. We are Dutch,' replied Luteyn.

'Good. Come in and sit here. This compartment was reserved, but my friends are not coming.'

We took our seats beside the big man who spoke very slowly to us, using simple phrases. His friendliness alarmed me.

'Where are you travelling?'

'To Ulm.'

'Why?'

'We are Dutch electrical workers transferred there from Leipzig.'

Luteyn was doing the talking. He had his genuine Dutch passport ready to produce in an emergency. Then the man turned to me and his stupid eyes examined my face, searching for something he did not understand.

'You are Dutch, too?'

'Yes.'

'How are things in Holland?'

'We have not been there for some months. We have been in Leipzig since the summer.'

It was Luteyn who spoke. The S.S. man turned to me.

'I am going to Munich,' he said unexpectedly. 'Then I go to Vienna for a conference.'

We nodded politely and the conversation stopped. Men and women passengers were walking up and down the corridor and were soon invited into the reserved compartment. They bowed respectfully to the high S.S. officer, took their seats and gave our shabby clothes a scornful stare.

There was no further conversation about Holland. I was glad of this. My sole visit to that country had been the journey in the barge up the River Waal to Germany as a prisoner in 1940. As soon as the passengers began to snore, Luteyn stayed awake according to our arrangement and I slept for a few hours until his turn came to sleep. I was awakened by a loud tapping on the glass of the door and two military policemen looked in. They checked the passes of the soldiers and even scrutinised the documents of the S.S. officer. They stopped for a moment to stare at our queerly tailored clothes. I wondered for a moment whether they would recognise the colour of R.A.F. trousers, but the S.S. officer intervened importantly.

'These are foreign workers (*fremdarbeiter*). Dutch,' he said with conviction.

The military police hesitated, then turned away as if suspicious

157

civilians were nothing to do with their department. Now it was Luteyn's turn to sleep and I listened to the endless rattle of the express as we passed through Plauen and Hof and sped southwards into Bavaria. Lifting the blind, I glimpsed the snow outside or studied the sleeping faces in the dim light of the compartment. Towards four in the morning the train began to slow and came to a halt amid the sounds of a large station. I woke Luteyn, rose and stretched my limbs, and walked over to the doorway. In the gloom there was shouting and the bustle of passengers. I leant out of the window and saw on a sign before me the word 'Regensburg.'

It was here that we were due to change for the train to Ulm and we stepped on to the platform in the sharp cold.

'Good-bye, Dutchmen,' said the S.S. man pompously from inside the compartment.

We went into a waiting-room and sat down at a table. Passengers with their luggage came with us, and promptly fell asleep with their heads resting on the tables. Opposite, a man in railway police uniform stared at us in unfriendly fashion. We did not wait for him to speak but walked out again on to the platform and entered the booking-hall. We sat on the floor with other travellers leaning against a wooden partition. A man and a girl smelling of spiced sausages and garlic lay near us in a close embrace.

When the train to Ulm had filled with passengers it left the station in a cloud of steam and we found seats in a compartment, again taking turns to keep awake. When dawn came I saw that we were travelling through the wintry countryside of Bavaria. The snow, collecting along the edges of the windows, framed a picture of white roofs and towers set in the hollows of the hills. Sometimes beside the track an *autobahn* stretched like a tape threading through the forests and long convoys of military vehicles moved into the mist.

At nine on the second morning of the escape the train drew into Ulm and we left, making our way towards the booking office. Luteyn calmly asked the girl for two tickets to Singen and the Swiss frontier. She frowned and my heart began to sink. She asked for papers and we showed our papers to her.

'I must fetch the railway police. Stay here.'

We did not wish to run away, hoping that our papers would satisfy them. A fat, red-faced railway policeman in his dark blue uniform asked us why we wished to go to the frontier zone. Luteyn explained that we were due to begin work in Ulm on the morrow and wished to spend a short vacation. The policeman, looking baffled, released us and we started to leave the station, walking across the big square in front. There was a shout behind us.

'Come back, gentlemen! I wish to speak to you again.'

The policeman took us to an office in the goods-yard where a thin, tight-lipped German railway police lieutenant sat at a desk. He examined our false papers with bewilderment. It appeared to me that the writing on it did not make sense to him. I could hardly stop myself from laughing as he lifted them to the light, looking, no doubt, for water marks. He was, however, impressed by Luteyn's Dutch passport and there seemed no inkling in his mind that we were escaped prisoners of war.

'I don't understand these men at all,' he said helplessly. 'Take them to the Labour Office. I wish someone would control these foreign workers more efficiently.'

We walked across the square outside the station escorted by another policeman with a revolver. We chatted gaily in German, complimenting the man on the beauties of the town of Ulm. He was flattered and asked us about our own country of Holland. So much did we win his confidence that when we reached the State Labour Office, where men in brown uniforms with spades stood guard at the entrance, he bade us walk up the steps on our own, saying he would wait for us. His parting words were:

'You speak good German. Go and report to the office on the first floor and I shall wait for you here.'

Smiling to ourselves and hardly able to believe our good fortune, we climbed to the top floor of the building and it was not long before we discovered some stairs on the far side from the entrance. Hurrying down them we left by another door. Avoiding the policeman and the guards with spades, we made for the back streets of Ulm, and Luteyn bought a map of the surrounding country in a small shop.

The cold had now become intense and, walking beyond the suburbs of Ulm, we left the snow-capped roofs of the university town behind us and hurried towards the town of Laupheim. It was nearly dusk when we reached the market-square and, asking the way to the station, we took tickets to Stockach, a village as near to the Swiss frontier as we dared to go. The country folk on the platform watched us in silence as we sat upon a bench sleepily waiting for the train. When it arrived we entered a wooden compartment too tired to be able to take turns to stay awake. The train jolted on into the night. We wakened only at the sound of a halt, and after passing the village of Pfullendorf we reached Stockach about nine in the evening.

Of Stockach I only remember white cottages in the moonlight and a doubtful station master watching us as we walked into the hills hoping to reach the frontier town of Singen when the moon went down and the frontier was in darkness. The road began to rise steeply through the forests and great banks of snow were on either side of us. Even by two o'clock in the morning we still had many miles to go, struggling along the icy road as the moon began to wane. The road slowly descended towards Singen.

It seemed hopeless to try to cross the frontier that night and we determined to look for somewhere to hide until the following evening. At five o'clock on the morning of January 8th, we were still moving towards Singen. Lights showed ahead of us in the roadway and to our tired eyes they seemed welcoming and kind. Then the figures of four men appeared. They were woodcutters walking to work from Singen. They hailed us and we wished them good morning. Something about us surprised them.

'Are you Poles?' said one of them.

'Yes,' replied Luteyn.

'I don't believe it,' said another. 'Poles are not allowed out of their camp at five in the morning.'

Evidently there was a Polish labour camp in the neighbourhood. The four woodcutters looked startled and undecided. As for me, I was near to surrender. My feet seemed to be frozen in my boots as if in blocks of ice. I hardly cared that we had come so far only to be recaptured. I could only think of warm fires and beds.

'Go, Hans, fetch the police,' said the oldest woodcutter. The man called Hans who wheeled a bicycle, mounted it and rode off towards Singen. The remainder confronted us uncertainly. They did not try to detain us but stood irresolute and dumb. We suddenly realised that they were frightened of us. Without a word we dashed to the side of the road and into the forest, running in the snow until we sank exhausted. My breath came painfully and my head began to swim. I could not look at the whiteness around me without pain. We rose to our feet after a minute and began to move across a clearing. There was no sign of the woodcutters. As I walked there came over me a kind of delirium between sleep and waking. I thought that I was on some parade ground in England. I felt a figure beside me and turned to see my old Colonel marching in the snow in his uniform and field boots. I spoke to him and addressed him respectfully.

'What the hell?' said Luteyn.

'It's all right,' I said ashamed.

Luteyn grunted impatiently, and a few paces across the clearing we came to a large wooden hut surrounded by a fence. There was the outline of a pathway, shrubs and flower beds in the snow, and beside the hut were beehives. We walked up to the hut and tried the doors which were all locked, but a small window in the wall was open. We lifted ourselves in and staggered crazily around the hut in the faint light of dawn. There was no sound of life. We found a kitchen and two rooms in one of which there was a bed. Tired and faint, we lay together on the bed in the intense cold and with an old blanket over us fell into a deep sleep, not waking until the afternoon.

When we awoke there had been another heavy fall of snow which luckily concealed our footsteps leading to the hut. From outside it seemed that we could hear the far-off sound of dogs and we got ready to escape into the woods. But as the hours passed no one came in sight and the sound of barking grew faint. Searching the hut, we found in one corner of the kitchen, spades and shovels, and hanging behind the door, two long white coats evidently used by the bee keeper.

According to our map, we were in the middle of a forest, two or three miles from Singen. We planned, therefore, to leave the hut at dusk and walk along the road to the town. West of the town and to the south lay woods through which ran the road and railway line to Schaffhausen in Switzerland. At some points the road formed the frontier between Switzerland and Germany.

Shortly before five o'clock on this afternoon of the eighth of January, we shouldered spades, and carrying the two white coats under our arms we cut through the forest to the road to Singen. For more than a mile we saw no one on the road, then the lights of bicycles came towards us and a voice called 'Halt'. In the glow of the bicycle lamps I could see two boys in the uniform of the Hitler Youth, each armed with truncheons. I felt no fear of them. Refreshed by sleep, I was determined they should not stop us. The boys spoke in a hectoring fashion.

'What are your names and where are you going?'

'We are Westphalians working in the neighbourhood and we are going back to our lodgings in Singen,' said the resourceful Luteyn. This was a good choice of disguise for the Dutch accent resembles that of the Westphalians. The boys seemed doubtful.

'What is wrong?' I said, trying to imitate Luteyn's accent.

'We have been told to look for two British prisoners who have escaped and are thought to be trying to cross the frontier tonight.'

We both laughed.

'They won't get far,' said Luteyn, 'it is much too cold for prisoners of war!'

The boys laughed uncertainly and rode off towards Singen and as we reached the town they turned again and came towards us. One said to the other:

'There are the Westphalians.'

As this conversation was taking place in the road I reflected that these boys alone stood between us and freedom. Afterwards I asked Luteyn what was in his mind.

'For me to kill one with my spade and you the other,' he said, 'what did you intend to do?'

'Exactly the same.'

We passed through Singen in the black-out, without incident, and skirting a great dark mound which seemed to be a slag heap we set off southwards through the wood, marching upon a compass bearing to the frontier. At two o'clock in the morning on the ninth of January we crossed the railway to Schaffhausen about two miles north of a point where the road forms the frontier. It was a fine, cold night and the moon was full. Wrapping ourselves in the white bee-keepers coats for camouflage, we slowly advanced until we could see a gap in the trees and lights of cars passing along the road ahead. Not far to the east were voices and lanterns and what appeared to be a frontier post.

For an hour we crouched in a ditch beside the road and watched a sentry pacing up and down only forty yards away. Here we ate the remainder of our chocolate and swallowed a few mouthfuls of snow. Black clouds began to hide the moon and the cold increased with a rising wind. I watched the German buttoning the collar of his overcoat and saw him move towards the sentry-box beside the frontier barrier.

Before us across the roadway was a smooth plain of snow surrounded by distant trees. Beyond this few hundred yards of open No Man's Land was freedom. At half-past four in the morning the sentry turned away from us. I could no longer hear his footsteps against the wind.

'Do you agree to cross now?' said Luteyn.

'This is the moment,' I whispered.

We crawled from the ditch and across the road still dressed in our white coats. We continued crawling across the field in front of us, ploughing on hands and knees through the deep snow. After what seemed an eternity we rose to our feet, and surged forward into Switzerland.

Goodbye To All That

ROBERT GRAVES

As a young platoon leader in World War I, Graves was pitched headlong into the hell of death and destruction on the Western Front in France . . . . .

ON SEPTEMBER 19TH WE relieved the Middlesex Regiment at Cambrin, and were told that these would be the trenches from which we attacked. The preliminary bombardment had already started, a week in advance. As I led my platoon into the line, I recognized with some disgust the same machine-gun shelter where I had seen the suicide on my first night in trenches. It seemed ominous. This was by far the heaviest bombardment from our own guns we had yet seen. The trenches shook properly, and a great deal of cloud of drifting shell-smoke obscured the German lines. Shells went over our heads in a steady stream; we had to shout to make our neighbours hear. Dying down a little at night, the racket began again every morning at dawn, a little louder each time. 'Damn it,' we said, 'there can't be a living soul left in those trenches.' But still it went on. The Germans retaliated, though not very vigorously. Most of their heavy artillery had been withdrawn from this sector, we were told, and sent across to the Russian front. More casualties came from our own shorts and blow-backs than from German shells. Much of the ammunition that our batteries were using came from the United States and contained a high percentage of duds; the driving bands were always coming off. We had fifty casualties in the ranks and three officer casualties, including Buzz Off – badly wounded in the head. This happened before steel helmets were issued; we would not have lost nearly so many with those. I got two insignificant wounds on the hand, which I took as a favourable omen.

On the morning of the 23rd, Thomas came back from battalion headquarters carrying a notebook and six maps, one for each of us company officers. 'Listen,' he said, 'and copy out all this skite on the back of your maps. You'll have to explain it to your platoons this afternoon. Tomorrow morning we go back to dump our blankets, packs, and greatcoats in Béthune. The next day, that's Saturday the 25th, we attack.' This being the first definitive news we had been given, we looked up half startled, half relieved. I still have the map, and these are the

163

orders as I copied them down:

FIRST OBJECTIVE – *Les Briques Farm* – The big house plainly visible to our front, surrounded by trees. To get this it is necessary to cross three lines of enemy trenches. The first is three hundred yards distant, the second four hundred, and the third about six hundred. We then cross two railways. Behind the second railway line is a German trench called the Brick Trench. Then comes the Farm, a strong place with moat and cellars and a kitchen garden strongly staked and wired.

SECOND OBJECTIVE – *The Town of Auchy* – This is also plainly visible from our trenches. It is four hundred yards beyond the Farm and defended by a first line of trench half way across, and a second line immediately in front of the town. When we have occupied the first line our direction is half-right, with the left of the battalion directed to Tall Chimney.

THIRD OBJECTIVE – *Village of Haisnes* – Conspicuous by high-spired church. Our eventual line will be taken up on the railway behind this village, where we will dig in and await reinforcements.

When Thomas had reached this point, The Actor's shoulders were shaking with laughter.

'What's up?' asked Thomas irritably.

The Actor giggled: 'Who in God's name is responsible for this little effort?'

'Don't know,' Thomas said. 'Probably Paul the Pimp, or someone like that.' (Paul the Pimp was a captain on the divisional staff, young, inexperienced, and much disliked. He 'wore red tabs upon his chest And even on his undervest.') 'Between the six of us, but you youngsters must be careful not to let the men know, this is what they call a "subsidiary attack". There will be no troops in support. We've just got to go over and keep the enemy busy while the folk on our right do the real work. You notice that the bombardment is much heavier over there. They've knocked the Hohenzollern Redoubt to bits. Personally, I don't give a damn either way. We'll get killed whatever happens.'

We all laughed.

'All right, laugh now, but by God, on Saturday we've got to carry out this funny scheme.' I had never heard Thomas so talkative before.

'Sorry,' The Actor apologized, 'carry on with the dictation.'

Thomas went on:

The attack will be preceded by forty minutes' discharge of the

164

accessory,* which will clear the path for a thousand yards, so that the two railway lines will be occupied without difficulty. Our advance will follow closely behind the accessory. Behind us are three fresh divisions and the Cavalry Corps. It is expected we shall have no difficulty in breaking through. All men will parade with their platoons; pioneers, servants, etc., to be warned. All platoons to be properly told off under N.C.O.s. Every N.C.O. is to know exactly what is expected of him, and when to take over command in case of casualties. Men who lose touch must join up with the nearest company or regiment and push on. Owing to the strength of the accessory, men should be warned against remaining too long in captured trenches where the accessory is likely to collect, but to keep to the open and above all to push on. It is important that if smoke-helmets have to be pulled down they must be tucked in under the shirt.

The Actor interrupted again. 'Tell me, Thomas, do you believe in this funny accessory?'

Thomas said: 'It's damnable. It's not soldiering to use stuff like that, even though the Germans did start it. It's dirty, and it'll bring us bad luck. We're sure to bungle it. Take those new gas-companies – sorry, excuse me this once, I mean accessory-companies – their very look makes me tremble. Chemistry-dons from London University, a few lads straight from school, one or two N.C.O.s of the old-soldier type, trained together for three weeks, then given a job as responsible as this. Of course they'll bungle it. How could they do anything else? But let's be merry. I'm going on again:

Men of company: what they are to carry:

Two hundred rounds of ammunition (bomb-throwers fifty, and signallers one hundred and fifty rounds).

Heavy tools carried in sling by the strongest men.

Waterproof sheet in belt.

Sandbag in right tunic-pocket.

Field dressing and iodine.

Emergency ration, including biscuit.

One tube-helmet, to be worn when we advance, rolled up on the head. It must be quite secure and the top part turned down. If possible each man will be provided with an elastic band.

One smoke helmet, old pattern, to be carried for preference behind the back where it is least likely to be damaged by stray bullets, etc.

* The gas-cylinders had by this time been put into position on the front line. A special order came round imposing severe penalties on anyone who used any word but 'accessory' in speaking of the gas. This was to keep it secret, but the French civilians knew all about the scheme long before this.

Wire-cutters, as many as possible, by wiring party and others; hedging gloves by wire party.

Platoon screens, for artillery observation, to be carried by a man in each platoon who is not carrying a tool.

Packs, capes, greatcoats, blankets will be dumped, not carried.

No one is to carry sketches of our position or anything to be likely of service to the enemy.

That's all. I believe we're going over first with the Middlesex in support. If we get through the German wire I'll be satisfied. Our guns don't seem to be cutting it. Perhaps they're putting that off until the intense bombardment. Any questions?'

That afternoon I repeated the whole rigmarole to the platoon, and told them of the inevitable success attending our assault. They seemed to believe it. All except Sergeant Townsend. 'Do you say, sir, that we have three divisions and the Cavalry Corps behind us?' he asked.

'Yes,' I answered.

'Well, excuse me, sir, I'm thinking it's only those chaps on the right that'll get reinforcements. If we get half a platoon of Mons Angels,* that's about all we will get.'

'Sergeant Townsend,' I said, 'you're a well-known pessimist. This is going to be a really good show.'

We spent the night repairing damaged trenches.

When morning came we were relieved by the Middlesex, and marched back to Béthune, where we dumped our spare kit at the Montmorency Barracks. The battalion officers messed together in a *château* near by. This billet was claimed at the same time by the staff of a new Army division, due to take part in the fighting next day. The argument ended amicably with the division and battalion messing together. It was, someone pointed out, like a brutal caricature of The Last Supper in duplicate. In the middle of the long table sat the two pseudo-Christs, our colonel and the divisional general. Everybody was drinking a lot; the subalterns, allowed whisky for a treat, grew rowdy. They raised their glasses with: 'Cheerio, we will be messing together tomorrow night in La Bassée!' Only the company commanders were looking worried. I remember 'C' Company commander especially, Captain A. L. Samson, biting his thumb and refusing to join in the excitement. I think it was Childe-Freeman of 'B' Company who said that night: 'The last time the regiment visited these parts we were under decent leadership. Old Marlborough had more sense than to attack the La Bassée lines; he masked them and went around.'

The G.S.O.1 of the New Army division, a staff-colonel, knew the

* According to the newspapers, a vision of angels had been seen by the British Army at Mons; but it was not vouchsafed to Sergeant Townsend, who was there, with most of 'A' Company.

adjutant well. They had played polo together in India. I happened to be sitting opposite them. The G.S.O.1 said, rather drunkenly: 'Charley, see that silly old woman over there? Calls himself General Commanding! Doesn't know where he is; doesn't know where his division is; can't even read a map properly. He's marched the poor sods off their feet and left his supplies behind, God knows how far back. They've had to use their iron rations and what they could pick up in the villages. And tomorrow he's going to fight a battle. Doesn't know anything about battles; the men have never been in trenches before, and tomorrow's going to be a glorious balls-up, and the day after tomorrow he'll be sent home.' Then he ended, quite seriously: 'Really, Charley, it's just like that, no exaggeration. You mark my words!'

That night we marched back again to Cambrin. The men were singing. Being mostly from the Midlands, they sang comic songs rather than Welsh hymns: *Slippery Sam*, *When we've Wound up the Watch on the Rhine*, and *I do like a S'nice S'mince Pie*, to concertina accompaniment. The tune of *S'nice S'mince Pie* ran in my head all next day, and for the week following I could not get rid of it. The Second Welsh would never have sung a song like *When we've Wound up the Watch on the Rhine*. Their only songs about the war were defeatist:

> *I want to go home,*
> *I want to go home,*
> *The coal-box and shrapnel they whistle and roar,*
> *I don't want to go to the trenches no more,*
> *I want to go over the sea*
> *Where the Kayser can't shoot bombs at me.*
> *Oh, I*
> *Don't want to die,*
> *I want to go home.*

There were several more verses in the same strain. Hewitt, the Welsh machine-gun officer, had written one in a more offensive spirit:

> *I want go home,*
> *I want to go home.*
> *One day at Givenchy the week before last*
> *The Allmands attacked and they nearly got past.*
> *They pushed their way up to the Keep,*
> *Through our maxim-gun sights we did peep,*
> *Oh, my!*
> *They let out a cry,*
> *They never got home.*

But the men would not sing it, though they all admired Hewitt.

The Béthune–La Bassée road was chocked with troops, guns, and transport, and we had to march miles north out of our way to circle round to Cambrin. Even so, we were held up two or three times by massed cavalry. Everything radiated confusion. A casualty clearing-station had been planted astride one of the principal cross-roads, and was already being shelled. By the time we reached Cambrin, the battalion had marched about twenty miles that day. Then we heard that the Middlesex would go over first, with us in support; and to their left the Second Argyll and Sutherland Highlanders, with the Cameronians in support. The young Royal Welch officers complained loudly at our not being given the honour of leading the attack. As the senior regiment, they protested, we were entitled to the 'Right of the Line'. An hour or so past midnight we moved into trench sidings just in front of the village. Half a mile of communication trench, known as 'Maison Rouge Alley', separated us from the firing line. At half-past five the gas would be discharged. We were cold, tired, sick, and not at all in the mood for a battle, but tried to snatch an hour or two of sleep squatting in the trench. It had been raining for some time.

A grey, watery dawn broke at last behind the German lines; the bombardment, surprisingly slack all night, brisked up a little. 'Why the devil don't they send them over quicker?' The Actor complained. 'This isn't my idea of a bombardment. We're getting nothing opposite us. What little there seems to be, is going into the Hohenzollern.'

'Shell shortage. Expected it,' was Thomas's laconic reply.

We were told afterwards that on the 23rd a German aeroplane had bombed the Army Reserve shell-dump and sent it up. The bombardment on the 24th, and on the day of the battle itself, compared very poorly with that of the previous days. Thomas looked strained and ill. 'It's time they were sending that damned accessory off. I wonder what's doing.'

The events of the next few minutes are difficult for me now to sort out. I found it more difficult still at the time. All we heard back there in the sidings was a distant cheer, confused crackle of rifle fire, yells, heavy shelling on our front line, more shouts and yells, and a continuous rattle of machine-guns. After a few minutes, lightly wounded men of the Middlesex came stumbling down Maison Rouge Alley to the dressing-station. I stood at the junction of the siding and the Alley.

'What's happened? What's happened?' I asked.

'Bloody balls-up,' was the most detailed answer I could get.

Among the wounded were a number of men yellow-faced and choking, their buttons tarnished green – gas cases. Then came the badly wounded. Maison Rouge Alley being narrow, the stretchers had dificulty in getting down. The Germans started shelling it with five-point-nines.

Thomas went back to battalion headquarters through the shelling to ask for orders. It was the same place that I had visited on my first night in the trenches. This cluster of dug-outs in the reserve line showed very plainly from the air as battalion headquarters, and should never have been occupied during a battle. Just before Thomas arrived, the Germans put five shells into it. The adjutant jumped one way, the colonel another, the R.S.M. a third. One shell went into the signals dug-out, killed some signallers, and destroyed the telephone. The colonel, slightly cut on the hand, joined the stream of wounded and was carried back as far as the Base with it. The adjutant took command.

Meanwhile 'A' Company had been waiting in the siding for the rum to arrive; the tradition of every attack being a double tot of rum beforehand. All the other companies got theirs. The Actor began cursing: 'Where the bloody hell's that storeman gone?' We fixed bayonets in readiness to go up and attack as soon as Captain Thomas returned with orders. Hundreds of wounded streamed by. At last Thomas's orderly appeared. 'Captain's orders, sir: "A" Company to move up to the front line.' At that moment the storeman arrived, without rifle or equipment, hugging the rum-bottle, red-faced and retching. He staggered up to The Actor and said: 'There you are, sir!', then fell on his face in the thick mud of a sump-pit at the junction of the trench and the siding. The stopper of the bottle flew out and what remained of the three gallons bubbled on the ground. The Actor made no reply. This was a crime that deserved the death penalty. He put one foot on the storeman's neck, the other in the small of his back, and trod him into the mud. Then he gave the order 'Company forward!' The company advanced with a clatter of steel, and that was the last I ever heard of the storeman.

It seems that at half past four an R.E. captain commanding the gas-company in the front line phoned through to divisional headquarters: 'Dead calm. Impossible discharge accessory.' The answer he got was: 'Accessory to be discharged at all costs.' Thomas had not over-estimated the gas-company's efficiency. The spanners for unscrewing the cocks of the cylinders proved, with two or three exceptions, to be misfits. The gas-men rushed about shouting for the loan of an adjustable spanner. They managed to discharge one or two cylinders; the gas went whistling out, formed a thick cloud a few yards off in No Man's Land, and then gradually spread back into our trenches. The Germans, who had been expecting gas, immediately put on their gas-helmets: semi-rigid ones, better than ours. Bundles of oily cotton-waste were strewn along the German parapet and set alight as a barrier to the gas. Then their batteries opened on our lines. The confusion in the front trench must have been horrible; direct hits broke several of the gas-cylinders, the trench filled with gas, the gas-company stampeded.

No orders could come through because the shell in the signals dug-out at battalion headquarters had cut communication not only between companies and battalion, but between battalion and division. The officers in the front trench had to decide on immediate action; so two

companies of the Middlesex, instead of waiting for the intense bombardment which would follow the advertised forty minutes of gas, charged at
once and got as far as the German wire – which our artillery had not yet
cut. So far it had been treated only with shrapnel, which had no effect on
it; the barbed-wire needed high-explosive, and plenty of it. The Germans
shot the Middlesex men down. One platoon is said to have found a gap
and got into the German trench. But there were no survivors of the
platoon to confirm this. The Argyll and Sutherland Highlanders went
over, also, on the Middlesex left; but two companies, instead of charging
at once, rushed back out of the gas-filled assault trench to the support
line, and attacked from there. It will be recalled that the trench system
had been pushed forward nearer the enemy in preparation for the battle.
These companies were therefore attacking from the old front line, but the
barbed-wire entanglements protecting it had not been removed, so that
the Highlanders got caught and machine-gunned between their own
assault and support lines. The other two companies were equally
unsuccessful. When the attack started, the German N.C.O.s had jumped
up on the parapet to encourage their men. These were Jäger, famous for
their musketry.

The survivors of the two leading Middlesex companies now lay in
shell-craters close to the German wire, sniping and making the Germans
keep their heads down. They had bombs to throw, but these were nearly
all of a new type issued for the battle. The fuses were lighted on the
match-box principle, and the rain had made them useless. The other two
companies of the Middlesex soon followed in support. Machine-gun fire
stopped them half-way. Only one German machine-gun remained in
action, the others having been knocked out by rifle or trench-mortar fire.
Why the single gun survived is a story in itself.

It starts with the privilege granted British colonial governors and high-
commissioners of nominating one or two officers from their countries for
attachment in wartime to the regular Army. Under this scheme, the
officers began as full lieutenants. The Captain-General of Jamaica (if that
is his correct style) nominated the eighteen-year-old son of a rich planter,
who went straight from Kingston to the First Middlesex. He was good-
hearted enough, but of little use as an officer, having never been out of the
island in his life or, except for a short service with the West India militia,
seen any soldiering. His company commander took a fatherly interest in
'Young Jamaica', and tried to teach him his duties. This company
commander was known as 'The Boy'. He had twenty years' service with
the Middlesex, and the unusual boast of having held every rank from
'boy' to captain in the same company. His father, I believe, had been the
regimental sergeant-major. But 'Jamaica', as a full lieutenant, ranked
senior to the other experienced subalterns in the company, who were only
second-lieutenants.

The Middlesex colonel decided to shift Jamaica off on some course of extra-regimental appointment at the earliest opportunity. Somewhere about May or June, when instructed to supply an officer for the brigade trench-mortar company, he had sent Jamaica. Trench-mortars being then both dangerous and ineffective, the appointment seemed suitable. At the same time, the Royal Welch had also been asked to detail an officer, and the colonel selected Tiley, an ex-planter from Malaya, and what is called a 'fine natural soldier'. Tiley had been chosen because, when attached to us from a Lancashire regiment, he showed his resentment at the manner of his welcome somewhat too plainly. But, by September, mortars had improved in design and become an important infantry arm; so Jamaica, being senior to Tiley, held the responsible position of brigade mortar officer.

When the Middlesex charged, The Boy fell mortally wounded as he climbed over the parapet. He tumbled back and began crawling down the trench to the stretcher-bearers' dug-out, past Jamaica's trench-mortar emplacement. Jamaica had lost his gun-team, and was boldly serving the trench-mortars himself. On seeing The Boy, however, he deserted his post and ran off to fetch a stretcher-party. Tiley, meanwhile, on the other flank opposite Mine Point, had knocked out all the machine-guns within range. He went on until his mortar burst. Only one machine-gun in the Pope's Nose, a small salient facing Jamaica, remained active.

At this point the Royal Welch Fusiliers came up Maison Rouge Alley. The Germans were shelling it with five-nines (called 'Jack Johnsons' because of their black smoke) and lachrymatory shells. This caused a continual scramble backwards and forwards, to cries of: 'Come on!' 'Get back you bastards!' 'Gas turning on us!' 'Keep your heads, you men!' 'Back like hell, boys!' 'Whose orders?' 'What's happening?' 'Gas!' 'Back!' 'Come on!' 'Gas!' 'Back!' Wounded men and stretcher-bearers kept trying to squeeze past. We were alternately putting on and taking off our gas-helmets, which made things worse. In many places the trench had caved in, obliging us to scramble over the top. Childe-Freeman reached the front line with only fifty men of 'B' Company; the rest had lost their way in some abandoned trenches half-way up.

The adjutant met him in the support line. 'Ready to go over, Freeman?' he asked.

Freeman had to admit that he had lost most of his company. He felt this disgrace keenly; it was the first time that he had commanded a company in battle. Deciding to go over with his fifty men in support of the Middlesex, he blew his whistle and the company charged. They were stopped by machine-gun fire before they had got through our own entanglements. Freeman himself died – oddly enough, of heart-failure – as he stood on the parapet.

A few minutes later, Captain Samson, with 'C' Company and the remainder of 'B', reached our front line. Finding the gas-cylinders still whistling and the trench full of dying men, he decided to go over too – he could not have it said that the Royal Welch had let down the Middlesex. A strong, comradely feeling bound the Middlesex and the Royal Welch, intensified by the accident that the other three battalions in the brigade were Scottish, and that our Scottish brigadier was, unjustly no doubt, accused of favouring them. Our adjutant voiced the extreme non-Scottish view 'The Jocks are all the same; both the trousered kind and the bare-arsed kind: they're dirty in trenches, they skite too much, and they charge like hell – both ways.' The First Middlesex, who were the original 'Diehards', had more than once, with the Royal Welch, considered themselves let down by the Jocks. So Samson charged with 'C' and the remainder of 'B' Company.

One of 'C' officers told me later what happened. It had been agreed to advance by platoon rushes with supporting fire. When his platoon had gone about twenty yards, he signalled them to lie down and open covering fire. The din was tremendous. He saw the platoon on his left flopping down too, so he whistled the advance again. Nobody seemed to hear. He jumped up from his shell-hole, waved, and signalled 'Forward!'

Nobody stirred.

He shouted: 'You bloody cowards, are you leaving me to go on alone?'

His platoon-sergeant, groaning with a broken shoulder, gasped: 'Not cowards, sir. Willing enough. But they're all f—ing dead.' The Pope's Nose machine-gun, traversing, had caught them as they rose to the whistle.

'A' Company, too, had become separated by the shelling. I was with the leading platoon. The Surrey-man got a touch of gas and went coughing back. The Actor accused him of scrimshanking. This I thought unfair; the Surrey-man looked properly sick. I don't know what happened to him, but I heard that the gas-poisoning was not serious and that he managed, a few months later, to get back to his own regiment in France. I found myself with The Actor in a narrow communication trench between the front and support lines. This trench had not been built wide enough for a stretcher to pass the bends. We came on The Boy lying on his stretcher, wounded in the lungs and stomach. Jamaica was standing over him in tears, blubbering: 'Poor old Boy, poor old Boy, he's going to die; I'm sure he is. He's the only one who treated me decently.'

The Actor, finding that we could not get by, said to Jamaica: 'Take that poor sod out of the way, will you? I've got to get my company up. Put him into a dug-out, or somewhere.'

Jamaica made no answer; he seemed paralysed by the horror of the occasion and kept repeating: 'Poor old Boy, poor old Boy!'

'Look here,' said The Actor, 'if you can't shift him into a dug-out we'll have to lift him on top of the trench. He can't live now, and we're late getting up.'

'No, no,' Jamaica shouted wildly.

The Actor lost his temper and shook Jamaica roughly by the shoulders. 'You're the bloody trench-mortar wallah, aren't you?' he shouted.

Jamaica nodded miserably.

'Well, your battery is a hundred yards from here. Why the hell aren't you using your gas-pipes to some purpose? Buzz off back to them!' And he kicked him down the trench. Then he called over his shoulder: 'Sergeant Rose and Corporal Jennings! Lift this stretcher up across the top of the trench. We've got to pass.'

Jamaica leaned against a traverse. 'I do think you're the most heartless beast I've ever met,' he said weakly.

We went up to the corpse-strewn front line. The captain of the gas-company, who was keeping his head and wore a special oxygen respirator, had by now turned off the gas-cocks. Vermorel-sprayers had cleared out most of the gas, but we were still warned to wear our masks. We climbed up and crouched on the fire-step, where the gas was not so thick – gas, being heavy stuff, kept low. Then Thomas brought up the remainder of 'A' Company and, with 'D', we waited for the whistle to follow the other two companies over. Fortunately at this moment the adjutant appeared. He was now left in command of the battalion, and told Thomas that he didn't care a damn about orders; he was going to cut his losses and not send 'A' and 'D' over to their deaths until he got definite orders from brigade. He had sent a runner back, and we must wait.

Meanwhile, the intense bombardment that was to follow the forty minutes' discharge of gas began. It concentrated on the German front trench and wire. A good many shells fell short, and we had further casualties from them. In No Man's Land, the survivors of the Middlesex and of our 'B' and 'C' Companies suffered heavily.

My mouth was dry, my eyes out of focus, and my legs quaking under me. I found a water-bottle full of rum and drank about half a pint; it quieted me, and my head remained clear. Samson lay groaning about twenty yards beyond the front trench. Several attempts were made to rescue him. He had been very badly hit. Three men got killed in these attempts; two officers and two men, wounded. In the end his own orderly managed to crawl out to him. Samson waved him back, saying that he was riddled through and not worth rescuing; he sent his apologies to the company for making such a noise.

We waited a couple of hours for the order to charge. The men were silent and depressed; only Sergeant Townsend was making feeble, bitter jokes about the good old British Army muddling through, and how he thanked God we still had a Navy. I shared the rest of my rum with him, and he cheered up a little. Finally a runner arrived with a message that the attack had been postponed.

Rumours came down the trench of a disaster similar to our own in the brick-stack sector, where the Fifth Brigade had gone over; and again at Givenchy, where men of the Sixth Brigade at the Duck's Bill salient had fought their way into the enemy trenches, but been repulsed, their supply of bombs failing. It was said, however, that things were better on the right, where there had been a slight wind to take the gas over. According to one rumour, the First, Seventh, and Forty-seventh Divisions had broken through.

My memory of that day is hazy. We spent it getting the wounded down to the dressing-station, spraying the trenches and dug-outs to get rid of the gas, and clearing away the earth where trenches were blocked. The trenches stank with a gas-blood-lyddite-latrine smell. Late in the afternoon we watched through our field-glasses the advance of reserves under heavy shell-fire towards Loos and Hill 70; it looked like a real break-through. They were troops of the New Army division, whose staff we had messed with the night before. Immediately to the right of us we had the Highland Division, whose exploits on that day Ian Hay has celebrated in *The First Hundred Thousand*; I suppose that we were 'the flat caps on the left' who 'let down' his comrades-in-arms.

At dusk, we all went out to get in the wounded, leaving only sentries in the line. The first dead body I came upon was Samson's, hit in seventeen places. I found that he had forced his knuckles into his mouth to stop himself crying out and attracting any more men to their death. Major Swainson, the second-in-command of the Middlesex, came crawling in from the German wire. He seemed to be wounded in lungs, stomach, and one leg. Choate, a Middlesex second-lieutenant, came back unhurt; together we bandaged Swainson and got him into the trench and on a stretcher. He begged me to loosen his belt; I cut it with a bowie-knife I had bought at Béthune for use during the battle. He said: 'I'm about done for.'* We spent all that night getting in the wounded of the Royal Welch, the Middlesex, and those Argyll and Sutherland Highlanders who had attacked from the front trench. The Germans behaved generously. I do not remember hearing a shot fired that night, though we kept on until it was nearly dawn and we could see plainly; then they fired a few warning shots, and we gave it up. By this time we had recovered all the wounded, and most of the Royal Welch dead. I was surprised at some of the attitudes in which the dead stiffened – bandaging friends' wounds, crawling, cutting wire. The Argyll and Sutherland had seven hundred casualties, including fourteen officers killed out of the sixteen who went over; the Middlesex, five hundred and fifty casualties, including eleven

* Major Swainson recovered, and was back at the Middlesex Depôt after a few weeks. On the other hand, Lawrie, a Royal Welch quartermaster-sergeant back at Cambrin, was hit in the neck that day by a spent machine-gun bullet which just pierced the skin, and died of shock a few hours later.

officers killed.

Two other Middlesex officers besides Choate came back unwounded; their names were Henry and Hill, recently commissioned second-lieutenants, who had been lying out in shell-holes all day under the rain, sniping and being sniped at. Henry, according to Hill, had dragged five wounded men into a shell-hole and thrown up a sort of parapet with his hands and the bowie-knife which he carried. Hill had his platoon-sergeant beside him, screaming with a stomach wound, begging for morphia; he was done for, so Hill gave him five pellets. We always carried morphia for emergencies like that.

Choate, Henry, and Hill, returning to the trenches with a few stragglers, reported at the Middlesex headquarters. Hill told me the story. The colonel and the adjutant were sitting down to a meat pie when he and Henry arrived. Henry said: 'Come to report, sir. Ourselves and about ninety men of all companies. Mr Choate is back, unwounded, too.'

They looked up dully. 'So you've survived, have you?' the colonel said. 'Well, all the rest are dead. I suppose Mr Choate had better command what's left of "A" Company; the bombing officer will command what's left of "B" [the bombing officer had not gone over, but remained with headquarters]: Mr Henry goes to "C" Company. Mr Hill to "D". The Royal Welch are holding the front line. We are here in support. Let me know where to find you if you're needed. Good night.'

Not having been offered a piece of meat pie or a drink of whisky, they saluted and went miserably out.

The adjutant called them back. 'Mr Hill! Mr Henry!'

'Sir?'

Hill said that he expected a change of mind as to the propriety with which hospitality could be offered by a regular colonel and adjutant to temporary second-lieutenants in distress. But it was only: 'Mr Hill, Mr Henry, I saw some men in the trench just now with their shoulder-straps unbuttoned and their equipment fastened anyhow. See that this does not occur in future. That's all.'

Henry heard the colonel from his bunk complaining that he had only two blankets and that it was a deucedly cold night.

Choate, in peacetime a journalist, arrived a few minutes later; the others had told him of their reception. After he had saluted and reported that Major Swainson, hitherto thought killed, was wounded on the way down to the dressing-station, he boldly leaned over the table, cut a large piece of meat pie and began eating it. This caused such a surprise that no further conversation took place. Choate finished his meat pie and drank a glass of whisky; saluted, and joined the others.

Meanwhile, I took command of what remained of 'B' Company. Only six company officers survived in the Royal Welch. Next morning we were only five. Thomas was killed by a sniper while despondently watching through field-glasses the return of the New Army troops on the right. Pushed blindly into the gap made by the advance of the Seventh and Forty-seventh Divisions on the previous afternoon, they did not know where they were or what they were supposed to do. Their ration supply broke down, so they flocked back, not in panic, but stupidly, like a crowd returning from a cup final, with shrapnel bursting above them. We could scarcely believe our eyes, it was so odd.

Thomas need not have been killed; but everything had gone so wrong that he seemed not to care one way or the other. The Actor took command of 'A' Company. We lumped 'A' and 'B' Companies together after a couple of days, for the sake of relieving each other on night watch and getting some sleep. I agreed to take the first watch, waking him up at midnight. When the time came, I shook him, shouted in his ear, poured water over him, banged his head against the side of the bed. Finally I threw him on the floor. I was desperate for a lie-down myself, but he had attained a depth of sleep from which nothing could rouse him; so I heaved him back on the bunk, and had to finish the night without relief. Even 'Stand-to!' failed to wake him. In the end I got him out of bed at nine o'clock in the morning, and he was furious with me for not having called him at midnight.

We had spent the day after the attack carrying the dead down for burial and cleaning the trench up as best we could. That night the Middlesex held the line, while the Royal Welch carried all the unbroken gas-cylinders along to a position on the left flank of the brigade, where they were to be used on the following night, September 27th. This was worse than carrying the dead; the cylinders were cast-iron, heavy and hateful. The men cursed and sulked. Only the officers knew of the proposed attack; the men must not be told until just beforehand. I felt like screaming. Rain was still pouring down, harder than ever. We knew definitely, this time, that ours would be only a diversion to help troops on our right make the real attack.

The scheme was the same as before: at 4 p.m. gas would be discharged for forty minutes, and after a quarter of an hour's bombardment we should attack. I broke the news to the men about three o'clock. They took it well. The relations of officers and men, and of senior and junior officers, had been very different in the excitement of battle. There had been no insubordination, but a greater freedom of speech, as though we were all drunk together. I found myself calling the adjutant 'Charley' on one occasion; he appeared not to mind in the least. For the next ten days my relations with my men were like those I had in the Welsh Regiment; later, discipline reasserted itself, and it was only occasionally that I found them intimate.

At 4 p.m. then, the gas went off again with a strong wind; the gas-men had brought enough spanners this time. The Germans stayed absolutely silent. Flares went up from the reserve lines, and it looked as though all the men in the front trench were dead. The brigadier decided not to take too much for granted; after the bombardment he sent out a Cameronian officer and twenty-five men as a feeling-patrol. The patrol reached the German wire; there came a burst of machine-gun and rifle fire, and only two wounded men regained the trench.

We waited on the fire-step from four to nine o'clock, with fixed bayonets, for the order to go over. My mind was a blank, except for the recurrence of *S'nice S'mince S'pie, S'nice S'mince S'pie ... I don't like ham, lamb or jam, and I don't like roley-poley ...*

The men laughed at my singing. The acting C.S.M. said: 'It's murder, sir.'

'Of course it's murder, you bloody fool,' I agreed. 'But there's nothing else for it, is there?' It was still raining. *But when I sees a s'nice s'mince s'pie, I asks for a helping twice ...*

At nine o'clock brigade called off the attack; we were told to hold ourselves in readiness to go over at dawn.

No order came at dawn, and no more attacks were promised us after this. From the morning of September 24th to the night of October 3rd, I had in all eight hours of sleep. I kept myself awake and alive by drinking about a bottle of whisky a day. I had never drunk it before, and have seldom drunk it since; it certainly helped me then. We had no blankets, greatcoats, or waterproof sheets, nor any time or material to build new shelters. The rain poured down. Every night we went out to fetch in the dead of the other battalions. The Germans continued indulgent and we had few casualties. After the first day or two the corpses swelled and stank. I vomited more than once while superintending the carrying. Those we could not get in from the German wire continued to swell until the wall of the stomach collapsed, either naturally or when punctured by a bullet; a disgusting smell would float across. The colour of the dead faces changed from white to yellow-grey, to red, to purple, to green, to black, to slimy.

On the morning of the 27th a cry arose from No Man's Land. A wounded soldier of the Middlesex had recovered consciousness after two days. He lay close to the German wire. Our men heard it and looked at each other. We had a tender-hearted lance-corporal named Baxter. He was the man to boil up a special dixie for the sentries of his section when they came off duty. As soon as he heard the wounded Middlesex man, he ran along the trench calling for a volunteer to help fetch him in. Of course, no one would go; it was death to put one's head over the parapet. When he came running to ask me I excused myself as being the only officer in the company. I would come out with him at dusk, I said – not now. So he went alone. He jumped quickly over the parapet, then strolled across No Man's Land, waving a handkerchief; the Germans fired to frighten him, but since he persisted they let him come up close. Baxter continued towards them and, when he got to the Middlesex man, stopped and pointed to show the Germans what he was at. Then he dressed the man's wounds, gave him a drink of rum and some biscuit that he had with him, and promised to be back again at nightfall. He did come back, with a stretcher-party, and the man eventually recovered. I recommended Baxter for the Victoria Cross, being the only officer who had witnessed the action, but the authorities thought it worth no more than a Distinguished Conduct Medal.

The Actor and I had decided to get in touch with the battalion on our right. It was the Tenth Highland Light Infantry. I went down their trench some time in the morning of the 26th and walked nearly a quarter of a mile without seeing either a sentry or an officer. There were dead men, sleeping men, wounded men, gassed men, all lying anyhow. The trench had been used as a latrine. Finally I met a Royal Engineer officer who said: 'If the Boche knew what an easy job he had, he'd just walk over and take this trench.'

So I reported to The Actor that we might find our flank in the air at any moment. We converted the communication trench which made the boundary between the two battalions into a fire-trench facing right; and mounted a machine-gun to put up a barrage in case the Highlanders ran. On the night of the 27th they mistook some of our men, who were out in No Man's Land getting in the dead, for the enemy, and began firing wildly. The Germans retaliated. Our men caught the infection, but were at once ordered to cease fire. 'Cease fire!' went along the trench until it reached the H.L.I., who misheard it as 'Retire!' A panic seized them and they went rushing way, fortunately down the trench, instead of over the top. They were stopped by Sergeant McDonald of the Fifth Scottish Rifles, a pretty reliable territorial battalion now in support to ourselves and the Middlesex. He chased them back at the point of the bayonet; and was decorated for this feat.

On October 3rd we were relieved by a composite battalion consisting of about a hundred men of the Second Warwickshire Regiment and about seventy Royal Welch fusiliers – all that was left of our own First Battalion. Hanmer Jones and Frank Jones-Bateman had both been wounded. Frank had his thigh broken with a rifle bullet while stripping the equipment off a wounded man in No Man's Land; the cartridges in the man's pouches had been set on fire by a shot and were exploding.* We went back to Sailly la Bourse for a couple of days, where the colonel rejoined us with his bandaged hand; and then farther back to Annezin, a little village near Béthune, where I lodged in a two-roomed cottage with a withered old woman called Adelphine Heu.

* He was recommended for a Victoria Cross, but got nothing because no officer evidence, which is a condition of award, was available.

178

The Moon's A Balloon
DAVID NIVEN

Recently married to his first wife, Primmie, David Niven was for three years the officer in charge of a 'Phantom' squadron, responsible for obtaining vital information from a network of sources behind enemy lines. While his wife and their first child remain in the comparative safety of a country cottage near Dorney, Niven is about to embark on a new stage of his distinguished war career . . . . .

BY THE BEGINNING OF 1944, the Americans were pouring into Britain and many old Hollywood friends appeared at Dorney. Bob Coote materialised in the Royal Canadian Air Force. Clark Gable, whose adored wife, Carole Lombard, had been killed in an air disaster, appeared as a major in a bombing squadron and Jimmy Stewart showed up – a colonel in the same line of business. John Ford and Douglas Fairbanks Jr were in the U.S. Navy. Willie Wyler and John Huston were with Combat Photographic Units. Garson Kanin was doing something very mysterious in the Army and joy of joys, John McClain arrived, a lieutenant in the U.S. Navy attached to the O.S.S.

Dorney features so often in this account that I feel I should explain that I was in other places too. At the end of a war one forgets, thank God, the numbing patches of boredom and frustration and remembers only the fright and the fun. I am chiefly concerned with the fun and Dorney, with Primmie, was where my fun lay.

The Free French frequently cooked their rations in our kitchen, among them Claude Dauphin and Jean Pierre Aumont. These two gave a party for us in London and Joseph Kessel ate a champagne glass, stem and all.

Guy Gibson, the master bomber, spent a weekend with us just after he had been awarded the Victoria Cross for blowing up the Eder and Mohne dams. He was in a rare state of excitement because Winston Churchill had invited him to dinner at 10 Downing Street on the Monday. Guy made a date with us for luncheon at one o'clock on the following day so he could report everything the great man said.

Primmie and I were at the Berkeley sharp at one – no Gibson. Two o'clock – no Gibson. We were just finishing our ersatz coffee around three o'clock when he came tottering in looking ghastly, eyes like dog's balls.

179

'How was it?' we asked.

'Marvellous – fabulous!' he croaked. 'God! I'm tired – that was the best yet!'

'What did he say?'

'Who?' said Gibson.

'Churchill,' I said with a touch of asperity.

Gibson looked stricken – Then he clutched his head.

'Jesus Christ! – I *forgot!*'

A month later on his one hundred and twentieth bombing mission, he was shot down.

By the early spring of 1944, it was obvious that the Second Front would soon be opened on the Continent. Training increased in tempo and there were so many American troops in Britain that only the barrage balloons kept the island from sinking beneath the waves under their weight.

Out of the blue, I was ordered to report to General Sir Frederick Morgan at a highly camouflaged headquarters in a wood near Sunningdale. Morgan, although I did not know it, had for months been drawing up the invasion plans that would soon be put to effect in Normandy. He came straight to the point.

'You've lived in America for some years?'

'Yes, sir.'

'Do you like Americans?'

'Very much, sir.'

'Good, because you're going to be seeing a great deal of them ... I'm taking you out of Phantom and promoting you to Lieutenant Colonel ... from now on you will be under the direct order of General Barker – an American.'

He told me where to go and I found General Ray Barker in a Nissen hut under the trees. He, it transpired, had been working with Morgan on the overall invasion plan.

'One thing we dread is a repetition of what happened between the British and the French in the last war,' he said. 'Sir John French and General Lanrezac were commanding adjoining armies. They didn't speak each other's language; they detested each other and tried to win private feuds to impress Field Marshal Joffre.

'Their feeling percolated down to the troops. The Germans repeatedly attacked this weak link in the chain and very nearly won the war as a result.'

General Barker was the finest type of contemporary American ... quiet, courteous and full of humour but underneath his evident compassion and gentleness, one could detect the steel ... I listened attentively as he went on ...

'When we land on the Continent, there will be Americans, British and Canadians to start with. Later there will be Poles and French. I am charged by General Eisenhower with seeing that this time, there are no weak links in the chain. Misunderstandings and rumours are bound to arise but they will have to be dealt with promptly at all levels from friction between army commanders, right down to arguments about what programmes should be beamed to the troops by the B.B.C. and the American Forces Network. After we invade you will be in the field doing odd jobs for me and from now on you take orders only from me.'

'A' Squadron gave me a silver tankard and I handed over to John Hannay, my second-in-command for the past two years. It was a big wrench but my love of change soon dispelled my disappointment and under the highly efficient John the squadron prospered.

A celebration luncheon with Ian Fleming at Boodle's revealed that the place was much changed. A direct hit had demolished the back of the building but the beautiful façade and famous ceilings were still intact. Most of the windows were boarded over. Food had become very scarce.

'My members don't take to whale steaks at all,' said Davy mournfully.

We were peering at the daily menu displayed in the darkened hall when the oldest member growled in my ear,

'Can't see the damn thing in this gloom – what's on the card today?'

'Moules marinières, sir,' I said.

'Good God!' he trumpeted, 'the bloody fellers have got us eatin' moles now!'

We held a belated christening party for little David and with the exception of Bob Laycock, all the godparents came to Dorney.

Larry and Vivien produced a Jacobean drinking mug with 'D.W.' engraved on it. I complained about this to Godmother Vivien who said, 'I'm not going to change it so from now on you'll just have to be called "Wiven", that's all.'

Godfather Noël Coward donated a silver cocktail shaker on which was inscribed –

'Because, my Godson dear, I rather
Think you'll turn out like your father.'

The day, however, was made by a retired Nannie – Miss Maple – who at seventy had decided that she could still 'do her bit' so she struggled with little David to enable Primmie to return to work at Hawker's. Some of my methods, however, had upset this redoubtable old lady and she suddenly appeared and announced to the assembled guests.

'It's bad enough when the Colonel takes Master David's olive oil for the salad dressing – but when he steals his concentrated California orange juice for the cocktails – it's going *too far*!'

I was so proud of Primmie, of her flower-like beauty of course, but everyone loved her and the reason was obvious.... She never thought an unkind thought about anyone. She was incapable of saying an unkind word. On the June night before I left for Normandy we clung together miserably. The parting was not made easier by the news that her uncle, Michael Laycock, had just been killed on the beaches and that her brother, Andrew, had been blown up when his destroyer hit a mine. His captain reported that 'blown up' was the correct description because Andrew was on the foredeck when it happened and the next moment the captain, high on the bridge, saw Andrew above his head. Miraculously, he fell in the sea and survived.

I lied to Primmie about leaving after breakfast and at dawn when she had finally fallen asleep, I slipped out of bed, dressed, looked down at her with the little boy asleep in his cot beside her, and tiptoed out of the house.

The *Empire Battleaxe* was a Liberty ship with elements of an American Division. I boarded her at Southampton.

'That's one helluvan encouraging send-off,' observed a G.I. as, over the side, we watched hundreds of wounded being helped or carried ashore from a tank landing craft – boys with shocked faces and staring eyes, in their bandages and hastily applied field dressings, grown old in a few short hours.

Once opposite the Normandy beach, we were ordered into the landing craft and, to the continuous roll of gunfire, ferried ashore. Beach Masters pointed to the white taped paths through the minefields and we went our separate ways.

There is no place in these pages for harrowing blood-soaked descriptions of man's inhumanity to man – all that has been raked over a thousand times by a thousand more competent writers since that June of 1944 so let me say at once that lying in a ditch that first night in Normandy, my most vivid recollection was the sound of the nightingales.

Before the war, eminent lady cellists were employed by the B.B.C. to sit in remote black woods to try and coax these timid little birds into song. The nightingales of Normandy were made of sterner stuff – they all but drowned out the gunfire with their racket.

Between British Second Army and American First there was a small bridge at Carentan. It was in fact the one vital link between our very meagre bridgeheads and, consequently, was shelled by the Germans at close range many times a day.

Several spare Bailey bridges were kept handy so that replacement was speedy and the lifeline kept open, but it was a hazardous crossing and I had to make it frequently. Foxholes were dug on either side of the bridge and once, trapped by the shelling, I was cowering in the bottom of one of them when, after what seemed an eternity, the lethal rain seemed to have let up. I peeked timidly out and couldn't believe my eyes. Like a cock-pheasant in the bracken, a familiar head was sticking out of a foxhole, a few yards away – John McClain.

After the barrage, my transport was no longer functioning so my old friend gave me a ride in his command car driven by a very disapproving American sergeant. McClain also pinned on my chest the Iron Cross.

Cherbourg was still in enemy hands and McClain, with a psychological warfare unit, had been bombarding the defenders with a verbal barrage via sound truck. General von Schlieben, in an attempt to shore up the morale of the defenders, had for some days been handing out decorations like Lady Bountiful at a village fête. He had radioed for more Iron Crosses to be delivered by parachute and they had been dropped in error on McClain and his outfit.

My work completed at First Army, McClain suggested a light luncheon at a little inn he had heard about from Captain Bob Low, an ex-*Time* reporter, now working in First Army Intelligence.

'Low says it's in a backwater,' he said, 'no krauts there – nobody – untouched by the war – let's go.'

Quetthou, on the coast about five miles south of Barfleur, was all that Bob Low had predicted and the inn, 'Aux Trois Cents Hommes', was unforgettable. The disapproving sergeant refused to join us and sat outside morosely chewing his 'C' rations, while McClain and I, the first Allied combatants they had seen, were treated like royalty by the three bosomy ladies who ran the place. We were given a sumptuous meal of omelettes, delicious little flat fish and Camembert cheese, washed down by bottles of Bordeaux which they dug up from the cabbage patch where they had been hidden from the Germans.

On the way back, we grew strangely silent as we approached Carentan because it became obvious from the noise that we were going to have to run the gauntlet of the bridge once again.

'Er . . . lookit, Sarge,' said McClain. 'Isn't there some way round by the beach so we can cut out that goddam bridge?'

The disapproving one was unbending.

'The way I see it Lieutenant – it's either got your name on it, or it hasn't.'

McClain's reply was really brave.

'Well – it may have your fucking name on it – but it doesn't have mine.'

The Normandy battles raged around Caen and St. Lô longer than had been expected and this frustration of their plans sparked the first differences of opinion between the Allied commanders. Finally, at the end of July, with the British and Canadians containing the bulk of the German armour, the Americans were able to break out on the Western flank and the charge on Paris and Brussels began.

I found 'B' Squadron of Phantom hidden in a wood behind the Orne. Dennis Russell was still in command. Hugh (Tam) Willia ns, that fine actor, was still in the squadron. They told me that Hugh Kindersley had been badly wounded and 'Tam' and I agreed that if we had known about the German Nebelwerfer – a six-barreled mortar – we would never have joined the Army in the first place. (After the war, like many others, 'Tam' found his place had been filled while he had been away and that he had been largely forgotten as an actor. He went bankrupt and then emerged triumphant as one of the most successful playwrights that London has seen.)

In a tent far to the rear lived a group of war correspondents typing out pages of self-glorification ... 'as the bullets sang past my head', etc. There were some heroic and exemplary war correspondents, of course – Ernie Pyle, Bob Capa and Chester Wilmot, to name a few – but anyone who says a bullet sings past, hums past, flies, pings or whines past, has never heard one – they go *crack*.

Just before the breakout at Falaise, General Barker recalled me for a few hours to England.

The D.C.3 lumbered off the makeshift runway on a cliff top above the landing beaches. After an alarming dip, it gained height and headed home. Below much of the damage wrought by the disastrous three-day storm at the end of June was still apparent. The 'Mulberry' harbour opposite St. Laurent was completely wrecked and of the 800 landing craft originally smashed ashore, at least half still lay there like beached whales.

An American intelligence colonel sitting on the bucket seat beside me, told me that the storm had reduced the unloading of vital stores and reinforcements to a trickle and for two weeks it had been touch and go whether we could hang on in Normandy.

We landed at Croydon at eight o'clock in the morning. Flying bombs were now being directed into London all day long and driving through the City, the damage was much greater than I expected.

General Barker concluded his business with me with great dispatch, then with his customary thoughtfulness, he said, 'Your plane goes back at seven this evening so go on home and give your wife a surprise.'

I caught the fast train to Reading, got off at Taplow and borrowed the station master's bicycle. I could be in Dorney by one and the five o'clock train back seemed days away.

Land-girls were cutting lettuce and digging potatoes in the fields on either side of the road. They looked up and waved as I pedalled past. My heart was bubbling with excitement. In my mind I rehearsed all sorts of stiff-upper-lip-returning-warrior platitudes. I wished I had a toy for the little boy.

Quietly, I leaned the bicycle against a tree and pushed the back door – it was locked. The front door was locked too. I walked round and round the house ... nobody was home. I opened a back window by breaking a pane and crawled through ... The family was gone and judging by the

184

state of the kitchen had been gone for some days.

Disconsolate and also alarmed, I mounted the bicycle and made enquiries in the village shops.

'Mrs. Niven picked up her ration books a week ago but nobody knows where she went.'

Back at the house, I called Bill Rollo in London at his office but he was out.

I had beer, bread and cheese and pickled onions in the village pub then went home again and waited for Bill to call back. While I was waiting, I mowed the lawn and weeded Primmie's little vegetable garden. At three o'clock Bill called and told me she had decided to evacuate the London area and take little David up to the peace and quiet of Quenby in Leicestershire.

I put through a call to Quenby but there was a three-hour delay. I pleaded with the operator but she was granite.

'We all 'ave our little problems these days don't we, luv?'

I drank the remainder of a bottle of gin in the kitchen and weaved off on the stationmaster's bicycle in time to catch the five o'clock for London and Normandy.

By mid-August the Canadians had entered Falaise. The Poles were above Chambois and with the British and Americans in full spate, the bulk of the German Seventh Army was wiped out in the Mortain Pocket. Sixteen of the twenty German generals involved, however, managed to escape to fight another day and this touched off more asperity between the Allied commanders with everyone accusing everyone else of being too slow, too quick or too cautious.

The Americans and Free French entered Paris on the twenty-fifth and the British, Canadians and Poles rushed headlong for the Channel ports and Belgium.

With the Germans in full retreat, conflicting plans were put forward for bringing the war to a speedy conclusion and even louder squabbles now broke out between those super prima donnas, Montgomery, Bradley and Patton. Distorted versions of their differences filtered down to the fighting troops and General Barker's department had a lot of fence-mending to do.

I was ordered to Paris to deliver some important documents to an American colonel. 'Meet him in the bar of the Hotel Crillon', was my highly sophisticated directive and I hastened south, most anxious to see my favourite city in the full orgiastic ecstasy of her liberation.

An American corporal was driving my jeep. We got lost in Neuilly till I realised I was only a stone's throw from Claude's apartment. I bade the corporal wait, and leaving him festooned with flowers in the centre of a singing, kissing, bottle-waving throng, I pushed my way into the building.

My welcome was rapturous but the set-up had changed. 'Monsieur' having been deported to a forced labour camp near Essen, Madame and Claude, in their misery, had buried their hatchets, pooled their resources and Claude had moved in upstairs with the family. They nourished me from the sparse supplies of food and drink, heated water in pails so I could have a hot bath and clucked over me like two hens.

Luckily, I had kept the documents with me because when I descended to keep my rendezvous at the Crillon the jeep and corporal had disappeared, borne off, he assured me later, on the crest of a wave of hysterical grateful citizenry ... Claude saved the day.

'It's nothing – you take Madame's bicycle ... I come with you!'

From some long-forgotten celebration, Madame produced two small Union Jacks and with Claude at my side, bells ringing, and flags fluttering bravely from the handle-bars, we free-wheeled down the whole length of the Champs Elyseés to the admiring plaudits of the crowd. Mounted on a woman's bicycle, I was probably the first British soldier the French of Paris had seen for five years.

The Guards Armoured Division entered Brussels on September 3rd. Antwerp was freed the next day. The reaction of the French of Paris to their liberation was that of an undertakers' convention compared to the behaviour of the Belgians. The tired faces of the soldiers glowed – it made everything seem worthwhile.

The autumn has been described by the war historians as a 'lull' – the soldiers didn't notice it – particularly the British airborne troops who had to fight for their lives at Arnhem, the Canadians struggling on the Leopold Canal or the Americans at Aachen.

'A' Squadron Phantom, with John Hannay at the helm, was living in great discomfort in flat, water-logged fields near Geldrop. I spent some days with them en route to a chore in Nimegen near the Meuse where I ran across Tony Bushell, Olivier's production manager in usual life, and now a company commander with the Welsh Guards. We were reminiscing in the tank park when the earth shook under an appalling explosion. Instinctively, I dived for cover. I looked out to see Bushell roaring with laughter.

'What the hell was that?' I asked.

'Oh, that's an old friend,' said Bushell. 'They've got a bloody great gun in a railway tunnel across the river. About once an hour they wheel it out and let off a big one – then they pop back in again. We're used to it.'

In early December in Brussels, I found Bobby Sweeney who had been distinguishing himself with the R.A.F. He was on leave.

'They tell me,' said Bobby, 'that the wild duck are really flighting in to the flooded farmland on the Scheldt Estuary, let's go and knock some off.'

A great organiser of comfort, Sweeney conjured up a jeep, guns and ammunition and we set off, accompanied by a carload of Bobbie's

Belgian friends. The shooting at dusk was spectacular. On the other side
of the river it must have been equally good because we could hear the
Germans taking full advantage of it.

The Belgian group returned to Brussels after dark but 'the Comfort
King' had a better idea.

'Nothing in the world like wild duck cooked absolutely fresh ... much
better than after they've been hung,' he said. 'One of the best restaurants
in Europe is the "Panier d'Or" in Bruges. The Canadians have probably
taken the place by now – let's go in there and if the "Panier d'Or" is still
standing, we'll get 'em to cook for us.'

At the outskirts of the beautiful little seventh-century Flemish town,
the Military Police told us that the Germans had indeed been pushed out
several hours before. In the centre of the town there was very little
damage and we found the 'Panier d'Or' intact.

Bobby was right about the duck – they were sensational but we both
underestimated the hospitality of the owner and his family.

They plied us for hours with every known kind of drink and before we
staggered out, they produced their 'Livre d'Or' for our signatures. A
special page was prepared and after five years of German names, the two
first Allied ones were scrawled with a flourish. Outside, a full moon was
riding in the cold winter sky. The town, with not a chink of light showing,
was unnaturally quiet – not a cat was stirring – it was eerie.

We started up the jeep and clattered through the deserted streets and
back over the bridge to the main road. A Canadian patrol stopped us and
told us the facts of life. During our long meal, the enemy had started a
vicious counter-attack and the Canadians had pulled back through the
town. Half an hour after we left the 'Panier d'Or', the centre of Bruges
was once more swarming with Germans.

In the middle of December, I was passing through Spa, American First
Army Headquarters in the Ardennes. I spent the day with Bob Low and
he showed me the map room of the Intelligence Section.

'What happens here?' I asked.

'You mean here in Spa?'

'Yes.'

After all these years I can quote what he said, word for word – it was
impossible to forget. He pointed out of the window.

'You see the trees on the top of those hills?'

'Yes.'

'Well, the other side of those hills, there is a forest and in that forest
they are now forming the Sixth Panzer Army and any day now the Sixth
Panzer Army is going to come right through this room and out the other
side, cross the Meuse, then swing right and go north to Antwerp.'

'Have you told anyone?' I laughed.

'We've been telling them for days,' said Low. 'Every day we have to give three appreciations of what we *think* may happen – that has been our number one appreciation.'

The next day I went down through the fog-shrouded Forest of the Ardennes to Marche. Within hours the last great German offensive of the war erupted. Ahead of it, Skorzeny's Trojan Horse Brigade, American-speaking and wearing American uniforms, infiltrated everywhere with captured American tanks and half-tracks. Sabotaging as they went, they rushed for the Meuse. The rumours of Skorzeny's men flew wildly. In my British uniform and jeep with 21st Army Group markings, I had some anxious moments at the hands of understandably trigger-happy G.I.'s. Identification papers mean nothing – 'Hands above your head, Buddy – all right – so who won the World Series in 1940?'

'I haven't the faintest idea but I do know I made a picture with Ginger Rogers in 1938.'

'O.K. beat it, Dave, but watch your step for Crissake.'

Time and again I was stopped, and, thanks entirely to Sam Goldwyn, survived.

At the end of February, the British Army was fighting bloody battles in the Reichwald where a sudden thaw had turned the frozen forest floor into a quagmire. Great battles were in progress for the Roehr and the Maas. During the first week of March, U.S. First Army reached the Rhine at Cologne and two days later U.S. Third Army did likewise at the junction of the Moselle, 9th U.S. Armoured Division that week made their miraculous discovery that the Ludendorf Railway Bridge at Remagen had not been blown, and secured the first small bridgehead across the Rhine, a bridgehead that cried out for exploitation. Montgomery was all set to cross in strength further down and surge across the Ruhr plain, but first a big build-up, he felt, was necessary. This stoked up all the old friction between Montgomery's dedication to 'tidy battles,' and the American genius for improvisation. The super prima donnas were at it in earnest this time and the heights, or rather the depths of idiocy were surely reached when, according to military historians, Patton telephoned Bradley and said,

'I want the world to know Third Army made it before Monty starts across.'

I crossed the Rhine at Wessel and I had never seen such destruction – the smoking town had ceased to exist. At Munster nothing was left standing except a bronze statue of a horse. In the open country between Hanover and Osnabrück, both of which were totally ruined, was a huge hastily erected prisoner-of-war cage. There must have been a hundred thousand men already inside when the American Unit I was then with passed them. The first warming rays of the sun were just touching the prisoners. It had rained heavily during the night and now a cloud of steam was rising from this dejected field-grey mass of humanity.

The Burgomaster of Hanover said that at least 60,000 corpses were still under the rubble of his city. Bremen was no better.

Hitler had started the whole horrible shambles but looking at the places where his chickens had come home to roost, I watched the miserable survivors picking around in the ruins of their towns and was unable to raise a glimmer of a gloat.

In a siding near Liebenau, I came across a freight train, its flat cars loaded with V.2 rockets destined for London. In the woods nearby, was a slave labour camp where they had been made. The notices in the camp were in Italian, French, Czech, Polish, Dutch, Yugoslav, Russian and Ukrainian. The liberated workers were wandering dazedly all over the place, asking how to get home, mingling with the dead-eyed prisoners from the concentration camps, gaunt and shuffling, conspicuous in their black and white stripes.

By May 8th, the war in Europe was officially over, but people were still being killed and Hitler's werewolves were still hopefully stretching piano wire at head height from trees on either side of the roads. To avoid decapitation, the wiser jeeps now carried sharpened iron stanchions welded to their radiators. The routes west out of Germany were becoming clogged with an estimated eight million homeward-bound displaced persons pushing their pathetic belongings on bicycles or dragging them in little home-made carts. One became hardened to the sight of people lying under trees or in ditches too exhausted or too hungry to take another step.

On a country road near Brunswick, I drove through an attractive red-roofed village on the outskirts of which was a large manor house. Two tow-headed little boys were playing in the garden. A mile or so away, I passed a farm wagon headed for the village. I glanced casually at the two men sitting up behind the horse. Both wore typical farmer headgear and sacks were thrown over their shoulders protecting them from a light drizzle. We were just past them when something made me slam on the brakes and back up. I was right, the man who was not driving was wearing field boots. I slipped out from behind the wheel, pulled my revolver from its holster and told the corporal to cover me with his Tommy gun.

I gestured to the men to put their hands over their heads and told them in fumbling German to produce their papers.

'I speak English,' said the one with the field boots, 'this man has papers – I have none.'

'Who are you?' I asked.

He told me his name and rank – 'General.'

'We are not armed,' he added, as I hesitated.

Sandhurst did it – I saluted, then motioned to them to lower their hands.

'Where are you coming from, sir?'

He looked down at me. I had never seen such utter weariness, such blank despair on a human face before. He passed a hand over the stubble of his chin.

'Berlin,' he said quietly.

'Where are you going, sir?'

He looked ahead down the road towards the village and closed his eyes.

'Home,' he said almost to himself, 'it's not far now ... only ... one more kilometre.'

I didn't say anything. He opened his eyes again and we stared at each other. We were quite still for a long time. Then I said,

'Go ahead, sir,' and added ridiculously ... 'please cover up your bloody boots.'

Almost as though in pain, he closed his eyes and raised his head, then with sobbing intake of breath, covered his face with both hands and they drove on.

On 13th May, Churchill spoke from London and the whole world listened – or did it?

'... we have yet to make sure that the simple and honourable purposes for which we entered the war are not brushed aside or overlooked in the months following our success, and that the words "freedom", "democracy" and "liberation" are not distorted from their true meaning as we have understood them. There would be little use in punishing the Hitlerites for their crimes if law and justice did not rule, and if totalitarian or police governments were to take the place of the German invaders ...'

I cannot claim to have exerted much presure on the squabbling field marshals and generals but way down the scale, attached to various units, I must have done what General Barker wanted. At any rate, in September, he pinned the American Legion of Merit on me and the British Army gave me –

1 suit, worsted grey

1 hat, Homburg, brown

2 shirts, poplin, with collars

1 tie, striped

1 Pair shoes, walking, black –

and above all my FREEDOM.

Such was the stringency of the clothing rationing that Major General Robert Laycock, D.S.O., Chief of Combined Operations, asked me if I could spare him my discarded khaki shirts.

The Warrior's Soul

JOSEPH CONRAD

THE OLD OFFICER WITH LONG white moustaches gave rein to his indignation.

'Is it possible that you youngsters should have no more sense than that! Some of you had better wipe the milk off your upper lip before you start to pass judgment on the few poor stragglers of a generation which has done and suffered not a little in its time.'

His hearers having expressed much compunction the ancient warrior became appeased. But he was not silenced.

'I am one of them – one of the stragglers, I mean,' he went on patiently. 'And what did we do? What have we achieved? He – the great Napoleon – started upon us to emulate the Macedonian Alexander, with a ruck of nations at his back. We opposed empty spaces to French impetuosity, then we offered them an interminable battle so that their army went at last to sleep in its positions lying down on the heaps of its own dead. Then came the wall of fire in Moscow. It toppled down on them.

'Then began the long rout of the Grand Army. I have seen it stream on, like the doomed flight of haggard, special sinners across the innermost frozen circle of Dante's Inferno ever widening before their despairing eyes.

'They who escaped must have had their souls doubly riveted inside their bodies to carry them out of Russia through that frost fit to split rocks. But to say that it was our fault that a single one of them got away is mere ignorance. Why! Our own men suffered nearly to the limit of their strength. Their Russian strength!

'Or course our spirit was not broken; and then our cause was good – it was holy. But that did not temper the wind much to men and horses.

'The flesh is weak. Good or evil purpose, Humanity has to pay the price. Why! In that very fight for that little village of which I have been telling you we were fighting for the shelter of those old houses as much as victory. And with the French it was the same.

'It wasn't for the sake of glory, or for the sake of strategy. The French knew that they would have to retreat before morning and we knew perfectly well that they would go. As far as the war was concerned there was nothing to fight about. Yet our infantry and theirs fought like wild cats, or like heroes if you like that better, amongst the houses – hot work

191

enough – while the supports out in the open stood freezing in a tempestuous north wind which drove the snow on earth and the great masses of clouds in the sky at a terrific pace. The very air was inexpressibly sombre by contrast with the white earth. I have never seen God's creation look more sinister than on that day.

'We, the cavalry (we were only a handful), had not much to do except turn our backs to the wind and receive some stray French round shot. This, I may tell you, was the last of the French guns and it was the last time they had their artillery in position. Those guns never went away from there either. We found them abandoned next morning. But that afternoon they were keeping up an infernal fire on our attacking column; the furious wind carried away the smoke and even the noise but we could see the constant flicker of the tongues of fire among the French front. Then a driving flurry of snow would hide everything except the dark red flashes in the white swirl.

'At intervals when the line cleared we could see away across the plain to the right a sombre column moving enlessly; the great rout of the Grand Army creeping on and on all the time while the fight on our left went on with a great din and fury. The cruel whirlwind of snow swept over that scene of death and desolation. And then the wind fell as suddenly as it had arisen in the morning.

'Presently we got orders to charge the retreating column; I don't know why unless they wanted to prevent us from getting frozen in our saddles by giving us something to do. We changed front half right and got into motion at a walk to take that distant dark line in flank. It might have been half-past two in the afternoon.

'You must know that so far in this campaign my regiment had never been on the main line of Napoleon's advance. All these months since the invasion the army we belonged to had been wrestling with Oudinot in the north. We had only come down lately driving him before us to the Beresina.

'This was the first occasion then that I and my comrades had a close view of Napoleon's Grand Army. It was an amazing and terrible sight. I had heard from others; I had seen the stragglers from it; small bands of marauders, parties of prisoners in the distance. But this was the very column itself! A crawling, stumbling, starved, half-demented mob. It issued from the forest a mile away and its head was lost in the murk of the fields. We rode into it at a trot, which was the most we could get out of our horses, and we stuck in that human mass as if in a moving bog. There was no resistance. I heard a few shots, half a dozen perhaps. Their very senses seemed frozen within them. I had time for a good look while riding at the head of my squadron. Well, I assure you, there were men walking on the outer edge so lost to everything but their misery that they never turned their heads to look at our charge. Soldiers!

'My horse pushed over one of them with his chest. The poor wretch had a dragoon's blue cloak, all torn and scorched, hanging from his shoulders, and he didn't even put his hand out to snatch at my bridle and save himself. He just went down. Our troops were pointing and slashing; well, and of course at first I myself. ... What would you have! An enemy is an enemy. Yet a sort of sickening awe crept into my heart. There was no tumult – only a low deep murmur dwelt over them interspersed with louder cries and groans while that mob kept on pushing and surging past us, sightless and without feeling. A smell of scorched rags and festering wounds hung in the air. My horse staggered in the eddies of swaying men. But it was like cutting down galvanized corpses that didn't care. Invaders! Yes ... God was already dealing with them.

'I touched my horse with the spurs to get clear. There was a sudden rush and a sort of angry moan when our second squadron got into them on our right. My horse plunged and somebody got hold of my leg. As I had no mind to get pulled out of the saddle I gave a back-handed slash without looking. I heard a cry and my leg was let go suddenly.

'Just then I caught sight of the subaltern of my troop at some little distance from me. His name was Tomassov. That multitude of resurrected bodies with glassy eyes was seething round his horse as if blind, growling crazily. He was sitting erect in his saddle not looking down at them and sheathing his sword deliberately.

'This Tomassov, well, he had a beard. Of course we all had beards then. Circumstances, lack of leisure, want of razors, too. No, seriously, we were a wild looking lot in those unforgotten days which so many, so very many of us did not survive. You know our losses were awful, too. Yes, we looked wild. *Des Russes sauvages* – what!

'So he had a beard – this Tomassov·I mean; but he did not look *sauvage*. He was the youngest of us all. And that meant real youth. At a distance he passed muster fairly well, what with the grime and the particular stamp of that campaign on our faces. But directly you were near enough to have a good look into his eyes that was where his lack of age showed though he was not exactly a boy.

'Those same eyes were blue, something like the blue of autumn skies, dreamy and gay, too – innocent believing eyes. A topknot of fair hair decorated his brow like a gold diadem in what one would call normal times.

'You may think I am talking of him as if he were the hero of a novel. Why, that's nothing to what the adjutant discovered about him. He discovered that he had "lover's lips" – whatever that may be. If the adjutant meant a nice mouth why, it was nice enough, but of course it was intended for a sneer. That adjutant of ours was not a very delicate fellow. "Look at those lover's lips," he would exclaim in a loud tone while Tomassov was talking.

'Tomassov didn't quite like that sort of thing. But to a certain extent he had laid himself open to banter by the lasting character of his impressions which were connected with the passion of love and, perhaps, were not of such a rare kind as he seemed to think them. What made his comrades tolerant of his rhapsodies was the fact that they were connected with France, with Paris!

'You of the present generation, you cannot conceive how much prestige there was then in those names for the whole world. Paris was the centre of wonder for all human beings gifted with imagination. There we were, the majority of us young and well connected, but not long out of our hereditary nests in the provinces; simple servants of God; mere rustics, if I may say so. So we were only too ready to listen to the tales of France from our comrade Tomassov. He had been attached to our mission in Paris the year before the war. High protections very likely – or maybe sheer luck.

'I don't think he could have been a very useful member of the mission because of his youth and complete inexperience. And apparently all his time in Paris was his own. The use he made of it was to fall in love, to remain in that state, to cultivate it, to exist only for it in a manner of speaking.

'Thus it was something more than a mere memory that he had brought with him from France. Memory is a fugitive thing. It can be falsified, it can be effaced, it can even be doubted. Why! I myself come to doubt sometimes that I too have been in Paris in my turn. And the long road there with battles for its stages would appear still more incredible if it were not for a certain musket ball which I have been carrying about my person ever since a little cavalry affair which happened in Silesia at the very beginning of the Leipsic campaign.

'Passages of love, however, are more impressive perhaps than passages of danger. You don't go affronting love in troops as it were. They are rarer, more personal and more intimate. And remember that with Tomassov all that was very fresh yet. He had not been home from France three months when the war began.

'His heart, his mind were full of that experience. He was really awed by it, and he was simple enough to let it appear in his speeches. He considered himself a sort of privileged person, not because a woman had looked at him with favour, but simply because, how shall I say it? He had had the wonderful illumination of his worship for her, as if it were heaven itself that had done this for him.

'Oh, yes, he was very simple. A nice youngster yet no fool; and with that, utterly inexperienced, unsuspicious and unthinking. You will find one like that here and there in the provinces. He had some poetry in him, too. It could only be natural, something quite his own, not acquired. I suppose Father Adam had some poetry in him of that natural sort. For the rest *un Russe sauvage* as the French sometimes call us, but not of that kind which, they maintain, eats tallow candle for a delicacy. As to the woman, the Frenchwoman, well though I have also been in France with a hundred thousand Russians, I have never seen her. Very likely she was not in Paris then. And in any case hers were not the doors that would fly open before simple fellows of my sort, you understand. Gilded salons were never in my way. I could not tell you how she looked, which is strange considering that I was, if I may say so, Tomassov's special confidant.

'He very soon got shy of talking before the others. I suppose the usual camp-fire comments jarred his fine feelings. But I was left to him and truly I had to submit. You can't very well expect a youngster in Tomassov's state to hold his tongue altogether; and I – I suppose you will hardly believe me – I am by nature a rather silent sort of person.

'Very likely my silence appeared to him sympathetic. All the month of September our regiment, quartered in villages, had come in for an easy time. It was then that I heard most of that – you can't call it a story. The story I have in my mind is not in that. Outpourings, let us call them.

'I would sit quite content to hold my peace, a whole hour perhaps, while Tomassov talked with exaltation. And when he was done I would still hold my peace. And there would be produced a solemn effect of silence which, I imagine, pleased Tomassov in a way.

'She was of course not a woman in her first youth. A widow maybe. At any rate I never heard Tomassov mention her husband. She had a salon, something very distinguished; a social centre in which she queened it with great splendour.

'Somehow, I fancy her court was composed mostly of men. But Tomassov, I must say, kept such details out of his discourses wonderfully well. Upon my word I don't know whether her hair was dark or fair, her eyes brown or blue; what was her stature, her features, or her complexion. His love soared above mere physical impressions. He never described her to me in set terms; but he was ready to swear that in her presence everybody's thoughts and feelings were bound to circle round her. She was that sort of woman. Most wonderful conversations on all sorts of subjects went on in her salon: but through them all there flowed unheard like a mysterious strain of music the assertion, the power, the tyranny of sheer beauty. So apparently the woman was beautiful. She detached all these talking people from their life interests, and even from their vanities. She was a secret delight and a secret trouble. All the men when they looked at her fell to brooding as if struck by the thought that their lives had been wasted. She was the very joy and shudder of felicity and she brought only sadness and torment to the hearts of men.

'In short, she must have been an extraordinary woman, or else Tomassov was an extraordinary young fellow to feel in that way and to talk like this about her. I told you the fellow had a lot of poetry in him and observed that all this sounded true enough. It would be just about the sorcery a woman very much out of the common would exercise, you know. Poets do get close to truth somehow – there is no denying that.

'There is no poetry in my composition, I know, but I have my share of common shrewdness, and I have no doubt that the lady was kind to the youngster, once he did find his way inside her salon. His getting in is the real marvel. However, he did get in, the innocent, and he found himself in distinguished company there, amongst men of considerable position. And you know what that means: thick waists, bald heads, teeth that are not – as some satirist puts it. Imagine amongst them a nice boy, fresh and simple, like an apple just off the tree; a modest, good-looking, impression-able, adoring young barbarian. My word! What a change! What a relief for jaded feelings! And with that having in his nature that dose of poetry which saves even a simpleton from being a fool.

'He became an artlessly, unconditionally devoted slave. He was rewarded by being smiled on and in time admitted to the intimacy of the house. It may be that the unsophisticated young barbarian amused the exquisite lady. Perhaps – since he didn't feed on tallow candles – he satisfied some need of tenderness in the woman? You know, there are many kinds of tenderness highly civilized women are capable of. Women with heads and imagination, I mean, and no temperament to speak of, you understand. But who is going to fathom their needs or their fancies? Most of the time they themselves don't know much about their innermost moods, and blunder out of one into another, sometimes with catastrophic results. And then who is more surprised than they? However, Tomassov's case was in its nature quite idyllic. The fashionable world was amused. His devotion made for him a kind of social success. But he didn't care. There was his one divinity, and there was the shrine where he was permitted to go in and out without regard for official reception-hours.

'He took advantage of that privilege freely. Well, he had no official duties, you know. The Military Mission was supposed to be more complimentary than anything else, the head of it being a personal friend of our Emperor Alexander; and he too was laying himself out for successes in fashionable life exclusively – as it seemed. As it seemed.

'One afternoon Tomassov called on the mistress of his thoughts earlier than usual. She was not alone. There was a man with her, not one of the thick-waisted, bald-headed personages, but a somebody all the same, a man over thirty, a French officer who to some extent was also a privileged intimate. Tomassov was not jealous of him. Such a sentiment would have appeared presumptuous to the simple fellow.

'On the contrary, he admired that officer. You have no idea of the French military men's prestige in those days, even with us Russian soldiers who had managed to face them perhaps better than the rest.

Victory had marked them on the forehead – it seemed for ever. They would have been more than human if they had not been conscious of it; but they were good comrades and had a sort of brotherly feeling for all who bore arms, even if it was against them.

'And this was quite a superior example, an officer of the Major-General's staff, and a man of the best society besides. He was powerfully built, and thoroughly masculine, though he was as carefully groomed as a woman. He had the courteous self-possession of a man of the world. His forehead, white as alabaster, contrasted impressively with the healthy colour of his face.

'I don't know whether he was jealous of Tomassov, but I suspect that he might have been a little annoyed at him as at a sort of walking absurdity of the sentimental order. But these men of the world are impenetrable and outwardly he condescended to recognize Tomassov's existence even more distinctly than was strictly necessary. Once or twice he had offered him some useful worldly advice with perfect tact and delicacy. Tomassov was completely conquered by that evidence of kindness under the cold polish of the best society.

'Tomassov, introduced into the *petit salon*, found these two exquisite people sitting on a sofa together and had the feeling of having interrupted some special conversation. They looked at him strangely, he thought; but he was not given to understand that he had intruded. After a time the lady said to the officer – his name was de Castel – "I wish you would take the trouble to ascertain the exact truth as to that rumour."

'"It's much more than a mere rumour," remarked the officer. But he got up submissively and went out. The lady turned to Tomassov and said: "You may stay with me."

'This express command made him supremely happy, though as a matter of fact he had had no idea of going.

'She regarded him with her kindly glances, which made something glow and expand within his chest. It was a delicious feeling, even though it did cut one's breath short now and then. Ecstatically he drank in the sound of her tranquil seductive talk full of innocent gaiety and of spiritual quietude. His passion appeared to him to flame up and envelop her in blue fiery tongues, from head to foot and over her head, while her soul reposed in the centre like a big white rose. ...

'H'm, good this. He told me many other things like that. But this is the one I remember. He himself remembered everything because these were the last memories of that woman. He was seeing her for the last time though he did not know it then.

'M. de Castel returned, breaking into that atmosphere of enchantment Tomassov had been drinking in even to complete unconsciousness of the external world. Tomassov could not help being struck by the distinction of his movements, the ease of his manner, his superiority to all the other

197

men he knew, and he suffered from it. It occurred to him that these two brilliant beings on the sofa were made for each other.

'De Castel, sitting down by the side of the lady, murmured to her discreetly, "There is not the slightest doubt that it's true," and they both turned their eyes to Tomassov. Roused thoroughly from his enchantment he became self-conscious; a feeling of shyness came over him. He sat smiling faintly at them.

'The lady, without taking her eyes off the blushing Tomassov, said with a dreamy gravity unusual to her:

'"I should like to know that your generosity can be supreme – without a flaw. Love at its highest should be the origin of every perfection."

'Tomassov opened his eyes wide with admiration at this, as though her lips had been dropping real pearls. The sentiment, however, was not uttered for the primitive Russian youth but for the exquisitely accomplished man of the world, de Castel.

'Tomassov could not see the effect it produced because the French officer lowered his head and sat there contemplating his admirably polished boots. The lady whispered in a sympathetic tone:

'"You have scruples?"

'De Castel, without looking up, murmured: "It could be turned into a nice point of honour."

'She said vivaciously: "That surely is artificial. I am all for natural feelings. I believe in nothing else. But perhaps your conscience...."

'He interrupted her: "Not at all. My conscience is not childish. The fate of those people is of no military importance to us. What can it matter? The fortune of France is invincible."

'"Well then ..." she uttered meaningly, and rose from the couch. The French officer stood up too. Tomassov hastened to follow their example. He was pained by his state of utter mental darkness. While he was raising the lady's white hand to his lips he heard the French officer say with marked emphasis:

'"If he has the soul of a warrior (at that time, you know, people really talked in that way), if he has the soul of a warrior he ought to fall at your feet in gratitude."

'Tomassov felt himself plunged into even denser darkness than before. He followed the French officer out of the room and out of the house; for he had a notion that this was expected of him.

'It was getting dusk, the weather was very bad, and the street was quite deserted. The Frenchman lingered in it strangely. And Tomassov lingered too without impatience. He was never in a hurry to get away from the house in which she lived. And besides something wonderful had happened to him. The hand he had reverently raised by the tips of its fingers had been pressed against his lips. He had received a secret favour! He was almost frightened. The world had reeled – and it had hardly steadied itself yet. De Castel stopped short at the corner of the quiet street.

'"I don't care to be seen too much with you in the lighted thoroughfares, M. Tomassov," he said in a strangely grim tone.

'"Why?" asked the young man, too startled to be offended.

'"From prudence," answered the other curtly. "So we will have to part here; but before we part I'll disclose to you something of which you will see at once the importance."

'This, please note, was an evening in late March of the year 1812. For a long time already there had been talk of a growing coolness between Russia and France. The word war was being whispered in drawing-rooms louder and louder, and at last was heard in official circles. Thereupon the Parisian police discovered that our military envoy had corrupted some clerks at the Ministry of War and had obtained from them some very important confidential documents. The wretched men (there were two of them) had confessed their crime and were to be shot that night. Tomorrow all the town would be talking of the affair. But the worst was that the Emperor Napoleon was furiously angry at the discovery, and had made up his mind to have the Russian envoy arrested.

'Such was de Castel's disclosure; and though he had spoken in low tones Tomassov was stunned as by a great crash.

'"Arrested," he murmured desolately.

'"Yes, and kept as a state prisoner – with everybody belonging to him. . . ."

'The French officer seized Tomassov's arm above the elbow and pressed it hard.

'"And kept in France," he repeated into Tomassov's very ear, and then letting him go stepped back a pace and remained silent.

'"And it's you, you, who are telling me this!" cried Tomassov in an extremity of gratitude that was hardly greater than his admiration for the generosity of his future foe. Could a brother have done for him more! He sought to seize the hand of the French officer, but the latter remained wrapped up closely in his cloak. Possibly in the dark he had not noticed the attempt. He moved back a bit and in his self-possessed voice a man of the world as though he were speaking across a card table or something of the sort, he called Tomassov's attention to the fact that if he meant to make use of the warning the moments were precious.

'"Indeed they are," agreed the awed Tomassov. "Goodbye then. I have no word of thanks to equal your generosity; but if ever I have an opportunity, I swear it, you may command my life. . . ."

'But the Frenchman retreated, had already vanished in the dark lonely street. Tomassov was alone and then he did not waste any of the precious minutes of that night.

'See how people's mere gossip and idle talk pass into history. In all the memoirs of the time if you read them you will find it stated that our envoy had a warning from some highly placed woman who was in love with him. Of course it's known that he had successes with women, and in the highest spheres too, but the truth is that the person who warned him was no other than our simple Tomassov – an altogether different sort of lover from himself.

'This then is the secret of our Emperor's representative's escape from arrest. He and all his official household got out of France all right – as history records.

'And amongst that household there was our Tomassov of course. He had, in the words of the French officer, the soul of a warrior. And what more desolate prospect for a man with such a soul than to be imprisoned on the eve of war; to be cut off from his duty, from honour, and – well – from glory too.

'Tomassov used to shudder at the mere thought of the moral torture he had escaped; and he nursed in his heart a boundless gratitude to the two people who had saved him from that cruel ordeal. They were wonderful! For him love and friendship were but two aspects of exalted perfection. He had found these fine examples of it and he vowed them indeed a sort of cult. It affected his attitude towards Frenchmen in general, great patriot as he was. He was naturally indignant at the invasion of his country, but this indignation had no personal animosity in it. His was fundamentally a fine nature. He grieved at the appalling amount of human suffering he saw around him. Yes, he was full of compassion for all forms of mankind's misery in a manly way.

'Less fine natures than his own did not understand this very well. In the regiment they had nicknamed him the Humane Tomassov.

'He didn't take offence at it. There is nothing incompatible between humanity and a warrior's soul. People without compassion are the civilians, government officials, merchants and such like. As to the ferocious talk one hears from a lot of decent people in war time – well, the tongue is an unruly member at best, and when there is some excitement going on there is no curbing its furious activity.

'So I had not been very surprised to see our Tomassov sheathe deliberately his sword right in the middle of that charge, you may say. As we rode away after it he was very silent. He was not a chatterer as a rule, but it was evident that this close view of the Grand Army had affected him deeply, like some sight not of this earth. I had always been a pretty tough individual myself – well, even I . . . and there was that fellow with a lot of poetry in his nature! You may imagine what he made of it to himself. We rode side by side without opening our lips. It was simply beyond words.

'We established our bivouac along the edge of the forest so as to get some shelter for our horses. However, the boisterous north wind had dropped as quickly as it had sprung up, and the great winter stillness lay on the land from the Baltic to the Black Sea. One could almost feel its cold lifeless immensity reaching up to the stars.

'Our men had lighted several fires for their officers and had cleared the snow around them. We had big logs of wood for seats; it was a very tolerable bivouac upon the whole, even without the exultation of victory. We were to feel that later, but at present we were oppressed by our stern and arduous task.

'There were three of us round my fire. The third one was that adjutant. He was perhaps a well-meaning chap but not so nice as he might have been had he been less rough in manner and less crude in his perceptions. He would reason about people's conduct as though a man were as simple a figure as, say, two sticks laid across each other; whereas a man is much more like the sea whose movements are too complicated to explain, and whose depths may bring up God only knows what at any moment.

'We talked a little about that charge. Not much. That sort of thing does not lend itself to conversation. Tomassov muttered a few words about a mere butchery. I had nothing to say. As I told you I had very soon let my sword hang idle at my wrist. That starving mob had not even *tried* to defend itself. Just a few shots. We had two men wounded. Two! And we had charged the main column of Napoleon's Grand Army.

'Tomassov muttered wearily: "What was the good of it?" I did not wish to argue, so I only just mumbled: "Ah, well!" But the adjutant struck in unpleasantly:

'"Why, it warmed the men a bit. It has made me warm. That's a good enough reason. But our Tomassov is so humane! And besides he has been in love with a Frenchwoman, and thick as thieves with a lot of Frenchmen, so he is sorry for them. Never mind, my boy, we are on the Paris road now and you shall soon see her!" This was one of his usual, as we believed them, foolish speeches. None of us but believed that the getting to Paris would be a matter of years – of years. And lo! less than eighteen months afterwards was rooked of a lot of money in a gambling hell in the Palais Royal.

'Truth, being often the most senseless thing in the world, is sometimes revealed to fools. I don't think that adjutant of ours believed in his own words. He just wanted to tease Tomassov from habit. Purely from habit. We of course said nothing, and so he took his head in his hands and fell into a doze as he sat on a log in front of the fire.

'Our cavalry was on the extreme right wing of the army, and I must confess that we guarded it very badly. We had lost all sense of insecurity by this time; but still we did keep up a pretence of doing it in a way. Presently a trooper rode up leading a horse, and Tomassov mounted stiffly and went off on a round of the outposts. Of the perfectly useless outposts.

'The night was still, except for the crackling of the fires. The raging wind had lifted far above the earth and not the faintest breath of it could be heard. Only the full moon swam out with a rush into the sky and suddenly hung high and motionless overhead. I remember raising my hairy face to it for a moment. Then, I verily believe, I dozed off too, bent double on my log with my head towards the fierce blaze.

'You know what an impermanent thing such slumber is. One moment you drop into an abyss and the next you are back in the world that you would think too deep for any noise but the trumpet of the Last Judgment. And then off you go again. Your very soul seems to slip down into a bottomless black pit. Then up once more into a startled consciousness. A mere plaything of cruel sleep one is, then. Tormented both ways.

'However, when my orderly appeared before me, repeating: "Won't your honour be pleased to eat? Won't your honour be pleased to eat?" I managed to keep my hold of it – I mean that gaping consciousness. He was offering me a sooty pot containing some grain boiled in water with a pinch of salt. A wooden spoon was stuck in it.

'At that time these were the only rations we were getting regularly. Mere chicken food, confound it! But the Russian soldier is wonderful. Well, my fellow waited till I had feasted and then went away carrying off the empty pot.

'I was no longer sleepy. Indeed, I had become awake with an exaggerated mental consciousness of existence extending beyond my immediate surroundings. Those are but exceptional moments with mankind, I am glad to say. I had the intimate sensation of the earth in all its enormous expanse wrapped in snow, with nothing showing on it but trees with their straight stalk-like trunks and their funeral verdure; and in this aspect of general mourning I seemed to hear the sighs of mankind falling to die in the midst of a nature without life. They were Frenchmen. We didn't hate them; they did not hate us; we had existed far apart – and suddenly they had come rolling in with arms in their hands, without fear of God, carrying with them other nations, and all to perish together in a long, long trail of frozen corpses. I had an actual vision of that trail: a pathetic multitude of small dark mounds stretching away under the moonlight in a clear still and pitiless atmosphere – a sort of horrible peace.

'But what other peace could there be for them? What else did they deserve? I don't know by what connection of emotions there came into my head the thought that the earth was a pagan planet and not a fit abode for Christian virtues.

'You may be surprised that I should remember all this so well. What is a passing emotion or half-formed thought to last in so many years of a man's changing inconsequential life? But what has fixed the emotion of that evening in my recollection so that the slightest shadows remain indelible was an event of strange finality, an event not likely to be forgotten in a lifetime – as you shall see.

'I don't suppose I had been entertaining those thoughts more than five minutes when something induced me to look over my shoulder. I can't think it was a noise; the snow deadened all the sounds. Something it must have been, some sort of signal reaching my consciousness. Anyway, I turned my head, and there was the event approaching me, not that I knew it or had the slightest premonition. All I saw in the distance were two figures approaching in the moonlight. One of them was our Tomassov. The dark mass behind him which moved across my sight were the horses which his orderly was leading away. Tomassov was a very familiar appearance, in long boots, a tall figure ending in a pointed hood. But by his side advanced another figure. I mistrusted my eyes at first. It was amazing! It had a shining crested helmet on its head and was muffled up in a white cloak. The cloak was not as white as snow. Nothing in the world is. It was white more like mist, with an aspect that was ghostly and martial, to an extraordinary degree. It was as if Tomassov had got hold of the God of War himself. I could see at once that he was leading this resplendent vision by the arm. Then I saw that he was holding it up. While I stared and stared, they crept on – for indeed they were creeping – and at last they crept into the light of our bivouac fire and passed beyond the log I was sitting on. The blaze played on the helmet. It was extremely battered, and the frost-bitten face, full of sores, under it was framed in bits of mangy fur. No God of War this, but a French officer. The great white cuirassier's cloak was torn, burnt full of holes. His feet were wrapped up in old sheepskins over remnants of boots. They looked monstrous and he tottered on them, sustained by Tomassov, who lowered him most carefully on to the log on which I sat.

'My amazement knew no bounds.

'"You have brought in a prisoner," I said to Tomassov, as if I could not believe my eyes.

'You must understand that unless they surrendered in large bodies we made no prisoners. What would have been the good? Our Cossacks either killed the stragglers or else let them alone, just as it happened. It came really to the same thing in the end.

'Tomassov turned to me with a very troubled look.

'"He sprang up from the ground somewhere as I was leaving the outpost," he said. "I believe he was making for it, for he walked blindly into my horse. He got hold of my leg and of course none of our chaps dare touch him then."

'"He had a narrow escape," I said.

'"He didn't appreciate it," said Tomassov, looking even more troubled than before. "He came along holding to my stirrup leather. That's what made me so late. He told me he was a staff officer; and then talking in a voice such, I suppose, as the damned alone use, a croaking of rage and pain, he said he had a favour to beg of me. A supreme favour. Did I understand him? he asked in a sort of fiendish whisper.

'"Of course I told him that I did. I said: Oui, je vous comprends."

'"Then," said he, "do it. Now! At once – in the pity of your heart."

'Tomassov ceased and stared queerly at me above the head of the prisoner.

'I said, "What did he mean?"

'"That's what I asked him," answered Tomassov in a dazed tone, "and he said that he wanted me to do him the favour to blow his brains out. As a fellow soldier," he said. "As a man of feeling – as – as a humane man."

'The prisoner sat between us like an awful gashed mummy as to the face, a martial scarecrow, a grotesque horror of rags and dirt, with awful living eyes, full of vitality, full of unquenchable fire, in a body of horrible affliction, a skeleton at the feast of glory. And suddenly those shining unextinguishable eyes of his became fixed upon Tomassov. He, poor fellow, fascinated, returned the ghastly stare of a suffering soul in that mere husk of a man. The prisoner croaked at him in French.

'"I recognize you, you know. You are her Russian youngster. You were very grateful. I call on you to pay the debt. Pay it, I say, with one liberating shot. You are a man of honour. I have not even a broken sabre. All my being recoils from my own degradation. You know me."

'Tomassov said nothing.

'"Haven't you got the soul of a warrior?" the Frenchman asked in an angry whisper, but with something of a mocking intention in it.

'What a look of contempt that scarecrow gave him out of his unquenchable eyes! He seemed to live only by the force of infuriated and impotent despair. Suddenly he gave a gasp and fell forward writhing in the agony of cramp in all his limbs; a not unusual effect of the heat of a camp fire. It resembled the application of some horrible torture. But he tried to fight against the pain at first. He only moaned low while we bent over him so as to prevent him rolling into the fire, and muttered feverishly at intervals: "Tuez moi, tuez moi ..." till vanquished by the pain he screamed in agony, time after time, each cry bursting through his compressed lips.

'The adjutant woke up on the other side of the fire and started swearing awfully at the beastly row that Frenchman was making.

'"What's this? More of your infernal humanity, Tomassov," he yelled at us. "Why don't you have him thrown out of this to the devil on the snow?"

'As we paid no attention to his shouts, he got up, cursing shockingly, and went away to another fire. Presently the French officer became easier. We propped him up against the log and sat silent on each side of him till the bugles started their call at the first break of day. The big flame, kept up all through the night, paled on the livid sheet of snow, while the frozen air all round rang with the brazen notes of cavalry trumpets. The Frenchman's eyes, fixed in a glassy stare, which for a moment made us hope that he had died quietly sitting there between us two, stirred slowly to right and left, looking at each of our faces in turn. Tomassov and I exchanged glances of dismay. Then de Castel's voice, unexpected in its renewed strength and ghastly self-possession, made us shudder inwardly.

'"Bonjour, Messieurs."

'His chin dropped on his breast. Tomassov addressed me in Russian. '"It is he, the man himself. ..." I nodded and Tomassov went on in a tone of anguish: "Yes, he! Brilliant, accomplished, envied by men, loved by that woman – this horror – this miserable thing that cannot die. Look at his eyes. It's terrible."

'I did not look, but I understood what Tomassov meant. We could do nothing for him. This avenging winter of fate held both the fugitives and the pursuers in its iron grip. Compassion was but a vain word before that unrelenting destiny. I tried to say something about a convoy being no doubt collected in the village – but I faltered at the mute glance Tomassov gave me. We knew what those convoys were like: appalling mobs of hopeless wretches driven on by the butts of Cossacks' lances, back to the frozen inferno, with their faces set away from their homes.

'Our two squadrons had been formed along the edge of the forest. The minutes of anguish were passing. The Frenchman suddenly struggled up to his feet. We helped him almost without knowing what we were doing.

'"Come," he said, in measured tones. "This is the moment." He paused for a long time, then with the same distinctness went on: "On my word of honour, all faith is dead in me."

'His voice lost suddenly its self-possession. After waiting a little while he added in a murmur – "And even my courage. ... Upon my honour."

'Another long pause ensued before with a great effort he whispered hoarsely: "Isn't this enough to move a heart of stone? Am I to go on my knees to you?"

'Again a deep silence fell upon the three of us. Then the French officer flung his last word of anger at Tomassov.

'"Milksop!"

'Not a feature of the poor fellow moved. I made up my mind to go and fetch a couple of our troopers to lead that miserable prisoner away to the village. There was nothing else for it. I had not moved six paces towards the group of horses and orderlies in front of our squadron when ... but you have guessed it. Of course. And I too, I guessed it, for I give you my word that the report of Tomassov's pistol was the most insignificant thing imaginable. The snow certainly does absorb sound. It was a mere feeble pop. Of the orderlies holding our horses I don't think one turned his head round.

'Yes. Tomassov had done it. Destiny had led that de Castel to the man who could understand him perfectly. But it was poor Tomassov's lot to be the predestined victim. You know what the world's justice and mankind's judgment are like. They fell heavily on him with a sort of inverted hypocrisy. Why! That brute of an adjutant, himself, was the first to set going horrified allusions to the shooting of a prisoner in cold blood! Tomassov was not dismissed from the service, of course. But after the siege of Dantzig he asked for permission to resign from the army, and went away to bury himself in the depths of his province where a vague story of some dark deed clung to him for years.

'Yes. He had done it. And what was it? One warrior's soul paying its debts a hundred-fold to another warrior's soul by releasing it from a fate worse than death – the loss of all faith and courage. You may look on it in that way. I don't know. And perhaps poor Tomassov did not know himself. But I was the first to approach that appalling dark group on the snow: the Frenchman extended rigidly on his back, Tomassov kneeling on one knee rather nearer to the feet than to the Frenchman's head. He had taken his cap off and his hair shone like gold in the light drift of flakes that had begun to fall. He was stooping over the dead man in a tenderly contemplative attitude. And his young, ingenuous face with lowered eyelids, expressed no grief, no sternness, no horror – but was set in the repose of a profound, as if endless and endlessly silent meditation.'

Fly For Your Life

LARRY FORRESTER

As one of the few professional pilots of the Second World War, the now legendary Robert Standford Tuck was determined, after the frustrations and false alarms of the 'phoney' war, to make a good showing in his first active engagement with the enemy.....

A FEW MINUTES BEFORE 11 a.m. on May 23rd 1940, he saw the shooting war for the first time. From 15,000 feet he saw the immense, black pall of smoke brooding over the Dunkerque beaches, the sullen flashes of the enemy guns inland, the occasional puffs of flak staining the morning sky, and – quite distinctly – the straggling columns of men, threading their way painfully through narrow, choked roads, down to the sea.

He saw several little ships, privately-owned motor launches and trip-round-the-bay pleasure boats from Brighton and Cromer and Broadstairs and Cowes; with their garish paint, somehow they seemed in the worst of taste now, like aging actresses emerging from the playhouse into the world of grim reality still wearing their stage make-up. Yet they plodded gamely to and fro among the bigger, sleeker vessels, the grey-uniformed soldier-ships that were too few for the huge task ahead.

He saw shells exploding on the cluttered beach and raising tall, white plumes in the shallow water. Smouldering trucks and carriers, ruptured convoys, abandoned stores piled ready for burning, gun pits being dug in the dunes, sandbags being filled for the last dour stand here on this broad, white strand which, only nine months before, had known the light touch of sandal and beachball and the barefoot scamperings of children.

All this he saw, and the curious thing, the thing he could not understand, was how remote and unreal it seemed. He might have been watching a newsreel or studying newspaper photographs. He knew that his brother Jack must be somewhere down there, fighting with the 78th Field Regiment, Royal Artillery, but even this extremely personal link with the chaos below awakened no bitterness or anger. He felt exactly as he would have felt if at that moment he had been flying a practice formation over Shropshire, or one of those pointless patrols over the empty North Sea which he had carried out so often during the last few months.

A flight of Hurris slanted past far below, heading home to refuel and re-arm. He wondered if Cæsar Hull was one of them. He envied Cæsar, for the tough little Rhodesian had fought in Norway and bagged five Huns. He envied *all* Hurricane pilots, for Hurris had been scrapping in France as well as Norway while the Spit boys were kept patrolling the backstreets of the air war – because Air Chief Marshal Sir Hugh (later Lord) Dowding, the C.-in-C. Fighter Command, had decided to hold them for Home Defence.

Up till today the war had been for the most part boring, exasperating for him. A regular officer with nearly 700 hours in his log book and 'exceptional' gradings in every branch of flying, and he'd had to sit at home while youngsters of considerably less experience went out to mix it with the Luftwaffe. . . . On the Spit squadrons tempers had flared. Pilots were frequently sent on wild goose chases, misdirected by inexperienced ground controllers and fired on by excitable A.A. batteries on the south and east coasts.

But on May 1st he had been posted from 65 to 92 Squadron, then based at Croydon, where the C.O., Squadron Leader Roger Bushell, had immediately given him command of a flight and promoted him to Flight Lieutenant.

'We'll be getting a crack at them soon, don't worry,' Bushell had said in his deep, refined voice, smiling a tight smile of anticipation. 'You're just the sort of bloke I need, and I'm bloody well going to work you till you're on your knees. We've got to lick this squadron into top shape in double-quick time. Go and dump your kit. I'll meet you at dispersal in ten minutes.'

Ninety-two had been formed on the outbreak of war from a nucleus of Royal Auxiliary Air Force pilots – businessmen and students who in peace-time had given up their weekends to fly, some of them at considerable personal expense. The remainder were Volunteer Reserve pilots, straight from the flying schools. They had only recently been given Spitfires Mark II. In theory, a fighter squadron's full complement at this stage was twenty-six pilots, but in fact 92 had just fourteen or fifteen.

Tuck had expected to find them very different from the 'professional' pilots of 65, and was astounded and delighted to discover the atmosphere of the Croydon mess even wilder and woollier than Hornchurch. Moreover, in some mysterious way these war-time chaps had managed to learn the entire range of Raff slang and idiom, all the rude songs, all the traditional nicknames ('Chippie' Wood, 'Shady' Lane, 'Dickie' Bird, etc.,) and, most surprisingly of all, they had the same cynical approach to anything that savoured even faintly of militarism, rhetoric or red tape. Even the youngest of them had acquired the languid arrogance of experienced pilots.

Because the Spit was new to most of them, and because each one realized the 'phoney war' was over and that very soon – perhaps within days, or hours – the squadron would go into battle, they had practised combat drill with a quiet ardour. Between flights they had squatted in a circle on the grass and listened to Tuck, wide-eyed and attentive as children listening to a bedtime story.

They were a cosmopolitan bunch, and the range of Commonwealth accents gave the mess a vocal tapestry of rare richness. There were two Canadians, 'Eddie' Edwards and John Bryson, a former member of the 'Mounties'; Howard Hill, from New Zealand; Pat Learmond from Ireland, and Paddy Green from South Africa. For administrative purposes the squadron at this time was sub-divided into two flights of six or seven, but in the air they flew in three sub-units of four. Tuck's flying section were all English – Bob Holland, Allan Wright and Sergeant 'Titch' Havercroft – so short that he had to have two rubber cushions under his parachute before he could see over the instrument panel. John Gillies (son of the distinguished plastic surgeon), Peter Cazenove, Roy Mottram, Hargreaves, Bill Williams and Tony Bartley completed the 'native' contingent. Green led the second flying section, and the C.O. headed the third. The two or three remaining aircraft, with their pilots, were held as reserve.

At this early stage of the war most fighter pilots still wore the white flying overalls which had been part of peace-time bullshine. Their leather helmets had built-in earphones, and a rubber attachment combining oxygen mask and microphone was clipped across the lower half of the face like a visor. With the new large, tinted goggles in place and the visor clipped on, the face was almost completely blanked out, and the general effect was decidedly sinister – robot-like.

The broad, tough canvas straps of the parachute harness ran over each shoulder, down the back, through between the legs and up over the belly. All four ends clipped into a strong spring lock in the vicinity of the navel. This lock had a quick-release device: after the 'chute had landed him safely on land or in the sea, the pilot had only to twist a circular metal plate on top of the lock and then rap it smartly with his palm or clenched fist to be instantly freed from the harness, the tangled lines and the drag of the billowing silk. There had been a few strange cases in France of pilots operating this device while still in mid-air, and plummeting to their deaths. The only possible explanation seemed to be that those men had been suffering great agony from wounds or burns, and released themselves deliberately.

The parachute pack was worn like a huge bustle, but very low-slung, so that it fitted into a recess in the bucket seat when the pilot sat down in his cockpit. A few weeks after Dunkerque a smaller, very ingeniously constructed pack was added, also serving as a cushion, which contained a rubber dinghy that could be swiftly inflated by compressed air bottles attached to it. The same inflation device was incorporated in the 'Mae West', a bright yellow, rubber lifebelt which was worn like a waistcoat under the parachute harness. (Later versions of both dinghy and 'Mae West' were constructed to inflate automatically once immersed, so that injured or unconscious pilots could remain afloat.)

Following the example of Hurricane squadrons in France, the majority of the 92 pilots carried revolvers – usually not in holsters, but stuck down the legs of their heavy flying boots. If a man landed in enemy territory there might be a slim chance of shooting his way out of trouble and getting through to the British lines, but – more important – a revolver provided the surest and quickest way of destroying a crash-landed fighter. A few bullets pumped into the fuel tank produced a consuming inferno.

Bushell, the chieftain of this motley tribe, was a South African who had practised in London as a criminal barrister before the war, and taken prominent part in one or two sensational cases. But he was better known as a champion skier who had coached the British Olympic Team.

Often he had a single tear coursing down his left cheek, the result of an eye injury received in a ski-ing accident a few years before. No one had ever seen him wipe the tear away – he simply ignored it, even when the eye streamed for hours on end. His sight was unimpaired, and this inconvenient ailment had only one result: he always held his head slightly tilted to the right.

It was hard to tell how old he was, though he must have been about thirty. Of medium height, dark and indelibly tanned, he was wonderfully compact and fit. At practice 'scrambles' when the pilots sprinted across the grass, vaulted into the cockpits and strained every fibre to get into the air in a matter of seconds, the 'old man' nearly always won the race.

Bushell's voice was strong and cultured, and his diction was like an actor's, yet there was no false, courtroom pomp about him and he could bellow cheerful vulgarities and roar the bawdiest choruses with the rest of them. He was never one to stand on ceremony, but a candid and open character, ready to joke or play the fool with all. Yet when there was serious talk, the affability and the humour fell away and he became direct, shrewd, commanding. He engendered a fine squadron spirit with his overwhelming, enveloping aura of personality and strength.

On the morning of the 23rd they had moved to a forward base, nearer the coast – Tuck's old home, Hornchurch. There they breakfasted, refuelled, got briefed. And now at last, after all the waiting and working, the patrols and the play-acting, the testing time had come – and here they were in combat formation with Bushell leading them over the blazing beaches and their gun-buttons set to 'fire', with their faces rigid and aching with the suspense and their necks in swivel-gear and their eyes smarting from scouring the furthermost corners of the sky for the first tiny glint of metal. Twelve Spitfires, marching proudly, challengingly, disdaining the cover of the stratocumulus cloud 5,000 feet higher, inviting the enemy to attack.

But as they flew down the coast on their specified 'offensive sortie' – Calais – Boulogne – Dunkerque – nothing rose to meet them but the occasional flak-puffs and the oily smoke – though they had been warned at briefing to expect formations of up to forty Me. 109s and had been given the impression that long, unbroken lines of Ju.87B Stukas were stretched across France, queueing-up to dive-bomb the cornered British troops.

They flew through a patch of turbulent air and their wings rocked a little, the whole formation buckling and writhing momentarily out of its purposeful shape. It was all over in four or five seconds, but it left Tuck very uneasy. The formation was too tight – he couldn't see any point in keeping so close together when at any moment they might have to tear their minds and eyes away from each other to concentrate on battle. . . .

'Turning right – go!' Bushell's voice sounded gruff over the r/t. He was probably just as browned-off as everyone else.

The twelve Spits banked in one even, co-ordinated movement, directly above Dunkerque town, and began wheeling through 180 degrees to go back the way they had come. They would fly up and down this coast until either they were attacked or their fuel tanks were nearly empty and they were forced to return to base. Tuck told thimself that somewhere along this stretch, between here and Calais, they must surely meet their enemy. And yet still he felt no apprehensive tightening of muscles or nerves. He just sat there, not really believing all this, observing every detail of the spectacle around him with mild amusement and a begrudging, slightly suspicious curiosity – as one inspects the scenery of a dream. He was, for instance, struck by the sheer, majestic beauty of the wheeling echelon of Spitfires, stepped up so neat and steep on the outside of the turn, each machine printed sharply on the grey-blue canvas of space.

The two aircraft closest to him were flown by Holland and Wright. By turning his head, he could look straight into either man's eyes, for at this moment they were keeping their positions in the turn by watching Tuck's wingtip. They seemed so close that he felt he could stretch out a hand and touch them; yet he knew that in fact they were all three infinitely remote from each other, that if one of the engines stopped or a shell set one of the machines ablaze, there was no way for the others to help and they might as well be a million miles away.

He shook himself free of the thought and as the formation completed the turn he gave Holland and Wright a cheerful wave. They acknowledged with vigorous, pumping V-signs.

Soon after that a short, strangled cry in his earphones jerked him forward against his harness, breath congealed, eyes straining. He had no

211

idea who had given that cry, and there was no chance to find out, for the very next second, glancing downwards over his left shoulder, he saw the Messerschmitts shearing in.

'Here they come – eight o'clock!' he yelled. And then Pat Learmond died. An eye-searing, woofing explosion, and his machine simply was not there any more. There was only a big, pulsating ball of flame, which seemed to keep position in the echelon and fly on for several seconds before it sank away under their wings. And during these seconds, while the Spit pilots were twisting in their seats to look round and see their attackers and where they were coming from, the orderly, businesslike formation began to buckle, stretch, break up. Bushell was rapping out orders, but now everybody was yelling at once and his words were lost in the babble.

The 109s were dropping out of the stratocumulus behind and slightly to the left, a long, straggly line of them, diving hard and building up terrific speed before they swept in from just under the tails. Tracer was lashing the Spitfires, chivvying pieces out of them. The leader – it must have been this one that got Learmond – came snarling clean through the heaving, splitting formation, then climbed hard for the cloud ahead. Bob decided to go after him, though he knew he had very little chance of catching up.

Climbing at full power, he couldn't match the high angle of ascent which the Messerschmitt had earned with his earlier dive. He was still a good 2,000 feet under the cloud when the German vanished into its woolly sanctuary. But he kept on, up through the glary white stratocumulus, not quite knowing what he hoped for now.

The cloud was a lot thinner than he'd expected. After only two or three hundred feet of it he broke out into peerless blue. And there was the Hun dead ahead, not more than 2,000 yards distant, racing eastwards for his base, skimming so low over the great slab of milky cloud that he blended with his own shadow, like a flatfish scuttling over sea-rippled sand.

Tuck realized that his shallower angle of climb had actually brought him closer to his quarry. The German was flying perfectly straight, so apparently he felt quite safe up here. He might even be cruising at normal revs, in which case Tuck could overhaul him by using full 'emergency' power.

He pushed the throttle forward hard – breaking through the light seals that guarded the 'emergency' slot – and settled the Spitfire as low as possible, cutting through occasional wisps and tors that thrust up from the unbroken cloud; sometimes, in places where the surface was smooth, he flew for seconds on end with only his head and the canopy in the clear. The Messerschmitt kept straight on, and very gradually it grew larger in his windscreen.

He hasn't seen me, he hasn't seen me...!

212

For the first time since take-off a full-blooded thrill flushed through him, but immediately he suppressed it: this was the time to be cool, relaxed, methodical, precise ... he must never let himself get excited or emotional in battle, never! To keep his place as an exceptional pilot, he must prove himself as level-headed and as skilful in combat as in all the other flying he had done thus far. He *had* to be exceptional – ever since Grantham there had been no other way of facing each day. If he were not exceptional, he would be nothing.

Grantham, Hornchurch, Duxford, Eastleigh, Northolt – all one long rehearsal. Well, now the curtain was rising – this was the moment he had been working for, training for all these years. He must not fumble. For him failure was out of the question. If was different for all the others on the squadron, volunteers and auxiliaries – this was his chosen profession in life!

The Messerschmitt made a gentle turn of about ten degrees to the right, a small course correction. He eased round after it and adjusted the reflector sight for the wingspan: Me. 109.

Sixteen hundred yards ... fifteen hundred. ... He was gaining steadily, and the Hun was still unaware of his presence. He could see the Luftwaffe markings very plainly now. There they were, big black crosses – exactly as he had been told, exactly as he had seen in photographs and aircraft recognition posters. For some curious reason he experienced a twinge of disappointment, almost as if he'd been hoping for something different, *un*familiar. As if this was, after all, turning out to be ordinary, routine. ...

The enemy's silhouette continued to expand. He'd been chasing him for over two minutes now, and they must be well inland. He kept glancing in his rear vision mirror, and sweeping the sky all around, but the vast blue vault was empty except for the two of them. He checked his fuel, oil and radiator temperatures, all in one swift, custom-learned sweep of the eyes. All was well, everything was ready; each tiny piece of mechanism was toiling nobly, performing its own intricate function. The Spitfire would not blunder – only he, the human element, could wreck the whole elaborate scheme by a single wrong decision, misjudgment or oversight.

He didn't give a thought to the other human element – the man in the Messerschmitt, the man who was going to die for the cardinal sin of not looking over his shoulder. There was nothing personal about this.

Tuck had visited Germany twice, during annual leaves in '37 and '38. He'd liked the people more than the French, because he thought them cleaner, less mercenary, more industrious; and he'd taken a great fancy to the beer. Lusty, brawling Nazidom he had seen in plenty, but he regarded it as merely a ludicrous, melodramatic, political fad which the Germans would soon tire of, just as the Americans would get over their yo-yo craze.

213

Then on his second visit, strolling in the countryside near Zeltweg one evening he'd come upon a fighter aerodrome. It wasn't big, but it had broad concrete runways, hangars, a magnificent control tower and neat, stone-built quarters and outbuildings. Encircling the whole field there was a thick pipeline, sunk flush in the ground, with cocks fitted at regular intervals – about twenty feet apart, he judged. Clearly this carried petrol, and enabled aircraft to refuel speedily, without the aid of bowser-lorries and without taxi-ing into dispersal. They could replenish their tanks and be off again in a matter of two or three minutes.

It was obviously an expensive installation. Only a government with deadly serious intentions would provide such a luxury.

It was then, in that moment, that he had realized war would come, and that to begin with Britain would have small answer to such efficiency; only her toughness, her obstinacy, and her little air force which still used plain grass fields and lived for the most part in rickety huts.

Twelve hundred yards ... eleven hundred.... Now the Messerschmitt's wingspan almost filled the space between the parallel lines of the reflector sight. Another few seconds would bring him up to maximum range.

All at once he noticed a broad, black highway running almost parallel with them across the white desert of cloud. It nagged at his attention, dragging his eyes away from the gunsight, puzzling him with its startling evenness and straightness. Then he caught the faintest scent of burning oil, and knew what the dark stripe was: the eastward-drifting stratocumulus was collecting the smoke that rose in a great pillar from the Dunkerque beaches and dragging it, like a black ribbon of mourning, slowly inland over France.

One thousand yards – maximum range!

The 109's wingtips touched the sight's glowing graticules. He put his thumb gently on the gun-button and willed himself to relax, to let every muscle liquefy, as his father had taught him back in the days when the school rifle team was training for Bisley. Get comfortable, hold your breath, keep perfectly still – even a man's own heartbeats could upset his aim at the vital instant when he exerted firing pressure!

He flicked a last glance at the turn-and-bank indicator. The needle was in the centre, perfectly still, as though painted on the dial. He took a deep breath.

And then he changed his mind.

Why open up at extreme range if he could get closer? At a thousand yards even perfect shooting might only damage the Messerschmitt. Every yard nearer increased the chances of complete destruction. Provided, of course, that the German didn't look round....

Nine hundred yards, seven hundred, six hundred. ... It seemed impossible that he could get this close without being seen – in fact, he was beginning to feel that by now the Hun must *hear* him. But the 109 was still sitting up there, flying unconcernedly down the mild May sunlight.

Five hundred.

A deep breath ... don't tense up, stay relaxed ... turn-and-bank needle centred ... keep the red dot right on his canopy and, gently, gently, *s-q-u-ee-ze.* ...

The eight Vickers .303 burst into life with a sound like the crash of a roller-coaster. The Spitfire quivered lightly in his hands. He could see the wicked little blue flashes his bullets made as they struck the 109's wings and canopy. For two ... three ... four seconds they hosed into it, and nothing was happening. The German flew on, straight and level, with the little blue flashes all over him like fairy-lights on a Christmas tree. And then the machine seemed to flinch, and give a nervous shudder. Its nose came up lazily and it climbed for a little, with the Spitfire following. Suddenly there was a puff of dark blue smoke and a few small pieces of metal came whipping back at the pursuer, spinning like boomerangs, as though in a final, hopeless gesture of defiance.

Tuck took his thumb from the button and ruddered smartly to the right as the burning Messerschmitt rose, steeply, slowed, and seemed to hang in the air, nose pointing to the sun. Then suddenly it flicked over to the left. Once, twice, three times it rolled, as correctly as if giving an aerobatics display, and then it started down in a weary spiral.

He dived through the cloud and waited underneath a long time before it appeared. Though it was against orders, he meant to follow it down, to see it crash – *he had to be absolutely certain*. But it was hard to follow: several times as it built up speed its elevators, trimmed for level flight, made it climb again for a few hundred feet, so that it came down in long, dipping stages. It was as if the Messerschmitt were trying to shake him off, to sneak away and die alone.

But finally it fell, in its red and black garland, into a ploughed field. And blew up.

He climbed back into the cloud and set course for home. He felt no elation, only a quiet satisfaction. He had carried out his first act of war – coolly, correctly, professionally.

Not even Wills nor Savile could have found fault!

Wills and Savile, Tatnall and Lywood – he thought of them now, with a grateful affection which had never entered his mind before. It was by their grace, by their special efforts, that he was riding up here with his broken gun-ports whistling, and one Me. to his credit. They'd had faith in him, when he'd had none himself. Such men were a little too old now, and too valuable as instructors, to hunt Messerschmitts themselves, but in fact they had a part in this victory to-day. He made up his mind to write and tell them so, but he never did – there was no time, for when he landed at base he found most of the squadron already refuelled and rearmed, standing by for another 'scramble'.

Paddy Green, John Bryson and Tony Bartley each had bagged a 109. That made the score five for the loss of poor Learmond, whose incandescent wreck had been seen to crash smack on the French beach. Bushell was kicking at the ground in disappointment. He'd followed a Hun for three minutes, then lost him in cloud before he could get a squirt at him.

They gulped tea and munched sandwiches, excitedly comparing their experiences. A van arrived with five of the new-type, bullet-proof windscreens, completed at the factory that morning. The ground crews worked with dæmonic energy, and Tuck's machine was one of the three they managed to refit.

The thick, non-splintering perspex was the only protection Air Ministry could offer: at this stage the Spitfire was entirely without armoured plating.

They were off again at 1.45. One of their reserve pilots had taken Learmond's place in Green's flight, but otherwise the formation was the same. At 8,000 feet over the French beaches several of them simultaneously spotted a pack of between thirty and forty twin-engined Messerschmitt 110s diving from almost directly overhead. Bushell immediately put the squadron into a turn to the left, forming a sort of defensive circle in which they could, at least to some extent, protect each other's tails. Tuck, again in that strangely cool, almost dreamy state of mind, couldn't help thinking of western movies he'd seen, in which covered wagons adopted the same tactics to fight off redskins....

The 110s were formidably armed. In the nose they had a fixed cannon and machine-guns, fired by the pilot. Behind the pilot, back-to-back with him, the rear-gunner manipulated a single free-swivelling, heavy machine-gun. They came through the formation spewing tracer fore and aft, and then suddenly friend and foe were milling round and round as one loose mass, in a macabre waltz. Now some of the Spitfires were opening up. The air was criss-crossed with their fire – a fantastic imbroglio of glowing, curving lines – and clearly there was a great risk of pilots on both sides being shot down by their comrades.

Wheeling round in the thick of this confusion, for a time Tuck could see nothing to shoot at. Then a 110 drifted majestically in front of him, startlingly close, in a gentle bank and skidding slightly. It seemed enormous, impregnable. Its rear gunner swung his long barrel round and Tuck instinctively ducked as the bullets ricocheted off his cowling and canopy, filling the cockpit with the bitter stench of cordite. Then he was firing back, holding the gun-sight's dot steady on the gunner's goggled face for seconds on end, watching the Spit's eight streams of metal tear into the Messerschmitt's cabin, fuselage, and port engine.

At last the tail-gunner stopped firing – Tuck thought by now the fellow must be carrying more than his own weight in bullets. The 110 was seesawing, bits were flying off the port wing, and a thin, straight line of black was trailing from the port engine. He kept his thumb on the button until it flicked over and plunged vertically down, blossoming like a red flower as flames burst from its shattered engine and spread along the wing.

He pulled up and put his neck into swivel-gear. The sky about him was a streaked and mottle hiatus. Spitfires and 110s were slashing across and up and down, turning, writhing, rolling through the lethal latticework of tracer. His earphones rang with a bewildering din – four and five voices shrieking at once.

'Look out – here's another!'

'Watch that bastard – smack underneath you, man, *under* you!'

'He's burning – I got him, I *got* him chaps!'

'Bloody hell, I've been hit. . . .'

'Jesus, where are they all coming from?'

'For God's sake, *somebody*. . . !'

This was all wrong – the r/t shouldn't be abused like this. Properly used, it ought to be a valuable life-preserver, the team-brain of the squadron. Why didn't they keep quiet until it was absolutely necessary to shout a warning? Why didn't they use call-signs, or even Christian names, and give heights and directions as they had been taught – 'Two coming in four o'clock, above you. . . .' In their excitement they'd abandoned all set procedure and resorted to meaningless, unprofessional clamour.

Infuriated, he yelled into his microphone: 'Shut up, for Christ's sake!' But it did no good.

Shadows flicked by close overhead – a 110 with Tony Bartley not more than fifty yards from its tail, pouring continuous fire into it. Bartley was taking a terrible chance: if the Hun exploded the Spit would be destroyed too. 'Bloody idiot!' Tuck muttered – but the term expressed affectionate admiration.

Then above the commingled dins there came a cry that almost split his helmet – a long, horrendous sound which might have been dragged up from secret ocean depths. To his right he saw Flight Sergeant Wooder's Spitfire a blazing brand. Under the perspex of its canopy there was not the vaguest sign of a human figure, only a seething mass of yellow flame. It was like looking through the peep-hole of a blast furnace.

The fiery wreck fell slowly, wilting, becoming shapeless, till it resembled nothing so much as a lump of rag which somebody had soaked in petrol, lit, and tossed over the side. Tuck watched in sickly fascination – until something struck his windscreen a tremendous, jarring blow. A 110 was charging towards him, head-on, bombarding him with its shells and bullets.

He blazed back at it, holding the collision course. The two machines hurtled to meet each other, converging at a speed of roughly 600 m.p.h.,

217

their gunports flashing like bared fangs. The first to break off would almost certainly be destroyed – because he would present an easy target to the other. It was a question of which pilot had the strongest nerve.

In the final second, when it seemed that the weird joust could only end in an annihilating crash, an irresistible reflex made Tuck close his eyes and yank his head down below the level of the windscreen. A split-second roar, like an express train bursting out of a tunnel. He never knew whether the Messerschmitt passed below or above him. When he raised his head again, and looked over his shoulder, he saw it far behind him, losing a little height, turning east – towards the land. He thought he glimpsed a faint, white trail from one of its engines. He wheeled the Spitfire and set off in pursuit.

On the top left and bottom right corners of his windscreen there were ugly, opaque blotches, staring in at him like big blind eyes. Two of the Hun's shells had smacked him squarely: if the fitters hadn't installed the new type screen just over an hour before, these hits would have come though and taken off his head. . . .

He caught up with the 110 a mile or two inland and opened fire from about 500 yards. The rear-gunner replied with great accuracy, and the bullets drummed on the Spitfire's nose and canopy like savage rain. The German pilot took violent evasive action, lifting and dropping his damaged machine in a mad gambado. But he couldn't shake off his resolute and agile tormentor, so he dived to treetop level in the hope that the Englishman wouldn't have the nerve to follow.

Tuck followed, hard and fast. Now the duel became an obstacle race, with each protagonist's attention divided between fighting and flying, with neglect or misjudgment in either department entailing equal peril. They squeezed sideways – banked and skidding – through narrow gaps in thickets of firs . . . lifted wingtips over church steeples . . . grazed farmhouse chimneys with their prop tips . . . weaved along a river so low that their slipstreams whipped up spray and set small boats rocking madly at their moorings. And all the time they were exchanging long bursts of fire, knocking pieces off each other, the pursuer drawing closer with each second until they were less than two hundred yards apart.

Once Tuck came near to losing the battle. The 110 went under some high tension cables and barely managed to pull up in time to clear some sharply rising ground beyond. Bob, on a split-second decision, pulled up earlier, rose over the cables like a hurdler – and in so doing exposed his belly as a succulent target for the Hun rear-gunner. In the dragging moments before he could get flat down on the deck again, scores of bullets ripped through his wings and the underside of the fuselage. But the Merlin's warlike roar didn't falter and the Spit flew on, cool and competent and unperturbed.

It was the rear-gunner's last enfilade. Tuck's next burst riddled him;

the long-barrelled gun dipped, swung loosely, then drooped dispiritedly over the side of the Messerschmitt's fuselage. At once the German pilot, realizing he was at the Spitfire's mercy, swung into a long, flat field and crash-landed in a whorl of dust.

Tuck circled about fifty feet over the wreck and saw the pilot scramble out and run clear. Jolly good luck to him! – he deserved to get away with it, after that wonderful bit of low flying!

No hard feelings. Flushed with success, excited from the long and hazardous chase, Tuck felt a positive affection for his vanquished foe. So he circled even lower, slid back his canopy and waved to him.

The German was standing perfectly still now, a few yards from the hulk of his aircraft, looking up at the wheeling conqueror. An erect, proud figure in a smart grey uniform and polished black boots. And then suddenly he raised his arms.

He's waving back. No hard feelings....

A bullet whined through the cockpit, chipping the edge of the windscreen's panel, less than six inches from Tuck's face. Another glanced off the outside of the screen – leaving a third opaque blotch. The German's raised arms held a Schmeisser automatic machine pistol.

Tuck felt betrayed. So this was the enemy – this was the sort of fight it was going to be.... His eyes narrowed and his teeth clamped hard.

He drew away from the field, then went in again, very low, and laid his sights on that defiant grey figure which still held the gun levelled at him. Coolly, carefully, he checked his turn-and-bank indicator, then squeezed the button. The ground all round the German erupted in wicked flashes, clods of earth and spurts of dust. It was a very short burst, for the Spitfire had very little ammo left, and after a second or so there was only the hiss of compressed air and the futile clankings of the empty breech blocks. Enough, though.

The Hun staggered two or three steps through the dust, like a man lost in a fog, then pitched on to his face. The oily smoke from his burning plane gradually drifted over and covered him.

The Naked And The Dead
NORMAN MAILER

Sergeant Croft's platoon, a motley assortment of Americans, is charged with an impossible and futile mission against the Japanese on the mythical Pacific island of Anopopei. Ordered to bring forward heavy guns, the inexperienced GIs struggle against exhaustion, fear and the unknown horrors of the jungle terrain . . . . .

THERE WERE ABOUT FIFTY men in the column, and they moved very slowly down a narrow trail through the jungle. After they had moved a hundred feet, they were no longer able to see the men in front of them. The branches of the trees on either side of the trail joined overhead, and they felt as though they were groping through an endless tunnel. Their feet sank into the deep mud and, after a few yards, their boots were covered with great slabs of muck. The men on the guns would lunge forward for a few feet and then halt, lunge forward and halt. Every ten yards a gun would bog down and the three men assigned to it would have to tug until their strength seeped from their fingers. They would wrestle the gun out of its rut and plunge it forward for fifteen feet before their momentum was lost. Then they would pull it and lift it for another few yards until it sank into a hole once more. The entire column labored and stumbled at a miserable pace along the trail. In the darkness they kept ganging up on each other, the men on one gun sometimes riding it up onto the muzzle of the one ahead, or falling behind so far that the file at last broke into separate wriggling columns like a worm cut into many parts and still living. The men at the rear had the worst of it. The guns and men that preceded them had churned the trail until it was almost a marsh, and there were places where two teams would have to combine on one gun and carry it above the ground until they had passed the worst of the slime.

The trail was only a few feet wide. Huge roots continually tripped the men, and their faces and hands became scratched and bleeding from the branches and thorns. In the complete darkness they had no idea of how the trail might bend, and sometimes on a down slope, when they could let the gun roll a little distance, they would land at the bottom with the field piece completely off the trail. Then they would have to fumble in the

220

brush, covering their eyes with their arms to protect them from the vines, and a painful struggle to bring the gun back on the path would begin.

Some Japanese might easily have been waiting in ambush, but it was impossible to keep silent. The guns squeaked and lumbered, made sucking sounds as their tires sank into the mud, and the men swore helplessly, panted with deep sobbing sounds like wrestlers at the end of a long bout. Voices and commands echoed hollowly, were lost in a chorus of profanity and hoarse sobbing, the straining sweating noises of men in great labor. By the time an hour had passed, nothing existed for them but the slender cannon they had to get down the track. The sweat drenched their clothing and filled their eyes, blinding them. They grappled and blundered and swore, advanced the little guns a few feet at a time with no consciousness any longer of what they were doing.

When one team was relieved by another, they would stagger alongside the guns trying to regain their wind, falling behind sometimes to rest for a little while. Every ten nimutes the column would stop to allow for stragglers to catch up. During the halts the men would sprawl in the middle of the trail not caring how the mud covered them. They felt as though they had been running for hours; they could not regain their breath, and their stomachs retched emptily. Some of the men began to throw away their equipment; one after another the men threw their helmets aside or dropped them on the trail. The air was unbearably hot under the canopy of the jungle, and the darkness gave no relief from the heat of the day; if anything, walking the trail was like fumbling through an endless closet stuffed with velvet garments.

During one of the halts, the officer leading the file worked his way back to find Croft. 'Where's Sergeant Croft?' he shouted, his words repeated by the men along the trail until it reached Croft.

'Here, sir.' They stumbled toward each other through the mud.

'How're your men?' the officer asked.

'Okay.'

They sat down beside the trail. 'Mistake trying this,' the officer gasped. 'Have to get through.'

Croft, with his lean ropy body, had borne the labor comparatively well, but his voice was unsteady and he had to talk with short quick spates of words. 'How far?' he asked.

'Have to go one mile . . . one mile yet. More than halfway there I think. Never should have tried it.'

'They need the guns bad?'

The officer halted for a moment and tried to speak normally. 'I think so . . . there's no tank weapons there . . . up on the line. We stopped a tank attack two hours ago . . . at Third Battalion. Orders came to move some thirty-sevens over to First Battalion. Guess they expect attack there.'

'Better get them through,' Croft said. He was contemptuous because the officer had to talk to him. The man ought to be able to do his own job.

'Have to, I guess.' The officer stood up and leaned for a moment against a tree. 'If you get a gun stuck, let me know. Have to cross a stream ... up ahead. Bad place, I think.'

He began to feel his way forward, and Croft turned around and worked his way back to the gun he was pulling. The column was over two hundred yards long by now. They started to move, and the labor continued. Once or twice a flare filtered a wan and delicate bluish light over them, the light almost lost in the dense foliage through which it had to pass. In the brief moment it lasted, they were caught at their guns in classic straining motions that had the form and beauty of a frieze. Their uniforms were twice blackened, by the water and the dark slime of the trail. And for the instant the light shone on them their faces stood out, white and contorted. Even the guns had a slender articulated beauty like an insect reared back on its wire haunches. Then darkness swirled about them again, and they ground the guns forward blindly, a line of ants dragging their burden back to their hole.

They had reached that state of fatigue in which everything was hated. A man would slip in the mud and remain there, breathing hoarsely, having no will to get to his feet. That part of the column would halt, and wait numbly for the soldier to join them. If they had breath they would swear.

'Fug the sonofabitchin' mud.'

'Get up,' somebody would cry.

'Fug you. Fug the goddam gun.'

'Let me lay here. I'm okay, they ain't a thing wrong with me, I'm okay, let me lay.'

'Fug you, *get up!*'

And they would labor forward a few more yards and halt. In the darkness, distance had no meaning, nor did time. The heat had left their bodies; they shivered and trembled in the damp night, and everything about them was sodden and pappy; they stank but no longer with animal smells; their clothing was plastered with the foul muck of the jungle mud, and a chill dank rotting smell somewhere between leaf mold and faeces filled their nostrils. They knew only that they had to keep moving, and if they thought of time it was in so many convulsions of nausea.

Wyman was wondering why he did not collapse. His breath came in long parched shudders, his pack straps galled, his feet were ablaze, and he could not have spoken, for his throat and chest and mouth seemed covered with a woolly felt. He was no longer conscious of the powerful and fetid stench that rose from his clothes. Somewhere deep inside himself was a wonder at the exhaustion his body could endure. He was normally a sluggish youth who worked no more than he was obliged to, and the sensations of labor, the muscle strains, the panting, the taste of fatigue were things he had always tried to avoid. He had had vague dreams about being a hero, assuming this would bring him some immense reward which would ease his life and remove the problems of supporting his mother and himself. He had a girl and he wanted to dazzle her with his ribbons. But he had always imagined combat as exciting, with no misery and no physical exertion. He dreamed of himself charging across a field in the face of many machine guns; but in the dream there was no stitch in his side from running too far while bearing too much weight.

He had never thought that he would be chained to an inanimate monster of metal with which he would have to grapple until his arms trembled helplessly and his body was ready to fall; certainly he had never imagined he would stumble down a path in the middle of the night with his shoes sucking and dragging in slime. He pushed at the gun, he lifted it with Goldstein and Toglio when it became mired in a hole, but the motions were automatic by now; he hardly even felt the added pain when they had to pull it out by the wheel hubs. His fingers were no longer able to close, and often he would tug helplessly until his hands slipped away with the gun still mired.

The column was proceeding even more slowly than it had at the start, and sometimes fifteen minutes would elapse before a gun could be moved a hundred yards. Every now and then a man would faint, and would be left by the side of the trail to make his way back alone when he recovered.

At last a message began to carry back along the trail, 'Keep going, we're almost there,' and for a few minutes it served as a stimulant so that the men labored with some hope again. But when each turning in the trail discovered only another ribbon of mud and darkness, the men began to feel a hopeless dejection. Sometimes for as much as a minute they would not move at all. It became harder and harder to pitch themselves against the guns again. Every time they stopped they felt like quitting.

There was a draw they had to cross a few hundred feet before they reached 1st Battalion, and its banks sloped very steeply down to a little stony brook, then ascended again abruptly to about fifteen feet above the bottom. This was the stream the officer had mentioned. When the men reached it, the column stopped completely, and the stragglers caught up. Each team of soldiers waited for the men and gun in front of them to cross the stream. In the night it was an extremely difficult business at best and took a long time. The men would go sliding down the bank trying to restrain their field piece from turning over at the bottom, and then they would have to lift it over the slippery rocks of the brook before attempting to wrestle it up the other side. The banks were slimy, and there was no foothold; time and again a team would force their gun up almost to the top of the draw only to slip back again futilely.

By the time Wyman and Toglio and Goldstein had to move their gun, a half hour had passed and they were a little rested. Their wind had returned and they kept shouting instructions to each other as they nosed the gun over the edge of the bank. It began to pull away from them, and they had to resist desperately to keep it from crashing to the bottom. The exertion drained most of the strength they had recovered, and after they had carried the piece across the stream, they were as exhausted as they had been at any time during the march.

They stopped for a few moments to gather whatever force was left in them and began to struggle up the bank. Toglio was wheezing like a bull, and his commands had a hoarse urgent sound as if he were wrenching them from deep inside his body. 'Okay, PUSH ... PUSH,' he growled, and the three of them strove numbly to roll the gun. It resisted them, moved sluggishly and treacherously, and the strength began to flow out of their trembling legs. 'HOLD IT!' Toglio shouted 'DON'T LET IT SLIP!' They braced themselves behind the gun, trying to wedge their feet into the wet clay of the bank. 'PUSH AGAIN!' he shouted, and they forced it upwards a few more feet. Wyman felt a band was stretching dangerously inside his body, and would snap at any moment. They rested again, and then shoved the gun another few yards. Slowly, minute by minute, they came closer to the top. They were perhaps four feet from the crest when Wyman lost the last reserves of his strength. He tried to draw some few shreds of effort from his quivering limbs, but he seemed to collapse all at once, and just lay stupidly behind the gun supporting it with no more than the weight of his sagging body. The gun began to slip, and he pulled away. Toglio and Goldstein were left at each of the hubs. When Wyman let go, they felt as though someone were pushing down against the gun. Goldstein held on until the sliding wheels pulled his fingers loose, one by one, and then he just had time to shout hoarsely, 'WATCH IT!' to Toglio, before the gun went crashing down to the bottom. The three men fell after it, rolling in its wake. The gun struck some rocks at the bottom, and one of the wheels was knocked completely awry. They felt for it in the darkness like pups licking the wounds of their mother. Wyman began to blubber with exhaustion.

The accident caused a great deal of confusion. Croft's team was on the gun waiting behind them, and he began to shout, 'What's holdin' you up? What's happening down there?'

'We had ... trouble,' Toglio shouted back. 'Wait!' He and Goldstein succeeded in turning the gun on its side. 'The wheel's shot,' Toglio shouted. 'We can't move the gun.'

Croft swore. 'Get her out of the way.'

They tried and couldn't budge it.

'We need help,' Goldstein shouted.

Croft swore again, and then he and Wilson slid down the bank. After a while they were able to tumble the gun over enough times to move it down the creek bed. Without saying anything, Croft went back to his gun, and Toglio and the others climbed up the far bank and went staggering down the trail till they reached 1st Battalion's bivouac. The men who had arrived before them were lying on the ground motionless. Toglio stretched out in the mud, and Wyman and Goldstein lay down beside him. None of them spoke for ten minutes. Occasionally, a shell might burst somewhere in the jungle about them and their legs might twitch, but this was the only sign they gave of being conscious. Men were moving about constantly, and the sounds of the fighting were closer, more vicious. Voices kept coming to them out of the darkness. Someone would shout, 'Where's the pack train for B Company?' and the answer would be muffled to the men lying on the ground. They hardly cared. Occasionally they would be aware of the sounds of the night; for a few instants they might concentrate on the constant thrumming that emanated from the jungle, but they always relapsed into a stupor, thinking of nothing once more.

Croft and Wilson and Gallagher brought their gun in a short while later, and Croft shouted for Toglio.

'What do you want? I'm here,' Toglio said. He hated to move.

Croft came towards him in the darkness and sat down beside him. His breath was coming in long slow gasps like a runner after a race. 'I'm going to see the Lieutenant ... tell him about the gun. How the hell did it happen?'

Toglio propped himself on an elbow. He loathed the explanations that were to come, and he was confused. 'I don't know,' he said. 'I heard Goldstein yell "Watch out" and then it just seemed to rip out of our hands.' Toglio hated to give excuses to Croft.

'Goldstein yelled, huh?' Croft asked. 'Where is he?'

'Here I am, Sergeant.' Goldstein's voice came out of the darkness beside them.

'Why'd you yell "Watch out"?'

'I don't know. I felt suddenly as if I couldn't hold it any more. Something pulled it away from me.'

'Who was the other man?'

Wyman roused himself. 'I guess I was.' His voice sounded weak.

'Did you let go?' Croft asked.

Wyman felt a trace of fear as he thought of admitting that to Croft. 'No,' he said. 'No, I don't think so. I heard Goldstein yell, and then the gun started to come down on me. It was rolling back so I got out of the way.' Already he was uncertain exactly how it had occurred, and a part of his mind was trying to convince him that he spoke the truth. With it, however, he felt a surprising flush of shame. 'I guess it was my fault,' he blurted out honestly, but his voice was so tired that it lacked sincerity, and Croft thought he was trying to protect Goldstein.

225

'Yeah,' Croft said. A spasm of rage worked through him, and he turned on Goldstein and said, 'Listen, Izzy.'

'My name isn't Izzy,' Goldstein said angrily.

'I don't give a damn what it is. The next time you pull a goddam trick like that, I'm going to put you in for a court-martial.'

'But I don't think I let go,' Goldstein protested weakly. By now, he too was no longer sure. The sequence of his sensations when the gun had begun to pull out of his hands was too confused for him to feel righteous. He had thought that Wyman stopped pushing first, but when Wyman declared he was to blame, Goldstein had a moment of panic. Like Croft, he believed Wyman was protecting him. 'I don't know,' he said. 'I don't think I did.'

'You don't think,' Croft cut him off. 'Listen, for as long as you've been in the platoon, Goldstein, you've done nothing but have ideas about how we could do something better. But when it comes down to a little goddam work, you're always dicking off. I've had enough of that bullshit from you.'

Once again Goldstein was feeling a helpless anger. A reaction he could not control, his agitation was even greater than his resentment and choked him so that he could not speak. A few tears of frustration welled in his eyes, and he turned away and lay down again. His anger was now directed toward himself and he felt a hopeless shame. Oh, I don't know, I don't know, he said.

Toglio had a mingled relief and pity. He was glad the onus of losing the gun was not his, and yet he was unhappy anyone should be blamed. The bond of common effort that the three men had known while struggling with the weapon was still with him, and he said to himself, poor Goldstein, he's a good guy; he just had hard luck.

Wyman was too exhausted to think clearly. After he declared it was his fault, he was relieved to discover he was not to be blamed after all. He was actually too depleted to think consecutively about anything, or indeed remember anything. By now, he was convinced it was Goldstein who had deserted the gun, and his main reaction was one of comfort. The image still most vivid to him was the agony he had felt in his chest and groin as they had started up the embankment, and he thought, I would have let go two seconds later if he didn't. For this reason, Wyman felt a dulled sense of affection for Goldstein.

Croft stood up. 'Well, that's one gun they ain't going to rescue for a little while,' he said. 'I bet it stays there for the whole compaign.' He was enraged enough to strike Goldstein. Without saying anything more, Croft left them and went in search of the officer who had led the column.

The men in the platoon settled down and began to sleep. Occasionally a shell would burst in the jungle nearby, but they hardly cared. The battle had been threatening all evening like a thunderstorm which never breaks, and by now it would have taken a barrage to move them. Besides, they were too weary to dig holes.

It took Red longer to fall asleep than any of the others. For many years his kidneys had bothered him whenever he had too much exposure to dampness. They were throbbing now, and he turned several times on the wet ground, trying to decide if it would be less painful to sleep with his back against the moist earth or exposed to the night air. He lay awake for a long time thinking, his mood turning through a small gamut from weariness to sadness. He was thinking of a time when he had been caught in a small town in Nebraska with no jobs to be had, and had had to wait until he could catch a boxcar out of town. It had seemed very important to him then not to beg for something to eat, and he wondered if he still had that pride. 'Oh, I've been tough in my life,' he muttered to himself. 'Lot of good it does me.' The air was cold on his back, and he turned over. It seemed to him that all his life he had been sleeping in bare wet places, seeking for warmth. He thought of an old hobo saying, 'Half a buck in your pocket and winter coming,' and felt some of the gloom he had known on cold October twilights. His stomach was empty, and he got up after a while and rummaged through his pack. He found a K ration and chewed the fruit bar, washing it down with water from his canteen. His blanket was still wet from the evening storm, but he wrapped it about him and found a little warmth. Then he tried to go to sleep again, but his kidneys were aching too much. At last he sat up, fumbled in the first aid kit on his cartridge belt, and withdrew the little paper bag of wound tablets. He swallowed half of them and drank about half the water remaining in his canteen. For a moment he thought of using them all, but then he remembered that he might be wounded and need them. It brought back his dejection, and he stared solemnly into the darkness, being able to discern after a time the bodies of the sleeping men around him. Toglio was snoring, and he heard Martinez mutter softly in Spanish and then cry out, 'I no kill Jap, God, I no kill him.' Red sighed and lay down again. What men sleep easy? he thought.

A trace of an old anger passed through him. I don't give a damn about anything, he said to himself, and listened uneasily to a shell sighing overhead. This time it sounded like the branches of a tree murmuring in a winter wind. He remembered once striding along a highway as evening came. It had been in the eastern coal-mining towns of Pennsylvania and he had watched the miners driving home in their battered Fords, their faces still dark with the day's accumulation of soot and coal dust. It had not looked anything like the mining country in Montana he had left years before, and yet it had been the same. He had walked along brooding about home, and someone had given him a ride and treated him to a drink in a noisy bar. That night had a beauty about it now, and he remembered for a moment the sensation of leaving a strange town on a

227

dark freight. Things like that were only glints of light in the long gray day of those years. He sighed again as if to grasp something of the knowledge he had felt for an instant. Nobody gets what he wants, he said to himself, and this deepened his mood of pleasurable sorrow. He was growing drowsy, and he burrowed his head under his forearm. A mosquito began to whine near his ear and he lay still, hoping it would go away. The ground seemed crawling with insects. The little buggers are one thing I'm used to, he thought. For some reason this made him smile.

It was beginning to rain, and Red covered his head with the blanket. His body was slowly sinking into a weary slumber in which different parts of him fell asleep at separate intervals, so that long after he had stopped thinking, a portion of his mind could feel the quivering of an exhausted limb or a cramp in one of his limbs. The shelling was becoming steady, and a half mile away from him a machine gun kept firing. Almost asleep, he watched Croft return and spread out a blanket. The rain continued. After a time, he no longer heard the artillery. But even when he was completely asleep, one last area of his mind noticed what was happening. Although he didn't remember it when he awoke, he heard a platoon of men march by, and was conscious of some other men beginning to push the antitank guns to the other side of the bivouac. There's a Jap road leads into the bivouac, he said in his sleep. They're going to protect it now. Probably he was feverish.

He dreamed until he heard a voice shout, 'Recon? Where's recon?' The dream ebbed away, and he lay there drowsily, listening to Croft spring to his feet and holler, 'Here, over here!' Red knew he would have to be moving in a few minutes, and he burrowed deeper into his blankets. His body ached and he knew that when he stood up he would be stiff. 'All right, men, on your feet.' Croft was shouting 'Come on, get up, we got to move.'

Red pulled the cover off his face. It was still raining and his hand came away wet from the top surface of the blanket. When he replaced the blanket in his pack, his pack also would become wet. 'Aaaahhhhrr.' He cleared his throat with disgust and spat once or twice. The taste in his mouth was foul. Gallagher sat up beside him and groaned. 'Goddam Army, why don't they let a guy sleep? Ain't we done enough tonight?'

'We're heroes,' Red said. He stood up and began to fold his blanket. It was sopping wet on one side and muddy on the other. He had slept with his rifle beside him, covered under the blanket, but it too was wet. Red wondered how long it had been since he was dry. 'Fuggin jungle,' he said.

'Come on, you men, snap it up,' Croft said. A flare lit the wet ugly shrubs about them and flickered dully against their wet black clothing. Red saw that Gallagher's face was covered with mud, and when he felt his own face, his hands came away soiled. 'Show me the way to go home,' he hummed. 'I'm tired and I want to go to bed.'

'Yeah,' Gallagher said. They made their packs together and stood up. The flare had gone out and they were blinded for a moment in the returning darkness. 'Where we going?' Toglio asked.

'Up to A Company. They expect an attack there,' Croft said.

'We sure are a hard-luck platoon,' Wilson sighed. 'At least we're done with them antitank guns. Ah swear Ah'd fight a tank with mah bare hands 'fore Ah'd rassle with one of them sonsofbitches again.'

The squad formed a single file and began to move out. First Battalion's bivouac was very small and in thirty seconds they had reached the gap in the barbed wire. Martinez led them cautiously down the trail leading to A Company. His drowsiness vanished quickly, and he became alert. Actually he could not see anything, but some sense seemed to guide him along the bends in the path so that he rarely stumbled or blundered off the trail. He was proceeding about thirty yards ahead of the other men and he was completely isolated. If some Japanese had been waiting in ambush along the path, he would have been the first to be trapped. Yet he had very little fear; Martinez's terror developed in a void; the moment he had to lead men, his courage returned. At this instant, his mind was poised over a number of sounds and thoughts. His ears were searching the jungle ahead of him for some noise which might indicate that men were waiting in the brush beside the trail; they were also listening with disgust to the stumbling and muttering of the men following behind him. His mind recorded the intermittent sounds of battle and tried to classify them; he looked at the sky whenever they passed through a partial clearing in order to find the Southern Cross and determine in which direction the trail was bending. Wherever he could, he made a mental note of some landmark they were passing and added it to the ones he had observed previously. After a time he kept repeating a jingle to himself which went, Tree over trail, muddy creek, rock on trail, bushes across. Actually there was no reason for him to do it; the trail led only from 1st Battalion to A Company. But this was a habit he had formed on his first patrols. He did it instinctively by now.

And another part of his mind had a quiet pride that he was the man upon whom the safety of the others depended. This was a sustaining force which carried him through dangers his will and body would have resisted. During the march with the antitank guns, there had been many times when he wanted to quit; unlike Croft, he had felt it no contest at all. He would have been perfectly willing to declare the task beyond his strength and give up, but there was part of his mind that drove him to do things he feared and detested. His pride with being a sergeant was the core about which nearly all his actions and thoughts were bound. Nobody sees in the darkness like Martinez, he said to himself. He touched a branch before his extended arm and bent his knees easily and walked under it. His feet were sore and his back and shoulders ached, but they were ills with which he no longer concerned himself; he was leading his squad, and that was sufficient in itself.

The rest of the squad, strung out behind, was experiencing a variety of emotions. Wilson and Toglio were sleepy, Red was alert and brooding – he had a sense of foreboding. Goldstein was miserable and bitter, and the tension of creeping down a trail in the black early hours of the morning made him gloomy and then sad. He thought of himself dying without friends nearby to mourn him. Wyman had lost his power to recuperate; he was so tired that he plodded along in a stupor, not caring where he went or what happened to him. Ridges was weary and patient; he did not think of what the next hours would bring him, nor did he lose himself in contemplation of his aching limbs; he just walked and his mind drifted slowly like a torpid stream.

And Croft; Croft was tense and eager and impatient. All night he had been baulked by the assignment of the squad to a labor detail. The sounds of battle he had been hearing all night were goading to him. His mind was buoyed by a recurrence of the mood he had felt after Hennessey's death. He felt strong and tireless and capable of anything; his muscles were as strained and jaded as any of the men's, but his mind had excluded his body. He hungered for the fast taut pulse he would feel in his throat after he killed a man.

On the map there was only a half mile between 1st Battalion and A Company, but the trail doubled and curved so often that it was actually a mile. The men in recon were clumsy now and uncertain of their footing. Their packs sagged, their rifles kept sliding off their shoulders. The trail was crude; originally a game wallow, it had been partially enlarged, and in places it was still narrow. A man could not walk without being scratched by the branches on either side. The jungle was impenetrable at that point, and it would have taken an hour to cut one's way a hundred feet off the path. In the night it was impossible to see anything and the smell of wet foliage was choking. The men had to walk in single file, drawn up close. Even at three feet they could not see one another, and they plodded down the trail with each man grasping the shirt of the man before him. Martinez could hear them and judge his distance according-ly, but the others stumbled and collided with one another like children playing a game in the dark. They were bent over almost double, and the posture was cruel. Their bodies were outraged; they had been eating and sleeping with no rhythm at all for the last few hours. They kept loosing gas whose smell was nauseating in the foul dense air. The men at the rear had the worst of it; they gagged and swore, tried not to breathe for a few seconds, and shuddered from fatigue and revulsion. Gallagher was at the end of the file, and every few minutes he would cough and curse. 'Cut out the gaddam farting,' he would shout, and the men in front would rouse themselves for a moment and laugh.

230

'Eatin' dust, hey, boy,' Wilson muttered, and a few of them began to giggle.

Some of them began to fall asleep as they walked. Their eyes had been closed almost the entire march, and they drowsed for the instant their foot was in the air and awakened as it touched the ground. Wyman had been plodding along for many minutes with no sensation at all; his body had grown numb. He and Ridges drowsed continually, and every now and then for ten or fifteen yards they would be completely asleep. At last they would weave off the trail and go pitching into the bushes stupidly before regaining their balance. In the darkness such noises were terrifying. It made the men uncomfortably aware of how close they were to the fighting. A half mile away some rifles were firing.

'Goddammit,' one of them would whisper, 'can't you guys keep quiet?'

The march must have taken them over half an hour, but after the first few minutes they no longer thought about time. Crouching and sliding through the mud with their hands on the man in front became the only thing they really knew; the trail was a treadmill and they no longer concerned themselves with where they were going. To most of them the end of the march came as a surprise. Martinez doubled back and told them to be quiet. 'They hear you coming for ten minutes,' he whispered. A hush settled over the men, and they trod the last hundred yards down the river.

There was no barbed wire, nor any clearing at A Company. The trail divided in a quadruple fork which led to different emplacements. A soldier met them where the path broke up and led the squad along one of the footpaths to a few pup tents pitched in the middle of some foliage. 'I got Second Platoon,' he told Croft. 'I'm just about a hundred yards down the river. Your squad can sleep in these holes tonight, and set up a guard right along here. They's two machine guns set up for you.'

'What's doing?' Croft whispered.

'I dunno. I heard they expect an attack all up and down the line above dawn. We had to send a platoon over to C Company early tonight, and we been holding down the whole outpost here with less than a platoon.' He made a rustling sound in the darkness as he wiped his hand against his mouth. 'C'mere, I'll show you the setup,' he said, grasping Croft's elbow. Croft slipped his arm free; he hated to have anyone touch him.

They went a few feet along the path, until the sergeant from A Company halted before a foxhole. There was a machine gun mounted in front, its muzzle just projecting through a fringe of bushes. Croft peered through the foliage and in the faint moonlight was able to see a stream of water and a strip of beach bordering it on either side. 'How deep is the river?' he asked.

'Aw, it's four, five feet maybe. That water ain't going to stop them.'

'Any outposts forward of here?' Croft asked.

231

'Nothing. And the Japs know right where we are. Had some patrols up.' The soldier wiped his mouth again and stood up. 'I'll show you the other machine gun.' They walked along a stubbly path cut through the jungle about ten feet from the river's edge. Some crickets were chirping loudly, and the soldier trembled a little. 'Here's the other one,' he said. 'This is the flank.' He peered through the bushes and stepped out onto the strip of beach. 'Look,' he said. Croft followed him. About fifty yards to their right, the bluffs of Watamai Range began. Croft looked up. The cliffs rose almost vertically for perhaps a thousand feet. Even in the darkness, he felt them hovering about him. He strained his eyes and thought he saw a swatch of sky where they ended but could not be certain. He had a curious thrill. 'I didn't know we were that close,' he said.

'Oh, yeah. It's good and it's bad. You don't have to worry about them coming around that end, but still we're the flank. If they ever hit here hard, there ain't much to hold them.' The soldier drew into the bushes again and exhaled his breath slowly. 'I'll tell you these two nights we been out here give me the creeps. Look at that river. When there's a lot of moonlight it just seems to shine, and you get jittery after a while looking at it.'

Croft remained outside the jungle edge, looking at the stream that curved away at the right and flowed parallel to the mountains. It took a turn toward the Japanese lines just a few yards before the first walls of the bluff began, and he would be able to see everything on that side. To the left the stream ran straight for a few hundred yards like a highway at night, sunk between high grassy banks. 'Where are you?' he asked.

The soldier pointed to a tree which projected a little from the jungle. 'We're just on this side of it. If you got to get to us, go back to the fork and then take the trail at the far right going away from here. Yell "Buckeye" when you come up.'

'Okay,' Croft said. They talked for a few more minutes, and then the other soldier hooked his cartridge belt. 'Jesus, I'll tell ya, it'll drive ya crazy spending a night here. Just wilderness, that's all, and you stuck out at the end of it with nothing but a lousy machine gun.' He slung his rifle and struck off down the trail. Croft looked at him for a moment and then went back to recon. The men were waiting by the three pup tents, and he showed them where the two machine guns were placed. Briefly he told them what he had learned and picked a guard. 'It's three A.M. now,' he told them. 'There's gonna be four of us on one post and five on the other. We'll do it in two-hour shifts. Then the post that's only got four men will get the extra one for the next time around.' He divided them up, taking the first shift at the flank gun himself. Wilson volunteered to take the other gun. 'After Ah'm done, Ah'm gonna want to sleep right on through,' Wilson said. 'Ah'm tired of gittin' up right when Ah'm havin' a good dream.'

The men smiled wanly.

'An' listen,' Croft added, 'If any trouble starts, the men that are sleeping are to git up goddam fast and move to help us. It's only a couple of yards from our tents to Wilson's machine gun, and it ain't much further to mine. It shouldn't be takin' you all more than about three hours to reach us.' Again, a couple of men smiled. 'Okay, that's about it,' Croft said. He left them and walked over to his machine gun.

He sat down on the edge of the hole and peered through the bushes at the river. The jungle completely surrounded him, and, now that he was no longer active, he felt very weary and a little depressed. To counteract this mood, he began to feel the various objects in the hole. There were three boxes of belt ammunition and a row of seven grenades lined up neatly at the base of the machine gun. At his feet were a box of flares and a flare gun. He picked it up and broke open the breech quietly, loaded it, and cocked it. Then he set it down beside him.

A few shells murmured overhead and began to fall. He was a little surprised at how near they landed to the other side of the river. Not more than a few hundred yards away, the noise of their explosion was extremely loud; a few pieces of shrapnel lashed the leaves on the trees above him. He broke off a stalk from a plant and put it in his mouth, chewing slowly and reflectively. He guessed that the weapons platoon of A Company had fired, and he tried to determine which trail at the fork would lead to them in case he had to pull back his men. Now he was patient and at ease; the danger of their position neutralized the anticipation for some combat he had felt earlier, and he was left cool and calm and very tired.

The mortar shells were falling perhaps fifty yards in front of the platoon at his left, and Croft spat quietly. It was too close to be merely harassing fire; someone had heard something in the jungle on the other side of the river or they would never have called for mortars so close to their own position. His hand explored the hole again and discovered a field telephone. Croft picked up the receiver, listened quietly. It was an open line, and probably confined to the platoons of A Company. Two men were talking in voices so low that he strained to hear them.

'Walk it up another fifty and then bring it back.'

'You sure they're Japs?'

'I swear I heard them talking.'

Croft stared tensely across the river. The moon had come out, and the strands of beach on either side of the stream were shining with a silver glow. The jungle wall on the other side looked impenetrable.

The mortars fired again behind him with a cruel flat sound. He watched the shells land in the jungle, and then creep nearer to the river in successive volleys. A mortar answered from the Japanese side of the river, and about a quarter of a mile to the left Croft could hear several machine guns spattering at each other, the uproar deep and irregular. Croft picked up the phone and whistled into it. 'Wilson,' he whispered. '*Wilson!*' There was no answer and he debated whether to walk over to Wilson's hole. Silently Croft cursed him for not noticing the phone, and then berated himself for not having discovered it before he briefed the others. He looked out across the river. Fine sergeant I am, he told himself.

His ears were keyed to all the sounds of the night, and from long experience he sifted out the ones that were meaningless. If an animal rustled in its hole, he paid no attention; if some crickets chirped, his ear disregarded them. Now he picked a muffled slithering sound which he knew could be made only by men moving through a thin patch of jungle. He peered across the river, trying to determine where the foliage was least dense. At a point between his gun and Wilson's there was a grove of a few coconut trees sparse enough to allow men to assemble; as he stared into that patch of wood, he was certain he heard a man move. Croft's mouth tightened. His hand felt for the bolt of the machine gun, and he slowly brought it to bear on the coconut grove. The rustling grew louder; it seemed as if men were creeping through the brush on the other side of the river to a point opposite his gun. Croft swallowed once. Tiny charges seemed to pulse through his limbs and his head was as empty and shockingly aware as if it had been plunged into a pail of freezing water. He wet his lips and shifted his position slightly, feeling as though he could hear the flexing of his muscles.

The Jap mortar fired again and he started. The shells were falling by the next platoon, the sound painful and jarring to him. He stared out on the moonlit river until his eyes deceived him; he began to think he could see the heads of men in the dark swirls of the current. Croft gazed down at his knees for an instant and then across the river again. He looked a little to the left or right of where he thought the Japanese might be; from long experience he had learned a man could not look directly at an object and see it in the darkness. Something seemed to move in the grove, and a new trickle of sweat formed and rolled down his back. He twisted uncomfortably. Croft was unbearably tense, but the sensation was not wholly unpleasant.

He wondered if Wilson had noticed the sounds, and then in answer to his question, there was the loud unmistakable clicking of a machine gun bolt. To Croft's keyed senses, the sound echoed up and down the river, and he was furious that Wilson should have revealed his position. The rustling in the brush became louder and Croft was convinced he could hear voices whispering on the other side of the river. He fumbled for a grenade and placed it at his feet.

Then he heard a sound which pierced his flesh. Someone called from across the river, 'Yank, Yank!' Croft sat numb. 'That's a Jap,' Croft told himself. He was incapable of moving for that instant.

'Yank!' It was calling to him. 'Yank. We you coming-to-get, Yank.'

The night lay like a heavy stifling mat over the river. Croft tried to breathe.

'*We you coming-to-get, Yank.*'

Croft felt as if a hand had suddenly clapped against his back, traveled up his spine over his skull to clutch at the hair on his forehead. 'Coming to get you, Yank,' he heard himself whisper. He had the agonizing frustration of a man in a nightmare who wants to scream and cannot utter a sound. 'We you *coming-to-get*, Yank.'

He shivered terribly for a moment, and his hands seemed congealed on the machine gun. He could not bear the intense pressure in his head.

'We you coming-to-get, Yank,' the voice screamed.

'COME AND GET ME YOU SONSOFBITCHES,' Croft roared. He shouted with every fibre of his body as though he plunged at an oaken door.

There was no sound at all for perhaps ten seconds, nothing but the moonlight on the river and the taut rapt buzzing of the crickets. Then the voice spoke again. 'Oh, we come, Yank, we come.'

Croft pulled back the bolt on his machine gun, and rammed it home. His heart was still beating with frenzy 'Recon ... RECON, UP ON THE LINE,' he shouted with all his strength.

A machine gun lashed at him from across the river, and he ducked in his hole. In the darkness, it spat a vindictive white light like an acetylene torch, and its sound was terrifying. Croft was holding himself together by the force of his will. He pressed the trigger of his gun and it leapt and bucked under his hand. The tracers spewed wildly into the jungle on the other side of the river.

But the noise, the vibration of his gun, calmed him. He directed it to where he had seen the Japanese gunfire and loosed a volley. The handle pounded against his fist, and he had to steady it with both hands. The hot metallic smell of the barrel eddied back to him, made what he was doing real again. He ducked in his hole waiting for the reply and winced involuntarily as the bullets whipped past.

BEE-YOWWWW! ... BEE-YOOWWWW! Some dirt snapped at his face from the ricochets. Croft was not conscious of feeling it. He had the surface numbness a man has in a fight. He flinched at sounds, his mouth tightened and loosened, his eyes stared, but he was oblivious to his body.

Croft fired the gun again, held it for a long vicious burst, and then ducked in his hole. An awful scream singed the night, and for an instant Croft grinned weakly. Got him he thought. He saw the metal burning through flesh, shattering the bones in its path. 'AII-YOHHHH.' The scream froze him again, and for an odd disconnected instant he experienced again the whole complex of sounds and smells and sights

235

when a calf was branded. 'RECON, UP ... UP!' he shouted furiously and fired steadily for ten seconds to cover their advance. As he paused he could hear some men crawling behind him, and he whispered, 'Recon?'

'Yeah.' Gallagher dropped into the hole with him. 'Mother of Mary,' he muttered. Croft could feel him shaking beside him.

'Stop it!' he gripped his arm tensely. 'The other men up?'

'Yeah.'

Croft looked across the river again. Everything was silent, and the disconnected abrupt spurts of fire were forgotten like vanished sparks from a grindstone. Now that he was no longer alone, Croft was able to plan. The fact that men were up with him, were scattered in the brush along the bank between their two machine guns, recovered his sense of command. 'They're going to attack soon,' he whispered hoarsely in Gallagher's ear.

Gallagher trembled again. 'Ohh. No way to wake up,' he tried to say, but his voice kept lapsing.

'Look,' Croft whispered. 'Creep along the line and tell them to hold fire until the Japs start to cross the river.'

'I can't, I can't,' Gallagher whispered.

Croft felt like striking him. 'Go!' he whispered.

'I can't.'

The Jap machine gun lashed at them from across the river. The bullets went singing into the jungle behind them, ripping at leaves. The tracers looked like red splints of lightning as they flattened into the jungle. A thousand rifles seemed to be firing at them from across the river, and the two men pressed themselves against the bottom of the hole. The sounds cracked against their eardrums. Croft's head ached. Firing the machine gun had partially deafened him. BEE-YOWWWW! A ricochet slapped some more dirt on top of them. Croft felt it pattering on his back this time. He was trying to sense the moment when he would have to raise his head and fire the gun. The firing seemed to slacken, and he lifted up his eyes cautiously. BEE-YOWWWW, BEE-YOWWWW! He dropped in the hole again. The Japanese machine gun raked through the brush at them.

There was a shrill screaming sound, and the men covered their heads with their arms. BAA-ROWWMM, BAA-ROWWMM, ROWWMM, ROWWMM. The mortars exploded all about them, and something picked Gallagher up, shook him, and then released him. 'O God,' he cried. A clod of dirt stung his neck. BAA-ROWWMM, BAA-ROWWMM.

'Jesus, I'm hit,' someone screamed, 'I'm hit. Something hit me.' BAA-ROWWMM.

Gallagher rebelled against the force of the explosions. 'Stop, I give up,' he screamed. 'STOP! ... I give up! I give up!' At that instant he no longer knew what made him cry out.

BAA-ROWWMM, BAA-ROWWMM.

'I'm hit, I'm hit,' someone was screaming. The Japanese rifles were firing again. Croft lay on the floor of the hole with his hands against the ground and every muscle poised in its place.

BAA-ROWWMM. TEEEEEEEEN! The shrapnel was singing as it scattered through the foliage.

Croft picked up his flare gun. The firing had not abated, but through it he heard someone shouting in Japanese. He pointed the gun in the air.

'Here they come,' Croft said.

He fired the flare and shouted, 'STOP 'EM!'

A shrill cry came out of the jungle across the river. It was the scream a man might utter if his foot was being crushed. 'AAAIIIIII, AAAIIIIIIII.'

The flare burst at the moment the Japanese started their charge. Croft had a split perception of the Japanese machine gun firing from a flank, and then began to fire automatically, not looking where he fired, but holding his gun slow, swinging it from side to side. He could not hear the other guns fire, but he saw their muzzle blasts like exhausts.

He had a startling frozen picture of the Japanese running toward him across the narrow river. 'AAAAIIIIIIIIIIH,' he heard again. In the light of the flare the Japanese had the stark frozen quality of men revealed by a shaft of lightning. Croft no longer saw anything clearly, he could not have said at that moment where his hands ended and the machine gun began; he was lost in a vast moil of noise out of which individual screams and shouts etched in his mind for an instant. He could never have counted the Japanese who charged across the river; he knew only that his finger was rigid on the trigger. He could not have loosened it. In those few moments he felt no sense of danger. He just kept firing.

The line of men who charged across the river began to fall. In the water they were slowed considerably and the concentrated fire from recon's side raged at them like a wind across an open field. They began to stumble over the bodies ahead of them. Croft saw one soldier reach into the air behind another's body as though trying to clutch something in the sky and Croft fired at him for what seemed many seconds before the arm collapsed.

He looked to his right and saw three men trying to cross the river where it turned and ran parallel to the bluff. He swung the gun about and lashed them with it. One man fell, and the other two paused uncertainly and began to run back toward their own bank of the river. Croft had no time to follow them; some soldiers had reached the beach on his side and were charging the gun. He fired point blank at them, and they collapsed about five yards from his hole.

Croft fired and fired, switching targets with the quick reflexes of an athlete shifting for a ball. As soon as he saw men falling he would attack another group. The line of Japanese broke into little bunches of men who wavered, began to retreat.

The light of the flare went out and Croft was blinded for a moment. There was no sound again in the darkness and he fumbled for another flare, feeling an almost desperate urgency. 'Where is it?' he whispered to Gallagher.

'What?'

'Shit.' Croft's hands found the flare box, and he loaded the gun again. He was beginning to see in the darkness, and he hesitated. But something moved on the river and he fired the flare. As it burst, a few Japanese soldiers were caught motionless in the water. Croft pivoted his gun on them and fired. One of the soldiers remained standing for an incredible time. There was no expression on his face; he looked vacant and surprised even as the bullets struck him in the chest.

Nothing was moving now on the river. In the light of the flare, the bodies looked as limp and unhuman as bags of grain. One soldier began to float downstream, his face in the water. On the beach near the gun, another Japanese soldier was lying on his back. A wide stain of blood was spreading out from his body, and his stomach, ripped open, gaped like the swollen entrails of a fowl. On an impulse Croft fired a burst into him, and felt a twitch of pleasure as he saw the body quiver.

A wounded man was groaning in Japanese. Every few seconds he would scream, the sound terrifying in the cruel blue light of the flare. Croft picked up a grenade. 'That sonofabitch is makin' too much noise,' he said. He pulled the pin and lobbed the grenade over to the opposite bank. It dropped like a beanbag on one of the bodies, and Croft pulled Gallagher down with him. The explosion was powerful and yet empty like a blast that collapses windowpanes. After a moment, the echoes ceased.

Croft tensed himself and listened to the sounds from across the river. There was the quiet furtive noise of men retreating into the jungle. 'GIVE 'EM A VOLLEY!' he shouted.

All the men in recon began to fire again, and Croft raked the jungle for a minute in short bursts. He could hear Wilson's machine gun pounding steadily. 'I guess we gave 'em something,' Croft told Gallagher. The flare was going out, and Croft stood up. 'Who was hit?' he shouted.

'Toglio.'

'Bad?' Croft asked.

'I'm okay,' Toglio whispered. 'I got a bullet in my elbow.'

'Can you wait till morning?'

There was silence for a moment, then Toglio answered weakly, 'Yeah, I'll be okay.'

Croft got out of his hole. 'I'm coming down,' he announced. 'Hold your fire.' He walked along the path until he reached Toglio. Red and Goldstein were kneeling beside him, and Croft spoke to them in a low voice. 'Pass this on,' he said. 'We're all gonna stay in our holes until mornin'. I don't think they'll be back tonight, but you cain't tell. And no one is gonna fall asleep. They's only about an hour till dawn, so you ain't got nothin' to piss about.'

'I wouldn't go to sleep anyway,' Goldstein breathed. 'What a way to wake up.' It was the same thing Gallagher had said.

'Yeah, well, I just wasn't ridin' on my ass either, waitin' for them to come,' Croft said. He shivered for a moment in the early morning air and realized with a pang of shame that for the first time in his life he had been really afraid. 'The sonsofbitchin' Japs,' he said. His legs were tired and he turned to go back to his gun. I hate the bastards, he said to himself, a terrible rage working through his weary body.

'One of these days I'm gonna really get me a Jap,' he whispered aloud. The river was slowly carrying the bodies downstream.

'At least,' Gallagher said, 'If we got to stay here a couple of days, the fuggers won't be stinkin' up the joint.'

The Reason Why

CECIL WOODHAM SMITH

October 25, 1854, the Crimea. The beleaguered garrison of Balaclava and its surrounding hills and plains have been the scene of confusion and incompetence all day. Inexperienced miltary leaders have continually thwarted their younger officers' desire to secure the position against the Russians. Finally, a fateful order is carried by one of these hot-headed young cavalrymen to the Cavalry Division Commander, Lord Lucan:

LORD RAGLAN WISHES THE CAVALRY TO
ADVANCE RAPIDLY TO THE FRONT –
FOLLOW THE ENEMY AND TRY TO PREVENT
THE ENEMY CARRYING AWAY THE GUNS.
TROOP HORSE ARTILLERY MAY
ACCOMPANY. FRENCH CAVALRY IS ON YOUR
LEFT. IMMEDIATE.

ANY OTHER HORSEMAN would have picked his way with care down that rough, precipitous slope, but Nolan spurred his horse, and up on the heights the watchers held their breath, as, slithering, scrambling, stumbling, he rushed down to the plain.

So far the day had been a terrible one for Edward Nolan; even its sole glory, the charge of the Heavy Brigade, had been gall and wormwood to his soul. He was a light-cavalryman, believing passionately in the superior efficiency of light over heavy horsemen – 'so unwieldy, so encumbered', he had written – and in this, the first cavalry action of the campaign, the light cavalry had done absolutely nothing. Hour after hour, in an agony of impatience, he had watched the Light Cavalry Brigade standing by, motionless, inglorious and, as onlookers had not scrupled to say, shamefully inactive.

For this he furiously blamed Lord Lucan, as he had furiously blamed Lord Lucan on every other occasion when the cavalry had been kept out of action, 'raging', in William Howard Russell's phrase, against him all over the camp. Irish-Italian, excitable, headstrong, recklessly courageous, Nolan was beside himself with irritation and anger as he swooped like an avenging angel from the heights, bearing the order which would

240

force the man he detested and despised to attack at last.

With a sigh of relief the watchers saw him arrive safely, gallop furiously across the plain and, with his horse trembling, sweating and blown from the wild descent, hand the order to Lord Lucan sitting in the saddle between his two brigades. Lucan opened and read it.

The order appeared to him to be utterly obscure. Lord Raglan and General Airey had forgotten that they were looking down from 600 feet. Not only could they survey the whole action, but the inequalities of the plain disappeared when viewed from above. Lucan from his position could see nothing; inequalities of the ground concealed the activity round the redoubts, no single enemy soldier was in sight; nor had he any picture of the movements of the enemy in his mind's eye, because he had unaccountably neglected to take any steps to acquaint himself with the Russian dispositions. He should, after receiving the third order, have made it his business to make some form of reconnaissance; he should, when he found he could see nothing from his position, have shifted his ground – but he did not.

He read the order 'carefully', with the fussy deliberateness which maddened his staff, while Nolan quivered with impatience at his side. It seemed to Lord Lucan that the order was not only obscure but absurd: artillery was to be attacked by cavalry; infantry support was not mentioned; it was elementary that cavalry charging artillery in such circumstances must be annihilated. In his own account of these fatal moments Lucan says that he 'hesitated and urged the uselessness of such an attack and the dangers attending it'; but Nolan, almost insane with impatience, cut him short and 'in a most authoritative tone' repeated the final message he had been given on the heights: 'Lord Raglan's orders are that the cavalry are to attack immediately'.

For such a tone to be used by an aide-de-camp to a Lieutenant-General was unheard of; moreover, Lord Lucan was perfectly aware that Nolan detested him and habitually abused him. It would have been asking a very great deal of any man to keep his temper in such circumstances, and Lord Lucan's temper was violent. He could see nothing, 'neither enemy nor guns being in sight', he wrote, nor did he in the least understand what the order meant. It was said later that Lord Raglan intended the third and fourth orders to be read together, and that the instruction in the third order to advance and recover the heights made it clear that the guns mentioned in the fourth order must be on those heights. Lord Lucan, however, read the two orders separately. He turned angrily on Nolan, 'Attack, sir? Attack what? What guns, sir?'

The crucial moment had arrived. Nolan threw back his head, and, 'in a most disrespectful and significant manner', flung out his arm and, with a furious gesture, pointed, not to the Causeway Heights and the redoubts with the captured British guns, but to the end of the North Valley, where

241

the Russian cavalry routed by the Heavy Brigade were now established with their guns in front of them. 'There, my lord, is your enemy, there are your guns,' he said, and with those words and that gesture the doom of the Light Brigade was sealed.

What did Nolan mean? It has been maintained that his gesture was merely a taunt, that he had no intention of indicating any direction, and that Lord Lucan, carried away by rage, read a meaning into his out-flung arm which was never there.

The truth will never be known, because a few minutes later Nolan was killed, but his behaviour in that short interval indicates that he did believe the attack was to be down the North Valley and on those guns with which the Russian cavalry routed by the Heavy Brigade had been allowed to retire.

It is not difficult to account for such a mistake. Nolan, the cavalry enthusiast and a cavalry commander of talent, was well aware that a magnificent opportunity had been lost when the Light Brigade failed to pursue after the charge of the Heavies. It was, indeed, the outstanding, the flagrant error of the day, and he must have watched with fury and despair as the routed Russians were suffered to withdraw in safety with the much-desired trophies, their guns. When he received the fourth order he was almost off his head with excitement and impatience, and he misread it. He leapt to the joyful conclusion that at last vengeance was to be taken on those Russians who had been suffered to escape. He had not carried the third order, and read by itself the wording of the fourth order was ambiguous. Moreover, Lord Raglan's last words to him, 'Tell Lord Lucan that the cavalry is to attack immediately', were fatally lacking in precision.

And so he plunged down the heights and with a contemptuous gesture, scorning the man who in his opinion was responsible for the wretched mishandling of the cavalry, he pointed down the North Valley. 'There, my lord, is your enemy; there are your guns.'

Lord Lucan felt himself to be in a hideous dilemma. His resentment against Lord Raglan was indescribable; the orders he had received during the battle had been, in his opinion, not only idiotic and ambiguous, but insulting. He had been treated, he wrote later, like a subaltern. He had been peremptorily ordered out of his first position – the excellent position chosen in conjunction with Sir Colin Campbell – consequently after the charge of the Heavies there had been no pursuit. He had received without explanation a vague order to wait for infantry. What infantry? Now came this latest order to take his division and charge to certain death. Throughout the campaign he had had bitter experience of orders from Lord Raglan, and now he foresaw ruin; but he was helpless. The Queen's Regulations laid down that 'all orders sent by aides-de-camp ... are to be obeyed with the same readiness, as if delivered personally by the general officers to whom such aides are attached'. The Duke of Wellington himself had laid this down. Had Lord Lucan refused to execute an order brought by a member of the Headquarters staff and delivered with every assumption of authority he would, in his own words, have had no choice but 'to blow his brains out'.

Nolan's manner had been so obviously insolent that observers thought he would be placed under arrest. Lord Lucan, however, merely shrugged his shoulders and, turning his back on Nolan, trotted off, alone, to where Lord Cardigan was sitting in front of the Light Brigade.

Nolan then rode over to his friend Captain Morris, who was sitting in his saddle in front of the 17th Lancers – the same Captain Morris who had urged Lord Cardigan to pursue earlier in the day – and received permission to ride beside him in the charge.

There was now a pause of several minutes, and it is almost impossible to believe that Nolan, sitting beside his close friend and sympathiser, did not disclose the objective of the charge. If Nolan had believed the attack was to be on the Causeway Heights and the redoubts, he must surely have told Captain Morris. Morris, however, who survived the charge though desperately wounded, believed the attack was to be on the guns at the end of the North Valley.

Meanwhile Lord Lucan, almost for the first time, was speaking directly and personally to Lord Cardigan. Had the two men not detested each other so bitterly, had they been able to examine the order together and discuss its meaning, the Light Brigade might have been saved. Alas, thirty years of hatred could not be bridged; each, however, observed perfect military courtesy. Holding the order in his hand, Lord Lucan informed Lord Cardigan of the contents and ordered him to advance down the North Valley with the Light Brigade, while he himself followed in support with the Heavy Brigade.

Lord Cardigan now took an astonishing step. Much as he hated the man before him, rigid as were his ideas of military etiquette, he remonstrated with his superior officer. Bringing down his sword in salute he said, 'Certainly, sir; but allow me to point out to you that the Russians have a battery in the valley on our front, and batteries and riflemen on both sides.'

Lord Lucan once more shrugged his shoulders. 'I know it,' he said; 'but Lord Raglan will have it. We have no choice but to obey'. Lord Cardigan made no further comment, but saluted again. Lord Lucan then instructed him to 'advance very steadily and keep his men well in hand'. Lord Cardigan saluted once more, wheeled his horse and rode over to his second-in-command, Lord George Paget, remarking aloud to himself as he did so, 'Well, here goes the last of the Brudenells.'

Most of the officers and men of the Light Brigade were lounging by their horses, the officers eating biscuits and hardboiled eggs and drinking rum and water from their flasks. One or two of the men had lighted pipes, and were told to put them out at once, and not disgrace their regiments by smoking in the presence of the enemy. Lord George Paget, who had just lighted a cigar, felt embarrassed. Was he setting a bad example? Ought he to throw away his excellent cigar, a rarity in Balaclava? While he was debating the point Lord Cardigan rode up and said, 'Lord George, we are ordered to make an attack to the front. You will take command of the second line, and I expect your best support – mind, your best support.' Cardigan, who was very much excited, repeated the last sentence twice very loudly, and Lord George, rather irritated, replied as loudly, 'You shall have it, my lord.' It was the first intimation Lord George had had of an intended attack; he thought it was permissible to keep his cigar, and noticed that it lasted him until he got to the guns.

Lord Cardigan now hastened at a gallop back to his troops and drew the brigade up in two lines: the first the 13th Light Dragoons, 11th Hussars and the 17th Lancers; the second the 4th Light Dragoons and the main body of the 8th Hussars. A troop of the 8th Hussars, under Captain Duberly, had been detached to act as escort to Lord Raglan.

At the last moment Lord Lucan irritatingly interfered and ordered the 11th Hussars to fall back in support of the first lines, so that there were now three lines, with the 13th Light Dragoons and the 17th Lancers leading. Lord Lucan's interference was made more annoying by the fact that he gave the order, not to Cardigan, but directly to Colonel Douglas, who commanded the 11th. Moreover, the 11th was Cardigan's own regiment, of which he was inordinately proud, and the 11th was taken out of the first line, while the 17th Lancers, Lucan's old regiment, remained.

Lord Cardigan meanwhile had placed himself quite alone, about two lengths in front of his staff and five lengths in advance of his front line. He now drew his sword and raised it, a single trumpet sounded, and without any signs of excitement and in a quiet voice he gave the orders, 'The Brigade will advance. Walk, march, trot,' and the three lines of the Light Brigade began to move, followed after a few minutes' interval by the Heavy Brigade, led by Lord Lucan. The troop of Horse Artillery was left behind because part of the valley was ploughed.

The North Valley was about a mile and a quarter long and a little less than a mile wide. On the Fedioukine Hills, which enclosed the valley to the north, were drawn up eight battalions of infantry, four squadrons of cavalry and fourteen guns; on the Causeway Heights to the south were the bulk of the eleven battalions, with thirty guns and a field battery which had captured the redoubts earlier in the day; at the end of the valley, facing the Light Brigade, the mass of the Russian cavalry which had been defeated by the Heavy Brigade was drawn up in three lines, with twelve guns unlimbered before them, strengthened by six additional squadrons of Lancers, three on each flank. The Light Brigade was not merely to run a gauntlet of fire; it was advancing into a deadly three-sided trap, from which there was no escape.

The Brigade was not up to strength, cholera and dysentery having taken their toll – the five regiments present could muster only about 700 of all ranks, and both regiments in the first line, the 17th Lancers and the 13th Light Dragoons, were led by captains, Captain Morris and Captain Oldham respectively.

Nevertheless, the Brigade made a brave show as they trotted across the short turf. They were the finest light horsemen in Europe, drilled and disciplined to perfection, bold by nature, filled with British self-confidence, burning to show the 'damned Heavies' what the Light Brigade could do.

As the Brigade moved, a sudden silence fell over the battlefield: by chance for a moment gun- and rifle-fire ceased, and the watchers on the heights felt the pause was sinister. More than half a century afterwards old men recalled that as the Light Brigade moved to its doom a strange hush fell, and it became so quiet that the jingle of bits and accoutrements could be clearly heard.

The Brigade advanced with beautiful precision, Lord Cardigan riding alone at their head, a brilliant and gallant figure. It was his great day: he was performing the task for which he was supremely well fitted, no power of reflection or intelligence was asked of him, dauntless physical courage was the only requirement, and he had, as Lord Raglan said truly, 'the heart of a lion'. He rode quietly at a trot, stiff and upright in the saddle, never once looking back: a cavalry commander about to lead a charge must keep strictly looking forward; if he looks back his men will receive an impression of uncertainty.

He wore the gorgeous uniform of the 11th Hussars and, living as he did on his yacht, he had been able to preserve it in pristine splendour. The bright sunlight lit up the brilliance of cherry colour and royal blue, the richness of fur and plume and lace; instead of wearing his gold-laced pelisse dangling from his shoulders, he had put it on as a coat, and his figure, slender as a young man's, in spite of his fifty-seven years, was outlined in a blaze of gold. He rode his favourite charger, Ronald, 'a thoroughbred chestnut of great beauty', and as he led his Brigade steadily down the valley towards the guns he was, as his aide-de-camp Sir George Wombwell wrote, 'the very incarnation of bravery'.

Before the Light Brigade had advanced fifty yards the hush came to an end: the Russian guns crashed out, and great clouds of smoke rose at the end of the valley. A moment later an extraordinary and inexplicable incident took place. The advance was proceeding at a steady trot when suddenly Nolan, riding beside his friend Captain Morris in the first line, urged on his horse and began to gallop diagonally across the front. Morris thought that Nolan was losing his head with excitement, and, knowing that a mile and a quarter must be traversed before the guns were reached, shouted, 'That won't do, Nolan! We've a long way to go and must be steady.' Nolan took no notice; galloping madly ahead and to the right, he crossed in front of Lord Cardigan – an unprecedented breach of military etiquette – and, turning in his saddle, shouted and waved his sword as if he would address the Brigade, but the guns were firing with great crashes, and not a word could be heard. Had he suddenly realised that his interpretation of the order had been wrong, and that in his impetuosity he had directed the Light Brigade to certain death? No one will ever know, because at that moment a Russian shell burst on the right of Lord Cardigan, and a fragment tore its way into Nolan's breast, exposing his heart. The sword fell from his hand, but his right arm was still erect, and his body remained rigid in the saddle. His horse wheeled and began to gallop back through the advancing Brigade, and then from the body there burst a strange and appalling cry, a shriek so unearthly as to freeze the blood of all who heard him. The terrified horse carried the body, still shrieking, through the 4th Light Dragoons, and then at last Nolan fell from the saddle, dead.

Lord Cardigan, looking strictly straight ahead and not aware of Nolan's death, was transported with fury. It was his impression that Nolan had been trying to take the command of the Brigade away from him, to lead the charge himself; and so intense was his rage that when he was asked what he thought about as he advanced towards the guns, he replied that his mind was entirely occupied with anger against Nolan.

The first few hundred yards of the advance of the Light Brigade covered the same ground, whether the attack was to be on the guns on the Causeway Heights or the guns at the end of the valley. The Russians assumed that the redoubts were to be charged, and the watchers on the heights saw the Russian infantry retire first from Redoubt No. 3 and then from No. 2 and form hollow squares to receive the expected charge; but the Light Brigade, incredibly, made no attempt to wheel. With a gasp of horror, the watchers saw the lines of horsemen continue straight on down the North Valley.

The Russian artillery and riflemen on the Fedioukine Hills and the slopes of the Causeway Heights were absolutely taken by surprise; it was not possible to believe that this small force trotting down the North Valley in such beautiful order intended to attempt an attack on the battery at the end of the valley, intended, utterly helpless as it was, to expose itself to a cross fire, of the most frightful and deadly kind, to which it had no possibility of replying. There was again a moment's pause, and then from the Fedioukine Hills on one side and the Causeway Heights on the other, battalion upon battalion of riflemen, battery upon battery of guns, poured down fire on the Light Brigade.

When advancing calvary are caught in a withering fire and are too courageous to think of retreat, it is their instinct to quicken their pace, to gallop forward as fast as individual horses will carry them and get to grips with the enemy as soon as possible. But Lord Cardigan tightly restrained the pace of the Light Brigade: the line was to advance with parade-ground perfection. The inner squadron of the 17th Lancers broke into a canter, Captain White, its leader, being, he said, 'frankly anxious to get out of such a murderous fire and into the guns as being the lesser of two evils', and he shot forward, level with his brigadier. Lord Cardigan checked him instantly; lowering his sword and laying it across Captain White's breast, he told him sharply not to ride level with his commanding officer and not to force the pace. Private Wightman of the 17th Lancers, riding behind, heard his stern, hoarse voice rising above the din of the guns 'Steady, steady, the 17th Lancers.' Otherwise during the whole course of the charge Lord Cardigan neither spoke nor made any sign.

All he could see at the end of the valley as he rode was a white bank of smoke, through which from time to time flashed great tongues of flame marking the position of the guns. He chose one which seemed to be about the centre of the battery and rode steadily for it, neither turning in his saddle nor moving his head. Erect, rigid and dauntless, his bearing contributed enormously to the steadiness, the astonishing discipline which earned the Charge of the Light Brigade immortality.

And now the watchers on the heights saw that the lines of horsemen, like toys down on the plain, were expanding and contracting with strange mechanical precision. Death was coming fast, and the Light Brigade was meeting death in perfect order; as a man or horse dropped, the riders on each side of him opened out; as soon as they had ridden clear the ranks closed again. Orderly, as if on the parade-ground, the Light Brigade rode on, but its numbers grew every moment smaller and smaller as they moved down the valley. Those on the heights who could understand what that regular mechanical movement meant in terms of discipline and courage were intolerably moved, and one old soldier burst into tears. It was at this moment that Bosquet, the French General, observed 'C'est magnifique mais ce n'est pas la guerre'.

The fire grew fiercer; the first line was now within range of the guns at the end of the valley, as well as the fire pouring from both flanks. Round-shot, grape and shells began to mow men down not singly, but by groups; the pace quickened and quickened again – the men could no longer be restrained, and the trot became a canter.

The Heavy Brigade were being left behind; slower in any case than the Light Cavalry, they were wearied by their earlier action and, as the pace of the Light Brigade quickened, the gap began to widen rapidly. At this moment the Heavy Brigade came under the withering cross-fire which had just torn the Light Brigade to pieces. Lord Lucan, leading the Brigade, was wounded in the leg and his horse hit in two places; one of

247

his aides was killed, and two of his staff wounded. Looking back, he saw that his two leading regiments – the Greys and the Royals – were sustaining heavy casualties. In the Royals twenty-one men had already fallen. Lord Lucan's indifference under fire was remarkable: it was on this occasion that an officer described as 'one of his most steady haters' admitted, 'Yes, damn him, he's brave', but he felt himself once more in a dilemma. Should he continue to advance and destroy the Heavy Brigade, or should he halt and leave the Light Brigade to its fate without support? He turned to Lord William Paulet, who was riding at his side and had just had his forage cap torn off his head by a musket ball. 'They have sacrificed the Light Brigade: they shall not the Heavy, if I can help it,' he said. Ordering the halt to be sounded, he retired the brigade out of range and waited, having decided in his own words that 'the only use to which the Heavy Brigade could be turned was to protect the Light Cavalry against pursuit on their return'.

With sadness and horror the Heavy Brigade watched the Light Brigade go on alone down the valley and vanish in smoke. Help now came from the French. As a result of General Canrobert's earlier order the Chasseurs d'Afrique were drawn up beneath the heights. Originally raised as irregular cavalry, this force, which had a record of extraordinary distinction, now consisted of French troopers, mounted on Algerian horses.

Their commander, General Morris, had seen the Light Brigade fail to wheel and advance down the valley to certain doom with stupefied horror. Nothing could be done for them, but he determined to aid the survivors. He ordered the Chasseurs d'Afrique to charge the batteries and infantry battalions on the Fedioukine Hills. Galloping as if by a miracle over broken and scrubby ground in a loose formation learned in their campaigns in the Atlas mountains of Morocco, they attacked with brilliant success. Both Russian artillery and infantry were forced to retreat, and at a cost of only thirty-eight casualties – ten killed and twenty-eight wounded – the fire from the Fedioukine Hills was silenced. Such remnants of the Light Brigade as might return would now endure fire only on one flank: from the Causeway Heights.

The first line of the Light Brigade was now more than halfway down the valley, and casualties were so heavy that the squadrons could no longer keep their entity: formation was lost and the front line broke into a gallop, the regiments racing each other as they rode down to death. 'Come on,' yelled a trooper of the 13th to his comrades, 'come on. Don't let those b——s of the 17th get in front of us.' The men, no longer to be restrained, began to shoot forward in front of their officers, and Lord Cardigan was forced to increase his pace or be overwhelmed. The gallop became headlong, the troopers cheering and yelling; their blood was up, and they were on fire to get at the enemy. Hell for leather, with whistling bullets and crashing shells taking their toll every moment, cheers changing to death-cries, horses falling with a scream, the first line of the Light Brigade – 17th Lancers and 13th Light Dragoons – raced down the valley to the guns. Close behind them came the second line. Lord George Paget, remembering Lord Cardigan's stern admonition, 'Your best support mind, your best support', had increased the pace of his regiment, the 4th Light Dragoons, and caught up the 11th Hussars. The 8th Hussars, sternly kept in hand by their commanding officer, Colonel Shewell, advanced at a steady trot, and refused to increase their pace. The second line therefore consisted of the 4th Light Dragoons and the 11th Hussars, with the 8th Hussars to the right rear.

As they, too, plunged into the inferno of fire, and as batteries and massed riflemen on each flank began to tear gaps in their ranks and trooper after trooper came crashing to the ground, they had a new and horrible difficulty to face. The ground was strewn with casualties of the first line – not only dead men and dead horses, but horses and men not yet dead, able to crawl, to scream, to writhe. They had perpetually to avoid riding over men they knew, while riderless horses, some unhurt, some horribly injured, tried to force their way into the ranks. Troop-horses in battle, as long as they feel the hand of their rider and his weight on their backs, are, even when wounded, singularly free from fear. When Lord George Paget's charger was hit, he was astonished to find the horse showed no sign of panic. But, once deprived of his rider, the troop-horse becomes crazed with terror. He does not gallop out of the action and seek safety: trained to range himself in line, he seeks the companionship of other horses, and, mad with fear, eyeballs protruding, he attempts to attach himself to some leader or to force himself into the ranks of the nearest squadrons. Lord George, riding in advance of the second line, found himself actually in danger. The poor brutes made dashes at him, trying to gallop with him. At one moment he was riding in the midst of seven riderless horses, who cringed and pushed against him as round-shot and bullets came by, covering him with blood from their wounds, and so nearly unhorsing him that he was forced to use his sword to free himself.

And all the time, through the cheers, the groans, the ping of bullets whizzing through the air, the whirr and crash of shells, the earth-shaking thunder of galloping horses' hooves, when men were not merely falling one by one but being swept away in groups, words of command rang out as on the parade-ground, 'Close in to your centre. Back the right flank! Keep up, Private Smith. Left squadron, keep back. Look to your dressing.' Until at last, as the ranks grew thinner and thinner, only one command was heard: 'Close in! Close in! Close in to the centre! Close in! Close in!'

Eight minutes had now passed since the advance began, and Lord

Cardigan, with the survivors of the first line hard on his heels, galloping furiously but steadily, was within a few yards of the battery. The troopers could see the faces of the gunners, and Lord Cardigan selected the particular space between two guns where he intended to enter. One thought, wrote a survivor, was in all their minds: they were nearly out of it at last, and close on the accursed guns, and Lord Cardigan, still sitting rigid in his saddle, 'steady as a church', waved his sword over his head. At that moment there was a roar, the earth trembled, huge flashes of flame shot out and the smoke became so dense that darkness seemed to fall. The Russian gunners had fired a salvo from their twelve guns into the first line of the Light Brigade at a distance of eighty yards. The first line ceased to exist. To the second line, riding behind, it was as if the line had simply dissolved. Lord Cardigan's charger Ronald was blown sideways by the blast, a torrent of flame seemed to belch down his right side, and for a moment he thought he had lost a leg. He was, he estimated, only two or three lengths from the mouths of the guns. Then wrenching Ronald's head round, he drove into the smoke and, charging into the space he had previously selected, was the first man into the battery. And now the Heavy Brigade, watching in an agony of anxiety and impatience, became aware of a sudden and sinister silence. No roars, no great flashes of flame came from the guns – all was strangely, menacingly quiet. Nothing could be seen: the pall of smoke hung like a curtain over the end of the valley; only from time to time through their glasses the watchers saw riderless horses gallop out and men stagger into sight to fall prostrate among the corpses of their comrades littering the ground.

Fifty men only, blinded and stunned, had survived from the first line. Private Wightman of the 17th Lancers felt the frightful crash, saw his captain fall dead; then his horse made a 'tremendous leap into the air', though what he jumped at Wightman never knew – the pall of smoke was so dense that he could not see his arm before him – but suddenly he was in the battery, and in the darkness there were sounds of fighting and slaughter. The scene was extraordinary: smoke so obscured the sun that it was barely twilight, and in the gloom the British troopers, maddened with excitement, cut and thrust and hacked like demons, while the Russian gunners with superb courage fought to remove the guns.

While the struggle went on in the battery, another action was taking place outside. Twenty survivors of the 17th Lancers – the regiment was reduced to thirty-seven men – riding behind Captain Morris had outflanked the battery on the left, and, emerging from the smoke, suddenly found themselves confronted with a solid mass of Russian cavalry drawn up behind the guns. Turning in his saddle, Morris shouted, 'Now, remember what I have told you, men, and keep together', and without a moment's hesitation charged. Rushing himself upon the

Russian officer in command, he engaged him in single combat and ran him through the body. The Russians again received the charge halted, allowed the handful of British to penetrate their ranks, broke and retreated in disorder, pursued by the 17th. Within a few seconds an overwhelming body of Cossacks came up, the 17th were forced to retreat in their turn, and, fighting like madmen, every trooper encircled by a swarm of Cossacks, they tumbled back in confusion towards the guns. Morris was left behind unconscious with his skull cut open in two places.

Meanwhile in those few minutes the situation in the battery had completely changed. In the midst of the struggle for the guns, Colonel Mayow, the Brigade Major, looked up and saw a body of Russian cavalry preparing to descend in such force that the men fighting in the battery must inevitably be overwhelmed. Shouting, 'Seventeenth! Seventeenth! this way! this way!' he collected the remaining survivors of the 17th and all that was left of the 13th Light Dragoons – some twelve men – and, placing himself at their head, charged out of the battery, driving the Russians before him until he was some 500 yards away.

At this moment the second line swept down. The 11th Hussars outflanked the battery, as the 17th had done; the 8th Hussars had not yet come up, but the 4th Light Dragoons under Lord George Paget crashed into the battery. So great was the smoke and the confusion that Lord George did not see the battery until his regiment was on top of it. As they rode headlong down, one of his officers gave a 'View halloo', and suddenly they were in and fighting among the guns. The Russian gunners, with great courage, persisted in their attempt to take the guns away, and the 4th Light Dragoons, mad with excitement, fell on them with savage frenzy. A cut-and-thrust, hand-to-hand combat raged, in which the British fought like tigers, one officer tearing at the Russians with his bare hands and wielding his sword in a delirium of slaughter. After the battle this officer's reaction was so great that he sat down and burst into tears. Brave as the Russians were, they were forced to give way; the Russian gunners were slaughtered, and the 4th Light Dragoons secured absolute mastery of every gun.

While this fierce and bloody combat was being waged, Colonel Douglas, outflanking the battery with the 11th Hussars, had charged a body of Lancers on the left with considerable success, only to find himself confronted with the main body of the Russian cavalry, and infantry in such strength that he felt he was confronted by the whole Russian army. He had hastily to retreat with a large Russian force following in pursuit.

Meanwhile the 4th Light Dragoons, having silenced the guns, had pressed on out of the battery and beyond it. Lord George had, he said, an idea that somewhere ahead was Lord Cardigan, and Lord Cardigan's admonition enjoining his best support was 'always ringing in his ears.' As they advanced they collided with the 11th in their retreat, and the two groups, numbering not more than seventy men, joined together. Their situation was desperate. Advancing on them were enormous masses of Russian cavalry – the leading horsemen were actually within a few hundred yards; but Lord George noticed the great mass was strangely disorderly in its movements and displayed the hesitation and bewilderment the Russian cavalry had shown when advancing on the Heavy Brigade in the morning. Reining in his horse, Lord George shouted at the top of his voice, 'Halt front; if you don't front, my boys, we are done'. The 11th checked, and, with admirable steadiness, the whole group 'halted and fronted as if they had been on parade'. So for a few minutes the handful of British calvary faced the advancing army. The movement had barely been completed when a trooper shouted, 'They are attacking us, my lord, in our rear', and, looking round, Lord George saw, only 500 yards away, a formidable body of Russian Lancers formed up in the direct line of retreat. Lord George turned to his major: 'We are in a desperate scrape; what the devil shall we do? Has anyone seen Lord Cardigan?'

When Lord Cardigan dashed into the battery he had, by a miracle, passed through the gap between the two guns unhurt, and in a few seconds was clear – the first man into the battery and the first man out. Behind him, under the pall of smoke, in murk and gloom, a savage combat was taking place, but Lord Cardigan neither turned back nor paused. In his opinion, he said later, it was 'no part of a general's duty to fight the enemy among private soldiers'; he galloped on, until suddenly he was clear of the smoke, and before him, less than 100 yards away, he saw halted a great mass of Russian cavalry. His charger was wild with excitement, and before he could be checked Lord Cardigan had been carried to within twenty yards of the Russians. For a moment they stared at each other, the Russians utterly astonished by the sudden apparition of this solitary horseman, gorgeous and glittering with gold. By an amazing coincidence, one of the officers, Prince Radzivill, recognised Lord Cardigan – they had met in London at dinners and balls – and the Prince detached a troop of Cossacks with instructions to capture him alive. To this coincidence Lord Cardigan probably owed his life. The Cossacks approached him, but did not attempt to cut him down and after a short encounter in which he received a slight wound on the thigh he evaded them by wheeling his horse, galloped back through the guns again, and came out almost where, only a few minutes earlier, he had dashed in.

By this time the fight in the guns was over, and the battery, still veiled with smoke, was a hideous, confused mass of dead and dying. The second line had swept on, and Lord George Paget and Colonel Douglas, with their handful of survivors, were now halted, with the Russian army both in front of them and behind them, asking 'Where is Lord Cardigan?'

Lord Cardigan, however, looking up the valley over the scene of the charge, could see no sign of his brigade. The valley was strewn with dead and dying; small groups of men wounded or unhorsed were struggling towards the British lines; both his aides-de-camp had vanished; he had ridden never once looking back, and had no idea of what the fate of his brigade had been. Nor had he any feeling of responsibility – in his own words, having 'led the Brigade and launched them with due impetus, he considered his duty was done'. The idea of trying to find out what had happened to his men or of rallying the survivors never crossed his mind. With extraordinary indifference to danger he had led the Light Brigade down the valley as if he were leading a charge in a review in Hyde Park, and he now continued to behave as if he were in a review in Hyde Park. He had, however, he wrote, some apprehension that for a general his isolated position was unusual, and he avoided any undignified appearance of haste by riding back very slowly, most of the time at a walk. By another miracle he was untouched by the fire from the Causeway Heights, which, although the batteries on the Fedioukine Hills had been silenced by the French, was still raking the unfortunate survivors of the charge in the valley. As he rode he continued to brood on Nolan's behaviour, and on nothing else. The marvellous ride, the dauntless valour of the Light Brigade and their frightful destruction, his own miraculous escape from death, made no impression on his mind; Nolan's insubordination occupied him exclusively, and when he reached the point where the Heavy Brigade was halted, he rode up to General Scarlett and immediately broke into accusations of Nolan, furiously complaining of Nolan's insubordination, his ride across the front of the brigade, his attempt to assume command and, Lord Cardigan finished contemptuously, 'Imagine the fellow screaming like a woman when he was hit.' General Scarlett checked him: 'Say no more, my lord; you have just ridden over Captain Nolan's dead body.'

Meanwhile the seventy survivors of the 4th Light Dragoons and 11th Hussars under Lord George Paget, unaware that their General had retired from the field, were preparing to sell their lives dearly. There seemed little hope for them: they were a rabble, their horses worn out, many men wounded. Nevertheless, wheeling about, and jamming spurs into the exhausted horses, they charged the body of Russian Lancers who barred their retreat, 'as fast', wrote Lord George Paget 'as our poor tired horses could carry us'. As the British approached, the Russians, who had been in close column across their path, threw back their right, thus presenting a sloping front, and, with the air of uncertainty Lord George had noticed earlier, stopped – did nothing. The British, at a distance of a horse's length only, were allowed to 'shuffle and edge away', brushing along the Russian front and parrying thrusts from Russian lances. Lord George said his sword crossed the end of lances three or four times, but all the Russians did was to jab at him. It seems probable that the

Russians, having witnessed the destruction of the main body of the Light Brigade, were not greatly concerned with the handfuls of survivors. So, without the loss of a single man, 'and how I know not', wrote Lord George, the survivors of the 4th Light Dragoons and the 11th Hussars escaped once more, and began the painful retreat back up the valley.

One other small body of survivors had also been fighting beyond the guns. The 8th Hussars, restrained with an iron hand by their commanding officer, Colonel Shewell, had reached the battery in beautiful formation to find the 4th Light Dragoons had done their work and the guns were silenced. Colonel Shewell then led his men through the battery and halted on the other side, enquiring, like Lord George Paget, 'Where is Lord Cardigan?' For about three minutes the 8th Hussars waited, then on the skyline appeared lances. The fifteen men of the 17th Lancers, who with the few survivors of the 13th Light Dragoons had charged out of the battery before the second line attacked, were now retreating, with a large Russian force in pursuit. Colonel Mayow, their leader, galloped up to Colonel Shewell. 'Where is Lord Cardigan?' he asked. At that moment Colonel Shewell turned his head and saw that he, too, was not only menaced in front: in his rear a large force of Russian cavalry had suddenly come up, and was preparing to cut off his retreat and the retreat of any other survivors of the Light Brigade who might still be alive beyond the guns. A stern, pious man, by no means popular with his troops, Colonel Shewell had the harsh courage of Cromwell's Bible soldiers. Assuming command, he wheeled the little force into line and gave the order to charge. He himself, discarding his sword – he was a poor swordsman – gripped his reins in both hands, put down his head and rushed like a thunderbolt at the Russian commanding officer. The Russian stood his ground, but his horse flinched. Shewell burst through the gap and was carried through the ranks to the other side. Riding for their lives, his seventy-odd troopers dashed after him. The Russians were thrown into confusion and withdrew, and the way was clear.

But what was to be done next? Colonel Shewell paused. No supports were coming up, Lord Cardigan was not to be seen; there was nothing for it but retreat, and, just ahead of Lord George Paget and Colonel Douglas with the 4th Light Dragoons and the 11th Hussars, the other survivors of the Light Brigade began slowly and painfully to trail back up the valley.

Confusion was utter. No one knew what had taken place, who was alive or who was dead; no control existed; no one gave orders; no one knew what to do next. At the time when the survivors of the Light Brigade had begun to trail up the valley, Captain Lockwood, one of Lord Cardigan's three aides-de-camp, suddenly rode up to Lord Lucan.

'My lord, can you tell me where is Lord Cardigan?' he asked. Lord Lucan replied that Lord Cardigan had gone by some time ago, upon which Captain Lockwood, misunderstanding him, turned his horse's head, rode down into the valley and was never seen again.

The retreat, wrote Robert Portal, was worse than the advance. Men and horses were utterly exhausted and almost none was unhurt. Troopers who had become attached to their horses refused to leave them behind, and wounded and bleeding men staggered along, dragging with them wounded and bleeding beasts. Horses able to move were given up to wounded men; Major de Salis of the 8th Hussars retreated on foot, leading his horse with a wounded trooper in the saddle. All formation had been lost, and it was a rabble who limped painfully along. Mrs Duberly on the heights saw scattered groups of men appearing at the end of the valley. 'What can those skirmishers be doing?' she asked. 'Good God! It is the Light Brigade!' The pace was heartbreakingly slow; most survivors were on foot; little groups of men dragged along step by step, leaning on each other. At first Russian Lancers made harassing attacks, swooping down, cutting off stragglers, and taking prisoners, but when the retreating force came under fire from the Causeway Heights the Russians sustained casualties from their own guns and were withdrawn. Nearly a mile had to be covered, every step under fire; but the fire came from one side only, and the straggling trail of men offered no such target as the brilliant squadrons in parade order which had earlier swept down the valley. The wreckage of men and horses was piteous. 'What a scene of havoc was this last mile – strewn with the dead and dying and all friends!' wrote Lord George Paget. Men recognised their comrades, 'some running, some limping, some crawling', saw horses in the trappings of their regiments 'in every position of agony struggling to get up, then floundering back again on their mutilated riders'. So, painfully, step by step, under heavy fire, the exhausted, bleeding remnants of the Light Brigade dragged themselves back to safety. As each group stumbled in, it was greeted with ringing cheers. Men ran down to meet their comrades and wrung them by the hand, as if they had struggled back from the depths of hell itself.

One of the last to return was Lord George Paget, and as he toiled up the slope he was greeted by Lord Cardigan, 'riding composedly from the opposite direction'. Lord George was extremely angry with Lord Cardigan; later he wrote an official complaint of his conduct. He considered it was Lord Cardigan's 'bounden duty', after strictly enjoining that Lord George should give his best support – 'your best support, mind' – to 'see him out of it'; instead of which Lord Cardigan had disappeared, leaving his Brigade to its fate. 'Halloa, Lord Cardigan! were you not there?' he said. 'Oh, wasn't I, though!' replied Lord Cardigan. 'Here, Jenyns, did you not see me at the guns?' Captain Jenyns, one of the few survivors of the 13th Light Dragoons, answered that he had: he had been very near Lord Cardigan at the time when he entered the battery.

Out of this conversation, and a feeling that Lord Cardigan's desertion of his brigade could not be reconciled with heroism, grew a legend that Lord Cardigan never had taken part in the charge. During his life-time he was haunted by the whisper, and as late as 1909 Wilfrid Scawen Blunt was told positively that 'Cardigan was not in the charge at all, being all the time on board his yacht, and only arrived on the field of battle as his regiment was on its way back from the Valley of Death'.

When the last survivors had trailed in, the remnants of the Light Brigade re-formed on a slope looking southward over Balaclava. The charge had lasted twenty minutes from the moment the trumpet sounded the advance to the return of the last survivor. Lord Cardigan rode forward. 'Men, it is a mad-brained trick, but it is no fault of mine', he said in his loud, hoarse voice. A voice answered, 'Never mind, my lord; we are ready to go again', and the roll-call began, punctuated by the melancholy sound of pistol-shots as the farriers went round despatching ruined horses.

Some 700 horsemen had charged down the valley, and 195 had returned. The 17th Lancers was reduced to thirty-seven troopers, the 13th Light Dragoons could muster only two officers and eight mounted men; 500 horses had been killed.

The Affair at Coulter's Notch

AMBROSE BIERCE

'DO YOU THINK, COLONEL, that your brave Coulter would like to put one of his guns in here!' the General asked.

He was apparently not altogether serious; it certainly did not seem a place where any artillerist, however brave, would like to put a gun. The Colonel thought that possibly his division commander meant good-humouredly to intimate that Captain Coulter's courage had been too highly extolled in a recent conversation between them.

'General,' he replied warmly, 'Coulter would like to put a gun anywhere within reach of those people,' with a motion of his hand in the direction of the enemy.

'It is the only place,' said the General. He was serious, then.

The place was a depression, a 'notch', in the sharp crest of a hill. It was a pass, and through it ran a turnpike, which, reaching this highest point in its course by a sinuous ascent through a thin forest, made a similar, though less steep, descent toward the enemy. For a mile to the left and a mile to the right the ridge, though occupied by Federal infantry lying close behind the sharp crest, and appearing as if held in place by atmospheric pressure, was inaccessible to artillery. There was no place but the bottom of the notch, and that was barely wide enough for the roadbed. From the Confederate side this point was commanded by two batteries posted on a slightly lower elevation beyond a creek, and a half-mile away. All the guns but one were masked by the trees of an orchard; that one – it seemed a bit of impudence – was directly in front of a rather grandiose building, the planter's dwelling. The gun was safe enough in its exposure – but only because the Federal infantry had been forbidden to fire. Coulter's Notch – it came to be called so – was not, that pleasant summer afternoon, a place where one would 'like to put a gun'.

Three or four dead horses lay there, sprawling in the road, three or four dead men in a trim row at one side of it, and a little back, down the hill. All but one were cavalrymen belonging to the Federal advance. One was a quartermaster. The General commanding the division and the Colonel commanding the brigade, with their staffs and escorts, had ridden into the notch to have a look at the enemy's guns – which had straightway obscured themselves in towering clouds of smoke. It was hardly

257

profitable to be curious about guns which had the trick of the cuttlefish, and the season of observation was brief. At its conclusion – a short remove backward from where it began – occurred the conversation already partly reported. 'It is the only place,' the General repeated thoughtfully, 'to get at them.'

The Colonel looked at him gravely. 'There is room for but one gun, General – one against twelve.'

'That is true – for only one at a time,' said the commander with something like, yet not altogether like, a smile. 'But then, your brave Coulter – a whole battery in himself.'

The tone of irony was now unmistakable. It angered the Colonel, but he did not know what to say. The spirit of military subordination is not favourable to retort, nor even deprecation. At this moment a young officer of artillery came riding slowly up the road attended by his bugler. It was Captain Coulter. He could not have been more than twenty-three years of age. He was of medium height, but very slender and lithe, sitting his horse with something of the air of a civilian. In face he was of a type singularly unlike the men about him; thin, high-nosed, grey-eyed, with a slight blond moustache, and long, rather straggling hair of the same colour. There was an apparent negligence in his attire. His cap was worn with the visor a trifle askew; his coat was buttoned only at the sword belt, showing a considerable expanse of white shirt, tolerably clean for that stage of the campaign. But the negligence was all in his dress and bearing; in his face was a look of intense interest in his surroundings. His grey eyes, which seemed occasionally to strike right and left across the landscape, like searchlights, were for the most part fixed upon the sky beyond the Notch; until he should arrive at the summit of the road, there was nothing else in that direction to see. As he came opposite his division and brigade commanders at the roadside he saluted mechanically and was about to pass on. Moved by a sudden impulse, the Colonel signed him to halt.

'Captain Coulter,' he said, 'the enemy has twelve pieces over there on the next ridge. If I rightly understand the General, he directs that you bring up a gun and engage them.'

There was a blank silence; the General looked stolidly at a distant regiment swarming slowly up the hill through rough undergrowth, like a torn and draggled cloud of blue smoke; the Captain appeared not to have observed him. Presently the Captain spoke, slowly and with apparent effort: –

'On the next ridge, did you say, sir? Are the guns near the house?'

'Ah, you have been over this road before! Directly at the house.'

'And it is – necessary – to engage them? The order is imperative?'

His voice was husky and broken. He was visibly paler. The Colonel was astonished and mortified. He stole a glance at the commander. In that set, immobile face was no sign; it was as hard as bronze. A moment later the General rode away, followed by his staff and escort. The Colonel, humiliated and indignant, was about to order Captain Coulter into arrest, when the latter spoke a few words in a low tone to his bugler, saluted, and rode straight forward into the Notch, where, presently, at the summit of the road, his field-glass at his eyes, he showed against the sky, he and his horse, sharply defined and motionless as an equestrian statue. The bugler had dashed down the road in the opposite direction at headlong speed and disappeared behind a wood. Presently his bugle was heard singing in the cedars, and in an incredibly short time a single gun with its caisson, each drawn by six horses and manned by its full complement of gunners, came bounding and banging up the grade in a storm of dust, unlimbered under cover, and was run forward by hand to the fatal crest among the dead horses. A gesture of the Captain's arm, some strangely agile movements of the men in loading, and almost before the troops along the way had ceased to hear the rattle of the wheels, a great white cloud sprang forward down the slope, and with a deafening report the affair at Coulter's Notch had begun.

It is not intended to relate in detail the progress and incidents of that ghastly contest – a contest without vicissitudes, its alternations only different degrees of despair. Almost at the instant when Captain Coulter's gun blew its challenging cloud twelve answering clouds rolled upward from among the trees about the plantation house, a deep multiple report roared back like a broken echo, and thenceforth to the end the Federal cannoneers fought their hopeless battle in an atmosphere of living iron whose thoughts were lightnings and whose deeds were death.

Unwilling to see the efforts which he could not aid and the slaughter which he could not stay, the Colonel had ascended the ridge at a point a quarter of a mile to the left, whence the Notch, itself invisible but pushing up successive masses of smoke, seemed the crater of a volcano in thundering eruption. With his glass he watched the enemy's guns, noting as he could the effects of Coulter's fire – if Coulter still lived to direct it. He saw that the Federal gunners, ignoring the enemy's pieces, whose position could be determined by their smoke only, gave their whole attention to the one which maintained its place in the open – the lawn in front of the house, with which it was accurately in line. Over and about that hardy piece the shells exploded at intervals of a few seconds. Some exploded in the house, as could be seen by thin ascensions of smoke from the breached roof. Figures of prostrate men and horses were plainly visible.

'If our fellows are doing such good work with a single gun,' said the Colonel to an aide who happened to be nearest, 'they must be suffering like the devil from twelve. Go down and present the commander of that piece with my congratulations on the accuracy of his fire.'

Turning to his Adjutant-General he said, 'Did you observe Coulter's damned reluctance to obey orders?'

'Yes, sir, I did.'

'Well, say nothing about it, please. I don't think the General will care to make any accusations. He will probably have enough to do in explaining his own connection with this uncommon way of amusing the rearguard of a retreating enemy.'

A young officer approached from below, climbing breathless up the acclivity. Almost before he had saluted he gasped out: –

'Colonel, I am directed by Colonel Harmon to say that the enemy's guns are within easy reach of our rifles, and most of them visible from various points along the ridge.'

The brigade commander looked at him without a trace of interest in his expression. 'I know it,' he said quietly.

The young adjutant was visibly embarrassed. 'Colonel Harmon would like to have permission to silence those guns,' he stammered.

'So should I,' the Colonel said in the same tone. 'Present my compliments to Colonel Harmon and say to him that the General's orders not to fire are still in force.'

The adjutant saluted and retired. The Colonel ground his heel into the earth and turned to look again at the enemy's guns.

'Colonel,' said the Adjutant-General, 'I don't know that I ought to say anything, but there is something wrong in all this. Do you happen to know that Captain Coulter is from the South?'

'No: *was* he, indeed?'

'I heard that last summer the division which the General then commanded was in the vicinity of Coulter's home – camped there for weeks, and – '

'Listen!' said the Colonel, interrupting with an upward gesture. 'Do you hear that?'

'That' was the silence of the Federal gun. The staff, the orderlies, the lines of infantry behind the crest – all had 'heard', and were looking curiously in the direction of the crater, whence no smoke now ascended except desultory cloudlets from the enemy's shells. Then came the blare of a bugle, a faint rattle of wheels; a minute later the sharp reports recommenced with double activity. The demolished gun had been replaced with a sound one.

'Yes,' said the Adjutant-General, resuming his narrative, 'the General made the acquaintance of Coulter's family. There was trouble – I don't know the exact nature of it – something about Coulter's wife. She is a red-hot Secessionist, as they all are, except Coulter himself, but she is a good wife and high-bred lady. There was a complaint to army headquarters. The General was transferred to this division. It is odd that Coulter's battery should afterwards have been assigned to it.'

The Colonel had risen from the rock upon which they had been sitting. His eyes were blazing with a generous indignation.

'See here, Morrison,' said he, looking his gossiping staff officer straight in the face, 'did you get that story from a gentleman or a liar?'

'I don't want to say how I got it, Colonel, unless it is necessary' – he was blushing a trifle – 'but I'll stake my life upon its truth in the main.'

The Colonel turned towards a small knot of officers some distance away. 'Lieutenant Williams!' he shouted.

One of the officers detached himself from the group, and, coming forward, saluted, saying: 'Pardon me, Colonel, I thought you had been informed. Williams is dead down there by the gun. What can I do, sir?'

Lieutenant Williams was the aide who had had the pleasure of conveying to the officer in charge of the gun his brigade commander's congratulations.

'Go,' said the Colonel, 'and direct the withdrawal of that gun instantly. Hold! I'll go myself.'

He strode down the declivity toward the rear of the Notch at a breakneck pace, over rocks and through brambles, followed by his little retinue in tumultuous disorder. At the foot of the declivity they mounted their waiting animals and took to the road at a lively trot, round a bend and into the Notch. The spectacle which they encountered there was appalling.

Within that defile, barely broad enough for a single gun, were piled the wrecks of no fewer than four. They had noted the silencing of only the last one disabled – there had been a lack of men to replace it quickly. The debris lay on both sides of the road; the men had managed to keep an open way between, through which the fifth piece was now firing. The men? – They looked like demons of the pit! All were hatless, all stripped to the waist, their reeking skins black with blotches of powder and spattered with gouts of blood. They worked like madmen, with rammer and cartridge, lever and lanyard. They set their swollen shoulders and bleeding hands against the wheels at each recoil and heaved the heavy gun back to its place. There were no commands; in that awful environment of whooping shot, exploding shells, shrieking fragments of iron, and flying splinters of wood, none could have been heard. Officers, if officers there were, were indistinguishable; all worked together – each while he lasted – governed by the eye. When the gun was sponged, it was loaded; when loaded, aimed and fired. The Colonel observed something new to his military experience – something horrible and unnatural: the gun was bleeding at the mouth! In temporary default of water, the man sponging had dipped his sponge in a pool of his comrades' blood. In all this work there was no clashing; the duty of the instant was obvious. When one fell, another, looking a trifle cleaner, seemed to rise from the earth in the dead man's tracks, to fall in his turn.

With the ruined guns lay the ruined men – alongside the wreckage, under it and atop of it; and back down the road – a ghastly procession! – crept on hands and knees such of the wounded as were able to move. The Colonel – he had compassionately sent his cavalcade to the right about – had to ride over those who were entirely dead in order not to crush those who were partly alive. Into that hell he tranquilly held his way, rode up alongside the gun, and, in the obscurity of the last discharge, tapped upon the cheek the man holding the rammer, who straightway fell, thinking himself killed. A fiend seven times damned sprang out of the smoke to take his place, but paused and gazed up at the mounted officer with an unearthly regard, his teeth flashing between his black lips, his eyes, fierce and expanded, burning like coats beneath his bloody brow. The Colonel made an authoritative gesture and pointed to the rear. The fiend bowed in token of obedience. It was Captain Coulter.

Simultaneously with the Colonel's arresting sign silence fell upon the whole field of action. The procession of missiles no longer streamed into that defile of death; the enemy also had ceased firing. His army had been gone for hours, and the commander of his rearguard, who had held his position perilously long in hope to silence the Federal fire, at that strange moment had silenced his own. 'I was not aware of the breadth of my authority,' thought the Colonel facetiously, riding forward to the crest to see what had really happened.

An hour later his brigade was in bivouac on the enemy's ground, and its idlers were examining, with something of awe, as the faithful inspect a saint's relics, a score of straddling dead horses and three disabled guns, all spiked. The fallen men had been carried away; their crushed and broken bodies would have given too great satisfaction.

Naturally, the Colonel established himself and his military family in the plantation house. It was somewhat shattered, but it was better than the open air. The furniture was greatly deranged and broken. The walls and ceilings were knocked away here and there, and there was a lingering odour of powder smoke everywhere. The beds, the closets of women's clothing, the cupboards were not greatly damaged. The new tenants for a night made themselves comfortable, and the practical effacement of Coulter's battery supplied them with an interesting topic.

During supper that evening an orderly of the escort showed himself into the dining-room, and asked permission to speak to the Colonel.

'What is it, Barbour?' said that officer pleasantly, having overheard the request.

'Colonel, there's something wrong in the cellar; I don't know what – somebody there. I was down there rummaging about.'

'I will go down and see,' said a staff officer, rising.

'So will I,' the Colonel said; 'let the others remain. Lead on, orderly.'

They took a candle from the table and descended the cellar stairs, the orderly in visible trepidation. The candle made but a feeble light, but presently, as they advanced, its narrow circle of illumination revealed a human figure seated on the ground against the black stone wall which they were skirting, its knees elevated, its head bowed sharply forward. The face, which should have been seen in profile, was invisible, for the man was bent so far forward that his long hair concealed it; and, strange to relate, the beard, of a much darker hue, fell in a great tangled mass and lay along the ground at his feet. They involuntarily paused; then the Colonel, taking the candle from the orderly's shaking hand, approached the man and attentively considered him. The long dark beard was the hair of a woman – dead. The dead woman clasped in her arms a dead babe. Both were clasped in the arms of the man, pressed against his breast, against his lips. There was blood in the hair of the woman; there was blood in the hair of the man. A yard away lay an infant's foot. It was near an irregular depression in the beaten earth which formed the cellar's floor – a fresh excavation with a convex bit of iron, having jagged edges, visible in one of the sides. The Colonel held the light as high as he could. The floor of the room above was broken through, the splinters pointing at all angles downward. 'This casemate is not bomb-proof,' said the Colonel gravely; it did not occur to him that his summing up of the matter had any levity in it.

They stood about the group awhile in silence; the staff officer was thinking of his unfinished supper, the orderly of what might possibly be in one of the casks on the other side of the cellar. Suddenly the man, whom they had thought dead, raised his head and gazed tranquilly into their faces. His complexion was coal black; the cheeks were apparently tattooed in irregular sinuous lines from the eyes downward. The lips, too, were white, like those of a stage negro. There was blood upon his forehead.

The staff officer drew back a pace, the orderly two paces.

'What are you doing here, my man?' said the Colonel, unmoved.

'This house belongs to me, sir,' was the reply, civilly delivered.

'To you? Ah, I see! And these?'

'My wife and child. I am Captain Coulter.'

The Fort at Zinderneuf

P. C. WREN

Fleeing from scandal after the disappearance of the 'Blue Water' diamond, two brothers, John and Michael (Beau), join the French Foreign Legion. At Zinderneuf, in the middle of the hostile desert, insurrection springs up against the cruel Lejaune, while the massed hordes of the Touaregs gather and move silently on the undermanned fort . . . . .

A VERY, VERY FAINT LIGHTENING of the darkness outside the windows showed that the false dawn was breaking. As I stared into the room, I found myself trying to recall a verse about 'Dawn's left hand' being in the sky and,

> *'Awake! for morning in the bowl of night*
> *Has flung the stone that puts the stars to flight:*
> *And lo! the Hunter of the East has caught*
> *The Sultan's turrets in a noose of light.'*

I tried to put it into Arabic, and wondered how the original sounded in the liquid Persian.... Was it 'turrets' or 'terrace'?...

What sort of a stone was Lejaune about to fling into the bowl of night?...

Would he order the four of us, when the other two returned, to open fire and begin a massacre of sleeping men? – an indiscriminate slaughter?...

He was quite capable of it. These were mutineers who had threatened his life, and, worse still, his sacred authority and discipline.

Why should he wait, he would argue, for a court martial to do it? Besides, if he waited, there would never be a court martial. He could not permanently arrest the whole lot with only five men, and guard his prisoners, garrison his fort, carry on all the work of the place, and mount sentries, with five men. What would happen when the five slept, ate, cooked, mounted guard on the roof? It couldn't be done. It was their lives or his, and the very existence of the fort.

Perhaps he'd only shoot the ringleaders?

What should I do if Lejaune ordered me to open fire on unarmed men in their beds? What would Michael do?

264

What was my duty in such a case, with orders from such an officer? Private conscience said, 'Absolutely impossible! Sheer murder! You are not an executioner.... Not the public hangman.

Military consciences said, 'Absolutely necessary. These men are guilty of the greatest military crime. It is Lejaune's duty to save the fort at any cost. *Your* duty is to obey your officer implicitly. If you refuse, you are a mutineer, as criminal as they.'

The windows grew lighter.

Maris and Cordier crept back, their work completed. Maris gave Lejaune the key of the armoury.

'St. André is on guard over the magazine, *mon Adjudant*,' whispered he, saluting.

'Good!' said Lejaune. 'Maris, Brown, and Cordier, remain here. Shoot instantly any man who puts his foot to the ground. If there's a rush, shoot Schwartz first. Your own lives depend on your smartness. They're all unarmed, remember.... Come with me, you, Smith, and I'll disarm the guard and sentries.... Use your wits if you want to see daylight again.'

He glared round the room.

'Aha, my little birds in a trap,' he growled. 'You'd plot against *me*. Me, *l'Adjudant Lejaune*, would you?... Ah! ...'

I followed him down the passage.

'I'll clear that dog of a sentry off the roof first,' he said. 'Then there'll be no shooting down on us when I disarm the guard....'

Leading the way, he went up the stairs that opened on to the flat roof, round which ran a thick, low, crenellated wall, embrasured for rifle-fire.

A sentry patrolled this roof at night, though the high look-out platform was not occupied, for obvious reasons, during the hours of darkness.

Lejaune relieved the sentry and posted me. He then took the man's rifle from him and ordered him to go below to the guard-room and request Sergeant Dupré to come up to the roof.

'Now,' said he to me as the man went, 'come here. Look,' and he pointed down into the courtyard to the open door of the guard-room. 'I shall order Sergeant Dupré to take the rifles of the guard and sentries, and then to send one man out of the guard-house with the lot. If any man comes out with only one rifle, shoot him at once. Shoot anybody who comes through that doorway, except a man with half a dozen rifles. And shoot to kill too.'

I raised my rifle and covered the lighted doorway below me, at the other side of the courtyard.

'You understand,' growled Lejaune. 'The moment Sergeant Dupré enters that guard-room, after I've spoken to him, you shoot anybody who carries one rifle. A man with a rifle is a proclaimed and confessed mutineer....'

I felt that he was right, and that it was my duty to obey him, little as I relished the idea of shooting comrades like bolting rabbits.

Should I shout, '*Drop that rifle!*' before I fired, and shoot if the man did not do it? I wondered if Lejaune would kill me if I did so.

I saw the relieved sentry cross the courtyard and enter the guard-room, and a moment later Sergeant Dupré came out.

'Watch!' growled Lejaune. 'That sentry will talk, and they may make a rush.'

Nothing stirred below.

Sergeant Dupré came up the stairs, out on to the roof, and saluted Lejaune.

'I want the rifles of the guard and sentries, Sergeant Dupré,' said Lejaune. 'Send one man, and only one, to me here, with the lot. Shoot instantly any man who hesitates for a second. No man is to leave the guard-room (except the one who carries all the rifles), or he'll be shot as he does so. . . .' And he pointed at me, standing with my rifle resting in an embrasure and covering the doorway below.

Sergeant Dupré saluted and turned about with a quiet, 'Very good, *mon Adjudant.*'

He descended the stairs and emerged into the courtyard, crossed it to the gate beneath the gate-house, and took the rifle from the sentry there. The man preceded him to the guard-room. Dupré visited the other sentries, repeating the procedure.

A minute after the Sergeant's last visit to the guard-room, a man came out. I was greatly relieved to see that he carried three or four rifles over each shoulder, the muzzles in his hands.

'Watch,' growled Lejaune. 'They may all rush out together now. Open rapid fire if they do,' and he himself also covered the doorway with the rifle he had taken from the sentry.

The man with the rifles, one Gronau, a big stupid Alsatian, came up the stairs. I did not look round, but kept my eyes fixed on the doorway through which a yellow light (from 'where the great guard-lantern guttered') struggled with that of the dawn.

I heard a clattering crash behind me and then I did look round, fully expecting to see that the man had felled Lejaune from behind.

Gronau had released the muzzles of the rifles, they had crashed down on the roof, and he was standing pointing, staring, his silly eyes goggling and his silly mouth wide open.

So obviously was he stricken by some strange vision, that Lejaune, instead of knocking him down, turned to look in the direction of his pointing hand.

I did the same.

The oasis was swarming with Arabs, swiftly and silently advancing to attack!

Even as I looked, a huge horde of camel-riders swept out to the left, another to the right, to make a detour and surround the fort on all sides.

There were hundreds and hundreds of them already in sight, even in that poor light of early dawn.

Lejaune showed his mettle instantly.

'Run like Hell,' he barked at Gronau. 'Back with those rifles,' and sent him staggering with a push. 'Send Sergeant Dupré here, quick.'

'Down to the barrack-room,' he snapped at me. 'Give the alarm. Take this key to St. André and issue the rifles. Send me the bugler. Jump, or I'll ...'

I jumped.

Even as I went, Lejaune's rifle opened rapid fire into the advancing hordes.

Rushing down the stairs and along the passage, I threw the key to St. André, who was standing like a graven image at the door of the magazine.

'*Arabs!*' I yelled. 'Out with the rifles and ammunition!'

Dashing on, I came to the door of the barrack-room.

Michael was pointing his rifle at Boldini's head. Maris was covering Schwartz, and Cordier was wavering the muzzle of his rifle over the room generally. Everybody was awake, and there was a kind of whispered babel, over which rose Michael's clear and cheerful:

'Show a foot anybody who wants to die. ...'

Nobody showed a foot, though all seemed to show resentment, especially Boldini, with a loaded rifle a yard from his ear.

Taking this in at a glance, I halted, drew breath and then bawled, '*Aux armes! Aux armes! Les Arbis! Les Arbis!*' and, with a shout to Michael and the other two, of:

'*Up with you – we're surrounded,*' I turned to dash back, conscious of a surge of unclad men from the beds, as their gaolers rushed after me. Whoops and yells of joy pursued us, and gleeful howls of:

'*Aux armes! Les Arbis!*' as the delighted men snatched at their clothes.

St. André staggered towards us beneath a huge bundle of rifles.

Dupré and the guard were clattering up the stairs.

As we rushed out on to the roof, Lejaune roared:

'Stand to! Stand to! Open fire at once! Rapid fire! Give them Hell, you devils! Give them Hell!' and, ordering Dupré to take command of the roof, he rushed below.

A couple of minutes later, a constant trickle of men flowed up from below, men in shirt-sleeves, men bareheaded and barefooted, men in nothing but their trousers – but every man with a full cartridge-pouch and his rifle and bayonet.

Lejaune must have worked like a fiend, for within a few minutes of Gronau's dropping of the rifles, every man in the fort was on the roof, and from every embrasure rifles poured their magazine-fire upon the yelling, swarming Arabs.

It had been a very near thing. A very close shave indeed.

But for Gronau's coming up and diverting attention from the inside of the fort to the outside, there probably would not have been a man of the garrison alive in the place by now – except those of the wounded sufficiently alive to be worth keeping for torture.

One wild swift rush in the half-light, and they would have been into the place – to find what? A disarmed garrison!

As I charged my magazine and fired, loaded and fired, loaded and fired, I wondered if these things were 'chance', and Gronau's arrival and idle glance round, at the last moment that gave a chance of safety, pure accidental coincidence.

A near thing indeed – and the issue yet in doubt, for it was a surprise attack. They had got terribly close, the oasis was in their hands, and there were many hundreds of them to our little half-company.

And they were brave. There was no denying that, as they swarmed up to the walls under our well-directed rapid-fire, an Arab falling almost as often as a legionary pulled the trigger.

While hundreds, along each side, fired at our embrasures at a few score yards' range, a large band attacked the gate with stones, axes, heavy swords, and bundles of kindling-wood to burn it down.

Here Lejaune, exposing himself fearlessly, led the defence, controlling a rapid volley-fire that had terrible effect, both physical and moral, until the whole attack ceased as suddenly as it had begun, and the Touaregs, as the sun rose, completely vanished from sight to turn the assault into a siege and to pick us off, in safety from behind the crests of the sand-hills.

I suppose this whirlwind dawn attack lasted no more than ten minutes from the moment that the first shot was fired by Lejaune, but it had seemed like hours to me.

I had shot at least a score of men, I thought. My rifle was hot and sweating grease, and several bullets had struck the deep embrasure in which I leaned to fire.

Below, the plain was dotted over with little heaps of white or blue clothing, looking more like scattered bundles of 'washing' than dead ferocious men who, a minute before, had thirsted and yelled for the blood of the infidel, and had fearlessly charged to drink it.

Our bugler blew the 'Cease fire,' and on the order, 'Unload! Stand easy,' I looked round as I straightened myself up, unloaded my rifle, and stood at ease.

It was a strange sight.

At every embrasure there was a caricature of a soldier – in some cases almost naked – at his feet a litter of spent cartridges, and, in one or two instances, a pool of blood. As I looked, one of these wild figures, wearing nothing but a shirt and trousers, slowly sank to the ground, sat a moment and then collapsed, his head striking with a heavy thud. It was Blanc, the sailor.

Lejaune strode over from his place in the middle of the roof.

'Here,' he shouted. 'No room nor time, yet, for shirkers,' and putting his arms round the man, dragged him from the ground and jerked him heavily into the embrasure.

There he posed the body, for Blanc appeared to be dead. Into the embrasure it leaned, chest on the upward sloping parapet, and elbows wedged against the outer edges of the massive uprights of the crenellation.

Lejaune placed the rifle on the flat top of the embrasure, a dead hand under it, a dead hand clasped round the small of the butt, the heel-plate against the dead shoulder, a dead cheek leaning against the butt.

'Continue to look useful, my friend, if you can't *be* useful.' he jeered; and as he turned away, he added:

'Perhaps you'll see that route to Morocco if you stare hard enough.'

'Now then, Corporal Boldini,' he called, 'take every third man below, get them fed and properly dressed, and double back here if you hear a shot, or the 'Assembly' blown. If there's no attack, take below one-half of the rest.... Then the remainder.... Have all *klim-bim* and standing-to again in thirty minutes.... You, St. André, and Maris, more ammunition. A hundred rounds per man.... Cordier, pails of water. Fill all water-flasks and then put filled pails there above the gate.... They may try another bonfire against it.... Sergeant Dupré, no wounded whatsoever will go below. Bring up the medical panniers.... Are all prisoners out of the cells?' ...

He glared around, a competent, energetic, courageous soldier. 'And where's the excellent Schwartz?' he went on. 'Here, you dog, up on to that look-out platform and watch those palm trees – till the Arabs get you.... Watch that oasis, I say.... You'll have a little while up there for the thinking out of some more plots....' And he laid his hand on the butt of his revolver, as he scowled menacingly at the big German.

Schwartz sprang up the ladder leading to the high look-out platform that towered far above the roof of the fort. It was the post of danger.

'Now use your eyes, all of you,' bawled Lejaune, 'and shoot as soon as you see anything to shoot at.'

Ten minutes or so later, Boldini returned with the men who he had taken below, now all dressed as for morning parade. They took their places and the Corporal hurried round the roof, touching each alternate man on the shoulder.

'Fall out, and go below,' he ordered.

Ten minutes or so later they were back, fed, clothed, and in their right minds. Gone like magic were all signs of *cafard*, mutiny, and madness. These were eager, happy soldiers, revelling in a fight.

With the third batch I went, hoping to be back before anything happened. Not a rifle-shot broke the stillness, as we hastily swallowed *soupe* and coffee, and tore at our bread.

'Talk about "They came to curse and remained to pray",' murmured Michael, with bulging cheeks. 'These jolly old Arabs removed our curse and remained for us to slay. There'll be no more talk of mutiny for a while.'

'Nor of anything else, old bean,' I replied, 'if they remain to pray.'

'Never get in here,' said Michael. 'They couldn't take this place without guns.'

'Wonder what they're doing?' I mused.

'Diggin' themselves in on the crests of the sand-hills,' said Michael. 'They can't rush us, so they're going to do some fancy shooting.'

'Yes. What about a regular siege?' I asked. 'And killing only one of us to a score of them that we kill? We should be too few to man the four walls eventually.'

'What about relief from Tokotu?' suggested Michael.

'Over a hundred miles away!' I replied, 'and no wires. Nor any chance to heliograph across a level desert, even if they could see so far.'

'Chance for the *médaille militaire*,' grinned Michael. 'Go to Lejaune and say, "*Fear not! Alone I will walk through the encircling foe and bring you relief.*" Then you walk straight through them, what?'

'Might be done at night,' I mused.

'I *don't* think,' said Michael. 'These merry men will sit round the place in a circle like a spiritualists' *séance*, holding hands, rather than let anyone slip through them.'

'Full moon too,' I observed. 'Anyhow, I'm grateful to the lads for rolling up....'

'Shame to shoot 'em,' agreed Michael, and then Boldini hounded us all back to the roof, and we resumed our stations.

All was ready, and the Arabs could come again as soon as they liked.

Lejaune paced round and round the roof like a tiger in a cage.

'Hi you, there!' he called up to Schwartz. 'Can you see nothing?'

'Nothing moving, *mon Adjudant*,' replied Schwartz.

A moment later he shouted something, and his voice was drowned in the rattle and crash of a sudden outbreak of rifle fire in a complete circle all round the fort. The Arabs had lined the nearest sand-hills on all sides of us, and lying flat below the crests, poured in a steady independent fire.

This was a very different thing from their first mad rush up to the very walls, when they hoped to surprise a sleeping fort and swarm up over the walls from each other's shoulders.

They were now difficult to see, and a man firing from his embrasure was as much exposed as an Arab lying flat behind a stone or in a trench scooped in the sand.

There was a man opposite to me, about a hundred yards distant, who

270

merely appeared as a small black blob every few minutes. He must have been lying on a slope or in a shallow sand trench, and he only showed his head for a few seconds when he fired. I felt that either he or I would get hurt, sooner or later, for he, among others, was potting at my embrasure.

It was certainly 'fancy shooting' as Michael had said, waiting for the small object, a man's head, to appear for five seconds at a hundred yards' range, and get a shot at it. It was certainly interesting too, and more difficult than rifle-range work, for one's nerves are not steadied nor one's aim improved by the knowledge that one is also being shot at oneself, and by several people.

With unpleasant frequency there was a sharp blow on the wall near my embrasure and sometimes the high wailing song of a ricochet, as the deflected and distorted bullet continued its flight at an angle to the line of its arrival.

The morning wore on and the sun gained rapidly in power.

Unreasonably and unreasoningly I did not expect to be hit, and I was not hit, but I was increasingly conscious of the terrific heat and of a severe headache. I wondered if high nervous tension made one more susceptible, or whether the day was really hotter than usual. . . .

Suddenly, the man on my right leapt back, shouted, spun round and fell to the ground, his rifle clattering at my feet.

I turned and stooped over him. It was the wretched Guantaio, shot through the middle of his face.

As I bent down, I was suddenly sent crashing against the wall, as Lejaune literally sprang at me.

'By God!' he roared. 'You turn from your place again and I'll blow your head off! *Duty*, you dog! Get to your duty! What have you to do with this carrion, you cursed, slinking, cowering, hiding shirker . . .' and as I turned back into my embrasure, he picked up the choking, moaning Guantaio and flung him into the place from where he had fallen.

'Stay there, you rotten dog,' he shouted, 'and if you slide out of it, I'll *pin* you up with bayonets through you,' and he forced the dying wretch into the embrasure so that he was wedged in position, with his head and shoulders showing through the aperture between the crenellations on either side of him.

'I'll have no skulking malingerers here,' he roared. 'You'll all stay in those embrasures alive or *dead*, while there's an Arab in sight. . . .'

Suddenly the Arab fire dwindled and slackened and then ceased. Either they had had enough of our heavy and accurate fire, or else some new tactics were going to be introduced. I imagined that a camel-man had ridden all round the sand-hills, out of sight, calling the leaders to colloquy with the Emir in command.

Our bugles sounded the 'Cease fire'.

'Stand easy! . . . Wounded lie down where they are,' rang out Lejaune's voice, and some half-dozen men sank to the ground in their own blood. I was thankful to see that Michael was not among them.

Sergeant Dupré with Cordier, who had been a doctor, went to each in turn, with bandages and stimulants.

'Corporal Boldini,' barked Lejaune, 'take the men down in three batches. Ten minutes for *soupe* and a half-litre of wine each. Come back at the '*pas gymnastique*' if you hear the 'Assembly' blown.... St. André, replenish ammunition. Each man to have a hundred.... Stop that bandaging, Cordier, and stir yourself....'

When my turn came, later, to go below, I was more thankful for the comparative darkness and coolness of the *caserne* than for the *soupe* and wine even, for my head was splitting.

'"*Moriturus te saluto*",' said Cordier, as he raised his mug of wine.

'Don't talk rot,' said I. 'You're no more *moriturus* than – *Madame la République*.'

'I shall be dead before sunset,' replied Cordier. 'This place will be a silent grave shortly ... "*Madame la République – morituri te salutant!*" ...' and he drank again.

'He's fey,' said Michael. 'Anyhow, better to die fighting than to be done in by Lejaune afterwards.... If I go, I'd like to take that gentle *adjudant* with me....'

'He's a topping soldier,' I said.

'Great,' agreed Michael. 'Let's forgive him.'

'We will, if he dies,' said I. 'I am afraid that he'll see to it that he *needs* some forgiving, if he and we survive this show, and he gets control again....'

'Yes,' said Michael. 'Do you know, I believe he's torn both ways when a man's hit. The brute in him says, "*That's one for you, you damned mutineer*", and the soldier in him says, "*One more of a tiny garrison gone*".'

'He's a foul brute,' I agreed. 'He absolutely *flung* two wounded, suffering men back into the embrasures – and enjoyed doing it.'

'Partly enjoyment and partly tactics,' said Michael wiping his lips, and lighting a cigarette. 'He's going to give the Arabs the idea that not a man has been killed. Or else that he has so many men in the fort that another takes the place of each one that falls.... The Touaregs have no field-glasses, and to them a man in an embrasure is a man....'

'What about when there are too few to keep up any volume of fire?' I asked.

'He may hope for relief before then,' hazarded Michael.

'He does,' put in St. André, who had just joined us and taken a seat at the table. 'Dupré told me so. The wily beggar has kept the two *goums* outside every night lately – presumably ever since he knew of the conspiracy. They had orders to go, hell for leather, to Tokotu, and say the fort was *attacked*, the moment they heard a rifle fired, *inside or out*.'

'By Jove!' I exclaimed. 'Of course! He wouldn't send to Tokotu to ask for help in quelling a mutiny of his own men, before it happened – but he wouldn't mind a column arriving because a *goum* had erroneously reported an attack on the fort.'

'Cunning lad!' agreed Michael. 'And he knew that when the conspiracy was about to bloom and he nipped it in the bud, he'd be pretty shorthanded after it, if he should be attacked – even by a small raiding party out for a lark!'

'Yes,' said Cordier. 'He saved his face and he saved the fort too. If a shot had been fired at the mutineers, the *goums* would have scuttled off as ordered, and the relief-column from Tokotu would have found an heroic Lejaune cowing and guarding a gang of mutineers.... As it is, they'll know to-morrow morning, at Tokotu, that the place is invested, and they'll be here the next day.'

'Question is – where shall *we* be by then?' I observed.

'In Hell, dear friends,' smiled Cordier.

'Suppose the *goums* were chopped in the oasis?' said Michael. 'Taken by surprise, as we were.'

'What I said to Dupré!' replied Cordier. 'But Lejaune was too old a bird. They camped in the oasis by day, but were ordered to be out at night, and patrol separately, one north to south on the east and the other on the west, a half-circle each, from sunset to sunrise, Dupré says ... Likely they'd have been chopped in the oasis in the daytime all right, sound asleep – but they wouldn't be caught at dawn. They were well outside the enveloping movement from the oasis when the Arabs surrounded the place, and the *goums* would be off to Tokotu at the first shot or sooner.... By the time ...'

'Up with you,' shouted Boldini, and we hurried back to the roof and resumed our stations. The wounded were again in their places, one or two lying very still in them, others able to stand.

On either side of me, a dead man stood wedged into his embrasure, his rifle projecting before him, his elbows and the slope of the parapet keeping him in position.

I could see no sign of life from my side of the fort. Nothing but sand and stones over which danced the blinding aching heat-haze.

Suddenly there was a cry from Schwartz on the look-out platform.

'The palms,' he shouted and pointed. 'They're climbing them.' He raised his rifle and fired.

Those were his last words. A volley rang out a minute later, and he fell.

Bullets were striking the wall against which I stood, upon its *inner* face. Arab marksmen had climbed to the tops of the palms of the oasis, and were firing down upon the roof. From all the sand-hills round, the circle of fire broke out again.

'Rapid fire at the palms,' shouted Lejaune. 'Sergeant Dupré, take half the men from the other three sides to that one. Bring those birds down from their trees quickly.... Brandt, up with you on to the look-out platform. Quick....'

I glanced round as I charged my magazine afresh. Brandt looked at the platform and then at Lejaune. Lejaune's hand went to the revolver in the holster at his belt, and Brandt climbed the ladder, and started firing as quickly as he could work the bolt of his rifle.

Michael was still on his feet, but, as I turned back, I saw his neighbour spin round and crash down, clutching with both streaming hands at his throat.

When I took another swift glance later, the man had been wedged into the embrasure and posed by Lejaune as a living defender of the fort.

Soon afterwards I heard a shout from above, and turning, saw Brandt stagger backwards on the high platform. He struck the railing, toppled over, and came with a horrible crash to the roof.

'Find a good place for that carrion, Sergeant Dupré,' shouted Lejaune. 'Make him ornamental if he can't he useful.'

I then heard him call the name of Haff.

'Up you go, Haff,' he shouted. 'You're another of these brave *risque touts*. Up you go!'

Schwartz, Brandt, Haff! Doubtless the next would be Delarey and Vogué.... And then Colonna, Gotto, and Bolidar.... Guantaio was dead.... Why didn't he send Michael up there? Presumably he hoped to keep him, St. André, Cordier, Maris, and me alive until the mutineer ringleaders and the diamond-stealers were dead. ... He wouldn't want to be left victorious over the Arabs, only to find himself defenceless in the hands of the mutineers and the thieves.

I glanced up at Haff and saw that he was lying behind Schwartz's body, and firing over it as though it were a parapet along the edge of the platform.

I wondered how long this second phase of the fight had lasted, and whether we could hold out till night fell and the Arabs could not see to shoot.... Would they shoot by moonlight? It was unlikely, the Arab being, as a rule, averse from any sort of night work except peaceful travelling. A dawn rush is his favourite manœuvre....

It was agony to fire my rifle, for my head ached with one of those terrible eye-strain heat-stroke pains that give the feeling that the head is opening and shutting, exposing the brain. Every explosion of my rifle was like a blow on the head with a heavy hammer. I had almost come to the end of my tether when once again the fire of the Arabs slackened and dwindled and died away.

On the 'Cease fire' bugle being ordered by Lejaune, I straightened up. I looked round as the words, 'Unload! Stand easy!' rang out.

Michael was all right, but a good half of the garrison was dead or dying, for quite half the men remained partly standing, partly lying, wedged into their embrasures as the others obeyed the orders shouted by Lejaune.

Among the dead were both Sergeant Dupré and Corporal Boldini, and both had been stuck up to simulate living men. Haff must be dead too, for Delarey had been sent up to the platform, and was lying flat behind a little pile of bodies.

St. André was alive, for Lejaune called out:

'St. André, take rank as Corporal. One half the men to go below for *soupe* and coffee. Double back quick if you hear the 'Assembly' blown ...' and St. André passed round the roof, touching each alternate man of those who were standing up, and saying, 'Fall out, and go below.'

In many embrasures was a man whom he did not touch.

Poor Cordier had spoken truly as concerned his own fate, for he remained at his post, staring out with dead eyes across the desert.

Maris was dead too. There were left three men – St. André, Michael, and myself, upon whom Lejaune could rely if the Arabs now drew off and abandoned the siege of the fort.

But this, the Arabs did not do.

Leaving a circle of what were presumably their best marksman, to pick off any of the defenders of the fort who showed themselves, the bulk of them retired out of sight behind the oasis and sand-hills beyond it.

By Lejaune's orders, the embrasures were occupied only by the dead, the living being ordered below in small parties, for rest and food.

St. André was told to see that every man left his bed and *paquetage* as tidy as for inspection, and that the room was in perfect order. Lejaune himself never left the roof, but had *soupe*, coffee, and wine brought up to him.

To the look-out platform he sent Vogué to join the bodies of his fellow conspirators, Schwartz, Haff, and Delarey.

Except for a crouching sentry in the middle of each wall of the roof, those who were not below, feeding and resting, sat with their backs to the wall, each beside his embrasure.

The fire of the Arab sharpshooters did no harm, and they wasted their ammunition on dead men.

And so the evening came and wore away and the moon rose.

Where we were, we lay, with permission to sleep, St. André having the duty of seeing that two sentries patrolled each wall and were changed every two hours.

By Lejaune's orders, Vogué, in the dusk before moonrise, pushed the bodies of Schwatz, Haff, and Delarey from the look-out platform to fall down to the roof. They were then posed in embrasures, as though living defenders of the fort. It seemed to give Lejaune special pleasure to thrust his half-smoked cigarette between Schwartz's teeth, and pull the dead man's *képi* rakishly to one side.

'There, my fine conspirator,' said he when the body was arranged to his liking. 'Stand there and do your duty satisfactorily for the first time in your life, now you're dead. Much more useful now than ever you were before.'

'He's a devil! He's a devil! He's mad – *mad!* ...' groaned Vogué as he dragged the body of Delarey past me.

'Up with him! Put him over there,' growled Lejaune, when Vogué had got the body in his arms. 'I'll allot your corpse the place next to his, and your pipe shall be stuck between your teeth. You are fond of a pipe, friend Vogué! Helps you to think out plots, eh? ... Up with him, you dog ...' and he kept his hand on the butt of his revolver as he baited the man. He then sent him back to the look-out platform, to be a target for the Touaregs when the moon rose, or the sun, if he lived to see it. ...

I had a talk with Michael when our turn came to go below for a rest and food.

'Looks like a thin time to-morrow,' said Michael. 'If they pot a few of us and then rush, they should get in.'

'Yes,' I agreed. 'They ought to keep up a heavy fire while their ammunition lasts, and then charge on camels in one fell swoop. And then climb up from the backs of the camels. A lot would be killed but a bigger lot would get in.'

'Don't give them the tip, anyhow,' grinned Michael. 'Two or three hundred of the devils inside the place, and it would be a short life and a merry for the half-dozen or so of us who were left by that time. ...'

'If we can stand them off to-morrow, the relief from Tokotu ought to roll up the next morning,' I said.

'If either of those *goums* got away and played the game,' agreed Michael. 'They may have been pinched though. ... The relief will find a thin house here, if they do come. ... It'll mean a commission for Lejaune all right.'

'Nice if he's confirmed in command here, and we survive!' I remarked.

'Yes,' said Michael, 'and talking of which, look here, old son. If I take the knock and you don't, I want you to do something for me. ... Something *most* important ... what?'

'You can rely on me, Beau,' I said.

'I know I can, John,' he replied. 'There's some letters. A funny *public* sort of letter, a letter for Claudia, and one for you, and one for Digby, in my belt – and there's a letter and a tiny packet for Aunt Patricia. If you possibly can, old chap, get that letter and packet to Aunt. No hurry about it – *but get it to her*. See? *Especially the letter*. The packet doesn't much matter, and it contains nothing of any value, but I'd die a lot more comfortable if I knew that Aunt Patricia was going to get that letter after my death. ...'

276

'Oh, shut it, Beau,' I said roughly. 'Your number's not up yet. Don't talk rot.'

'I'm only asking you to do something *if* I'm pipped,' said Michael.

'And, of course, I'll do it if I'm alive,' I replied. . . . 'But suppose we're both killed?'

'Well – the things are addressed and stamped, and it's usual to forward such letters and packets found on dead soldiers, as you know. Depends on what happens. . . . If we die and Lejaune survives, I doubt their being dispatched. Or rather, I don't doubt at all. . . . Or if the Arabs get in, there's not much chance of anything surviving. . . . But if we're both killed and the relief gets in here before the Arabs do, the officer in charge would do the usual thing. . . . Anyhow, we can only hope for the best. . . .

'Anything I can do for you if it's the other way round, John?' he added.

'Well, love to Dig, you know, and there's a letter for Isobel, and you might write to her if ever you get back to civilisation and say we babbled of her, and sang, "*Just before the battle, Mother*," and "*Bring a flower from Maggie's grave*," and all that. . . .'

Michael grinned.

'I'll say the right things about you to Isobel, old son,' he said, 'and if otherwise, you'll see that Aunt gets my letter, eh? Be sure I'm dead though. . . . I mean if I were captured alive by Arabs, or anything humorous like that, I don't want her to get it while I'm alive. . . . Of course, all five of the letters are important, but I *do* want Aunt to get hers. . . .'

And then St. André ordered our little party up to the roof, and brought down the other one.

The Arabs had ceased their desultory firing, and might have been a hundred miles away. Only the sight of a little smoke from their camp-fires and the occasional scent of the burning camel-dung and wood betrayed their presence, for none were in sight, and they made no sound. No one doubted, however, that a very complete chain of watchful sentries ringed us round, and made it utterly impossible for anyone to leave the fort and bring help to his besieged comrades.

The fact that Lejaune sent no one to make the attempt seemed to confirm the story that Dupré had told Cordier as they bandaged the wounded, and to show that Lejaune believed that the *goums* had got away.

It would be a wellnigh hopeless enterprise, but there was just a chance in a thousand that a daring and skilful scout might be able to crawl to where their camels were, and get away on one. Nor was Lejaune the man to take any count of the fact that it was almost certain torture and death for the man who attempted it.

I decided that, on the one hand, he felt pretty sure the *goums* had got away to Tokotu directly the Arabs appeared, and that, on the other hand, the two or three men whom he could trust were just the men whom he could not spare.

Unless St. André, Michael, and I were with him, his fate would be the same whether he drove the Arabs off or not, and doubtless he would rather go down fighting Arabs, than be murdered by his own men.

I was ordered on duty as sentry, and, for two hours, patrolled my side of the roof with my eyes on the moonlit desert, where nothing moved and whence no sound came.

When relieved, I had a little chat with St. André after he had posted my relief.

'Dawn will be the dangerous time; they'll rush us then,' he said, 'and it will want quick shooting to keep them down if they come all together and on all four sides at once. They must be a hundred to one.... I wonder if they'll bring ropes and poles, or ride their camels right up to the walls....'

'If they don't count the cost, I don't see how we can keep them out,' I said.

'Nothing could keep them out,' replied St. André. 'But if they fail at dawn they won't try again until the next dawn. They'll just pepper us all day and tire us out.... They think they have all the time they want.'

'Haven't they?' I asked.

'No,' replied St. André. 'Lejaune is certain that one of the *goums* got away. The Arabs couldn't get them *both*, he says, as they were at opposite sides of the fort, and half a mile apart always, at night.'

'What about their ammunition?' I asked. 'The Touaregs', I mean.'

'The more they spend the more determined they'll be to get ours, and the more likely to put their money on a swift dawn-rush with cold steel....'

I lay down and fell asleep, to be awakened by the bugle and Lejaune's shout of '*Stand to!*'

There was no sign of dawn and none of the Arabs.

From the centre of the roof, Lejaune addressed the diminished garrison of Fort Zinderneuf.

'Now, my merry birds,' said he, 'you're going to *sing*, and sing like the happy joyous larks you are. We'll let our Arab friends know that we're not only awake, but also merry and bright. Now then – the *Marching Song of the Legion* first. Altogether, you warbling water-rats – *Now*.' And led by his powerful bellow, we sang at the tops of our voices.

Through the Legion's extensive repertoire he took us, and between songs the bugler blew every call that he knew.

'Now *laugh*, you merry, happy, jolly, care-free, humorous swine. *Laugh*. ... You, Vogué, up there – roar with laughter, or I'll make you roar with pain, by God.... Out with it. *Now*....'

A wretched laugh, like that of a hungry hyena, came down from the look-out platform.

It was so mirthless a miserable cackle, and so ludicrous, that we laughed genuinely.

'Again, you grinning dog,' roared Lejaune. 'Laugh till your sides ache, you gibbering jackal. Laugh till the tears run down your horrible face, you shivering she-ass. Laugh!... *Now*....'

Again the hideous quavering travesty of a laugh rang out, and the men below roared heartily at the ridiculous noise.

'Now then, you twittering sniggering *soupe*-snatchers, laugh in turn,' shouted Lejaune. 'From the right – you start, Gotto.'

Gotto put up a pretty good roar.

'Now beat *that*, next. Out with it, or, by God, I'll give you something to laugh at,' Lejaune continued.

And so round that circle of doomed men, among the dead men, ran the crazy laughter, the doomed howling noisily, the dead smiling secretly out to the illuminated silent desert.

'Now all together with me,' roared Lejaune, and great guffaws rang out, desecrating the silence and the beauty of the moonlit scene.

It was the maddest, most incredible business – that horrible laughter among the dead, from men about to die.

Certainly the Arabs must have thought us mad and certainly they were not far wrong. Anyhow, they knew we were awake and must have gathered that we were cheerful and defiant.

For Lejaune was justified of his madness, and no dawn attack came.

Whether the Touaregs regarded us as 'The afflicted of Allah,' and feared to rush the place, or whether they realised that there could be no element of surprise in the attack, I do not know, but it was never made.

And when the sun rose and they again lined the sand-hills and opened their heavy fire upon the fort, every embrasure was occupied by an apparently unkillable man, and every Arab who exposed himself paid the penalty.

But not all those who lined the walls of Zinderneuf were beyond scathe by Arab bullets. Now and then there would be a cry, an oath, a gurgling grunt or cough, and a man would stagger back and fall, or die where he crouched, a bullet through his brain.

And, in every case, Lejaune would prop and pose and arrange the body, dead or dying, in the embrasure whence it had fallen, and to the distant Arab eyes it must have seemed that the number of the defenders was undiminished.

As the morning wore on, Lejaune took a rifle, and, crouching beside each dead man in turn, fired several shorts from each embrasure, adding to the illusion that the dead were alive, as well as to the volume of fire.

Later still, he set one man to each wall to do the same thing, to pass continually up and down, firing from behind the dead.

When the Arab fire again slackened and then ceased, toward midday, and our bugle blew the '*Cease fire*,' I hardly dared to turn round.

With a sigh of relief, I saw Michael among the few who rose from their embrasures at the order '*Stand easy*.'

It was a terribly tiny band. Of all those who had sprung from their beds with cries of joy, at the shout of '*Aux armes!*' yesterday morning, only Lejaune, St. André, Michael, Colonna, Marigny, Vogué, Moscowski, Gotto, Vaerren, and I were still alive.

The end was inevitable, unless relief came from Tokotu before the Arabs assaulted the place. All they had to do now, was to run in and climb. Ten men cannot hold back a thousand.

If we survived to see the arrival of a relieving force it would be the dead who saved us, these dead who gave the impression of a numerous, fearless, ever-watchful garrison, who would cause an attack across open ground to wither beneath the blast of their rifles like grass beneath a flame.

'Half the men below, for *soupe* and coffee and half a litre of wine, Corporal St. André,' ordered Lejaune. 'Back as soon as you can – or if the "*Assembly*" is blown ...' and St. André took each alternate man.

Soon coffee and *soupe* were ready, although the cook was dead, and we sat at table as though in a dream, surrounded by the tidy beds of dead men.

'Last lap!' said Michael, as I gave him a cigarette. 'Last cigarette! Last bowl of *soupe!* Last mug of coffee! Last swig of wine! Well, well! It's as good an end as any – if a bit early.... Look out for the letter, Johnny,' and he patted the front of his sash.

'Oh, come off it,' I growled. 'Last nothing. The relief is half-way here by now.'

'Hope so,' replied Michael. 'But I don't greatly care, old son. So long as you see about the letter for me.'

'Why *I*, rather than you, Beau?' I asked. 'Just as likely that you do my posting for me.'

'Don't know, Johnny. Just feel it in my bones,' he replied. 'I feel I'm in for it and you're not, and thank the Lord for the latter, old chap,' and he gave my arm a little squeeze above the elbow. (His little grip of my arm, and squeeze, had been one of my greatest rewards and pleasures, all my life.)

As we returned to the roof at the end of our meal, Michael held out his hand to me.

'Well, good-bye, dear old Johnny,' he said. 'I wish to God I hadn't dragged you into this – but I think you'll come out all right. Give my love to Dig.'

I wrung his hand.

'Good-bye, Beau,' I replied. 'Or rather, *au 'voir*.... Of course, you didn't "drag" me into this. I had as much right to assume the blame for the theft of the "Blue Water" as you and Dig had. ... And it's been a great lark....'

He patted my shoulder as we clattered up the stairs.

Lejaune assigned one side of the roof to Michael and the opposite one to me. Vogué and Vaerren respectively were sent to the other two. Our orders were to patrol the wall and shoot from behind a dead man, if we saw an Arab.

St. André took Colonna, Marigny, Moscowski, and Gotto below.

Lejaune himself went up to the look-out platform with his field-glasses and swept the horizon in the direction of Tokotu. Apparently he saw no sign of help.

Nothing moved on the sand-hills on my side of the fort, and I watched them over the heads of my dead comrades....

How much longer could this last?

Would the Touaregs draw off from this fort-with-an-inexhaustible-garrison?

Would the relief come in time? If not, would they be in time to avenge us? It would be amusing if the Arabs, having got into the fort, were caught in it by the Senegalese and mounted troops from Tokotu – a poetic justice – for not a man of them would escape!

Where *did* all the flies come from? ... Horrible! ...

St. André and his party returned to the roof, and now two men were posted to each wall, St. André and Lejaune remaining in the centre of the roof to support whichever side of the fort should need it most when the attack came.

When it did come, it was a repetition of the siege-tactics and attrition warfare, a desultory fire of sharpshooters, and most of it aimed at the dead.

Up and down his half of the wall, each of the defenders hurried, firing from a different embrasure each time.

The Arabs must have been completely deceived, for they came no nearer, and fired impartially at the silent corpse-guarded embrasures and at those from which our eight rifles cracked.

Glancing round, as I darted from one embrasure to another, I saw that both Lejaune and St. André were in the firing-line now, and that Lejaune had one wall of the fort to himself. There were only seven of us left. Michael was among them.

The Arab fire died down.

Lejaune himself picked up the bugle and sounded the '*Cease fire*'. I saw that Vogué, Moscowski, and Marigny were dead and propped up in their places. St. André was dabbing his face with a rag, where a bullet had torn his cheek and ear.

Colonna, Gotto, and I were sent below to get food, and we spoke not a

281

single word. When we returned, Michael, Vaerren, and St. André went down in their turn.

Lejaune walked up and down the roof, humming '*C'est la reine Pomaré*,' to all appearance cool and unconcerned.

Not an Arab was to be seen, and not a shot was fired.

I wondered whether they withdrew for meals or for prayers – or whether they fired so many rounds per man from their trenches on the sand-hills, and then awaited their reliefs from the oasis.

Certainly it was a leisurely little war – on their side; and no doubt they were well advised to conduct it so. They must have lost terribly in their first attack, and they had learnt wisdom.

A shot rang out.

'*Stand to!*' shouted Lejaune, and blew the '*Assembly*' two or three times, as though calling up reserves from below to the already well-manned walls.

That fort and its garrison must have been a sore puzzle to the gentle Touareg.

The firing recommenced and grew hotter, and an ominous change took place in the Arab tactics.

While a heavy fire was maintained from the crests of the sand-hills, men crawled forward *en tirailleur* and scratched shallow holes in the sand, behind stones. ... Nearer and nearer they came. ... They were going to assault again.

I rushed from embrasure to embrasure, up and down my side of the roof, pausing only just long enough to bring my fore-sight on to an Arab. Time after time I saw that I hit one of the running or crouching crawling figures drawing ever closer to the wall.

Lejaune was like a man possessed, loading and firing, dashing from place to place, and rushing from one side of the fort to the other, to empty the magazine of his rifle....

Why from one side to the other? ... As I loaded and fired, emptied and recharged my magazine, I found myself asking this question.

Glancing round, I saw the reason. There was no one defending the two walls that ran to left and right of mine.

Lejaune was firing a burst from one, and then dashing across to the other – defending two walls at once.

Only one man was defending the wall behind me. Swiftly I looked across.

It was not Michael....

Only Lejaune, St. André, and I were on our feet.

This was the end....

Michael was gone – but I should follow him in a minute.

Cramming another clip of cartridges into my hot rifle, I looked across again.

The opposite wall was now undefended.

Rushing across the roof from left to right, Lejaune shouted:

'Both walls, damn you! To and fro, curse you! Shoot like hell, blast you!' and I dashed across and emptied my magazine from that side, a shot from a different embrasure each time.

Back again I ran, and got off a burst of fire along the opposite wall.

And when I was nearly spent, panting like a hunted fox, dripping with sweat, and nearly blind with eye-strain and headache, the Arab fire again dwindled and died, and there was perfect silence – an incredible dreadful silence, after those hours of deafening racket.

And so Lejaune and I (*Lejaune and I!*) held Fort Zinderneuf for a while, two against a thousand.

The Cruel Sea

NICHOLAS MONSARRAT

*Detailed to escort a convoy of valuable merchant ships, the corvette
Compass Rose finds herself and her charges at the mercy of the relentless
tracker planes of the Luftwaffe – a cold and unfair cruelty which in turn
engenders a new brutality in its victims . . . . .*

THE SMILING WEATHER of that late summer helped them to settle down to
sea-going again, after the relaxation of their refit. It was a curious
business, this tuning-up of men and machinery, and in some cases it
caught both of them unawares. *Compass Rose* hit the knuckle of the jetty –
fortunately, not very hard – on her way out of dock, owing to a small
defect in her reversing gear; and one seaman, to his lasting shame, was
actually sea-sick on the five-minute trip across the river to top up at the
oiler . . . But these were odd items in a quick process of re-establishment:
when they picked up their convoy off the Bar Light Vessel they were
already halfway back to the old routine, and by the time they were two
days out, clear of land, and heading in a wide south-westerly circle for
Gibraltar, the ship was fighting fit again. The weather gave them a
wonderful succession of sunlit days and calm nights; and conscious of
their luck in sailing for hour after hour over a deep blue, mirror-calm sea,
the sort of warm and lazy trip that cost a guinea a day in peace-time, they
quickly made the transfer from land to seafaring. It was, from many
angles, good to be back on the job again: clear of the dubious and
emotional tie of land, they were once more part of an increased escort –
two destroyers and five corvettes – charged with the care of twenty-one
deep-laden ships bound for Gibraltar. This was their real task, and they
turned to it again with the readiness of men who, knowing that the task
was crucial, were never wholly convinced that the Navy could afford to
let them take a holiday.

The treachery of that perfect weather, the lure of the easy transition,
were not long in the declaring.

It started with a single aircraft, possibly an old friend, a four-engined
Focke-Wulf reconnaissance plane which closed the convoy from the
eastwards and then began to go round them in slow circles, well out of
range of any gun-fire they could put up. It had happened to them before,

and there was little doubt of what the plane was doing – pin-pointing the convoy, shadowing it, noting exactly its course and speed, and then reporting back to some central authority, as well as tipping off any U-boats that might be nearby. The change this time lay in the fact that it was occurring so early in their voyage, and that, as they watched the plane circling and realized its mission, the sun was pouring down from a matchless sky onto a sea as smooth and as lovely as old glass, hardly disturbed at all by the company of ships that crossed it on their way southwards. Unfair to peace-loving convoys, they thought as they closed their ranks and trained their glasses on the slowly-circling messenger of prey: leave us alone on this painted ocean, let us slip by, no one will know . . .

At dusk the plane withdrew, droning away eastwards at the same level pace: up on the bridge, preparing to darken ship and close down for the night, they watched it go with gloomy foreboding.

'It's too easy,' said Ericson broodingly, voicing their thoughts. 'All it's got to do is to fly round us, sending out some kind of homing signal, and every U-boat within a hundred miles just steers straight for us.' He eyed the sky, innocent and cloudless. 'I wish it would blow up a bit. This sort of weather doesn't give us a chance.'

There was nothing out of the ordinary that night, except a signal at eleven o'clock addressed by the Admiralty to their convoy. 'There are indications of five U-boats in your area, with others joining,' it warned them with generous scope, and left them to make the best they could of it. As soon as darkness fell the convoy changed its course from the one the aircraft had observed, going off at a sharp tangent in the hope of escaping the pursuit: perhaps it was successful, perhaps the U-boats were still out of range, for the five hours of darkness passed without incident, while on the Radar-screen the compact square of ships and the out-lying fringe of escorts moved steadily forwards, undisturbed, escaping notice. *Viperous*, making her routine dash round the convoy at first light, signalled: 'I think we fooled them,' as she swept past *Compass Rose*. The steep wave of her wash had just started them rolling when they heard the drone of an aircraft, and the spy was with them again.

The first ship was torpedoed and set on fire at midday. She was a big tanker – all the twenty-one ships in the convoy were of substantial size, many of them bound for Malta and the eastern Mediterranean: it was a hand-picked lot, a valuable prize well worth the pursuit and the harrying. And pursued and harried they were, without quarter: the swift destruction of that first ship marked the beginning of an eight-day battle which took steady toll of the convoy, thinning out the ships each night with horrible regularity, making of each dawn a disgusting nursery-rhyme, a roll-call of the diminishing band of nigger-boys.

CALL TO ARMS

They fought back, they did their best: but the odds against them were too high, the chinks in their armour impossible to safeguard against so many circling enemies.

'There are nine U-boats in your area,' said the Admiralty at dusk that night, as generous as ever; and the nine U-boats between them sank three ships, one of them in circumstances of special horror. She was known to be carrying about twenty Wrens, the first draft to be sent to Gibraltar: aboard *Compass Rose* they had watched the girls strolling about the deck, had waved to them as they passed, had been glad of their company even at long range. The ship that carried them was the last to be struck that night: she went down so swiftly that the flames which engulfed the whole of her after-part hardly had time to take hold before they were quenched. The noise of that quenching was borne over the water towards *Compass Rose*, a savage hissing roar, indescribably cruel. 'By God, it's those poor kids!' exclaimed Ericson, jolted out of a calm he could not preserve at so horrible a moment. But there was nothing that they could do: they were busy on a wide search ordered by *Viperous*, and they could not leave it. If there were anything left to rescue, someone else would have to do it.

Four of the girls *were* in fact picked up by another merchant-ship which had bravely stopped and lowered a boat for the job. They were to be seen next morning, sitting close together on the upper deck, staring out at the water: there was no gay waving now, from either side ... But the ship that rescued them was one of the two that were sunk that same night: she too went down swiftly, and *Compass Rose*, detailed this time to pick up survivors could only add four to her own total of living passengers, and six to the dead. Among these dead was one of the wrens, the only one that any ship found out of the draft of twenty: included in the neat row of corpses which Tallow laid out on the quarter-deck, the girl's body struck a note of infinite pity. She was young: the drenched fair hair, the first that had ever touched the deck of *Compass Rose*, lay like a spread fan, outlining a pinched and frightened face which would, in living repose, have been lovely. Lockhart, who had come aft at dawn to see to the sewing-up of those that were to be buried, felt a constriction in his throat as he looked down at her. Surely there could be no sadder, no filthier aspect of war ... But there were many other things to do besides mourn or pity. They buried her with the rest, and added her name to the list in the log, and continued the prodigal southward journey.

Six ships were gone already: six ships in two days, and they still had a week to go before they were near the shelter of land. But now they had a stroke of luck: a succession of two dark nights which, combined with a violent evasive alteration of course, threw the pursuit off the scent. Though they were still on the alert, and the tension, particularly at night, was still there, yet for forty-eight hours they enjoyed a wonderful sense of respite: the convoy, now reduced to fifteen ships, cracked on speed,

286

romping along towards the southern horizon and the promise of safety. Aboard *Compass Rose*, a cheerful optimism succeeded the sense of ordained misfortune which had begun to take a hold; and the many survivors whom they had picked up, wandering about the upper deck in their blankets and scraps of clothing or lining the rails to stare out at the convoy, lost gradually the strained refugee look which was so hard on the naval conscience. Hope grew: they might see harbour after all ...

So it was for two days and two nights; and then the aircraft, casting wide circles in the clear dawn sky, found them again.

Rose, the young signalman, heard it first: a stirring in the upper air, a faint purring whisper which meant discovery. He looked round him swiftly, his head cocked on one side: he called out: 'Aircraft, sir – somewhere ...' and Ferraby and Baker, who had the forenoon watch, came to the alert in the same swift nervous movement. The throbbing grew, and achieved a definite direction – somewhere on their port beam, away from the convoy and towards the distant Spanish coast. 'Captain, sir!' called Baker down the voice-pipe. 'Sound of aircraft –' but Ericson was already mounting the bridge-ladder, brought up from his sea-cabin by the hated noise. He looked round him, narrowing his eyes against the bright day, and then: 'There it is!' he exclaimed suddenly, and pointed. On their beam, emerging from the pearly morning mist that lay low on the horizon all round them, was the plane, the spying eye of the enemy.

They all stared at it, every man on the bridge, bound together by the same feeling of anger and hatred. It was so unfair ... U-boats they could deal with – or at least the odds were more level: with a bit of luck in the weather, and the normal skill of sailors, the convoy could feint and twist and turn and hope to escape their pursuit. But this predatory messenger from another sphere, destroying the tactical pattern, eating into any distance they contrived to put between themselves and the enemy – this betrayer could never be baulked. They felt, as they watched the aircraft, a helpless sense of nakedness, an ineffectual rage: clearly, it was all going to happen again, in spite of their care and watchfulness, in spite of their best endeavour, and all because a handful of young men in an aircraft could span half an ocean in a few hours, and come plummeting down upon their slower prey.

Swiftly the aircraft must have done its work, and the U-boats could not have been far away; within twelve hours, back they came, and that night cost the convoy two more ships out of the dwindling fleet. The hunt was up once more, the pack exultant, the savage rhythm returning and quickening ... They did their best: the escorts counter-attacked, the convoy altered course and increased its speed: all to no purpose. The sixth day dawned, the sixth night came: punctually at midnight the alarm-bells sounded and the first distress-rocket soared up into the night sky, telling of a ship mortally hit and calling for help. She burned for a long time, that ship, reddening the water, lifting sluggishly with the swell, becoming at last a flickering oily pyre which the convoy left slowly astern. Then there was a pause of more than two hours, while they remained alert at Action-Stations and the convoy slid southwards under a black moonless sky; and then, far out on the seaward horizon, five miles away from them, there was a sudden return of violence. A brilliant orange flash split the darkness, died down, flared up again, and then guttered away to nothing. Clearly it was another ship hit – but this time, for them, it was much more than a ship; for this time, this time it was *Sorrel*.

They all knew it must be *Sorrel*, because at that distance it could not be any other ship, and also because of an earlier signal which they had relayed to her from *Viperous*. 'In case of an attack tonight', said the signal, '*Sorrel* will proceed five miles astern and to seaward of the convoy, and create a diversion by dropping depth-charges, firing rockets, etc. This may draw the main attack away from the convoy.' They had seen the rockets earlier that night, and disregarded them: they only meant that *Sorrel*, busy in a corner, was doing her stuff according to plan ... Probably that plan had been effective, if the last two hours' lull were anything to go by: certainly it had, from one point of view, been an ideal exercise, diverting at least one attack from its proper mark. But in the process, someone had to suffer: it had not cancelled the stalking approach, it did not stop the torpedo being fired: *Sorrel* became the mark, in default of a richer prize, meeting her lonely end in the outer ring of darkness beyond the convoy.

Poor *Sorrel*, poor sister-corvette ... Up on the bridge of *Compass Rose*, the men who had known her best of all were now the mourners, standing separated from each other by the blackness of night but bound by the same shock, the same incredulous sorrow. How could it have happened to *Sorrel*, to an escort like themselves...? Immediately he saw the explosion, Ericson had rung down to the wireless office. '"*Viperous* from *Compass Rose*"', he dictated. '"*Sorrel* torpedoed in her diversion position. May I leave and search for survivors?"' Then: 'Code that up,' he snapped to the telegraphist who was taking down the message. 'Quick as you can. Send it by R/T.' Then, the message sent, they waited, silent in the darkness of the bridge, eyeing the dim bulk of the nearest ship, occasionally turning back to where *Sorrel* had been struck. No one said a word: there were no words for this. There were only thoughts, and not many of those.

The bell of the wireless-office rang sharply, breaking the silence, and Leading-Signalman Wells, who was standing by the voice-pipe, bent down to it.

'Bridge!' he said, and listened for a moment. Then he straightened up, and called to the Captain across the grey width of the bridge. 'Answer from *Viperous*, sir ... "Do not leave convoy until daylight".'

There was silence again, a sickened, appalled silence. Ericson set his teeth. He might have guessed ... It was the right answer, of course, from the cold technical angle: *Viperous* simply could not afford to take another escort from the screen, and send her off on a non-essential job. It was the right answer, but by Christ it was a hard one! ... Back there in the lonely darkness, ten miles and more away by now, men were dying, men of a special sort: people they knew well, sailors like themselves: and they were to be left to die, or, at best, their rescue was to be delayed for a period which must cost many lives. *Sorrel*'s sinking had come as an extraordinary shock to them all: she was the first escort that had ever been lost out of their group, and she was, of all the ones that could have gone, their own chummy-ship, the ship they had tied up alongside after countless convoys, for two years on end: manned by their friends, men they played tombola with or met in pubs ashore: men they could always beat at football ... For *Sorrel* to be torpedoed was bad enough; but to leave her crew to sink or swim in the darkness was the most cruel stroke of all.

'Daylight,' said Morell suddenly, breaking the oppressive silence on the bridge. 'Two more hours to wait.'

Ericson found himself answering: 'Yes' – not to Morell's words, but to what he had meant. It was a cold night. With two hours to wait, and then the time it would take them to run back to where *Sorrel* had gone down, there would be very few men to pick up.

There were in fact fifteen – fifteen out of a ship's company of ninety.

They found them without much difficulty, towards the end of the morning watch, sighting the two specks which were Carley rafts across three miles or more of flat unruffled sea. However familiar this crude seascape had become to them, it was especially moving to come upon it again now: to approach the loaded rafts and the cluster of oily bodies washing about among *Sorrel*'s wreckage: to see, here and there in this filthy aftermath, their own uniforms, their own badges and caps, almost their own mirrored faces ... The men on the rafts were stiff and cold and soaked with oil, but as *Compass Rose* approached, one of them waved with wild energy, foolishly greeting a rescuer not more than twenty yards away from him. Some of the men were clearly dead, from cold or exhaustion, even though they had gained the safety of the rafts: they lay with their heads on other men's knees, cherished and warmed until death and perhaps for hours beyond it. Ericson, looking through his binoculars at the ragged handful that remained, caught sight of the grey face of *Sorrel*'s captain, Ramsay, his friend for many years. Ramsay was holding a body in his arms, a young sailor, ugly and pitiful in death, the head thrown back, the mouth hanging open. But the living face above the dead one was hardly less pitiful. The whole story – the lost ship, the lost crew, the pain and exhaustion of the last six hours – all these were in Ramsay's face as he sat, holding the dead body, waiting for rescue.

It was a true captain's face, a captain in defeat who mourned his ship, and bore alone the monstrous burden of its loss.

Lockhart, waiting in the waist of the ship while the survivors were helped aboard, greeted him with impulsive warmth as he climbed stiffly over the side.

'Very glad to see you, sir!' he exclaimed eagerly. Everything about Ramsay – his expression, his weary movements, his reeking oil-soaked uniform – was suddenly and deeply moving, so that to have saved his life, even in these tragic circumstances, seemed a triumph and a blessing. 'We were all hoping –' he stopped awkwardly, watching Ramsay's face. He knew immediately that it would be wrong, terribly wrong, to say: 'We were all hoping that we'd pick *you* up, anyway.' That was not what Ramsay himself was feeling, at that moment. Rather the reverse.

'Thanks, Number One.' Ramsay, straightening up, turned round and gestured vaguely towards the men still on the rafts. 'Look after them, won't you? One or two of them are pretty far gone.'

Lockhart nodded. 'I'll see to all that, sir.'

'I'll go up to the bridge, then.' But he lingered by the rails, watching with hurt eyes as the remnants of his crew were helped or hauled or lifted tenderly in-board. In the middle of the crowd of men working, he was unassailably withdrawn and private in his grief. When the living were seen to, and they were starting on the dead, he turned away and walked slowly towards the bridge-ladder, his oily bare feet slurring and slopping along the deck. Lockhart was glad to be kept busy and preoccupied at that moment. It was not one to be intruded on, upon any pretext.

To Ericson, up on the bridge, Ramsay presently held out his hand and said:

'Thanks, George. I'll never forget that.' The West Country accent was very prominent.

'Sorry we couldn't be here earlier,' said Ericson shortly. 'But I couldn't leave the screen before daylight.'

'It wouldn't have made much difference,' answered Ramsay. He had turned away, and was once more watching the bodies coming in-board, and the other bodies that disfigured the even surface of the sea round *Compass Rose*. 'Most of them were caught below, anyway. We broke in half. Went down in a couple of minutes.'

Ericson said nothing. Presently Ramsay turned back to him and said, half to himself:

'You never think that *you'll* be the one to catch it. It's something you can't be ready for, no matter how much you think about it. When it does happen –' he broke off, as if at some self-reproach which he did not know how to voice, and then the moment itself was interrupted by Signalman Rose, alert at one of the voice-pipes.

'Signal from *Viperous*, sir,' he called out. 'Addressed to us. "Rejoin the convoy forthwith".'

'Something must be happening,' said Ericson. He walked to the head of the bridge-ladder, and looked down at the waist of the ship. The two rafts were cleared now, but there were still twenty or more bodies floating within a circle of half a mile of them. 'I'd like to—' he began uncertainly.

Ramsay shook his head. 'It doesn't matter, George,' he said quietly. 'What's the odds, anyway? Leave them where they are.'

He did not look at anyone or anything as *Compass Rose* drew away.

What had happened, as they discovered when they caught up the convoy, towards midday, was that another ship had been torpedoed, in broad daylight, and *Viperous* was rightly anxious to close up all the escorts as soon as possible. There could be no pause, no respite in this long chasing battle: certainly the dead had no claim – not even when, as now, they were beginning to outnumber the living. By noon of that seventh day, the tally of ships was eleven – eleven out of the original twenty-one; behind them were ten good merchant-ships sunk, and countless men drowned, and one of the escorts lost as well. It was horrible to think of the hundreds of miles of sea that lay in their wake, strewn with the oil and the wreckage and the corpses they were leaving behind them: it was like some revolting paper-chase, with the convoy laying a trail from an enormous suppurating satchel of blood and treasure. But some of it – the Wrens, and *Sorrel*, and the screams of the men caught in the first ship lost, the burning tanker – some of it did not bear thinking about at all.

It was not a one-sided battle, with repeated hammer strokes on the one hand and a futile dodging on the other, but it was not much better than that, in the way it was working out; there were too many U-boats in contact with them, not enough escorts, not enough speed or manoeuvre-ability in the convoy to give it a level chance. They had fought back all that they could. *Compass Rose* had dropped more than forty depth-charges on her various counter-attacks, some of which should have done some damage: the other escorts had put up a lively display of energy: *Viperous* herself, after one accurate attack, had sufficient evidence in the way of oil and wreckage to claim a U-boat destroyed. But as far as the overall picture was concerned, all this was simply a feeble beating of the air: with so many U-boats in their area, miracles were necessary to escape the appalling trap the convoy had run into, and no miracles came their way. There was no chance of winning, and no way of retreat; all they could do was to close their ranks, make the best speed they could, and sweat it out to the end.

Compass Rose had never been so crowded, so crammed with survivors. It was lucky, indeed, that they had the new sick-bay and the Sick-Berth Attendant to deal with their wounded and exhausted passengers: Lockhart could never have coped with the continual flow, singlehanded.

But apart from the number of people requiring attention, they had collected a huge additional complement of rescued men – far outnumbering, indeed, their own crew. There were fourteen Merchant Navy officers in the wardroom, including three ship's captains: there were a hundred and twenty-one others – seamen, firemen, cooks, Lascars, Chinese – thronging the upper deck by day and at night crowding into the messdecks to eat and sleep and wait for the next dawn. During the dark hours, indeed, the scene in the darkened fo'c'sle was barely describable. Under the shaded yellow lamp was a scene from the Inferno, a nightmare of tension and confusion and discomfort and pain.

The place was crammed to the deckhead: men stood or sat or knelt or lay, in every available space: they crouched under the tables, they wedged themselves in corners, they stretched out on top of the broad ventilating shafts. There were men being sea-sick, men crying out in their sleep, men wolfing food, men hugging their bits of possessions and staring at nothing: wounded men groaning, apparently fit men laughing uneasily at nothing, brave men who could still summon a smile and a straight answer. It was impossible to pick one's way from one end of the fo'c'sle to the other, as Lockhart did each night when he made the Rounds, without being shocked and appalled and saddened by this slum corner of the war: and yet somehow one could be heartened also, and cheered by an impression of patience and endurance, and made to feel proud ... Individuals, here and there, might have been pushed close to defeat or panic; but the gross crowding, the rags, the oil, the bandages, the smell of men in adversity, were *still* not enough to defeat the whole company. They were all sailors there, not to be overwhelmed even by this sudden and sustained nightmare: they were being mucked about, it was true, but it would have to be a lot worse than this before they changed their minds about the sea.

There was another sort of nightmare, which kept recurring to Lockhart as he looked at the throng of survivors, and at *Compass Rose*'s seamen making their cheerful best of the invasion, and met a puzzled or frightened face here and there in the crowd. Suppose, like *Sorrel*, they were hit: suppose they went down in a minute or so, in two broken halves, as *Sorrel* had done: what would happen in there, what sort of trapped and clawing shambles would develop as they slid to the bottom? The details could not really be faced, though it was possible that other people in the fo'c'sle were occupying their spare time in facing them. Once, when Lockhart was adjusting a survivor's bandaged arm, the man said:

'Be all right for swimming, eh?'

Lockhart smiled. 'Sure thing. But you won't be doing any more swimming on this trip.'

The man looked straight at him, and jerked his head. 'You're dead right there. If anything happens to this lot, we're snug in our coffin already.'

The afternoon that they rejoined the convoy, another signal came from the Admiralty. 'There are now eleven U-boats in your area,' it ran. 'Destroyers *Lancelot* and *Liberal* will join escort at approximately 1800.'

'Two L Class destroyers – that's grand!' said Baker enthusiastically, down in the wardroom at tea-time. 'They're terrific ships. Brand new, too.'

'They'd better be very terrific indeed,' said Morell, who was reading a copy of the signal. 'Eleven U-boats works out at one to each ship left in the convoy. I very much doubt,' he added suavely, 'whether Their Lordships really intended such a nice balance of forces.'

Morell considered for a moment, 'I must admit,' he said finally, 'that this is *not* a reassuring occasion. Whatever we do, those damned U-boats get inside the screen every time. We've lost almost half our ships, and we're still two days away from Gibraltar.' He paused, 'It's odd to think that even if nothing else happens, this is probably the worst convoy in the history of sea-warfare.'

'Something to tell your grandchildren.'

'Yes, indeed. In fact, if you guarantee me grandchildren I shall recover my spirits very quickly.'

'How can he guarantee that you have grandchildren?' asked Baker who was, aboard *Compass Rose* at least, a dull conversationalist.

'If they're as stupid as you,' said Morell, with a flash of impatience so rare that he must in truth have been nervous, 'I hope I don't have any.'

They were all feeling the same, thought Lockhart in the offended silence that followed: irritable, on edge, inclined to intolerance with each other. The tiredness and strain that had mounted during the past week was reaching an almost unbearable pitch. There could be no cure for it save gaining harbour with the remnants of their convoy, and that was still two days ahead. He suddenly wanted, more than anything else in the world, to be at peace and in safety. Like the rest of them, like all the escorts and all the merchant-ships, he had very nearly had enough.

The two destroyers joined punctually at six o'clock, coming up from the south-east to meet the convoy, advancing swiftly towards it, each with an enormous creaming bow-wave. They both exhibited, to a special degree, that dramatic quality which was the pride of all destroyers: they were lean, fast, enormously powerful – nearer to light cruisers than destroyers – and clearly worth about three of any normal escort. They made a cheerful addition to the ships in company, thrashing valiantly at the slightest scare or none at all, darting round and through the convoy at a full thirty-five knots, signalling in three directions at once, and refusing to stay still in any one position for more than five minutes at a time.

'Proper show off,' said Leading-Signalman Wells, watching them through his glasses as they sped past on some purely inventive errand. But there was a touch of envy in his voice as he added: 'All very well for them to dash about like a couple of brand-new tarts – they haven't had the last week along o' this lot.'

At dusk the two newcomers settled down, one ahead and one astern of the convoy, completing the atmosphere of last-minute rescue which had accompanied their arrival. They were doubtless well aware of the effect they had produced. But theatrical or not, their presence did seem to make a difference: though there was an attack that night, all that the circling pack of U-boats could account for was one ship, the smallest ship in the convoy. She was hit astern, and she went down slowly: out of her whole company the only casualty was a single Lascar seaman who jumped (as he thought) into the sea with a wild cry and landed head first in one of the life-boats. In the midst of the wholesale slaughter, this comedy exit had just the right touch of fantasy about it to make it seem really funny ... But even so, this ship was the eleventh to be lost, out of the original twenty-one: it put them over the halfway mark, establishing a new and atrocious record of U-boat successes. And the next night, the eighth and last of the battle, when they were within three hundred miles of Gibraltar, made up for any apparent slackening in the rate of destruction.

That last night cost three more ships, and one of them – yet another loaded tanker to be torpedoed and set on fire – was the special concern of *Compass Rose*. It was she who was nearest when the ship was struck, and she circled round as the oil, cascading and spouting from the tanker's open side, took fire and spread over the surface of the water like a flaming carpet in a pitch-black room. Silhouetted against this roaring backcloth which soon rose to fifty feet in the air, *Compass Rose* must have been visible for miles around: even in swift movement she made a perfect target, and Ericson, trying to decide whether to stop and pick up survivors, or whether the risk would not be justified, could visualize clearly what they would look like when stationary against this wall of flame. *Compass Rose*, with her crew and her painfully collected ship-load of survivors, would be a sitting mark from ten miles away ... But they had been detailed as rescue-ship: there were men in the water, there were boats from the tanker already lowered and pulling away from the tower of flame: there was a job to be done, a work of mercy, if the risk were acceptable – if it was worth hazarding two hundred lives in order to gain fifty more, if prudence could be stretched to include humanity.

It was Ericson's decision alone. It was a captain's moment, a pure test of nerve: it was, once again, the reality that lay behind the saluting and the graded discipline and the two-and-a-half stripes on the sleeve. While Ericson, silent on the bridge, considered the chances, there was not a man in the ship who would have changed places with him.

The order, when it came, was swift and decisive.

'Stop engines!'

'Stop engines, sir ... Engines stopped, wheel amidships, sir.'

'Number One!'

'Sir?' said Lockhart.

'Stand by to get those survivors in-board. We won't lower a boat – they'll have to swim or row towards us. God knows they can see us easily enough. Use a megaphone to hurry them up.'

'Aye, aye, sir.'

As Lockhart turned to leave the bridge, the Captain added, almost conversationally:

'We don't want to waste any time, Number One.'

All over the ship a prickling silence fell, as *Compass Rose* slowly came to a stop and waited, rolling gently, lit by the glare from the fire. From the bridge, every detail of the upper deck could be picked out: there was no flickering in this huge illumination, simply a steady glow which threw a black shadow on the sea behind them, which showed them naked to the enemy, which endowed the white faces turned towards it with a photographic brilliance. Waiting aft among his depth-charge crews, while the flames roared and three boats crept towards them, and faint shouting and bobbing lights here and there on the water indicated a valiant swimmer making for safety, Ferraby was conscious only of a terror-stricken impatience. Oh God, oh God, oh God, he thought, almost aloud: let them give this up, let them get moving again ... Twenty feet away from him in the port waist, Lockhart was coolly directing the preliminaries to the work of rescue – rigging a sling for the wounded men, securing the scrambling-nets that hung over the side, by which men in the water could pull themselves up.

Ferraby watched him, not with admiration or envy but with a futile hatred. Damn you, he thought, once more almost saying the words out loud: how can you be like that, why don't you feel like me – or if you do, why don't you show it? He turned away from the brisk figures and the glowing heat of the flames, his eyes traversing the arch of black sky overhead, a sky blotched and streaked by smoke and whirling sparks; he looked behind him, at the outer darkness which the fire could not pierce, the place where the submarines must be lying and watching them. No submarine within fifty miles could miss this beacon, no submarine within five could resist chancing a torpedo, no submarine within two could fail to hit the silhouetted target, the stationary prey. It was wicked to stop like this, just for a lot of damned merchant-navy toughs ...

A boat drew alongside, bumping and scraping: Lockhart called out: 'Hook on forrard!' there were sounds of scrambling: an anonymous voice, foreign, slightly breathless, said: 'God bless you for stopping!' The work of collection began.

It did not take long, save in their own minds; but coming towards the end of the long continued ordeal of the voyage, when there was no man in the ship who was not near to exhaustion, those minutes spent motionless in the limelight had a creeping and paralytic tension. It seemed impossible for them to take such a reckless chance, and not be punished for it; there was, in the war at sea, a certain limiting factor to bravery, and beyond that, fate stood waiting with a ferocious rebuke. 'If we don't buy it this time,' said Wainwright, the torpedo-man, standing by his depth-charges and staring at the flames, 'Jerry doesn't *deserve* to win the war.' It did seem, indeed, that if *Sorrel* could be hit when she was zigzagging at fourteen knots, there wouldn't be much trouble with *Compass Rose*; and as the minutes passed, while they collected three boatloads of survivors and a handful of swimmers, and the huge circle of fire gave its steady illumination, they seemed to be getting deeper and deeper into a situation from which they would never be able to retreat. The men who had work to do were lucky: the men who simply waited, like Ericson on the bridge or the stokers below the water-line, knew, in those few agonizing minutes, the meaning of fear.

It never happened: that was the miracle of that night. Perhaps some U-boat fired and missed, perhaps those within range, content with their success, had submerged for safety's sake and broken off the attack: at any rate, *Compass Rose* was allowed her extraordinary hazard, without having to settle the bill. When there were no more men to pick up, she got under way again: the returning pulse of her engine, heard and felt throughout the ship, came like some incredible last-minute respite, astonishing them all. But the pulse strengthened and quickened, in triumphant chorus, and she drew away from the flames and the smell of oil with her extra load of survivors snatched from the very mouth of danger, and her flaunting gesture unchallenged. They had taken the chance, and it had come off; mixed with the exhilaration of that triumph was a sober thankfulness for deliverance, a certain humility. Perhaps it would not do to think too much about it: perhaps it was better to bury the moment as quickly as possible, and forget it, and not take that chance again.

Another ship, on the opposite wing, went down at four o'clock, just before dawn; and then, as daylight strengthened and the rags of the convoy drew together again, they witnessed the last cruel item of the voyage.

Lagging behind with some engine defect, a third ship was hit, and began to settle down on her way to the bottom. She sank slowly, but owing to bad organization, or the villainous list which the torpedoing gave her, no boats got away; for her crew, it was a time for swimming, for jumping into the water, and striking out away from the fatal downward suction, and trusting to luck. *Compass Rose*, dropping back to come to her aid, circled round as the ship began to disappear; and then, as she dipped below the level of the sea and the swirling ripples began to spread outwards from a central point which was no longer there, Ericson turned his ship's bows towards the centre of disaster, and the bobbing heads which dotted the surface of the water. But it was not to be a straightforward rescue; for just as he was opening his mouth to give the order for lowering a boat, the Asdic-set picked up a contact, an undersea echo so crisp and well-defined that it could only be a U-boat.

Lockhart, at his Action-Station in the Asdic-compartment, felt his heart miss a beat as he heard that echo. At last .. He called through the open window: 'Echo bearing two-two-five – moving left!' and bent over the Asdic-set in acute concentration. Ericson increased the revolutions again, and turned away from the indicated bearing, meaning to increase the range: if they were to drop depth-charges, they would need a longer run-in to get up speed. In his turn, he called out: 'What's it look like, Number One?' and Lockhart, hearing the harsh pinging noise and watching the mark on the recording set, said: 'Submarine, sir – can't be anything else.' He continued to call out the bearing and the range of the contact: Ericson prepared to take the ship in, at attacking speed, and to drop a pattern of depth-charges on the way; and then, as *Compass Rose* turned inwards towards the target, gathering speed for the onslaught, they all noticed something which had escaped their attention before. The place where the U-boat lay, the point where they must drop their charges, was alive with swimming survivors.

The Captain drew in his breath sharply at the sight. There were about forty men in the water, concentrated in a small space: if he went ahead with the attack he must, for certain, kill them all. He knew well enough, as did everyone on board, the effect of depth-charges exploding under water – the splitting crash which made the sea jump and boil and spout skywards, the aftermath of torn seaweed and dead fish which always littered the surface after the explosion. Now there were men instead of fish and seaweed, men swimming towards him in confidence and hope ... And yet the U-boat was there, one of the pack which had been harassing and bleeding them for days on end, the destroying menace which *must* have priority, because of what it might do to other ships and other convoys in the future: he could hear the echo on the relay-loudspeaker, he acknowledged Lockhart's developed judgement where the Asdic-set was concerned. As the seconds sped by, and the range closed, he fought against his doubts, and against the softening instinct of mercy: the book said: 'Attack at all costs,' and this was a page out of the book, and the men swimming in the water did not matter at all, when it was a question of bringing one of the killers to account.

But for a few moments longer he tried to gain support and confidence for what he had to do.

'What's it look like now, Number One?'

'The same, sir – solid echo – exactly the right size – *must* be a U-boat.'

'Is it moving?'

'Very slowly.'

'There are some men in the water, just about there.'

There was no answer. The range decreased as *Compass Rose* ran in: they were now within six hundred yards of the swimmers and the U-boat, the fatal coincidence which had to be ignored.

'What's it look like now?' Ericson repeated.

'Just the same – seems to be stationary – it's the strongest contact we've ever had.'

'There are some chaps in the water.'

'Well, there's a U-boat just underneath them.'

All right, then, thought Ericson, with a new unlooked-for access of brutality to help him: all right, we'll go for the U-boat. With no more hesitation he gave the order: 'Attacking – stand by!' to the depth-charge positions aft: and having made this sickening choice he swept into the attack with a deadened mind, intent only on one kind of kill, pretending there was no other.

Many of the men in the water waved wildly as they saw what was happening: some of them screamed, some threw themselves out of the ship's path and thrashed furiously in the hope of reaching safety: others, slower-witted or nearer to exhaustion, still thought that *Compass Rose* was speeding to their rescue, and continued to wave and smile almost to their last moment ... The ship came in like an avenging angel, cleaving the very centre of the knots of swimmers: the amazement and horror on their faces was reflected aboard *Compass Rose*, where many of the crew, particularly among the depth-charge parties aft, could not believe what they were being called upon to do. Only two men did not share this horror: Ericson, who had shut and battened down his mind except to a single thought – the U-boat they must kill: and Ferraby, whose privilege it was to drop the depth-charges. 'Serve you bloody well right!' thought Ferraby as *Compass Rose* swept in among the swimmers, catching some of them in her screw, while the firing bell sounded and charges rolled over the stern or were rocketed outwards from the throwers: 'Serve you right – you nearly killed us last night, making us stop next door to that fire – now it's your turn.'

There was a deadly pause, while for a few moments the men aboard *Compass Rose* and the men left behind in her wake stared at each other, in pity and fear and a kind of basic disbelief; and then with a huge hammer-crack the depth-charges exploded.

Mercifully, the details were hidden in the flurry and roar of the explosion; and the men must all have died instantly, shocked out of life by the tremendous pressure of the sea thrown up upon their bodies. But one freak item of horror impressed itself upon the memory. As the tormented water leapt upwards in a solid grey cloud, the single figure of a man was tossed high on the very plume of the fountain, a puppet figure of whirling arms and legs seeming to make, in death, wild gestures of anger and reproach. It appeared to hang a long time in the air, cursing them all, before falling back into the boiling sea.

When they ran back to the explosion area, with the Asdic silent and the contact not regained, it was as if to some aquarium where poisoned water had killed every living thing. Men floated on the surface like dead goldfish in a film of blood. Most of them were disintegrated, or pulped out of human shape. But half a dozen of them, who must have been on the edge of the explosion, had come to a tidier end: split open from chin to crutch, they had been as neatly gutted as any herring. Some seagulls were already busy on the scene, screaming with excitement and delight. Nothing else stirred.

No one looked at Ericson as they left that place: if they had done so, they might have been shocked by his expression and his extraordinary pallor. Now deep in self-torture, and appalled by what he had done, he had already decided that there had been no U-boat there in the first place: the contact was probably the torpedoed ship, sliding slowly to the bottom, or the disturbed water of her sinking. Either way, the slaughter which he had inflicted was something extra, a large entirely British-made contribution to the success of the voyage.

By the time they were past the Straits, and had smelt the burnt smell of Africa blowing across from Ceuta, and had shaped a course for Gibraltar Harbour, they were all far off balance.

It had gone on too long, it had failed too horribly, it had cost too much. They had been at Action-Stations for virtually eight days on end, missing hours of sleep, making do with scratch meals of cocoa and corned-beef sandwiches, living all the time under recurrent anxieties which often reached a desperate tension. There had hardly been a moment of the voyage when they could forget the danger that lay in wait for them and the days of strain that stretched ahead, and relax and find peace. They had been hungry and dirty and tired from one sunrise to the next: they had lived in a ship crammed and disorganized by nearly three times her normal complement. Through it all, they had had to preserve an alertness and a keyed-up efficiency, hard enough to maintain even in normal circumstances.

The deadly part was that it had all been in vain, it had all been wasted: there could have been no more futile expense of endurance and nervous energy. Besides *Sorrel*, which was in a special category of disaster, they had lost fourteen ships out of the original twenty-one – two-thirds of the entire convoy wiped out by a series of pack-attacks so adroit and so ferocious that counter-measures had been quite futile. That was the most wretched element of the voyage – the inescapable sense of futility, the conviction that there were always more U-boats than escorts and that the U-boats could strike, and strike home, practically as they willed.

The escorts, and *Compass Rose* among them, seemed to have been beating the air all the time: they could do nothing save count the convoy's losses at each dawn, and make, sometimes, a vain display of force which vanished like a trickle of water swallowed by an enormous sea. In the end, they had all sickened of the slaughter, and of the battle too.

To off-set the mortal bleeding of the convoy, by far the worst of this or any other war, *Viperous* had sunk one U-boat: a second had probably been destroyed; and *Compass Rose* herself had collected 175 survivors – nearly twice the number of her own crew. But this seemed nothing much, when set alongside the total loss of lives: it seemed nothing much, when measured against the men they had depth-charged and killed, instead of saving: it seemed nothing much, when shadowed by the stricken figure of *Sorrel's* captain, wordless and brooding at the back of their bridge as *Compass Rose* slid into the shelter of Gibraltar Harbour, under the huge Rock that dwarfed and mocked the tiny defeated ships below.

Waterloo

W. M. THACKERAY

Mrs O'Dowde and the lovely young Amelia are waiting in a fever of suspense and fear for news of their husbands in the field in the army under the Duke of Wellington. Others, like the cowardly braggart Jos Sedley and the cool and calculating Rebecca Crawley, react rather differently to the desperate situation . . . . .

WE OF PEACEFUL LONDON city have never beheld – and please God never shall witness – such a scene of hurry and alarm, as that which Brussels presented. Crowds rushed to the Namur gate, from which direction the noise proceeded, and many rode along the level *chaussée*, to be in advance of any intelligence from the army. Each man asked his neighbour for news; and even great English lords and ladies condescended to speak to persons whom they did not know. The friends of the French went abroad, wild with excitement, and prophesying the triumph of their Emperor. The merchants closed their shops, and came out to swell the general chorus of alarm and clamour. Women rushed to the churches, and crowded the chapels, and knelt and prayed on the flags and steps. The dull sound of the cannon went on rolling, rolling. Presently carriages with travellers began to leave the town, galloping away by the Ghent barrier. The prophecies of the French partisans began to pass for facts. 'He has cut the armies in two,' it was said. 'He is marching straight on Brussels. He will overpower the English, and be here to-night.' 'He will overpower the English,' shrieked Isidor to his master, 'and will be here to-night.' The man bounded in and out from the lodgings to the street, always returning with some fresh particulars of disaster. Jos's face grew paler and paler. Alarm began to take entire possession of the stout civilian. All the champagne he drank brought no courage to him. Before sunset he was worked up to such a pitch of nervousness as gratified his friend Isidor to behold, who now counted surely upon the spoils of the owner of the laced coat.

The women were away all this time. After hearing the firing for a moment, the stout Major's wife bethought her of her friend in the next chamber, and ran in to watch, and if possible to console, Amelia. The idea that she had that helpless and gentle creature to protect, gave additional strength to the natural courage of the honest Irishwoman. She passed five hours by her friend's side, sometimes in remonstrance, sometimes talking cheerfully, oftener in silence, and terrified mental supplication. 'I never let go her hand once,' said the stout lady afterwards, 'until after sunset, when the firing was over.' Pauline, the *bonne*, was on her knees at church hard by, praying for *son homme à elle*.

When the noise of the cannonading was over, Mrs O'Dowd issued out of Amelia's room into the parlour adjoining, where Jos sate with two emptied flasks, and courage entirely gone. Once or twice he had ventured into his sister's bedroom, loking very much alarmed, and as if he would say something. But the Major's wife kept her place, and he went away without disburthening himself of his speech. He was ashamed to tell her that he wanted to fly. But when she made her appearance in the dining-room, where he sate in the twilight in the cheerless company of his empty champagne bottles, he began to open his mind to her.

'Mrs O'Dowd,' he said, 'hadn't you better get Amelia ready?'

'Are you going to take her out for a walk?' said the Major's lady; 'sure she's too weak to stir.'

'I – I've ordered the carriage,' he said, 'and – post-horses; Isidor is gone for them,' Jos continued.

'What do you want with driving to-night!' answered the lady. 'Isn't she better on her bed? I've just got her to lie down.'

'Get her up,' said Jos; 'she must get up, I say:' and he stamped his foot energetically. 'I say the horses are ordered – yes, the horses are ordered. It's all over, and – '

'And what?' asked Mrs O'Dowd.

'I'm off for Ghent,' Jos answered. 'Everybody is going; there's a place for you! We shall start in half-an-hour.'

The Major's wife looked at him with infinite scorn. 'I don't move till O'Dowd gives me the route,' said she. 'You may go if you like, Mr Sedley; but faith, Amelia and I stop here.'

'She *shall* go,' said Jos, with another stamp of his foot. Mrs O'Dowd put herself with arms akimbo before the bedroom door.

'Is it her mother you're going to take her to?' she said; 'or do you want to go to Mamma, yourself, Mr Sedley? Good marning – a pleasant journey to ye, sir. *Bon voyage*, as they say, and take my counsel, and shave off them mustachios, or they'll bring you into mischief.'

'D——n!' yelled out Jos, wild with fear, rage, and mortification; and Isidor came in at this junction, swearing in his turn. '*Pas de chevaux, sacrebleu!*' hissed out the furious domestic. All the horses were gone. Jos was not the only man in Brussels seized with panic that day.

But Jos's fears, great and cruel as they were already, were destined to increase to an almost frantic pitch before the night was over. It had been mentioned how Pauline, the *bonne*, had *son homme à elle* also in the ranks of the army that had gone out to meet the Emperor Napoleon. This lover was a native of Brussels, and a Belgian hussar. The troops of his nation signalised themselves in this war for anything but courage, and young Van Cutsum, Pauline's admirer, was too good a soldier to disobey his Colonel's orders to run away. Whilst in garrison at Brussels young Regulus (he had been born in the revolutionary times) found his great comfort, and passed almost all his leisure moments in Pauline's kitchen; and it was with pockets and holsters crammed full of good things from her larder, that he had taken leave of his weeping sweetheart, to proceed upon the campaign a few days before.

As far as his regiment was concerned, this campaign was over now. They had formed a part of the division under the command of his sovereign apparent, the Prince of Orange, and as respected length of swords and mustachios, and the richness of uniform and equipments, Regulus and his comrades looked to be as gallant a body of men as ever trumpet sounded for.

When Ney dashed upon the advance of the allied troops, carrying one position after the other, until the arrival of the great body of the British army from Brussels changed the aspect of the combat of Quatre Bras, the squadrons among which Regulus rode showed the greatest activity in retreating before the French, and were dislodged from one post after another which they occupied with perfect alacrity on their part. Their movements were only checked by the advance of the British in their rear. Thus forced to halt, the enemy's cavalry (whose bloodthirsty obstinacy cannot be too severely reprehended) had at length an opportunity of coming to close quarters with the brave Belgians before them; who preferred to encounter the British rather than the French, and at once turning tail rode through the English regiments that were behind them, and scattered in all directions. The regiment in fact did not exist any more. It was nowhere. It had no headquarters. Regulus found himself galloping many miles from the field of action, entirely alone; and whither should he fly for refuge so naturally as to that kitchen and those faithful arms in which Pauline had so often welcomed him!

At some ten o'clock the clinking of a sabre might have been heard up the stair of the house where the Osbornes occupied a storey in the Continental fashion. A knock might have been heard at the kitchen door; and poor Pauline, come back from church, fainted almost with terror as she opened it and saw before her her haggard hussar. He looked as pale as the midnight dragoon who came to disturb Leonora. Pauline would have screamed, but that her cry would have called her masters, and discovered her friend. She stifled her scream, then, and leading her hero into the kitchen, gave him beer, and the choice bits from the dinner, which Jos had not had the heart to taste. The hussar showed he was no ghost by the prodigious quantity of flesh and beer which he devoured –

and during the mouthfuls he told his tale of disaster.

His regiment had performed prodigies of courage, and had withstood for a while the onset of the whole French army. But they were overwhelmed at last, as was the whole British army by this time. Ney destroyed each regiment as it came up. The Belgians in vain interposed to prevent the butchery of the English. The Brunswickers were routed and had fled – their Duke was killed. It was a general *débâcle*. He sought to drown his sorrow for the defeat in floods of beer.

Isidor, who had come into the kitchen, heard the conversation, and rushed out to inform his master. 'It is all over,' he shrieked to Jos. 'Milor Duke is a prisoner; the Duke of Brunswick is killed; the British army is in full flight; there is only one man escaped, and he is in the kitchen now – come and hear him.' So Jos tottered into that apartment, where Regulus still sate on the kitchen table, and clung fast to his flagon of beer. In the best French which he could muster, and which was in sooth a very ungrammatical sort, Jos besought the hussar to tell his tale. The disasters deepened as Regulus spoke. He was the only man of his regiment not slain on the field. He had seen the Duke of Brunswick fall, the black hussars fly, the Ecossais pounded down by the cannon.

'And the – th?' gasped Jos.

'Cut in pieces,' said the hussar – upon which Pauline cried out, 'O my mistress, *ma bonne petite dame*,' went off fairly into hysterics, and filled the house with her screams.

Wild with terror, Mr Sedley knew not how or where to seek for safety. He rushed from the kitchen back to the sitting-room, and cast an appealing look at Amelia's door, which Mrs O'Dowd had closed and locked in his face; but he remembered how scornfully the latter had received him, and after pausing and listening for a brief space at the door, he left it, and resolved to go into the street, for the first time that day. So, seizing a candle, he looked about for his gold-laced cap, and found it lying in its usual place, on a console-table, in the anteroom, placed before a mirror at which Jos used to coquet, always giving his side-locks a twirl, and his cap the proper cock over his eye, before he went forth to make appearance in public. Such is the force of habit, that even in the midst of his terror he began mechanically to twiddle with his hair, and arrange the cock of his hat. Then he looked amazed at the pale face in the glass before him, and especially at his mustachios, which had attained a rich growth in the course of near seven weeks, since they had come into the world. They *will* mistake me for a military man, thought he, remembering Isidor's warning, as to the massacre with which all the defeated British army was threatened; and staggering back to his bed-chamber, he began wildly pulling the bell which summoned his valet.

Isidor answered that summons. Jos had sunk in a chair – he had torn off his neckcloths, and turned down his collars, and was sitting with both his hands lifted to his throat.

'*Coupez-moi*, Isidor,' shouted he: '*vite! Coupez-moi!*'

Isidor thought for a moment he had gone mad, and that he wished his valet to cut his throat.

'*Les moustaches*,' gasped Jos; '*les moustaches – coupy, rasy, vite!*' – his French was of this sort – voluble, as we have said, but not remarkable for grammar.

Isidor swept off the mustachios in no time with the razor, and heard with expressible delight his master's orders that he should fetch a hat and a plain coat. '*Ne porty ploo – habit militair – bonny – bonny a voo, prenny dehors*' – were Jos's words – the coat and cap were at last his property.

This gift being made, Jos selected a plain black coat and waistcoat from his stock, and put on a large white neckcloth, and a plain beaver. If he could have got a shovel-hat he would have worn it. As it was, you would have fancied he was a flourishing, large parson of the Church of England.

'*Venny maintenong*,' he continued, '*sweevy – ally – party – dong la roo.*' And so having said, he plunged swiftly down the stairs of the house, and passed into the street.

Although Regulus had vowed that he was the only man of his regiment, or of the allied army, almost, who had escaped being cut to pieces by Ney, it appeared that his statement was incorrect, and that a good number more of the supposed victims had survived the massacre. Many scores of Regulus's comrades had found their way back to Brussels, and – all agreeing that they had run away – filled the whole town with an idea of the defeat of the allies. The arrival of the French was expected hourly; the panic continued, and preparation for flight went on everywhere. No horses! thought Jos, in terror. He made Isidor inquire of scores of persons, whether they had any to lend or sell, and his heart sank within him, at the negative answers returned everywhere. Should he take the journey on foot? Even fear could not render that ponderous body so active.

Almost all the hotels occupied by the English in Brussels face the Parc, and Jos wandered irresolutely about in this quarter, with crowds of other people, oppressed as he was by fear and curiosity. Some families he saw more happy than himself, having discovered a team of horses, and rattling through the streets in retreat; others again there were whose case was like his own, and who could not for any bribes or entreaties procure the necessary means of flight. Amongst these would-be fugitives, Jos remarked the Lady Bareacres and her daughter, who sate in their carriage in the *porte-cochère* of their hotel, all their imperials packed, and the only drawback to whose flight was the same want of motive power which kept Jos stationary.

Rebecca Crawley occupied apartments in this hotel; and had before this period had sundry hostile meetings with the ladies of the Bareacres family. My Lady Bareacres cut Mrs Crawley on the stairs when they met by chance; and in all places where the latter's name was mentioned, spoke perseveringly ill of her neighbour. The Countess was shocked at the familiarity of General Tufto with the aide-de-camp's wife. The Lady Blanche avoided her as if she had been an infectious disease. Only the Earl himself kept up a sly occasional acquaintance with her, when out of the jurisdiction of his ladies.

Rebecca had her revenge now upon these insolent enemies. It became known in the hotel that Captain Crawley's horses had been left behind, and when the panic began, Lady Bareacres condescended to send her maid to the Captain's wife with her Ladyship's compliments, and a desire to know the price of Mrs Crawley's horses. Mrs Crawley returned a note with her compliments, and an intimation that it was not her custom to transact bargains with the ladies' maids.

This curt reply brought the Earl in person to Becky's apartment; but he could get no more success than the first ambassador. 'Send a lady's maid to *me!*' Mrs Crawley cried in great anger; 'Why didn't my Lady Bareacres tell me to go and saddle the horses! Is it her Ladyship that wants to escape, or her Ladyship's *femme de chambre*?' And this was all the answer that the Earl bore back to his Countess.

What will not necessity do? The Countess herself actually came to wait upon Mrs Crawley on the failure of her second envoy. She entreated her to name her own price; she even offered to invite Becky to Bareacres House, if the latter would but give her the means of returning to that residence. Mrs Crawley sneered at her.

'I don't want to be waited on by bailiffs in livery,' she said; 'you will never get back though most probably – at least not you and your diamonds together. The French will have those. They will be here in two hours, and I shall be half-way to Ghent by that time. I would not sell you my horses, no, not for the two largest diamonds that your Ladyship wore at the ball.' Lady Bareacres trembled with rage and terror. The diamonds were sewed into her habit, and secreted in my Lord's padding and boots. 'Woman, the diamonds are at the banker's, and I *will* have the horses,' she said. Rebecca laughed in her face. The infuriate Countess went below, and sate in her carriage; her maid, her courier, and her husband, were sent once more through the town, each to look for cattle; and woe betide those who came last! Her ladyship was resolved on departing the very instant the horses arrived from any quarter – with her husband or without him.

Rebecca had the pleasure of seeing her Ladyship in the horseless carriage, and keeping her eyes fixed upon her, and bewailing, in the loudest tone of voice, the Countess's perplexities. 'Not to be able to get horses!' she said, 'and to have all those diamonds sewed into the carriage cushions! What a prize it will be for the French when they come! – the carriage and the diamonds, I mean; not the lady!' She gave this information to the landlord, to the servants, to the guests, and the innumerable stragglers about the courtyard. Lady Bareacres could have shot her from the carriage window. It was while enjoying the humiliation of her enemy that Rebecca caught sight of Jos, who made towards her directly he perceived her.

That altered, frightened, fat face, told his secret well enough. He too wanted to fly, and was on the look-out for the means of escape. '*He* shall buy my horses,' thought Rebecca, 'and I'll ride the mare.'

Jos walked up to his friend, and put the question for the hundredth time during the past hour, 'Did she know where horses were to be had?'

'What, *you* fly?' said Rebecca, with a laugh. 'I thought you were the champion of all the ladies, Mr Sedley.'

'I—I'm not a military man,' gasped he.

'And Amelia? – Who is to protect that poor little sister of yours?' asked Rebecca. 'You surely would not desert her?'

'What good can I do her, suppose – suppose the enemy arrive?' Jos answered. 'They'll spare the women; but my man tells me that they have taken an oath to give no quarter to the men – the dastardly cowards.'

'Horrid!' cried Rebecca, enjoying his perplexity.

'Besides, I don't want to desert her,' cried the brother. 'She *shan't* be deserted. There is a seat for her in my carriage, and one for you, dear Mrs Crawley, if you will come; and if we can get horses' – sighed he –

'I have two to sell,' the lady said. Jos could have flung himself into her arms at the news. 'Get the carriage, Isidor,' he cried; 'we've found them – we have found them!'

'My horses never were in harness,' added the lady. 'Bullfinch would kick the carriage to pieces, if you put him in the traces.'

'But he is quiet to ride?' asked the civilian.

'As quiet as a lamb, and as fast as a hare,' answered Rebecca.

'Do you think he is up to my weight?' Jos said. He was already on his back, in imagination, without ever so much as a thought for poor Amelia. What person who loved a horse-speculation could resist such a temptation?

In reply, Rebecca asked him to come into her room, whither he followed her quite breathless to conclude the bargain. Jos seldom spent a half-hour in his life which cost him so much money. Rebecca, measuring the value of the goods which she had for sale by Jos's eagerness to purchase as well as by the scarcity of the article, put upon her horses a price so prodigious as to make even the civilian draw back. 'She would sell both or neither,' she said resolutely. Rawdon had ordered her not to part with them for a price less that that which she specified. Lord Bareacres below would give her the same money – and with all her love and regard for the Sedley family, her dear Mr Joseph must conceive that poor people must live – nobody, in a word, could be more affectionate, but more firm about the matter of business.

Jos ended by agreeing, as might be supposed of him. The sum he had to give her was so large that he was obliged to ask for time: so large as to be a little fortune to Rebecca, who rapidly calculated that with this sum and the sale of the residue of Rawdon's effects, and her pension as a widow should he fall, she would now be absolutely independent of the world, and might look her weeds steadily in the face.

Once or twice in the day she certainly had herself thought about flying. But her reason gave her better counsel. 'Suppose the French do come,' thought Becky, 'what can they do to a poor officer's widow? Bah! The time of sacks and sieges are over. We shall be let to go home quietly, or I may live pleasantly abroad with a snug little income.'

Meanwhile Jos and Isidor went off to the stables to inspect the newly purchased cattle. Jos bade his man saddle the horses at once. He would ride away that very night, that very hour. And he left the valet busy in getting the horses ready, and went homewards himself to prepare for his departure. It must be secret. He would go to his chamber by the back entrance. He did not care to face Mrs O'Dowd and Amelia, and own to them that he was about to run.

By the time Jos's bargain with Rebecca was completed, and his horses had been visited and examined, it was almost morning once more. But though midnight was long past, there was no rest for the city: the people were up, the lights in the houses flamed, crowds were still about the doors, and the streets were busy. Rumours of various natures went still from mouth to mouth: one report averred that the Prussians had been utterly defeated; another that it was the English who had been attacked and conquered; a third that the latter had held their ground. This last rumour gradually got strength. No Frenchmen had made their appearance. Stragglers had come in from the army bringing reports more and more favourable: at last an aide-de-camp actually reached Brussels with dispatches for the Commandant of the place, who placarded presently through the town an official announcement of the success of the allies at Quatre Bras, and the entire repulse of the French under Ney after a six hours' battle. The aide-de-camp must have arrived some time while Jos and Rebecca were making their bargain together, or the latter was inspecting his purchase. When he reached his own hotel, he found a score of its numerous inhabitants on the threshold discoursing of the news; there was no doubt as to its truth. And he went up to communicate it to the ladies under his charge. He did not think it was necessary to tell them how he had intended to take leave of them, how he had bought horses, and what a price he had paid for them.

But success or defeat was a minor matter to them, who had only thought for the safety of those they loved. Amelia, at the news of the victory, became still more agitated even than before. She was for going that moment to the army. She besought her brother with tears to conduct her thither. Her doubts and terrors had reached their paroxysm; and the poor girl, who for many hours had been plunged into stupor, raved and ran hither and thither in hysteric insanity – a piteous sight. No man writhing in pain on the hard-fought field fifteen miles off, where lay, after their struggles, so many of the brave – no man suffered more keenly than this poor harmless victim of the war. Jos could not bear the sight of her pain. He left his sister in the charge of her stouter female companion, and descended once more to the threshold of the hotel, where everybody still lingered, and talked, and waited for more news.

It grew to be broad daylight as they stood here, and fresh news began to arrive from the war, brought by men who had been actors in the scene. Waggons and long country carts laden with wounded came rolling into the town; ghastly groans came from within them, and haggard faces looked up sadly from out of the straw. Jos Sedley was looking at one of these carriages with a painful curiosity – the moans of the people within were frightful – the wearied horses could hardly pull the cart. 'Stop! Stop!' a feeble voice cried from the straw, and the carriage stopped opposite Mr Sedley's hotel.

'It is George, I know it is!' cried Amelia, rushing in a moment to the balcony, with a pallid face and loose flowing hair. It was not George, however, but it was the next best thing: it was news of him. It was poor Tom Stubble, who had marched out of Brussels so gallantly twenty-four hours before, bearing the colours of the regiment, which he had defended very gallantly upon the field. A French lancer had speared the young Ensign in the leg, who fell, still bravely holding to his flag. At the conclusion of the engagement, a place had been found for the poor boy in a cart, and he had been brought back to Brussels.

'Mr Sedley, Mr Sedley!' cried the boy faintly, and Jos came up almost frightened at the appeal. He had not at first distinguished who it was that called him.

Little Tom Stubble held out his hot and feeble hand. 'I'm to be taken in here,' he said. 'Osborne – and – and Dobbin said I was; and you are to give the man two Napoleons: my mother will pay you.' This young fellow's thoughts during the long feverish hours passed in the cart, had been wandering to his father's parsonage, which he had quitted only a few months before, and he had sometimes forgotten his pain in that delirium.

The hotel was large, and the people kind, and all the inmates of the cart were taken in and placed on various couches. The young Ensign was conveyed upstairs to Osborne's quarters. Amelia and the Major's wife had rushed down to him, when the latter had recognised him from the balcony. You may fancy the feelings of these women when they were told that the day was over, and both their husbands were safe; in what mute rapture Amelia fell on her good friend's neck, and embraced her; in what grateful passion of prayer she fell on her knees, and thanked the Power which had saved her husband.

Our young lady, in her fevered and nervous condition, could have had no more salutary medicine prescribed for her by any physician than that which chance put in her way. She and Mrs O'Dowd watched incessantly by the wounded lad, whose pains were very severe, and in the duty thus forced upon her, Amelia had not time to brood over her personal anxieties, or to give herself up to her own fears and forebodings after her wont. The young patient told in his simple fashion the events of the day, and the actions of our friends of the gallant –th. They had suffered severely. They had lost very many officers and men. The Major's horse had been shot under him as the regiment charged, and they all thought that O'Dowd was gone, and that Dobbin had got his majority, until on their return from the charge to their old ground, the Major was discovered seated on Pyramus's carcase, refreshing himself from a case-bottle. It was Captain Osborne that cut down the French lancer who had speared the Ensign. Amelia turned so pale at the notion, that Mrs O'Dowd stopped the young Ensign in his story. And it was Captain Dobbin who at the end of the day, though wounded himself, took up the lad in his arms and carried him to the surgeon, and thence to the cart which was to bring him back to Brussels. And it was he who promised the driver two louis if he would make his way to Mr Sedley's hotel in the city; and tell Mrs Captain Osborne that the action was over, and that her husband was unhurt and well.

'Indeed, but he has a good heart that William Dobbin,' Mrs O'Dowd said, 'though he is always laughing at me.'

Young Stubble vowed there was not such another officer in the army, and never ceased his praises of the senior captain, his modesty, his kindness, and his admirable coolness in the field. To these parts of the conversation, Amelia lent a very distracted atention: it was only when George was spoken of that she listened, and when he was not mentioned, she thought about him.

In tending her patient, and in thinking of the wonderful escapes of the day before, her second day passed away not too slowly with Amelia. There was only one man in the army for her: and as long as he was well, it must be owned that its movements interested her little. All the reports which Jos brought from the streets fell very vaguely on her ears; though they were sufficient to give that timorous gentleman, and many other people then in Brussels, every disquiet. The French had been repulsed certainly, but it was after a severe and doubtful struggle, and with only a division of the French army. The Emperor, with the main body, was away at Ligny, where he had utterly annihilated the Prussians, and was now free to bring his whole force to bear upon the allies. The Duke of Wellington was retreating upon the capital, and a great battle must be fought under its walls probably, of which the chances were more than doubtful. The Duke of Wellington had but twenty thousand British troops on whom he could rely, for the Germans were raw militia, the Belgians disaffected; and with this handful his Grace had to resist a hundred and fifty thousand men that had broken into Belgium under Napoleon. Under Napoleon! What warrior was there, however famous and skilful, that could fight at odds with him?

Jos thought of all these things, and trembled. So did all the rest of Brussels – where people felt that the fight of the day before was but the prelude to the greater combat which was imminent. One of the armies opposed to the Emperor was scattered to the winds already. The few English that could be brought to resist him would perish at their posts, and the conqueror would pass over their bodies into the city. Woe be to those whom he found there! Addresses were prepared, public functionaries assembled and debated secretly, apartments were got ready, and tricoloured banners and triumphal emblems manufactured, to welcome the arrival of His Majesty the Emperor and King.

The emigration still continued, and wherever families could find means of departure, they fled. When Jos, on the afternoon of the 17th of June, went to Rebecca's hotel, he found that the great Bareacres carriage had at length rolled away from the *porte-cochère*. The Earl had procured a pair of horses somehow, in spite of Mrs Crawley, and was rolling on the road to Ghent. Louis the Desired was getting ready his portmanteau in that city too. It seemed as if Misfortune was never tired of worrying into motion that unwieldy exile.

Jos felt that the delay of yesterday had been only a respite, and that his dearly bought horses must of a surety be put into requisition. His agonies were very severe all this day. As long as there was an English army between Brussels and Napoleon, there was no need of immediate flight; but he had his horses brought from their distant stables, to the stables in the court-yard of the hotel where he lived; so that they might be under his own eyes, and beyond the risk of violent abduction. Isidor watched the stable-door constantly, and had the horses saddled, to be ready for the start. He longed intensely for that event.

After the reception of the previous day, Rebecca did not care to come near her dear Amelia. She clipped the bouquet which George had brought her, and gave fresh water to the flowers, and read over the letter which he had sent her. 'Poor wretch,' she said, twirling round the little bit of paper in her fingers, 'how I could crush her with this! – And it is for a thing like this that she must break her heart, forsooth – for a man who is stupid – a coxcomb – and who does not care for her. My poor good Rawdon is worth ten of this creature.' And then she fell to thinking what she should do if – if anything happened to poor good Rawdon, and what a great piece of luck it was that he had left his horses behind.

In the course of this day too, Mrs Crawley, who saw not without anger the Bareacres party drive off, bethought her of the precaution which the Countess had taken, and did a little needlework for her own advantage; she stitched away the major part of her trinkets, bills, and banknotes about her person, and so prepared, was ready for any event – to fly if she thought fit, or to stay and welcome the conqueror, were he Englishman or Frenchman. And I am not sure that she did not dream that night of becoming a duchess and Madame la Maréchale, while Rawdon, wrapped in his cloak, and making his bivouac under the rain at Mount Saint John, was thinking, with all the force of his heart, about the little wife whom he had left behind him.

The next day was a Sunday. And Mrs Major O'Dowd had the satisfaction of seeing both her patients refreshed in health and spirits by some rest which they had taken during the night. She herself had slept on a great chair in Amelia's room, ready to wait upon her poor friend or the Ensign, should either need her nursing. When morning came, this robust woman went back to the house where she and her Major had their billet; and here performed an elaborate and splendid toilette, befitting the day. And it is very possible that whilst alone in that chamber, which her husband had inhabited, and where his cap still lay on the pillow, and his cane stood in the corner, one prayer at least was sent up to Heaven for the welfare of the brave soldier, Michael O'Dowd.

When she returned she brought her prayer-book with her, and her uncle the Dean's famous book of sermons, out of which she never failed to read every Sabbath; not understanding all, haply, not pronouncing many of the words aright, which were long and abstruse – for the Dean was a learned man, and loved long Latin words – but with great gravity, vast emphasis, and with tolerable correctness in the main. How often has my Mick listened to these sermons, she thought, and me reading in the cabin of a calm! She proposed to resume this exercise on the present day, with Amelia and the wounded Ensign for a congregation. The same service was read on that day in twenty thousand churches at the same hour; and millions of British men and women, on their knees, implored protection of the Father of all.

They did not hear the noise which disturbed our little congregation at Brussels. Much louder than that which had interrupted them two days previously, as Mrs O'Dowd was reading the service in her best voice, the cannon of Waterloo began to roar.

When Jos heard that dreadful sound, he made up his mind that he would bear this perpetual recurrence of terrors no longer, and would fly at once. He rushed into the sick man's room, where our three friends had paused in their prayers, and further interrupted them by a passionate appeal to Amelia.

'I can't stand it any more, Emmy,' he said; 'I won't stand it; and you must come with me. I have bought a horse for you – never mind at what price – and you must dress and come with me, and ride behind Isidor.'

'God forgive me, Mr Sedley, but you are no better than a coward,' Mrs O'Dowd said, laying down the book.

'I say come, Amelia,' the civilian went on; 'never mind what she says; why are we to stop here and be butchered by the Frenchmen?'

'You forget the –th, my boy,' said the little Stubble, the wounded hero, from his bed – 'and – and you won't leave me, will you, Mrs O'Dowd?'

'No, my dear fellow,' said she, going up and kissing the boy. 'No harm shall come to you while *I* stand by. I don't budge till I get the word from Mick. A pretty figure I'd be, wouldn't I, stuck behind that chap on a pillion?'

This image caused the young patient to burst out laughing in his bed, and even made Amelia smile. 'I don't ask her,' Jos shouted out – 'I don't ask that – that Irishwoman, but you, Amelia; once for all, will you come?'

'Without my husband, Joseph?' Amelia said, with a look of wonder, and gave her hand to the Major's wife. Jos's patience was exhausted.

'Good-bye, then,' he said, shaking his fist in a rage, and slamming the door by which he retreated. And this time he really gave his order for march: and mounted in the courtyard. Mrs O'Dowd heard the clattering hoofs of the horses as they issued from the gate; and looking on, made many scornful remarks on poor Joseph as he rode down the street with Isidor after him in the laced cap. The horses, which had not been exercised for some days, were lively, and sprang about the street. Jos, a clumsy and timid horseman, did not look to advantage in the saddle. 'Look at him, Amelia dear, driving into the parlour window. Such a bull in a china-shop *I* never saw.' And presently the pair of riders disappeared at a canter down the street leading in the direction of the Ghent road, Mrs O'Dowd pursuing them with a fire of sarcasm so long as they were in sight.

All that day, from morning until past sunset, the cannon never ceased to roar. It was dark when the cannonading stopped all of a sudden.

All of us have read of what occurred during that interval. The tale is in every Englishman's mouth; and you and I, who were children when the great battle was won and lost, are never tired of hearing and recounting the history of that famous action. Its remembrance rankles still in the bosoms of millions of the countrymen of those brave men who lost the day. They pant for an opportunity of revenging that humiliation; and if a contest, ending in a victory on their part, should ensue, elating them in their turn, and leaving its cursed legacy of hatred and rage behind to us, there is no end to the so-called glory and shame, and to the alternations of successful and unsuccessful murder, in which two high-spirited nations might engage. Centuries hence, we Frenchmen and Englishmen might be boasting and killing each other still, carrying out bravely the Devil's code of honour.

All our friends took their share and fought like men in the great field. All day long, whilst the women were praying ten miles away, the lines of the dauntless English infantry were receiving and repelling the furious charges of the French horsemen. Guns which were heard at Brussels were ploughing up their ranks, and comrades falling, and the resolute survivors closing in. Towards evening, the attack of the French, repeated and resisted so bravely, slackened in its fury. They had other foes besides the British to engage, or were preparing for a final onset. It came at last: the columns of the Imperial Guard marched up the hill of Saint Jean, at length and at once to sweep the English from the height which they had maintained all day, and spite of all: unscared by the thunder of the artillery, which hurled death from the English line – the dark rolling column pressed on and up the hill. It seemed almost to crest the eminence, when it began to wave and falter. Then it stopped, still facing the shot. Then at last the English troops rushed from the post from which no enemy had been able to dislodge them, and the Guard turned and fled.

No more firing was heard at Brussels – the pursuit rolled miles away. Darkness came down on the field and city; and Amelia was praying for George, who was lying on his face, dead, with a bullet through his heart.

Enemy Coast Ahead
GUY GIBSON V.C.

As the culmination of long scientific research and precision training, Gibson's crack bomber squadron launched their now famous attack on the Möhne, Eder and Sorpe dams on 16 May, 1943. Three formations, eighteen planes in all, were to wreak havoc throughout the Ruhr Valley, destroying and halting production of munitions which would otherwise have contributed greatly to prolonging the war . . . . .

WE HAD BEEN FLYING for about an hour and ten minutes in complete silence, each one busy with his thoughts, while the waves were slopping a few feet below with monotonous regularity. And the moon dancing on those waves had become almost a hypnotising crystal. As Terry spoke he jerked us into action. He said, 'Five minutes to go to the Dutch coast, skip.'

I said, 'Good,' and looked ahead. Pulford turned on the spotlights and told me to go down much lower; we were about 100 feet off the water. Jim Deering, in the front turret, began to swing it from either way, ready to deal with any flak ships which might be watching for mine-layers off the coast. Hutch sat in his wireless cabin ready to send a flak warning to the rest of the boys who might run into trouble behind us. Trevor took off his Mae West and squeezed himself back into the rear turret. On either side the boys tucked their blunt-nosed Lancs in even closer than they were before, while the crews inside them were probably doing the same sort of things as my own. Someone began whistling nervously over the intercom. Someone else said, 'Shut up.'

Then Spam said, 'There's the coast.'

I said, 'No, it's not; that's just low cloud and shadows on the sea from the moon.'

But he was right and I was wrong, and soon we could see the Dutch islands approaching. They looked low and flat and evil in the full moon, squirting flak in many directions because their radar would now know we were coming. But we knew all about their defences, and as we drew near this squat and unfriendly expanse we began to look for the necessary landmarks which would indicate how to get through that barrage. We began to behave like a ship threading its way through a minefield, in danger of destruction on either side, but safe if we were lucky and on the right track. Terry came up beside me to check up on Spam. He opened the side windows and looked out to scan the coast with his night glasses. 'Can't see much,' he said. 'We're too low, but I reckon we must be on track because there's so little wind.'

'Hope so.'

'Stand by, front gunner; we're going over.'

'OK. All lights off. No talking. Here we go.'

With a roar we hurtled over the Western Wall, skirting the defences and turning this way and that to keep to our thin line of safety; for a moment we held our breath. Then I gave a sigh of relief; no one had fired a shot. We had taken them by surprise.

'Good effort, Terry. Next course.'

'105 degrees magnetic.'

We had not been on the new course for more than two minutes before we came to more sea again; we had obviously just passed over a small island, and this was wrong. Our proper track should have taken us between the two islands, as both were fairly heavily defended, but by the grace of God the gunners on the one we had just passed over were apparently asleep. We pulled up high to about 300 feet to have a look and find out where we were, then scrammed down on the deck again as Terry said, 'OK – there's the windmill and those wireless masts. We must have drifted to starboard. Steer new course – 095 degrees magnetic, and be careful of a little town that is coming up straight ahead.'

'OK, Terry, I'll go around it.'

We were turning to the left now, and as we turned I noticed with satisfaction that Hoppy and Mickey were still flying there in perfect formation.

We were flying low. We were flying so low that more than once Spam yelled at me to pull up quickly to avoid high-tension wires and tall trees. Away on the right we could see the small town, its chimneys outlined against the night sky; we thought we saw someone flash us a 'V', but it may have been an innkeeper poking his head out of his bedroom window. The noise must have been terrific.

Our new course should have followed a very straight canal, which led to a T-shaped junction, and beyond that was the Dutch frontier and Germany. All eyes began looking out to see if we were right, because we could not afford to be wrong. Sure enough, the canal came up slowly from underneath the starboard wing and we began to follow it carefully, straight above it, for now we were mighty close to Eindhoven, which had the reputation of being very well defended. Then, after a few minutes, that too had passed behind and we saw a glint of silvery light ahead. This was the canal junction, the second turning point.

It did not take Spam long to see where we were; now we were right on track, and Terry again gave the new course for the River Rhine. A few minutes later we crossed the German frontier, and Terry said, in his matter-of-fact way: 'We'll be at the target in an hour and a half. The next thing to see is the Rhine.'

But we did not all get through. One aircraft, P/O Rice, had already hit the sea, bounced up, lost both its outboard engines and its weapon, and had flown back on the inboard two. Les Munro had been hit by flak a little later on, and his aircraft was so badly damaged that he was forced to return to base. I imagined the feelings of the crews of these aircraft who, after many weeks of intense practice and expectation, at the last moment could only hobble home and land with nothing accomplished. I felt very sorry for them. This left sixteen aircraft going on; 112 men.

The journey into the Ruhr Valley was not without excitement. They did not like our coming. And they knew we were coming. We were the only aircraft operating that night; it was too bright for the main forces. And so, deep down in their underground plotting-rooms, the Hun controllers stayed awake to watch us as we moved steadily on. We had a rough idea how they worked, these controllers, moving fighter squadrons to orbit points in front of us, sounding air-raid sirens here and there, tipping off the gun positions along our route and generally trying to make it pretty uncomfortable for the men who were bound for 'Happy Valley'. As yet they would not know where we were going, because our route was planned to make feint attacks and fox their control. Only the warning sirens would have sounded in all the cities from Bremen southwards. As yet, the fighters would be unable to get good plots on us because we were flying so low, but once we were there the job would have to take quite a time and they would have their chance.

We flew on. Germany seemed dead. Not a sign of movement, of light or a moving creature stirred the ground. There was no flak, there was nothing. Just us.

And so we came to the Rhine. This is virtually the entrance to the Ruhr Valley; the barrier our armies must cross before they march into the big towns of Essen and Dortmund. It looked white and calm and sinister in the moonlight. But it presented no difficulties to us. As it came up, Spam said, 'We are six miles south. Better turn right, skip. Duisburg is not far away.'

As soon as he mentioned Duisburg my hands acted before my brain, for they were more used to this sort of thing, and the Lanc banked steeply to follow the Rhine up to our crossing point. For Duisburg is not a healthy place to fly over at 100 feet. There are hundreds of guns there, both light and heavy, apart from all those searchlights, and the defences have had plenty of experience ...

As we flew up – 'How did that happen?'

'Don't know, skip. Compass u/s?'

'Couldn't be.'

317

'Hold on, I will just check my figures.'

Later – 'I'm afraid I mis-read my writing, skip. The course I gave you should have been another ten degrees to port.'

'OK, Terry. That might have been an expensive mistake.'

During our steep turn the boys had lost contact, but now they were just beginning to form up again; it was my fault the turn had been too steep, but the name Duisburg or Essen, or any of the rest of them, always does that to me. As we flew along the Rhine there were barges on the river equipped with quick-firing guns and they shot at us as we flew over, but our gunners gave back as good as they got; then we found what we wanted, a sort of small inland harbour, and we turned slowly towards the east. Terry said monotonously, 'Thirty minutes to go and we are there.'

As we passed on into the Ruhr Valley we came to more and more trouble, for now we were in the outer light-flak defences, and these were very active, but by weaving and jinking we were able to escape most of them. Time and again searchlights would pick us up, but we were flying very low and, although it may sound foolish and untrue when I say so, we avoided a great number of them by dodging behind the trees. Once we went over a brand-new aerodrome which was very heavily defended and which had not been marked on our combat charts. Immediately all three of us in front were picked up by the searchlights and held. Suddenly Trevor, in the rear turret, began firing away trying to scare them enough to turn out their lights, then he shouted that they had gone behind some tall trees. At the same time Spam was yelling that he would soon be shaving himself by the tops of some corn in a field. Hutch immediately sent out a flak warning to all the boys behind so that they could avoid this unattractive area. On either side of me, Mickey and Hoppy, who were a little higher, were flying along brightly illuminated; I could see their letters quite clearly, 'TAJ' and 'MAJ', standing out like broadway signs. Then a long string of tracer came out from Hoppy's rear turret and I lost him in the momentary darkness as the searchlights popped out. One of the pilots, a grand Englishman from Derbyshire, was not so lucky. He was flying well out to the left. He got blinded in the searchlights and, for a second, lost control. His aircraft reared up like a stricken horse, plunged on to the deck and burst into flames; five seconds later his mine blew up with a tremendous explosion. Bill Astell had gone.

The minutes passed slowly as we all sweated on this summer's night, sweated at working the controls and sweated with fear as we flew on. Every railway train, every hamlet and every bridge we passed was a potential danger, for our Lancasters were sitting targets at that height and speed. We fought our way past Dortmund, past Hamm – the well-known Hamm which has been bombed so many times; we could see it quite clearly now, its tall chimneys, factories and balloons capped by its umbrella of flak like a Christmas tree about five miles to our right; then we began turning to the right in between Hamm and the little town of Soest, where I nearly got shot down in 1940. Soest was sleepy now and did not open up, and out of the haze ahead appeared the Ruhr hills.

'We're there,' said Spam.

'Thank God,' said I, feelingly.

As we came over the hill, we saw the Möhne Lake. Then we saw the dam itself. In that light it looked squat and heavy and unconquerable; it looked grey and solid in the moonlight, as though it were part of the countryside itself and just as immovable. A structure like a battleship was showering out flak all along its length, but some came from the powerhouse below it and nearby. There were no searchlights. It was light flak, mostly green, yellow and red, and the colours of the tracer reflected upon the face of the water in the lake. The reflections on the dead calm of the black water made it seem there was twice as much as there really was.

'Did you say these gunners were out of practice?' asked Spam, sarcastically.

'They certainly seem awake now,' said Terry.

They were awake all right. No matter what people say, the Germans certainly have a good warning system. I scowled to myself as I remembered telling the boys an hour or so ago that they would probably only be the German equivalent of the Home Guard and in bed by the time we arrived.

It was hard to say exactly how many guns there were, but tracers seemed to be coming from about five positions, probably making twelve guns in all. It was hard at first to tell the calibre of the shells, but after one of the boys had been hit, we were informed over the RT that they were either 20-mm type or 37-mm, which, as everyone knows, are nasty little things.

We circled around stealthily, picking up the various landmarks upon which we had planned our method of attack, making use of some and avoiding others; every time we came within range of those bloody-minded flak-gunners they let us have it.

'Bit aggressive, aren't they?' said Trevor.

'Too right they are.'

I said to Terry, 'God, this light flak gives me the creeps.'

'Me, too,' someone answered.

For a time there was a general bind on the subject of light flak, and the only man who didn't say anything was Hutch, because he could not see it and because he never said anything about flak, anyway. But this was not the time for talking. I called up each member of our formation and found, to my relief, that they had all arrived, except, of course, Bill Astell. Away to the south, Joe McCarthy had just begun his diversionary attack on the Sorpe. But not all of them had been able to get there; both Byers and Barlow had been shot down by light flak after crossing the coast; these had been replaced by other aircraft of the rear formation. Bad luck, this being shot down after crossing the coast, because it could have happened to anybody; they must have been a mile or so off track and had got the hammer. This is the way things are in flying; you are either lucky or you aren't. We, too, had crossed the coast at the wrong place and had got away with it. We were lucky.

Down below, the Möhne Lake was silent and black and deep, and I spoke to my crew.

'Well, boys, I suppose we had better start the ball rolling.' This with no enthusiasm whatsoever. 'Hello, all Cooler aircraft. I am going to attack. Stand by to come in to attack in your order when I tell you.'

Then to Hoppy: 'Hello, "M Mother". Stand by to take over if anything happens.'

Hoppy's clear and casual voice came back. 'OK, Leader. Good luck.'

Then the boys dispersed to the pre-arranged hiding-spots in the hills, so that they should not be seen either from the ground or from the air, and we began to get into position for our approach. We circled wide and came around down moon, over the high hills at the eastern end of the lake. On straightening up we began to dive towards the flat, ominous water two miles away. Over the front turret was the dam silhouetted against the haze of the Ruhr Valley. We could see the towers. We could see the sluices. We could see everything. Spam, the bomb-aimer, said, 'Good show. This is wizard.' He had been a bit worried, as all bomb-aimers are, in case they cannot see their aiming points, but as we came in over the tall fir trees his voice came up again rather quickly. 'You're going to hit them. You're going to hit those trees.'

'That's all right, Spam. I'm just getting my height.'

To Terry: 'Check height, Terry.'

To Pulford: 'Speed control, Flight-Engineer.'

To Trevor: 'All guns ready, gunners.'

To Spam: 'Coming up, Spam.'

Terry turned on the spotlights and began giving directions – 'Down – down – down. Steady – steady.' We were then exactly sixty feet.

Pulford began working the speed; first he put on a little flap to slow us down, then he opened the throttles to get the air-speed indicator exactly against the red mark. Spam began lining up his sights against the towers. He had turned the fusing switch to the 'ON' position. I began flying.

The gunners had seen us coming. They could see us coming with our spotlights on for over two miles away. Now they opened up and the tracers began swirling towards us; some were even bouncing off the smooth surface of the lake. This was a horrible moment: we were being dragged along at four miles a minute, almost against our will, towards the things we were going to destroy. I think at that moment the boys did not want to go. I know I did not want to go. I thought to myself, 'In another minute we shall all be dead – so what?' I thought again, 'This is terrible – this feeling of fear – if it is fear.' By now we were a few hundred yards away, and I said quickly to Pulford, under my breath, 'Better leave the throttles open now and stand by to pull me out of the seat if I get hit.' As I glanced at him I thought he looked a little glum on hearing this.

The Lancaster was really moving and I began looking through the special sight on my windscreen. Spam had his eyes glued to the bomb-sight in front, his hand on his button; a special mechanism on board had already begun to work so that the mine would drop (we hoped) in the right spot. Terry was still checking the height. Joe and Trev began to raise their guns. The flak could see us quite clearly now. It was not exactly inferno. I have been through far worse flak fire than that; but we were very low. There was something sinister and slightly unnerving about the whole operation. My aircraft was so small and the dam was so large; it was thick and solid, and now it was angry. My aircraft was very small. We skimmed along the surface of the lake, and as we went my gunner was firing into the defences, and the defences were firing back with vigour, their shells whistling past us. For some reason, we were not being hit.

Spam said, 'Left – little more left – steady – steady – steady – coming up.' Of the next few seconds I remember only a series of kaleidoscopic incidents.

The chatter from Joe's front guns pushing out tracers which bounced off the left-hand flak tower.

Pulford crouching beside me.

The smell of burnt cordite.

The cold sweat underneath my oxygen mask.

The tracers flashing past the windows – they all seemed the same colour now – and the inaccuracy of the gun positions near the power-station; they were firing in the wrong direction.

The closeness of the dam wall.

Spam's exultant, 'Mine gone'.

Hutch's red Very lights to blind the flak-gunners.

The speed of the whole thing.

Someone was saying over the RT, 'Good show, leader. Nice work.'

Then it was all over, and at last we were out of range, and there came over us all, I think, an immense feeling of relief and confidence.

Trevor said, 'I will get those bastards,' and he bagan to spray the dam with bullets until at last he, too, was out of range. As we circled round we could see a great 1000-feet column of whiteness still hanging in the air where our mine had exploded. We could see with satisfaction that Spam had been good, and it had gone off in the right position. Then, as we came closer, we could see that the explosion of the mine had caused a great disturbance upon the surface of the lake and the water had become broken and furious, as though it were being lashed by a gale. At first we thought that the dam itself had broken, because great sheets of water were slopping over the top of the wall like a gigantic basin. This caused some delay, because our mines could only be dropped in calm water, and we would have to wait until all became still again.

We waited.

We waited about ten minutes, but it seemed hours to us. It must have seemed even longer to Hoppy, who was the next to attack. Meanwhile, all the fighters had now collected over our target. They knew our game by now, but we were flying too low for them; they could not see us and there were no attacks.

At last – 'Hello, "M Mother". You may attack now. Good luck.'

'OK. Attacking.'

Hoppy, the Englishman, casual, but very efficient, keen now on only one thing, which was war. He began his attack.

He began going down over the trees where I had come from a few moments before. We could see his spotlights quite clearly, slowly closing together as he ran across the water. We saw him approach. The flak, by now, had got an idea from which direction the attack was coming, and they let him have it. When he was about 100 yards away someone said, hoarsely, over the RT: 'Hell! he has been hit.'

'M Mother' was on fire; an unlucky shot had got him in one of the inboard petrol tanks and a long jet of flame was beginning to stream out. I saw him drop his mine, but his bomb-aimer must have been wounded, because it fell straight on to the power-house on the other side of the dam. But Hoppy staggered on, trying to gain altitude so that his crew could bale out. When he had got to about 500 feet there was a vivid flash in the sky and one wing fell off; his aircraft disintegrated and fell to the ground in cascading, flaming fragments. There it began to burn quite gently and rather sinisterly in a field some three miles beyond the dam.

Someone said, 'Poor old Hoppy!'

Another said, 'We'll get those bastards for this.'

A furious rage surged up inside my own crew, and Trevor said, 'Let's go in and murder those gunners.' As he spoke, Hoppy's mine went up. It went up behind the power-house with a tremendous yellow explosion and left in the air a great ball of black smoke; again there was a long wait while we watched for this to clear. There was so little wind that it took a long time.

Many minutes later I told Mickey to attack; he seemed quite confident, and we ran in beside him and a little in front; as we turned, Trevor did his best to get those gunners as he had promised.

Bob Hay, Mickey's bomb-aimer, did a good job, and his mine dropped in exactly the right place. There was again a gigantic explosion as the whole surface of the lake shook, then spewed forth its cascade of white water. Mickey was all right; he got through. But he had been hit several times and one wing-tank lost all its petrol. I could see the vicious tracer from his rear-gunner giving one gun position a hail of bullets as he swept over. Then he called up, 'OK. Attack completed.' It was then that I thought that the dam wall had moved. Of course we could not see anything, but if Jeff's theory had been correct, it should have cracked by now. If only we could go on pushing it by dropping more successful mines, it would surely move back on its axis and collapse.

Once again we watched for the water to calm down. Then in came Melvyn Young in 'D Dog'. I yelled to him, 'Be careful of the flak. It's pretty hot.'

He said, 'OK.'

I yelled again, 'Trevor's going to beat them up on the other side. He'll take most of it off you.'

Melvyn's voice again. 'OK. Thanks.' And so as 'D Dog' ran in we stayed at a fairly safe distance on the other side, firing with all guns at the defences, and the defences, like the stooges they were, firing back at us. We were both out of range of each other, but the ruse seemed to work, and we flicked on our identification lights to let them see us even more clearly. Melvyn's mine went in, again in exactly the right spot, and this time a colossal wall of water swept right over the dam and kept on going. Melvyn said, 'I think I've done it. I've broken it.' But we were in a better position to see than he, and it had not rolled down yet. We were all getting pretty excited by now, and I screamed like a schoolboy over the RT: 'Wizard show, Melvyn. I think it'll go on the next one.'

Now we had been over the Möhne for quite a long time, and all the while I had been in contact with Scampton Base. We were in close contact with the Air Officer Commanding and the Commander-in-Chief of Bomber Command, and with the scientist, observing his own greatest scientific experiment in Damology. He was sitting in the operations room, his head in his hands, listening to the reports as one after another the aircraft attacked. On the other side of the room the Commander-in-Chief paced up and down. In a way their job of waiting was worse than mine. The only difference was that they did not know that the structure was shifting as I knew, even though I could not see anything clearly.

When at last the water had all subsided I called up No 5 – David Maltby – and told him to attack. He came in fast, and I saw his mine fall within feet of the right spot; once again the flak, the explosion and wall of water. But this time we were on the wrong side of the wall and could see what had happened. We watched for about five minutes, and it was rather hard to see anything, for by now the air was full of spray from these explosions, which had settled like mist on our windscreens. Time was getting short, so I called up Dave Shannon and told him to come in.

As he turned I got close to the dam wall and then saw what had happened. It had rolled over, but I could not believe my eyes. I heard someone shout, 'I think she has gone! I think she has gone!' Other voices took up the cry and quickly I said, 'Stand by until I make a recco.' I remembered that Dave was going in to attack and told him to turn away and not to approach the target. We had a closer look. Now there was no doubt about it; there was a great breach 100 yards across, and the water, looking like stirred porridge in the moonlight, was gushing out and rolling into the Ruhr Valley towards the industrial centres of Germany's Third Reich.

Nearly all the flak had now stopped, and the other boys came down from the hills to have a closer look to see what had been done. There was no doubt about it at all – the Möhne Dam had been breached and the gunners on top of the dam, except for one man, had all run for their lives towards the safety of solid ground; this remaining gunner was a brave man, but one of the boys quickly extinguished his flak with a burst of well-aimed tracer. Now it was all quiet, except for the roar of the water which steamed and hissed its way from its 150-foot head. Then we began to shout and scream and act like madmen over the RT, for this was a tremendous sight, a sight which probably no man will ever see again.

Quickly I told Hutch to tap out the message, 'Nigger', to my station, and when this was handed to the Air Officer Commanding there was (I heard afterwards) great excitement in the operations room. The scientist jumped up and danced round the room.

Then I looked again at the dam and at the water, while all around me the boys were doing the same. It was the most amazing sight. The whole valley was beginning to fill with fog from the steam of the gushing water, and down in the foggy valley we saw cars speeding along the roads in front of this great wave of water, which was chasing them and going faster than they could ever hope to go. I saw their headlights burning and I saw water overtake them, wave by wave, and then the colour of the headlights underneath the water changing from light blue to green from green to dark purple, until there was no longer anything except the water bouncing down in great waves. The floods raced on, carrying with them as they went – viaducts, railways, bridges and everything that stood in their path. Three miles beyond the dam the remains of Hoppy's aircraft were still burning gently, a dull red glow on the ground. Hoppy had been avenged.

Then I felt a little remote and unreal sitting up there in the warm cockpit of my Lancaster, watching this mighty power which we had unleashed; then glad, because I knew that this was the heart of Germany, and the heart of her industries, the place which itself had unleashed so much misery upon the whole world.

We knew, as we watched, that this flood-water would not win the war; it would not do anything like that, but it was a catastrophe for Germany.

I circled round for about three minutes, then called up all aircraft and told Mickey and David Maltby to go home and the rest to follow me to Eder, where we would try to repeat the performance.

We set our course from the southern tip of the Möhne Lake, which was already fast emptying itself – we could see that even now – and flew on in the clear light of the early morning towards the south-east. We flew on over the little towns tucked away in the valleys underneath the Ruhr Mountains. Little places, these, the Exeters and Baths of Germany; they seemed quiet and undisturbed and picturesque as they lay sleeping there on the morning of May 17th. The thought crossed my mind of the amazing mentality of German airmen, who went out of their way to bomb such defenceless districts. At the same time a bomb or two on board would not have been out of place to wake them up as a reprisal.

At the Sorpe Dam, Joe McCarthy and Joe Brown had already finished their work. They had both made twelve dummy runs and had dropped their mines along the lip of the concrete wall in the right spot. But they had not been able to see anything spectacular, for these earthen dams are difficult nuts to crack and would require a lot of explosive to shift them. It looked as if we would not have enough aircraft to finish that job successfully because of our losses on the way in. However, the Sorpe was not a priority target, and only contributed a small amount of water to the Ruhr Valley Catchment Area.

After flying low across the treetops, up and down the valleys, we at last reached the Eder Lake and, by flying down it for some five minutes we arrived over the Eder Dam. It took some finding because fog was already beginning to form in the valleys, and it was pretty hard to tell one part of the reservoir filled with water, from another valley filled with fog. We circled up for a few minutes waiting for Henry, Dave and Les to catch up; we had lost them on the way. Then I called up on the RT.

'Hello, Cooler aircraft – can you see the target?'

Dave answered faintly, 'I think I'm in the vicinity. I can't see anything. I cannot find the dam.'

'Stand by – I will fire a red Very light – right over the dam.' No sooner had Hutch fired his Very pistol than Dave called up again. 'OK – I was a bit south. I'm coming up.'

The other boys had seen the signal, too, and after a few minutes we rendezvous'd in a left-hand orbit over the target. But time was getting short now; the glow in the north had begun to get brighter, heralding the coming dawn. Soon it would be daylight, and we did not want this in our ill-armed and un-armoured Lancasters.

I said, 'OK, Dave. You begin your attack.'

It was very hilly all round. The dam was situated, beautifully, I thought, in a deep valley with high hills all around densely covered with fir trees. At the far end, overlooking it, was rather a fine Gothic castle with magnificent grounds. In order to make a successful approach, our aircraft would have to dive steeply over this castle, dropping down on to the water from 1,000 feet to 60 feet – level out – let go the mine – then do a steep climbing turn to starboard to avoid a rocky mountain about a mile on the other side of the dam. It was much more inaccessible than the Möhne Valley and called for a much higher degree of skill in flying. There did not seem to be any defences, though, probably because it was an out-of-the-way spot and the gunners would not have got the warning. Maybe they had just been warned and were now getting out of their beds in the nearby village before cycling up the steep hill to get to their gun emplacements. Dave circled wide and then turned to go in. He dived down rather too steeply and sparks came from his engine, as he had to pull out at full boost to avoid hitting the mountain on the north side. As he was doing so ...

'Sorry, leader, I made a mess of that. I'll try again.'

He tried again. He tried five times, but each time he was not satisfied and would not allow his bomb-aimer to drop his mine. He spoke again on the RT. 'I think I had better circle round a bit and try and get used to this place.'

'OK, Dave. You hang around for a bit, and I'll get another aircraft to have a crack – Hello, "Z Zebra"' (this was Henry). 'You can go in now.'

Henry made two attempts. He said he found it very difficult, and gave the other boys some advice on the best way to go about it. Then he called up and told us that he was going in to make his final run. We could see him running in. Suddenly he pulled away; something seemed to be wrong, but he turned quickly, climbed up over the mountain and put his nose right down, literally flinging his machine into the valley. This time he was running straight and true for the middle of the wall. We saw his spotlights together, so he must have been at 60 feet. We saw the red ball of his Very light shooting out behind his tail, and we knew he had dropped his weapon. A split second later we saw someone else; Henry Maudslay had dropped his mine too late. It had hit the top of the parapet and had exploded immediately on impact with a slow, yellow, vivid flame which lit up the whole valley like daylight for just a few seconds. We could see him quite clearly banking steeply a few feet above it. Perhaps the blast was doing that. It all seemed so sudden and vicious and the flame seemed so very cruel. Someone said, 'He has blown himself up.'

Trevor said, 'Bomb-aimer must have been wounded.'

It looked as though Henry had been unlucky enough to do the thing we all might have done.

I spoke to him quickly, 'Henry – Henry. "Z Zebra" – "Z Zebra". Are you OK?' No answer. I called again. Then we all thought we heard a very faint, tired voice say, 'I think so – stand by.' It seemed as though he was dazed, and his voice did not sound natural. But Henry had disappeared. There was no burning wreckage on the ground; there was no aircraft on fire in the air. There was nothing. Henry had disappeared. He never came back.

Once more the smoke from his explosion filled the valley, and we all had to wait for a few minutes. The glow in the north was much brighter, and we would have to hurry up if we wanted to get back.

We waited patiently for it to clear away.

At last to Dave – 'OK. Attack now, David. Good luck.'

Dave went in and, after a good dummy run, managed to put his mine up against the wall, more or less in the middle. He turned on his landing light as he pulled away, and we saw the spot of light climbing steeply over the mountain as he jerked his great Lancaster almost vertically over the top. Behind me there was that explosion which, by now, we had got used to, but the wall of the Eder Dam did not move.

Meanwhile, Les Knight had been circling very patiently, not saying a word. I told him to get ready, and when the water had calmed down he began his attack. Les, the Australian, had some difficulty, too, and after a while Dave began to give him some advice on how to do it. We all joined in on the RT, and there was a continuous back-chat going on.

'Come on, Les. Come in down the moon; dive towards the point and then turn left.'

'OK, Digger. It's pretty difficult.'

'Not that way, Dig. This way.'

'Too right it's difficult. I'm climbing up to have another crack.'

After a while I called up rather impatiently and told them that a joke was a joke and that we would have to be getting back. Then Les dived in to make his final attack. His was the last weapon left in the squadron. If he did not succeed in breaching the Eder now, then it would never be breached; at least, not tonight.

I saw him run in. I crossed my fingers. But Les was a good pilot and he made as perfect a run as any seen that night. We were flying above him, and about 400 yards to the right, and saw his mine hit the water. We saw where it sank. We saw the tremendous earthquake which shook the base of the dam, and then, as if a gigantic hand had punched a hole through cardboard, the whole thing collapsed. A great mass of water began running down the valley into Kassel. Les was very excited. He kept his radio transmitter on by mistake for quite some time. His crew's remarks were something to be heard, but they couldn't be put into print here. Dave was very excited and said, 'Good show, Dig!' I called them up and told them to go home immediately. I would meet them in the Mess afterwards for the biggest party of all time.

The valley below the Eder was steeper than the Ruhr, and we followed the water down for some way. We watched it swirling and slopping in a 30-foot wall as it tore round the steep bends of the countryside. We saw it crash down in six great waves, swiping off power-stations and roads as it went. We saw it extinguish all the lights in the neighbourhood as though a great black shadow had been drawn across the earth. It all reminded us of a vast moving train. But we knew that a few miles farther on lay some of the Luftwaffe's largest training bases. We knew that it was a modern field with every convenience, including underground hangars and underground sleeping quarters ... We turned for home.

Dave and Les, still jabbering at each other on RT, had by now turned for home as well. Their voices died away in the distance as we set our course for the Möhne Lake to see how far it was empty. Hutch sent out a signal to Base using the code word, 'Dinghy', telling them the good news – and they asked us if we had any more aircraft available to prang the third target. 'No, none,' I said. 'None,' tapped Hutch.

Now we were out of RT range of our base and were relying on WT for communication. Gradually, by code words, we were told of the movements of the other aircraft. Peter Townsend and Anderson of the rear formation had been sent out to make one attack against the Sorpe. We heard Peter say that he had been successful, but heard nothing from Anderson.

'Let's tell Base we're coming home, and tell them to lay on a party,' suggested Spam.

We told them we were coming home.

We had reached the Möhne by now and circled twice. We looked at the level of the lake. Already bridges were beginning to stick up out of the lowering water. Already mudbanks with pleasure-boats sitting on their sides could be seen. Below the dam the torpedo nets had been washed to one side of the valley. The power-station had disappeared. The map had completely changed as a new silver lake had formed, a lake of no strict dimensions; a lake slowly moving down towards the west.

Base would probably be panicking a bit, so Hutch sent out another message telling them that there was no doubt about it. Then we took one final look at what we had done and afterwards turned north to the Zuider Zee.

Trevor asked a question – Trevor, who had fired nearly 12,000 rounds of ammunition in the past two hours. 'I am almost out of ammo,' he called, 'but I have got one or two incendiaries back here. Would you mind if Spam tells me when a village is coming up, so that I can drop one out? It might pay for Hoppy, Henry and Bill.'

I answered, 'Go ahead.'

We flew north in the silence of the morning, hugging the ground and wanting to get home. It was quite light now, and we could see things that we could not see on the way in – cattle in the fields, chickens getting airborne as we rushed over them. On the left someone flew over Hamm at 500 feet. He got the chop. No one knew who it was. Spam said he thought it was a German night-fighter which had been chasing us.

I suppose they were all after us. Now that we were being plotted on our retreat to the coast, the enemy fighter controllers would be working overtime. I could imagine the Führer himself giving orders to 'stop those air pirates at all costs'. After all, we had done something which no one else had ever done. Water when released can be one of the most powerful things in the world – similar to an earthquake – and the Ruhr Valley had never had an earthquake.

Someone on board pointed out that Duisburg had been pranged the night before and that our water might put the fires out there. Someone else said – rather callously, I thought – 'If you can't burn 'em, drown 'em.' But we had not tried to do this; we had merely destroyed a legitimate industrial objective so as to hinder the Ruhr Valley output of war munitions. The fact that people were in the way was incidental. The fact that they might drown had not occurred to us. But we hoped that the dam wardens would warn those living below in time, even if they were Germans. No one likes mass slaughter, and we did not like being the authors of it. Besides, it brought us in line with Himmler and his boys.

Terry looked up from his chart-board. 'About an hour to the coast,' he said.

I turned to Pulford. 'Put her into maximum cruising. Don't worry about petrol consumption.' Then to Terry – 'I think we had better go the shortest way home, crossing the coast at Egmond – you know the gap there. We're the last one, and they'll probably try to get us if we lag behind.'

Terry smiled and watched the air-speed needle creep round. We were now doing a smooth 240 indicated, and the exhaust stubs glowed red hot with the power she was throwing out. Trevor's warning light came on the panel, then his voice – 'Unidentified enemy aircraft behind.'

'OK. I'll sink to the west – it's dark there.'

As we turned – 'OK. You've lost it.'

'Right on course. Terry, we'd better fly really low.'

These fighters meant business, but they were hampered by the conditions of light during the early morning. We could see them before they saw us.

Down went the Lanc until we were a few feet off the ground, for this was the only way to survive. And we wanted to survive. Two hours before we had wanted to burst dams. Now we wanted to get home – quickly. Then we could have a party.

Some minutes later Terry spoke. 'Thirty minutes to the coast.'

'OK. More revs.'

The needle crept round. It got very noisy inside.

We were flying home – we knew that. We did not know whether we were safe. We did not know how the other boys had got on. Bill, Hoppy, Henry, Barlow, Byers and Ottley had all gone. They had all got the hammer. The light flak had given it to most of them, as it always will to low-flying aircraft – that is, the unlucky ones. They had all gone quickly, except perhaps for Henry. Henry, the born leader. A great loss, but he gave his life for a cause for which men should be proud. Boys like Henry are the cream of our youth. They die bravely and they die young.

And Burpee, the Canadian? His English wife about to have a baby. His father who kept a large store in Ottawa. He was not coming back because they had got him, too. They had got him somewhere between Hamm and the target. Burpee, slow of speech and slow of movement, but a good pilot. He was Terry's countryman, and so were his crew. I like their ways and manners, their free-and-easy outlook, their openness. I was going to miss them a lot – even when they chewed gum.

I called up Melvyn on the RT. He had been with me all the way round as deputy-leader when Mickey had gone home with his leaking petrol tank. He was quite all right at the Eder. Now there was no reply. We wondered what had happened.

Terry said, 'Fifteen minutes to go.'

Fifteen minutes. Quite a way yet. A long way, and we might not make it. We were in the black territory. They had closed the gates of their fortress and we were locked inside; but we knew the gap – the gap by those wireless masts at Egmond. If we could find that, we should get through safely.

Back at the base they would be waiting for us. We did not know that when they received the code word 'Dinghy' there was a scene in the operations room such as the WAAF Ops Clerks had never seen before. The Air Officer Commanding had jumped up and had shaken Jeff by the hand, almost embracing him. The Commander-in-Chief had picked up the phone and asked for Washington. At Washington another US–Great Britain conference was in progress. Sir Charles Portal, the CAS, was giving a dinner-party. He was called away to the telephone. Back at Scampton, the C-in-C yelled, 'Downwood successful – yes.' At Washington, CAS was having difficulty in hearing. At last the members of the dinner-party heard him say quietly, 'Good show'. From then on the dinner-party was a roaring success.

We did not know anything about the fuss, the Press, the publicity which would go round the world after this effort. Or of the honours to be given to the squadron or of trips to America and Canada, or of visits by important people. We did not care about anything like that. We only wanted to get home.

We did not know that we had started something new in the history of aviation, that our squadron was to become a byword throughout the

RAF as a precision-bombing unit – a unit which could pick off anything from viaducts to gun emplacements, from low level or high level, by day or by night. A squadron consisting of crack crews using all the latest new equipment and largest bombs, even earthquake bombs. A squadron flying new aeroplanes, and flying them as well as any in the world.

Terry was saying, 'Rotterdam's 20 miles on the port bow. We will be getting to the gap in five minutes.' Now they could see where we were going, the fighters would be streaking across Holland to close that gap. Then they could hack us down.

I called up Melvyn, but he never answered. I was not to know that Melvyn had crashed into the sea a few miles in front of me. He had come all the way from California to fight this war and had survived sixty trips at home and in the Middle East, including a double ditching. Now he had ditched for the last time. Melvyn had been responsible for a good deal of the training that made this raid possible. He had endeared himself to the boys, and now he was gone.

Of the sixteen aircraft which had crossed the coast to carry out this mission, eight had been shot down, including both Flight-Commanders. Only two men escaped to become prisoners of war. Only two out of fifty-six, for there is not much chance at 50 feet.

They had gone. Had it been worth it? Or were their lives just thrown away on a spectacular mission? Militarily, it was cheap at the price. The damage done to the German war effort was substantial. But there is another side to the question. We would soon begin our fifth year of war – a war in which the casualties had been lighter than the last; nevertheless, in Bomber Command there have been some heavy losses. These fifty-five boys who had lost their lives were some of many. The scythe of war, and a very bloody one at that, had reaped a good harvest in Bomber Command. As we flew on over the low fields of Holland, past dykes and ditches, we could not help thinking, 'Why must we make war every twenty-five years? Why must men fight? How can we stop it? Can we make countries live normal lives in a peaceful way?' But no one knows the answer to that one.

The answer may lie in being strong. A powerful, strategic bomber force based so that it would control the vital waterways of the world, could prevent and strangle the aggressor from the word 'Go'. But it rests with the people themselves; for it is the people who forget. After many years they will probably slip and ask for disarmament so that they can do away with taxes and raise their standard of living. If the people forget, they bring wars on themselves, and they can blame no one but themselves.

Yes, the decent people of this world have to remember war. Movies and radio records should remind this and the future generations of what happened between 1936 and 1942. It should be possible to keep this danger in everyone's mind so that we can never be caught on the wrong foot again. So that our children will have a chance to live. After all, that is why we are born. We aren't born to die.

But we ourselves must learn. We must learn to know and respect our great Allies who have made the chance of victory possible. We must learn to understand them, their ways and their customs. We British are apt to consider ourselves the yardstick upon which everything else should be based. We must not delude ourselves. We have plenty to learn.

We must learn about politics. We must vote for the right things, and not necessarily the traditional things. We want to see our country remain as great as it is today – for ever. It all depends on the people, their common-sense and their memory.

Can we hope for this? Can all this be done? Can we be certain that we can find the answer to a peaceful world for generations to come?

'North Sea ahead, boys,' said Spam.

There it was. Beyond the gap, in the distance, lay the calm and silvery sea, and freedom. It looked beautiful to us then – perhaps the most wonderful thing in the world.

We climbed up a little to about 300 feet.

Then – 'Full revs and boost, Pulford.'

As he opened her right up, I shoved the nose down to get up extra speed and we sat down on the deck at about 260 indicated.

'Keep to the left of this little lake,' said Terry, map in hand.

This was flying.

'Now over this railway bridge.'

More speed.

'Along this canal ...' We flew along that canal as low as we had flown that day. Our belly nearly scraped the water, our wings would have knocked horses off the towpath.

'See those radio masts?'

'Yeah.'

'About 200 yards to the right.'

'OK.'

The sea came closer. It came closer quickly as we tore towards it. There was a sudden tenseness on board.

'Keep going; you're OK now.'

'Right. Stand by, front gunner.'

'Guns ready.'

Then we came to the Western Wall. We whistled over the anti-tank ditches and beach obstacles. We saw the yellow sand-dunes slide below us silently, yellow in the pale morning.

Then we were over the sea with the rollers breaking on the beaches and the moon casting its long reflection straight in front of us – and there was England.

We were free. We had got through the gap. It was a wonderful feeling of relief and safety. Now for the party.

'Nice work,' said Trevor from the back.

'Course home?' I asked.

Behind us lay the Dutch coast, squat, desolate and bleak, still squirting flak in many directions.

We would be coming back.

Into Battle

FREDERIC MANNING

Those who survived the horrors of the Somme – including the three friends, Privates Bourne, Shem and Martlow – had before them only the daunting prospect of another push 'over the top' .....

We see yonder the beginning of day, but I think we shall never see the end of it.... I am afeard there are few die well that die in a battle.

SHAKESPEARE

THE DRUMMING OF THE guns continued, with bursts of great intensity. It was as though a gale streamed overhead, piling up great waves of sound, and hurrying them onward to crash in surf on the enemy entrenchments. The windless air about them, by its very stillness, made that unearthly music more terrible to hear. They cowered under it, as men seeking shelter from a storm. Something rushed downward on them with a scream of exultation, increasing to a roar before it blasted the air asunder and sent splinters of steel shrieking over their heads, an eruption of mud spattering down on the trench, and splashing in brimming shell-holes. The pressure among the men increased. Someone shouldering a way through caused them to surge together, cursing, as they were thrown off their balance to stumble against their neighbours.

'For Christ's sake walk on your own bloody feet an' not on mine!' came from some angry man, and a ripple of idiot mirth spread outwards from the centre of the disturbance. Bourne got a drink of tea, and though it was no more than warm, it did him good; at least, it washed away the gummy dryness of his mouth. He was shivering, and told himself it was the cold. Through the darkness the dripping mist moved slowly, touching them with spectral fingers as it passed. Everything was clammy with it. It condensed on their tin hats, clung to their rough serge, their eye-lashes, the down on their cheek-bones. Even though it blinded everything beyond the distance of a couple of yards, it seemed to be faintly luminous itself. Its damp coldness enhanced the sense of smell. There was a reek of mouldering rottenness in the air, and through it came the sour, stale odour from the foul clothes of the men. Shells streamed overhead, sighing, whining, and whimpering for blood; the upper air fluttered with them; but Fritz was not going to take it all quietly, and with its increasing roar another shell leaped toward them, and they cowered under the wrath. There was the enormous grunt of its eruption, the sweeping of harp-strings and part of the trench wall collapsed inwards, burying some men in the landslide. It was difficult to get them out, in the crowded conditions of the trench.

Bourne's fit of shakiness increased, until he set his teeth to prevent them chattering in his head; and after a deep, gasping breath, almost like a sob, he seemed to recover to some extent. Fear poisoned the very blood; but, when one recognised the symptoms, it became objective, and one seemed to escape partly from it that way. He heard men breathing irregularly beside him, as he breathed himself; he heard them licking their lips, trying to moisten their mouths; he heard them swallow, as though overcoming a difficulty in swallowing; and the sense that others suffered equally or more than himself, quietened him. Some men moaned, or even sobbed a little, but unconsciously, and as though they struggled to throw off an intolerable burden of oppression. His eyes met Shem's, and they both turned away at once from the dread and question which confronted them. More furtively he glanced in Martlow's direction; and saw him standing with bent head. Some instinctive wave of pity and affection swelled in him, until it broke into another shuddering sigh, and the boy looked up, showing the whites of his eyes under the brim of his helmet. They were perplexed, and his under-lip shook a little. Behind him Bourne heard a voice almost pleading: 'Stick it out, chum.'

'A don't care a—,' came the reply, with a bitter harshness rejecting sympathy.

'Are you all right, kid?' Bourne managed to ask in a fairly steady voice; and Martlow only gave a brief affirmative nod. Bourne shifted his weight on to his other foot, and felt the relaxed knee trembling. It was the cold. If only they had something to do, it might be better. It had been a help simply to place a ladder in position. Suspense seemed to turn one's mind to ice, and bind even time in its frozen stillness; but at an order it broke. It broke, and one became alert, relieved. They breathed heavily in one another's faces. They looked at each other more quietly, forcing themselves to face the question.

'We've stuck it before,' said Shem.

They could help each other, at least up to that point where the irresistible thing swept aside their feeble efforts, and smashed them beyond recovery. The noise of the shells increased to a hurricane fury. There was at last a sudden movement with some purpose behind it. The men began to fix bayonets. Someone thrust a mug into Shem's hands.

'Three men. Don't spill the bloody stuff, you won't get no more.'

Shem drank some of the rum and passed it to Bourne.

335

'Take all you want, kid,' said Bourne to Martlow; 'I don't care whether I have any or not.'

'Don't want much,' said Martlow, after drinking a good swig. 'It makes you thirsty, but it warms you up a bit.'

Bourne emptied the mug, and handed it back to Jakes to fill again and pass to another man. It had roused him a little.

'It'll soon be over, now,' whispered Martlow.

Perhaps it was lighter, but the stagnant fog veiled everything. Only there was a sound of movement, a sudden alertness thrilled through them all with an anguish inextricably mingled with relief. They shook hands, the three among themselves and then with others near them.

Good luck, chum. Good luck. Good luck.

He felt his heart thumping at first. And then, almost surprised at the lack of effort which it needed, he moved towards the ladder.

Martlow, because he was nearest, went first. Shem followed behind Bourne, who climbed out a little clumsily. Almost as soon as he was out he slipped sideways and nearly fell. The slope downward, where others, before he did, had slipped, might have been greased with vaseline; and immediately beyond it, one's boots sank up to the ankle in mud which sucked at one's feet as they were withdrawn from it, clogging them, as in a nightmare. It would be worse when they reached the lower levels of this ill-drained marsh. The fear in him now was hard and icy, and yet apart from that momentary fumbling on the ladder, and the involuntary slide, he felt himself moving more freely, as though he had full control of himself.

They were drawn up in two lines, in artillery formation; C and D Companies in front, and A and B Companies to the rear. Another shell hurtled shrieking over them, to explode behind Dunmow with a roar of triumphant fury. The last effects of its blast reached them, whirling the mist into eddying spirals swaying fantastically: then he heard a low cry for stretcher-bearers. Some lucky beggar was out of it, either for good and all, or for the time being. He felt a kind of envy; and dread grew in proportion to the desire, but he could not turn away his thought: it clung desperately to the only possible solution. In this emotional crisis, where the limit of endurance was reached, all the degrees which separate opposed states of feeling vanished, and their extremities were indistinguishable from each other. One could not separate the desire from the dread which restrained it; the strength of one's hope strove to equal the despair which oppressed it; one's determination could only be measured by the terrors and difficulties which it overcame. All the mean, peddling standards of ordinary life vanished in the collision of these warring opposites. Between them one could only attempt to maintain an equilibrium which every instant disturbed and made unstable.

If it had been clear, there would have been some light by now, but darkness was prolonged by fog. He put up a hand, as though to wipe the filthy air from before his eyes, and he saw the stupid face of Jakes, by no means a stupid man, warped into a lop-sided grin. Bloody fool, he thought, with unreasoning anger. It was as though Jakes walked on tiptoe, stealing away from the effects of some ghastly joke he had perpetrated.

'We're on the move,' he said softly, and grinned with such a humour as skulls might have.

Then suddenly that hurricane of shelling increased terrifically, and in the thunder of its surf, as it broke over the German lines, all separate sounds were engulfed: it was one continuous fury, only varying as it seemed to come from one direction now, and now from another. And they moved. He didn't know whether they had heard any orders or not: he only knew they moved. It was treacherous walking over that greasy mud. They crossed Monk Trench, and a couple of other trenches, crowding together, and becoming confused. After Monk was behind them, the state of the ground became more and more difficult: one could not put a foot to the ground without skating and sliding. He saw Mr Finch at one crossing, looking anxious and determined, and Sergeant Tozer; but it was no more than a glimpse in the mist. A kind of maniacal rage filled him. Why were they so slow? And then it seemed that he himself was one of the slowest, and he pressed on. Suddenly the Hun barrage fell: the air was split and seared with shells. Fritz had been ready for them all right, and had only waited until their intentions had been made quite clear. As they hurried, head downward, over their own front line, they met men, some broken and bleeding, but others whole and sound, breaking back in disorder. They jeered at them, and the others raved inarticulately, and disappeared into the fog again. Jakes and Sergeant Tozer held their own lot together, and carried them through this moment of demoralization: Jakes roared and bellowed at them, and they only turned bewildered faces to him as they pressed forward, struggling through the mud like flies through treacle. What was all the bloody fuss about? they asked themselves, turning their faces, wide-eyed, in all directions to search the baffling fog. It shook, and twitched, and whirled about them: there seemed to be a dancing flicker before their eyes as shell after shell exploded, clanging, and the flying fragments hissed and shrieked through the air. Bourne thought that every bloody gun in the German army was pointed at him. He avoided some shattered bodies of men too obviously dead for help. A man stumbled past him with an agonized and bleeding face. Then more men broke back in disorder, throwing them into some confusion, and they seemed to waver for a moment. One of the fugitives charged down on Jakes, and that short but stocky fighter smashed the butt of his rifle to the man's jaw, and sent him sprawling. Bourne had a vision of Sergeant-Major Glasspool.

'You take your bloody orders from Fritz!' he shouted as a triumphant frenzy thrust him forward.

For a moment they might have broken and run themselves, and for a moment they might have fought men of their own blood, but they struggled on as Sergeant Tozer yelled at them to leave that bloody tripe alone and get on with it. Bourne, floundering in the viscous mud, was at once the most abject and the most exalted of God's creatures. The effort and rage in him, the sense that others had left them to it, made him pant and sob, but there was some strange intoxication of joy in it, and again all his mind seemed focused into one hard bright point of action. The extremities of pain and pleasure had met and coincided too.

He knew, they all did, that the barrage had moved too quickly for them, but they knew nothing of what was happening about them. In any attack, even under favourable conditions, the attackers are soon blinded; but here they had lost touch almost from the start. They paused for a brief moment, and Bourne saw that Mr Finch was with them, and Shem was not. Minton told him Shem had been hit in the foot. Bourne moved closer to Martlow. Their casualties, as far as he could judge, had not been heavy. They got going again, and, almost before they saw it, were on the wire. The stakes had been uprooted, and it was smashed and tangled, but had not been well cut. Jakes ran along it a little way, there was some firing, and bombs were hurled at them from the almost obliterated trench, and they answered by lobbing a few bombs over, and then plunging desperately among the steel briars, which tore at their puttees and trousers. The last strand of it was cut or beaten down, some more bombs came at them, and in the last infuriated rush Bourne was knocked off his feet and went practically headlong into the trench; getting up, another man jumped on his shoulders, and they both fell together, yelling with rage at each other. They heard a few squeals of agony, and he saw a dead German, still kicking his heels on the broken boards of the trench at his feet. He yelled for the man who had knocked him down to come on, and followed the others. The trench was almost obliterated: it was nothing but a wreckage of boards and posts, piled confusedly in what had become a broad channel for the oozing mud. They heard some more bombing a few bays further on, and then were turned back. They met two prisoners, their hands up, and almost unable to stand from fear, while two of the men threatened them with a deliberate, slow cruelty.

'Give 'em a chance! Send 'em through their own bloody barrage!' Bourne shouted, and they were practically driven out of the trench and sent across no man's land.

On the other flank they found nothing; except for the handful of men they had encountered at first, the trench was empty. Where they had entered the trench, the three first lines converged rather closely, and they thought they were too far right. In spite of the party of Germans they had met, they assumed that the other waves of the assaulting troops were ahead of them, and decided to push on immediately, but with some misgivings. They were now about twenty-four men. In the light, the fog was coppery and charged with fumes. They heard in front of them the terrific battering of their own barrage and the drumming of the German guns. They had only moved a couple of yards from the trench, when there was a crackle of musketry. Martlow was perhaps a couple of yards in front of Bourne, when he swayed a little, his knees collapsed under him, and he pitched forward on to his face, his feet kicking and his whole body convulsive for a moment. Bourne flung himself down beside him, and, putting his arms round his body, lifted him, calling him.

'Kid! You're all right, kid?' he cried eagerly.

He was all right. As Bourne lifted the limp body, the boy's hat came off, showing half the back of his skull shattered where the bullet had come through it; and a little blood welled out on to Bourne's sleeve and the knee of his trousers. He was all right; and Bourne let him settle to earth again, lifting himself up almost indifferently, unable to realize what had happened, filled with a kind of tenderness that ached in him, and yet extraordinarily still, extraordinarily cold. He had to hurry, or he would be alone in the fog. Again he heard some rifle-fire, some bombing, and, stooping, he ran towards the sound, and was by Minton's side again, when three men ran towards them, holding their hands up and screaming; and he lifted his rifle to his shoulder and fired; and the ache in him became a consuming hate that filled him with exultant cruelty, and he fired again, and again. The last man was closest to him, but as drunk and staggering with terror. He had scarcely fallen, when Bourne came up to him and saw that his head was shattered, as he turned it over with his boot. Minton looking at him with a curious anxiety, saw Bourne's teeth clenched and bared, the lips snarling back from them in exultation.

'Come on. Get into it,' Minton cried in his anxiety.

And Bourne struggled forward again, panting, and muttering in a suffocated voice.

'Kill the bastards! Kill the bloody —ing swine! Kill them!'

All the filth and ordure he had ever heard came from between his clenched teeth; but his speech was thick and difficult. In a scuffle immediately afterwards a Hun went for Minton, and Bourne got him with the bayonet, under the ribs near the liver, and then, unable to wrench the bayonet out again, pulled the trigger, and it came away easily enough.

'Kill the bastards!' he muttered thickly.

He ran against Sergeant Tozer in the trench.

'Steady, ol' son! Steady. 'ave you been 'it? You're all over blood.'

'They killed the kid,' said Bourne, speaking with sudden clearness, though his chest heaved enormously. 'They killed him. I'll kill every

339

bastard I see.'

'Steady. You stay by me. I want you. Mr Finch 'as been 'it, see? You two come as well. Where's that bloody bomber?'

They searched about a hundred yards to the right, bombing a dug-out from which no answer came, and again they collided with some small party of Huns, and, after some ineffective bombing, both sides drew away from each other. Jakes, with about ten men, had apparently got into the third line, and after similar bombing fights with small parties of Germans had come back again.

'Let's 'ave a dekko, sir,' said Sergeant Tozer, taking Mr Finch's arm.

'It's all right,' said the young man, infuriated; but the sergeant got his arm out of the sleeve, and bandaged a bullet-wound near the shoulder. They were now convinced they could not go on by themselves. They decided to try and get into touch with any parties on the left. It was useless to go on, as apparently none of the other companies were ahead of them, and heavy machine-gun fire was coming from Serre. They worked up the trench to the left, and after some time, heard footsteps. The leading man held up a hand, and they were ready to bomb or bayonet, when a brave voice challenged them.

'Who are ye?'

'Westshires!' they shouted, and moved on, to meet a corporal and three men of the Gordons. They knew nothing of the rest of their battalion. They were lost, but they thought one of their companies had reached the front line. These four Gordons were four of the quickest and coolest men you could meet. There was some anxiety in the expression of their eyes, but it was only anxiety as to what they should do. Mr Finch ordered them to stay with him; and almost immediately they heard some egg-bombs. Some Huns were searching the trench. Sergeant Tozer, with the same party, went forward immediately. As soon as some egg-bombs had burst in the next bay, they rushed it, and flung into the next. They found and bayoneted a Hun, and pursued the others some little distance, before they doubled back on their tracks again. Then Mr Finch took them back to the German front line, intending to stay there until he could link up with other parties. The fog was only a little less thick than the mud; but if it had been one of the principal causes of their failure, it helped them now. The Hun could not guess at their numbers; and there must have been several isolated parties playing the same game of hide-and-seek. The question for Mr Finch to decide was whether they should remain there. They searched the front line to the left, and found nothing but some dead, Huns and Gordons.

Bourne was with the Gordons who had joined them, and one of them, looking at the blood on his sleeve and hands, touched him on the shoulder.

'Mon, are ye hurt?' he whispered gently.

'No. I'm not hurt, chum,' said Bourne, shaking his head slowly, and then he shuddered and was silent. His face became empty and expressionless.

Their own barrage had moved forward again; but they could not get into touch with any of their own parties. Then, to show how little he knew about what was happening, Fritz began to shell his own front line. They had some casualties immediately; a man called Adams was killed, and Minton was slightly wounded in the shoulder by a splinter. It was quite clear by this time that the other units had failed to penetrate even the first line. To remain where they were was useless, and to go forward was to invite either destruction or capture.

'Sergeant,' said Mr Finch, with a bitter resolution, 'we shall go back.'

Sergeant Tozer looked at him quietly.

'You're wounded, sir,' he said kindly. 'If you go back with Minton, I could hang on a bit longer, and then take the men back on my own responsibility.'

'I'll be blowed if I go back with only a scratch, and leave you to stick it. You're a bloody sportsman, sergeant. You're the best bloody lot o' men . . .'

His words trailed off shakily into nothing for a moment.

'That's all right, sir,' said Sergeant Tozer, quietly; and then he added with an angry laugh: 'We've done all we could: I don't care a blast what the other beggar says.'

'Get the men together, sergeant,' said Mr Finch huskily.

The sergeant went off and spoke to Jakes, and to the corporal of the Gordons. As he passed Bourne, who had just put a dressing on Minton's wound, he paused.

'What 'appened to Shem?' he asked.

'Went back. Wounded in the foot.'

''e were wounded early on, when Jerry dropped the barrage on us,' explained Minton, stolidly precise as to facts.

'That beggar gets off everything with 'is feet,' said Sergeant Tozer.

''e were gettin' off with 'is 'ands an' knees when I seed 'im,' said Minton, phlegmatically.

There was some delay as they prepared for their withdrawal. Bourne thought of poor old Shem, always plucky, and friendly, without sentiment, and quiet. Quite suddenly, as it were spontaneously, they climbed out of the trench and over the wire. The clangour of the shelling increased behind them. Fritz was completing the destruction of his own front line before launching a counter-attack against empty air. They moved back very slowly and painfully, suffering a few casualties on the way, and they were already encumbered with wounded. One of the Gordons was hit, and his thigh broken. They carried him tenderly, soothing him with the gentleness of women. All the fire died out of them as they dragged themselves laboriously through the clinging mud. Presently they came to where the dead lay more thickly; they found some helplessly wounded, and helped them. As they were approaching their own front line, a big shell, burying itself in the mud, exploded so close to Bourne that it blew him completely off his feet, and yet he was unhurt. He picked himself up, raving a little. The whole of their front and support trenches were being heavily shelled. Mr Finch was hit again in his already wounded arm. They broke up a bit, and those who were free ran for it to the trench. Men carrying or helping the wounded continued steadily enough. Bourne walked by Corporal Jakes, who had taken his place in carrying the wounded Gordon: he could not have hurried anyway; and once, unconsciously, he turned and looked back over his shoulder. Then they all slid into the wrecked trench.

Hearing that all their men had been ordered back to Dunmow, Mr Finch led the way down Blenau. His wounds had left him pallid and suffering, but he looked as though he would fight anything he met. He made a report to the adjutant, and went off with some other wounded to the dressing-station. The rest of them went on, crowded into a dug-out, and huddled together without speaking, listening to the shells bumping above them. They got some tea, and wondered what the next move would be. Bourne was sitting next to the doorway, when Jakes drew him out into a kind of recess, and handed him a mess-tin with some tea and rum in it.

'Robinson's gone down the line wounded, an' Sergeant Tozer's takin' over,' he whispered.

Presently Sergeant Tozer joined them, and looked at Bourne, who sat there, drinking slowly and looking in front of him with fixed eyes. He spoke to Jakes about various matters of routine, and of further possibilities.

'There's some talk o' renewing the attack,' he said shortly.

Jakes laughed with what seemed to be a cynical enjoyment.

'O' course it's all our bleedin' fault, eh?' he asked grimly.

Sergeant Tozer didn't answer, but turned to Bourne.

'You don't want to think o' things,' he said, with brutal kindness. 'It's all past an' done wi', now.'

Bourne looked at him in a dull acquiescence. Then he emptied the tin, replaced it on the bench, and, getting up, went to sit by the door again. He sat with his head flung back against the earth, his eyes closed, his arms relaxed, and hands idle in his lap, and he felt as though he were lifting a body in his arms, and looking at a small impish face, the brows puckered with a shadow of perplexity, bloody from a wound in the temple, the back of the head almost blown away; and yet the face was quiet, and unmoved by any trouble. He sat there for hours, immobile and indifferent, unaware that Sergeant Tozer glanced at him occasionally.

The shelling gradually died away, and he did not know it. Then Sergeant Tozer got up angrily.

''ere, Bourne. Want you for sentry. Time that other man were relieved.'

He took up his rifle, and climbed up, following the sergeant into the frosty night. Then he was alone, and the fog frothed and curdled about him. He became alert, intent, again; his consciousness hardening in him. After about half an hour, he heard men coming along the trench; they came closer; they went by the corner.

'Stand!' he cried in a long, low note of warning.

'Westshire. Officer and rations.'

He saw Mr White, to whom Captain Marsden came up and spoke. Some men passed him, details and oddments, carrying bags of rations. Suddenly he found in front of him the face of Snobby Hines, grinning excitedly.

'What was it like, Bourne?' he asked, in passing.

'Hell,' said Bourne briefly.

Snobby moved on, and Bourne ignored the others completely. Bloody silly question, to ask a man what it was like. He looked up to the sky, and through the travelling mist saw the half-moon with a great halo round it. An extraordinary peace brooded over everything. It seemed only the more intense because an occasional shell sang through it.

Acknowledgments

The Publishers gratefully acknowledge permission granted by the following to reprint the copyright material included in this volume:

Fair Stood The Wind For France by H. E. Bates. From the novel of the same name, published by Michael Joseph Ltd. Reprinted by permission of Laurence Pollinger Ltd and the Estate of H. E. Bates.

How Brigadier Gerard Won His Medal by Sir Arthur Conan Doyle. From 'The Exploits of Brigadier Gerard'. Copyright in the name of Jean Conan Doyle.

The Invaders by Richard Hillary. From 'The Last Enemy' by Richard Hillary. Reprinted by permission of the Publishers, Macmillan, London and Basingstoke.

The War of the Worlds by H. G. Wells. From the novel of the same name. Reprinted by permission of the Publishers, William Heinemann Ltd, the Estate of the late H. G. Wells and A. P. Watt Ltd.

All Quiet On The Western Front by Erich Maria Remarque. Copyright 1938 by Ullstein, A.G.: copyright renewed 1966 by Erich Maria Remarque. 'All Quiet on the Western Front' copyright 1929, copyright renewed 1957, 1958 by Erich Maria Remarque. All rights reserved. Reprinted with permission of Putnam & Co. Ltd at The Bodley Head.

Catch 22 by Joseph Heller. From the novel of the same name. Copyright © 1961 by Joseph Heller. Reprinted by permission of the Author, the Publishers, Jonathan Cape Ltd, and Candida Donadio & Associates.

Buller's Guns by Richard Hough. Chapter XV in the novel of the same name. Copyright © 1981 by Richard Hough. Reprinted by permission of the Publishers, Weidenfeld & Nicolson Ltd and William Morrow & Company.

Arctic Convoy by Alistair MacLean. An excerpt from 'H.M.S. Ulysses' by Alistair MacLean. Copyright © 1956 by Alistair MacLean. Reprinted by permission of the Publishers, Collins & Sons Company Ltd and Doubleday & Company, Inc.